ACKNOW

CW01507496

To my wife, Jemma, you've always believed in me, and finally, that belief has reached its goal. Now that I've accomplished this, don't let me slack off going forward.

Damien Buckley, in recent months, not only have you become a friend, but you have also been a source of motivation and guidance, becoming a dear mentor. Thank you for putting up with all the questions and my constant inability to believe in myself.

Bella, what a star you've been! Your encouragement, constructive criticism, and ideas have been invaluable, providing endless help throughout. Thank you doesn't seem enough.

Julia, thank you for helping me complete a week's worth of work in one night and for bringing me even closer to finishing.

Gordon and everyone else who has supported my journey, thank you so, so much. I'll have number two out as soon as possible.

THE JADE PANDORA

TWO KINGS, ONE THRONE

A. D. STEVENS

Thankyou For your purchase
I hope it quacks you up

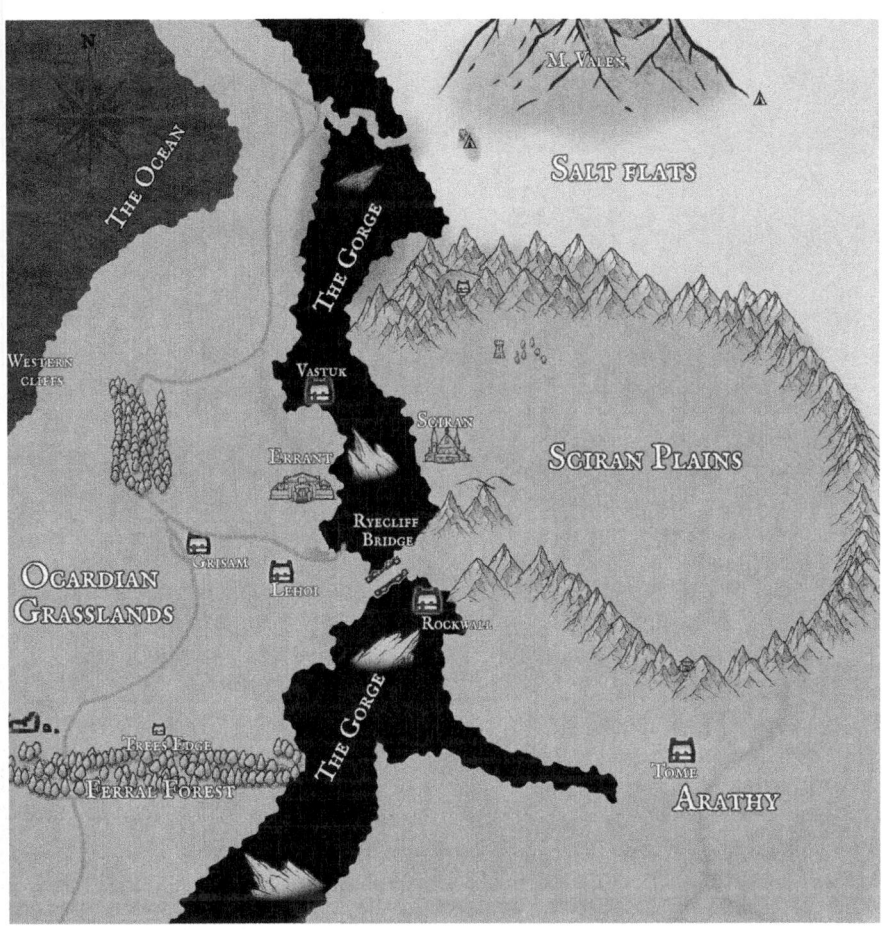

PROLOGUE

Zenith walked these fields daily, his family's land, a land where gods had walked in ages past—the place of many ancient stories that had never been told or had yet to unfold.

Another ordinary spring day, working hard in the soil getting the field ready for sowing, moving his Mullok-drawn plough in lines, turning the earth, preparing it to plant the next crop. He spent this time far from his stepbrother, Merrik, and the other farmhands, especially on days when he felt like reminiscing about his father. Often pondering how different it could have been for him and his brother had tragedy not struck all those years ago, stealing their parents from them. Under mysterious circumstances, a sudden, unexplained plague took not only them but many others from the village.

This occurred after the loss of his grandfather, only six months prior.

There wandering, following the plough in its straight-line monotony from one end of the field to the other, thinking more as he laboured step after step in the fields, getting ready to produce a bountiful harvest year after year.

His father, Ake, would often say, "Your mother, Zenith, was worth more than any throne in the world. I quite happily traded my crown for Calluses and never needed to look back."

Ake was always one to be among the people, enjoying life before ascending the throne. Living as a village farmer to be with their mother. The woman who had captured his heart falling deeply in love, whilst out to meet the people as an envoy to the throne. Ake was truly a prince among men. The people of Grissam reflected this in the stories and memories they shared. Ake had fallen for their mother in a heartbeat, instantly refusing to leave Grissam from that very day to be with her always.

This was the way his father always told it, possibly to make it seem more fantastical and romantic as a bedtime story for him and Merrik.

Ake had spent years building the farm with his own hands, never seeking handouts from Zenith's grandfather, King Barathor. Ake never used his rank as a reason to shy away from hard graft.

Zenith fondly remembered the years he had spent watching with his stepbrother, learning from their father about the life he had chosen. Zenith never got any sense that Ake lacked completeness in his choice.

Laughing to himself as he remembered his father's mantra. *A man must follow his heart first, feelings second and his duty third. Easier said than done when you're knee deep in a muddy field, following a Mullock's arse.*

This advice had always guided him well enough and was one of the main reasons that Zenith never envied his uncle the king. The king saw them as commoners and completely ignored them. Even though Zenith didn't envy his uncle's lofty status, he didn't know him, nor want to; even as a child, they had never interacted. His uncle Quinten wasn't the most caring of people; in fact, most would say he was materialistic and selfish.

Although he had a right to be royal by blood and could claim the titles and estates of his late father, he saw no point; he had his remaining family around him, which was all that mattered.

His mother and father had loved him dearly, and so had their grandfather, the previous king. He visited his grandfather many times with Ake whilst he was alive. The time he spent with Barathor was always intriguing and fun. Ultimately, they would always return to Grissam; the luxury of royalty never suited his or Ake's free spirits and love of nature.

Whilst on his deathbed, his grandfather announced that he would be passing the throne to his father's younger, inexperienced, less qualified brother, Quinten. This was unprecedented. Quinten had never been for, or of, the people. King Barathor knew this; many speculated that his death was the result of foul play and that he had been forced into declaring Quinten as his successor to the throne, but no proof was ever found.

Even with his family history, this life suited him fine. Days of hard labour tending to the fields, doing what was necessary to yield the best crop.

Nights practising his husbandry skills, taming beasts of all types from the wilds surrounding the village limits, using them to improve the people's lives or releasing them as needed. Simple creatures like the winged squirrel, which the smiths always wanted for their ability to harness the wind element, and the wild cats, which they domesticated to hunt mice and other small animals in the barns and buildings. Other larger creatures, such as boars and bears, would be used to maintain the forest's equilibrium under the foresters as protectors.

A skill he had become well known for, as no others could match him, even veteran tamers. It was a skill he'd had since birth; nobody knew why. It was like he had been born for more than a farmer's life. He often felt a sense of longing for more. A vast part of who he was seemed outside of his grasp.

It was as if he had a task in life that he had yet to fulfil, something that made him want to leave, but had not given him reason to. If the choice did come, he didn't know if he genuinely wanted it; it would mean leaving all he knew and loved.

The sun hit harder as midday arrived, bringing him out of his thoughts. His thirst was genuinely beginning to devour him, forcing him to stop and walk to the field's edge. Picking up his skin of water, placing it up to his dry lips, his Adam's apple permeating the skin of his throat whilst gulping and drinking deeply. A voice came from the distance. He didn't hear them clearly, just a muffled sound on the wind.

Turning around, he saw him. A man stood tall and proud, covered entirely by a red hooded robe, with a large staff in one hand and a sheathed sword in the other.

Zenith, confused and a little off guard, stared at the hooded figure. He called out to him, receiving no response. Zenith attempted to return to his work. He sensed no ill intent in the air around them, as if the man wasn't really present. Zenith found he was becoming intrigued by him and approached. That led to one of the most essential gifts he would ever receive, the Echidna Flame.

This would see Zenith leave his beloved home to seek new friends, encounter mythical beasts and face all manner of horrific creatures, in the quest to truly become one with his newfound powers and fight alongside those he loved.

1

AT JOURNEY'S END TO START ANEW

Three Years had passed since he met the monk and left his home to search for his weapons kin; those years had seen him travel all over the Occardian Grasslands.

Zenith looked to cross the gorge. Heading to places he had never heard of, or even dreamed of, as his entire world grew with each passing day.

Procrastinating, at his in-room window instead of being out in the street, trying to gather more information on where he could search next. He gazed off into the distance, the gleaming setting of the Sun dancing upon the meandering River Ko, which wound its way past the main road, leading off to the west—the vastness of the fields and the bright colours of the windmills. The spinning blades in the distance twirled reds and yellows, merging into oranges; the fields were a darkened green, with flicks of amber dancing on the waving blades. Even compared to the morning dew glistening on the grassy fields around his home village. It almost put to shame the memories he held dear.

Realising that something was wrong, striking like a smith's hammer on the inside of his chiselled brow. He had felt uneasy before, but had never really known why. He still didn't, but at the very least, there were physical signs now.

Zenith knew that something was wrong, sitting uneasily within him, his stomach knotting a little as he realised no one else seemed to have noticed.

"That doesn't make sense", Zenith muttered to himself silently. "The sun shouldn't be in the north this time of year...it just shouldn't." Even though where it now hung itself created such a fantastic ambience.

Zenith sat there pondering: *Is it the land or the Sun that had moved its place among the stars? Or is it a greater power at work?*

In the confines of his dank and dark inn room, a musty smell rose from the sheets of his bed. The smell of gruel filled the air around him, reminding him of his own home, where his stepbrother Merik now ran their grain and dairy farm in his stead.

It had been many days since Zenith had seen home; he had not passed through there in almost three full years, wondering if his journey would ever bring him back.

Lying on the bed of straw wrapped in a damp woollen blanket, he felt his mind drift back home. The smell of freshly mown grass in the summer and the scent of the spring breeze. This was but a distant memory now, oh, how he longed to be there labouring hard with his brother alongside him, as they had always done since the passing of their father years ago.

As the morning came, so did the noise of the Lehoi market and the smell of the first baked goods. No one had noticed the difference in the weather and continued as they usually would. Today would be the day Zenith's true journey began, although nobody, especially not Zenith, knew it.

It must have been the seventh bell of the day; it was time to leave. As he rode, he wished Lehoi a fond farewell; it had been his home for the last month, while the bridge at Ryecliff was repaired. There was no other way to cross the Rysand gorge.

The ride gave him a chance to reflect on all the years prior, he had been alone and travelling, looking for any information he could find about the weapons of the Rysander.

As he rode, he remembered the legend of Rysand. The god of good and how the gorge was created, in the teachings of Rysandia, wondering if the legend could provide any more clues to their whereabouts. Thinking about it and the information it gave him.

The Legend of Rysand stated that during the time of creation, when the twin gods Rysand and Rycore walked upon the land, they attended to the needs of humanity. Rysand blessed those who became his loyal followers, Rycore following his brother's lead.

The brothers eventually grew further apart after Rycore became jealous of Rysand and the bountiful paradise that he had created for his followers. Rycore began to twist man into creatures of evil. Changing their physical forms into grotesque lizard-like beings and mashing multiple souls into one.

When Rysand saw what his brother had created, he decided that men needed to learn to fight, so they could defend themselves against all evil.

The wars started, and the chaos that ensued was so beastly that Rysand knew the time had come for his intervention. He pleaded with his brother to stop the chaos, but he would not. Rycore refused, wanting his creations to walk alone on Apprite.

The creators came to war with each other, each fighting for their creations.

In his desperation, Rysand created the jade Pandora as a Weapon of phenomenal power. His horse still, moving at a slow and constant pace, giving him a chance to start recalling the Legend line by line. He'd done it so many times to beat the loneliness of the road, the words just naturally formed, muttered just loud enough that he could hear him self.

Rysand and Rycore stood side by side,
> *Created a world of diversity,*
> *Both in control,*
> *Among their creation,*
> *One followed, one forgotten,*
> *Together as a whole,*
> *Apart at war,*
> *Jealous and enraged,*
> *Rycore twisted and mutilated the souls of man,*
> *The creatures rose to fight and kill,*
> *Rysand, afraid of the chaos, pursued his twin,*
> *Words not strong,*
> *The war began,*
> *Brother against brother,*
> *Man against man,*
> *A weapon created to bring the balance,*
> *A land severed there to remind us of the evil restrained,*
> *The darkness removed his twin, and he would rest*
> *evermore,*
> *God and weapon at rest, the war was done,*
> *Life was fresh, peace restored."*

Finally, recalling the end of the story. In the final days of the war, Rysand used the jade Pandora to strike down Rycore. So incomprehensible was the weapon's power that it cleaved Rycore in two, at the same time cutting deeply, revealing nothing but rock in the once-beautiful plains of Sciran. So deep that it almost split the lands in two.

After the death of Rycore, his armies descended into the darkness of the world. Although Rysand believed he won, he had drained his energy so much that he left the world to sleep until his power was needed again.

By the time Zenith had remembered the legend, he had ridden half the distance to Rysand gorge. His horse was tired and needed rest and water. A nearby stream was a convenient enough spot to stop for a while.

He would at least be among other travellers, able to see a crowd from the track. They all stood staring at the same point. Questioning. *Why?* Worrying him and rousing his curiosity.

Leading his horse by hand, he approached. Hearing screaming and shouted vulgarities, as he did, seeing at the centre a woman come into focus. Although only in silhouette, her body's shape seemed smooth and well-defined. Even standing there, she portrayed a calm and collected demeanour; she seemed somewhat different from any other woman he had met before.

Much more aware and attentive to her surroundings, her clothing was unusual; it was feminine, yet seemed unrestrictive, covering her head to toe like a soldier's battle gear.

A strange energy surrounded him, as he approached like a weight pressing upon him that was hard to resist. It pushed him towards her, or so he thought.

At her waist, seeing a weapon in a clasp, one of a kind he had never seen, a five-bladed star. He wondered how it was used. There was no handle he could see to hold. His sword was regular by comparison, even though legend had it that it was forged by a mage, infused with the fur of a mythical beast. A rare sword indeed, but still just a sword.

Zenith managed to gain control of himself, making sure to

stand a while away from the group, who seemed interested in the woman, questioning silently as he watched. *Are their intentions good?*

Stood quietly while his horse drank for what seemed like an entire hour. In an instant, the silence vanished around him, broken by the crack of lightning. He turned to see what had happened. "What in gods-?". Zenith jerked the horse's reins, pulling it out of the way, screaming, "Shift it, horse!" Instinctively drawing his sword in fear, sparks flying when the weapons collided, cursing to himself. "I could have died just standing here minding my own business".

Thinking in a split second. *The virtue of Rysand must smile upon me*, as he raised his sword to the light, just in time, the weapon the woman was carrying struck the blade and fell to the floor. Lightning struck a small tree to the side of him; at the very moment, the blades collided.

Realising this, he jerked his body back to where the crowd was gathered. Bodies lay strewn in the stream and on the ground, some limbs missing, some bodies burning, blood pouring crimson from others into the crystal-clear waters of the river, the stench of death filling the air. His mind raced with too many unanswered questions.

What had such power to cause this and to leave this woman uninjured? Had this five-bladed star that now lay on the ground done this? Had it scorched the earth and severed the bodies of these men now bereft of life?

Still fixed and motionless, the woman stood amongst them. *Could she have done this? Why would she have done this?* These were questions Zenith needed answered.

Unable to move, staring at the woman, these answers could prove dangerous to his life. Yet questions flooded his thoughts. *The power it feels was nearer now; is it the weapon or the woman?* He watched as the woman approached him.

Fear, replaced with contempt for this slayer of men. As she removed her helmet and greeted him with a smile, he started to relax, noticing and muttering. *This woman did not want my death; she seems overly intrigued by my sword, as I am the star.* As the woman gazed at the sword through her Hazel-green eyes.

"That is the Echidna flame! Is it not?" The woman asked, seemingly shocked by the man before her.

"It is", Zenith responded cautiously, then adding, "and I'm guessing you didn't come here for the weather", trying to break the tension with sarcastic humour. The woman seemed to ignore his comments and spoke plainly.

"I am Lemma of Sciran, the kingdom of the plains. I have been searching the Occardian Grasslands for the bearer of the Echidna flame".

Astonished and thrown to his back foot at this proclamation, all he could muster was, "It is... I am..." with a stutter.

Lemma's eyes danced over him, studying him further, realising that he was no soldier, possibly a farm boy. By the leathers and a cape he wore, surprisingly, no armour, yet a sword sheathed at his waist.

"How did you stop the star of Sciran?" Pausing for a moment, she demanded, "Answer me!!" Fear was now back in place. *Why was a warrior of the plains looking for him? For that matter, why was she here, and how was she on this side of the gorge?* Speaking plainly, Zenith answered.

"I am Zenith of Grissam, bearer of the Echidna flame." The power he felt earlier dulled as if eased by the presence of Lemma and the sense of kinship.

As the afternoon drew closer, the air getting ever hotter, they decided to take shade under the tree that he had seen struck by lightning earlier. Soon, in deep conversation with

Lemma over the questions he wished to ask and in some respect answer.

The afternoon drew on, and Lemma and Zenith discussed many things. The mythical sword had a profound influence. "How did you come to wield the Echidna flame?" she asked curiously.

"It was around three years ago; I was working on the farm when a man approached me carrying the sword." Zenith's mind regressed to that day as he spoke.

"It was the first trimester of spring, and the fields needed to be tilled for planting. As the stranger approached, my body shivered, as though held by a power I had never felt. The man spoke to me." Zenith paused and changed his voice, attempting to imitate the man's voice. Lemma chuckled at the attempt, thinking. *I hope the monk didn't sound like this strangled chicken voice he uses.*

"I am Brother Thaddeus from the order of Ayr Rose; I have been charged to find you, the one who will wield the Echinda Flame"

Zenith stopped using the imitated voice and recounted what the monk had told him of the sword.

"On that day, the Monk explained to me that the Echidna flame was forged at the time of the creation by a magical smith, using the fur of a godly beast to imbue the sword with strength. The one chosen by the sword was to be gifted with increased strength, agility and the swordsmanship of a seasoned warrior." Zenith continued. "It also gave the wielder the ability to sense danger before they could see it."

He also remembered that it was part of a set of three weapons, the Rysendar, the other two of which were lost. Not unfindable, the weapons could sense each other, their users attuned to each other as if they were near kindred spirits. He started recounting Thaddeus' words.

. . .

Three weapons forged.

One of strength and foresight
One agile and a window to the soul
One pure and good emanating the light of a god
The Rysendar, a weapon created by man blessed by the creator.
Two will wield, and one lost the kinship unbroken.
Knowing no bounds.
Apart, they are strong.
In unity, their power is unknown.

The fourth bell of late afternoon rang clear in the distance as Zenith finished his story. Now, he wanted to know what Lemma wanted.

"Why do you seek me? For what purpose?" Zenith asked.

Lemma began to explain, "I have travelled from Sciran in search of the bearer of the Echidna flame. My kingdom is in dire straits. You wouldn't have realised as of yet. Your mind is untrained, the star and Echidna flame are kin; they are linked. They're of the same set forged in the war of creation."

Was this true? Have I found one of my weapons kin? I do feel a sense of kinship with Lemma and the star; perhaps this was how my quest will truly begin. Zenith pondered. Sat in silence.

As Lemma continued, she explained, "Sciran is in grave terror, dark things were moving, and it seemed Rycore was reviving before I left. The star allows me to sense Rycore's influence in man and the twisting of souls." This had been the case of the group now lying silent not far from them, or so Lemma said.

Zenith felt and thought, *I feel no lie in her words, so I'll believe her for now.*

Lemma continued for a brief time, then as the fifth bell sounded, she sprang to her feet. "It's time to go, we must leave at once!"

The two mounted their horses in an instant and were off at a gallop toward the Ryecliff bridge. Surely it was fixed by now? And would see them in Sciran sooner. Better that than Lemma resting on her laurels, chatting; she had found the one she sought.

They would be there by the eighth bell at this rate, later than expected by Zenith. Substantially earlier than Lemma's expectations, as she had not planned to leave for a few more days if her search failed.

By the Eighth bell, they arrived. The bridge was finished, but it was too late to cross. The gorge seemed to cover almost half of the continent; it would take the better part of a day to cross, so it would be better to wait until the first light of the day. Zenith knew of a coach house not far from the bridge. Spending a night there seemed the easiest option for both of them. Some food and time to talk further would not be so bad. He'd stayed in worse places.

On their horses, they turned down the well-trodden path that lay to the side of the gorge. Zenith felt troubled by a sense of being stalked; a rustle in some bushes alongside the path piqued his curiosity. Peering as he guided his horse closer to the foliage, startling him and his horse. A strange creature bolted from the bushes, too swift to be seen, somewhat resembling a black wolf. The horse bucked upward, Zenith gripping the reins, fighting gravity to stay seated in the saddle. Lemma Pulled alongside, allowing his horse to see that hers remained calm, reassuring it, uttering whispered words that they remained safe.

After their short delay, they arrived at the inn, spending their evening talking over wine and fruit, an otherwise exceptional meal for an inn of this standard. The entertainment was plentiful, featuring singers who sang both old and new songs, as well as a play. A comedy derived from the legend of creation, but with a different end from the one Zenith had been taught to believe.

The jade Pandora was not a weapon, but a seal locking away the jealous god Rycore. A result of the clash of the creation. This was in direct conflict with Zenith's own beliefs. *How can there be two different legends, which of them is true?* Zenith noted Lemma seemed perplexed by this rendition of the legend as well.

The play finished, Lemma remarked the eleventh bell of the clock, bidding Zenith a good night. Zenith sat there, confused over what he had just seen and the differences from what he believed. Maybe his dreams would help him understand better that night.

He summoned a servant girl and asked for a final goblet of warm mead before bed, then headed up to his room.

Lying there on his bed of straw, the final amber rays of the inn room's fire brushed over the lintel of the window that his bed lay under. The fresh smell of his lavender linen soothed his aching body, summoning him to his sleep from the confusion he felt. Dreams always cleared his mind, hoping that the questions of faith playing in his mind would be answered. His eyes closed, listening to the sounds of the evening birds, and the sound of happy travellers below helped ease him into a sound sleep.

Ravaged by visions of creatures he had never known attacking a place he had never seen, made his mind anxious and distressed. Yet, there was a sense of kinship here. A man grey in colour, a warrior's body hardened through many battles. Other soldiers surrounding him called out to him, asking him to be at his side. *What did he hold, a staff?* Bloodied body of man and beast asunder at his feet, this man was a mighty fighter, the likes of which he had never seen.

Unable to wake from his sleep, his mind pulled away, heading for the safety of the known, smelling the grass of home. The smell of the ocean was near. *Where am I?* He didn't know, yet he felt safe, as if kept close to his mother's breast at birth. The place seemed familiar, yet perceived through another man's eyes in the distance, there was something considerable in its height and greater in its girth, colourless in its appearance, as if covered in a thick, unrelenting fog.

The rays of the sun rose slowly through the window of the room, as if not to wake the souls sleeping within, but it was too late.

Lemma had risen with the third ring of the morning bell. Readying for the journey ahead, back to Sciran with Zenith. Only hoping the horror she had left behind had not worsened or overrun the kingdom entirely.

She knew Zenith was the only hope, but still she had only found the Echidna flame, whilst she held the star of Sciran. *What of the staff of Angelus? Is it utterly lost or just somewhere that I've never been?* Her mind was in a state of perplexity. *I have travelled the whole of the known lands. The only place left is inside the Rysand gorge, but no one knows of any way down or what horrific creatures lie there.* The gorge was completely unexplored; anyone who descended into it never returned.

The fourth ring of the morning bell rang out, waking Zenith, sweat dripping from his brow, his long, flowing hair swept back and held by the moisture clinging to it, unsure of what the day ahead would bring. Terrible visions of death and destruction haunted his dreams in a place he had never seen before, with barely any light. He worried and asked the air. "Where could such a place be? And who in all the benevolence was the man who called to me? He called me in such a way that it seemed almost real. What did my dream mean?"

They made ready, their journey set before them, the Ryecliff Bridge crossing the expanse to Sciran. Zenith had planned to go here next to search for information, but now he had been given a much more urgent reason to.

The sun had started to brighten the day, as it was still in the north, Zenith glanced at Lemma, who was also studying this with some intent.

"Why does the Sun feel wrong? What has happened?" Lemma remarked rhetorically, confusion in her tone.

Zenith didn't know how to answer, his mind full of confusion. *Only God knows, and the answer doesn't seem to be friendly. Is this the doing of Rycore? Is he still alive, now waking from his slumber? Does Rysand know?* These questions tormented Zenith's mind after the events of the play the night before and the fear his dreams provoked.

The morning drew on; all they could see above them was a picture-perfect blue sky with not a cloud in sight. In contrast, below the gorge, full of mist and dark jagged rocks. Ahead, the bridge seemed as though it stretched further into the distance, the end not coming into sight. They had ridden for what seemed like an age but had gotten nowhere.

Lemma had become conscious of things being out of place, voicing the concern to Zenith. Why haven't we seen the planes of Sciran yet? It's half a day's travel, and midday is almost upon us; it's as if something is stopping us from reaching our destination. Is it some mystic force?" Zenith answered. "Could we have just travelled that slowly?" Lemma shook her head in disagreement. "We have not seen another soul on the bridge; this bridge is the main trade route from the Scirainian plains to the cities and towns of the Ocard Grasslands."

Pulled from the conversation to a sudden stop, the two looked ahead to see what appeared like a group of men, but strange in their appearance, unlike men as they knew them.

Zenith's blade reacted to a sense of danger aroused in the air.

"Stop", Zenith said abruptly. "Lemma, they aren't here for pleasantries, I assure you; they are here for our heads!"

"I too feel it, their souls are twisted to a point I have never felt before, they're not as men should be. I need to see you fight so I can see how you fare. I'll aid you if you need me," Lemma retorted in anticipation of battle.

The disfigured creatures charged towards them, weapons drawn and ready.

A thirst for blood resounded within their war cry. As Zenith drew his weapon, he was readying for battle. Lemma, calm and steady, watched on, ready to join the fry.

His blood cooling, serenity spread over Zenith as he ran headlong into combat, hacking and slashing, his foes' arms severed from the elbow down. The metallic smell of blood filled the air as limbs fell into the mist below.

The bridge swung from side to side, making their attacks feel uncontrolled, as he fought for their survival. Pulling aside assailant and fallen foe alike. Screaming over his shoulder, smugly. "Are you impressed yet?" Lemma just shouted back nonchalantly. "Pay Attention."

Zenith drew their penultimate attacker in. One final attack would bring this onslaught to an end. As he drove his blade upwards into his assailant's torso, the forceful thrust slashed his body in two. Bloody organs fell onto the fresh wood of the bridge, vibrant red soaking in as a permanent reminder of the attack, and a mark of the chaos to come.

As the last aggressor stood in the path, blocking their way and stopping them from moving ahead. Zenith swung with a mighty blow, cleanly removing the assailant's head, off into the mist below. As the body fell with an axe in hand, slicing through the ropes supporting the freshly repaired bridge, the side of the bridge collapsed. They had no chance of holding, falling from their point on high, into the mist, praying that they had a chance of survival.

Their eternal fall abruptly ended with an almighty crash; they landed cold as ice, lifeless. There they lay on a ledge, the horses gone and all their belongings with them.

2

THE GORGE

"Tripas, where are you? Get here, lad, what are you doing? You know that we are heading to Rockwall today, and you chose now to disappear?"

"Here, Sir Cathal, I was arranging the Tri-glorg to carry the equipment like you said". Tripas appearing and answering without warning. Caught off guard, moved on to the following question: "Have you made sure you have everything for camp? Those powers over fire of yours will only get us so far." Tripas held up a small pack containing kindling and sticks to reassure Cathal.

The path to Rockwall was long and steep. Almost a full day's climb up the gorge walls. Sharp and ragged rocks protruding from all sides. Cathal looked at the Tri-glorg's, wondering. *Did we pack too much iron? Will the tri-glorg be able to carry it that far?* Shaking his head of the negativity and changing it to a more productive thought process.

That's of no consequence; we will make it and sell the iron. The village required food, timber and tools to rebuild after the last Slither attack.

The hike was long and arduous; they made good time, fully laden, as the Tri-glorg's six legs marched forward, three on each side. The long, round body bobbing up and down, its short, stumpy tail swiping side to side, following its tether attached to its four horns on its head, guided by Tripas and Cathal. Tripas didn't understand why the Tri-glorg looked the way it did, so he asked Cathal, after all, he was his teacher. "Sir Cathal, why does the tri-glorg look so reptilian?" Cathal wasn't overly sure of the best answer, but he tried his best. "Tripas, my lad, to my understanding, they are bread from an ancient giant lizard, a cousin of sorts to the Slither, sharing an ancestry." Astounded, Tripas asked the obvious. "They're Slithers?" Cathal shook his head. "No, just a relative, not anything like them." Stopping the conversation there, knowing they were soon in Slither territories, thinking. "Can we pass unscathed?"

Tripas, still unhindered by the sense he needed to be quiet, spoke again, "Sire Cathal, are we secure? Are we out of harm's way?"

Cathal scolded the boy, "Don't be so harebrained, lad, of course we are, as long as we pass before nightfall, so move yourself".

Their pace doubled as the path levelled off. In the distance, they could hear the howls of Slithers. Cathal, cursing under staggered breaths.

"Why are they out in the day? They never dare be in the light; it burns them." *Something must be wrong.* Cathal contemplated as he pulled his staff from its scabbard on his back.

Just above a whisper, he spoke to Tripas. "Boy, make ready for a fight, I hear Slithers ahead" Slowing their pace, to get a greater vantage point from which to see their enemy. Numerous Slithers stood between them and the path to Rockwall. Tripas raised his concerns to Cathal.

"Why are so many there? Scores of them in one place is unheard of unless they aim to raid."

In the midst of the number, Cathal observes an inner ring, surrounding something. *What is it, friend, foe, treasure?*

Whatever way he looked, he could not see in this circle; inconveniently, they were tied together closely as if they had a common goal. Tripas asked, enquiring, "What's in the middle of them?" Cathal answered. "I don't know, but I have to know. I won't wait for the path to clear; we need to be away from here before nightfall." The Slither stood there, scaled black bodies shoulder to shoulder, forming an impenetrable wall.

The two resorted to the fact that they needed to charge headlong. Cathal anyway. Tripas could hang back, pick them off with a bow and arrow. Clearing the bulk before Cathal went into the centre ring.

Issuing his command, Cathal spoke, "Now, lad, start firing" One by one, the group fell, unable to see where their assailants were, running this way and that. Screams of vile pain ensued. Slither after Slither, fell to the ground, blue gooey blood and bodily fluids flowing from them. The centre ring still held fast, even though many of them had been pierced with arrows. "Hold your fire, lad, my turn now," called Cathal.

Dashing staff in hand, Cathal struck the first of the group, delivering a solid blow to the back that sent it hurtling into the air and onto a mass of jagged rocks below, looking on into the ring, a Toplander cold and lifeless in the middle. A momentary lapse of concentration left him stunned as a Slither clubbed him on the back, only to be dropped with a mighty stab from behind at the hand of Tripas. Who had seen the attack coming but failed to intercept it. The three remaining Slithers vanished into the murk that surrounded this place.

Lying in front of him were two lifeless bodies. Tripas gawped and shakily spoke, "Toplanders here?" Cathal shook his head, disappointed. "Their luck must have run dry to be this far down. It's fantastic that they remain intact. Any that had fallen before had always been missing a limb or two. All the same, living is highly doubtful."

A sudden sense of well-being filled the air; his staff glowing in the darkness. Cathal was unsure what to do and tapped his foot as he considered his questions. *What is this ancient magic at work? Or just an illusion.*

Illusion or not, his staff wanted him to approach with or without him; they seemed drawn together like kin of old, like a mother would greet her young after many nights of severance. Cathal's mind was in a flurry of thoughts. *The staff pulls strongly; it feels like I have to reunify an ancient bond. What is it?*

Equally strong was his sense of passion, which made it feel as though there was no other choice but to go to the Toplanders and check them. By some miracle, they were alive, unconscious but alive.

Bellowing out, he called on Tripas, "Tripas, come quick, they are alive; we must help them, take them to Rockwall and seek healers for them."

His sensibilities were forced. Great urgency and panic in his speech. "Hurry, boy, hurry." Rapidly, the bodies of the Toplanders were loaded onto the tri-glorg. The load was already hefty, but the beast was bred for burden and didn't seem to mind. On, they continued after the third bell, from noon, they left the Slither territories behind. Here, they could rest and examine the bodies with greater ease, to see if they could help revive them.

The day was drawing close. The darkness crept up like the ruin of the day. Now they would have to stop on this ledge until morning and then continue their journey.

Tripas, although only a stable lad, was adept with the elements, able to control them in a fashion. Untrained in any academic way, just a natural connection to the elements, he lit a fire upon the cold, moist rock where they stood using the kindling he had bought along.

Light defying the natural darkness of the gorge, as if gasping for air, it burned bright and warm nonetheless. Cathal complimented and ordered him. "Well done, lad. Now attend to the man, cover his cut and lay his head on a blanket. I shall do the same for the lady".

Zenith was unable to move; he could not understand his plight. "Why can't I move?" he spoke quietly to himself. Hearing two strange voices. One he recognised, sending his mind whirring uncontrollably. *That voice, I know it, I swear it's the one from my dream. Why do I feel like I'm floating? Where is Lemma? She must have some idea of what is happening. I can sense her, not see her; is that something like what I felt when I met Lemma? What is it? Where is it?"*

At this, feeling as though he had drifted back into his body, the questions in his mind drove him to awaken. Awake, he realised that he had no horse or any of his possessions. It was him, alone in the dark.

Flames of a fire caught Zenith's eye, where two figures resided, neither of which was Lemma. *Who are they? Did they save me?* So many questions floated about his head. Still pondering this, he looked to his sword, seeing it glowing red, like a dragon's breath.

The sword seems to be drawn to the fire or the figures there: *Why? What does it sense this time? The third of the set was lost or destroyed in the war of creation. Maybe it's called to the star.*

Raising his head, Zenith was able to make out another figure, lifeless, not too far from him. Seeing it was Lemma and whispering to himself, "Is she dead or alive? I must know."

Rolling over, able to clamber to his knees and walk on them, jarring them as they scraped on the rocks to where Lemma lay, lifeless and unconscious.

Zenith examined her; her body seemed fine, thinking. *What of her mind? is it still with her? Has she joined Rysand in the rest of the benevolent?* Shaking her gently, Zenith felt Lemma's chest rise and fall, realising she was simply asleep, surmising she must have awoken earlier than him and felt too weary to do much else. He would have done the same had it not made him so anxious, not knowing her situation. He didn't know why, but even in this short time, he had become protective of her.

Examining the star was next; it seemed intact like the Echidna flame, still glowing red in its sheath. The star had its own golden glow. Zenith asked the air. "Why do they react in such a way? Maybe the figures at the fire can explain it."

Cathal and Tripas, meanwhile, were feasting at the fire on mead and meat, a traveller's meal they called it. Unaware their guests had awoken, they chatted amongst themselves. Just on the edge of his peripheral vision, teetering at the corner of his eye. Cathal spotted a light in the dark, a hazy red glow, and a gold light that shone near the floor, moving slightly, where they laid the Toplanders down to rest, in hopes they could recover some of their stamina. In this moment, the dull light of his staff had begun showing. Sparking to life even brighter, catching him off guard, as silver light filled the air around him. Gasping out loud and thinking to himself.

"What is this? This staff has never acted this way before! It never seemed to have any magic at all. It is a lump of metal. Has something new awakened in it? A strange new power." Speaking to Tripas in his confusion. "My body feels stronger, my mind wiser beyond its years." Tripas just sat there gawping with an open mouth, staring at the staff. Cathal felt a sudden surge of pain in his head; the vision of the man and woman he had found thumped away in the back of his head. Forcing him to think about them. *Who are they? That's it, are they awake? I need them awake to know what was happening with this staff. Maybe they can tell me something.*

Cathal approached Zenith and Lemma slowly. Spotting Cathal approaching them first, Zenith spoke in a probing yet assertive tone.

"You there... Where are we? "

"This is the road to Rockwall. Who are you? Why are you here!? "Demanded Cathal.

"I am Zenith of Grissam, this is Lemma of the plains, who do we address, kind sir? I presume you are the one who dressed our wounds".

"Who am I!? I'm Sir Cathal, commander of the Bastion, protector of the village of Vastuk, and indeed I did dress your wounds." His demeanour softened as he spoke.

Introductions over, the three were distracted by the vibrations of their weapons, each of them trying to escape their sheaths and scabbards alike, glowing furiously.

Zenith realised that the sword wished to be freed from his side; it felt right to him. He unclipped the sheath, and the sword sprang from it, hanging there in mid-air, waiting for something.

Zenith's excitement was palpable as he spoke, his voice trembling, "Lemma Free the star. I think his staff is the third." Cathal looked between the two of them. "What in all Apprite are you two on about?"

Lemma whispered, "The Rysendar, the weapons of god, and your staff, Cathal, may be the missing one."

Lemma reached down to her hips, unclipping the clasp on the stars' scabbard, unsheathing the star to hang in mid-air as if waiting to be joined by another. Gesturing to the staff, Lemma Questioned.

"Where did you get that staff? What is its name?"

Thrown by the question of his staff's name and where he had got it from, Cathal responded tentatively.

"This staff has no name. I know it is a family heirloom that has been handed down for hundreds of years. Why do you ask such strange questions?"

Zenith spoke, beginning to recount the tale the monk had told him so many years ago, as he did, Cathal listened intensely, the Echidna flame and star still hanging impatiently waiting.

"I believe your staff is their third, the staff of Angelus, a weapon of pure good and light".

Confusion was evident on Cathal's face; "It's not magical!" Still thinking about it, he had heard that name, but only in his history lessons back in his childhood.

"Did you say Angelus?".

Now, Zenith and Lemma were the ones whose heads were spinning. Angelus was an ancient warrior who fought in the battle of creation and disappeared with Rysand, or so it was said. Zenith looked over at Cathal with a questioning look.

"What does it mean to you?"

Cathal began his tale speaking earnestly.

"Angelus was the founder of the kingdom of Sithos. The staff was his weapon; it had no powers when he died, and he passed it on to my family for safekeeping. Until the day it may be needed again." Cathal then moved on to explain.

The legend of the staff helping to restore order to chaos when needed; there was no mention of any other weapons. His memories of the kingdom's history made no mention of any other weapon. Well, at least that he could recall. Cathal recounted the passages that came to mind.

. . .

*At a time of war, many fought for the creation of good
and evil.*

*Their bloodshed to claim a land on which they all
resided.*

*Angelus, the general of the armies of good, laid siege
upon the last
stronghold of Rycore*

*Many soldiers, along. They fought with their deity on
their side.*

*At the final blow, Rycore fell, and only Angelus
remained standing.*

Many men were injured or killed.

His deity was wounded and drained of all his vigour.

*Enough power left to heal Angelus and to retreat to on
high
To rest until needed again.*

*Angelus was left all alone, inside the place of the last
battle
The citadel of evil had been severed away.*

Building a new world in the dark of war and chaos.

A place of peace and religion.

*His staff was a sign of strength and protection
His kingdom formed; his temple built.*

*Now, the time had come to rest and relive the days of
Old.*

His staff drained until the day it was met and revived.

All was well, Rycore gone, the staff unneeded.

*Until the next general was chosen
Angelus was able to join his deity in eternal rest.*

Safe in knowledge, his time was past.

His people's lives, safe.

. . .

Looking closely at the staff, it did seem as though it was trying to escape its binding on his side.

"What's it doing?" Lemma gasped as the staff broke free of its bindings. "Choosing for him," Zenith whispered, unable to tear his eyes away from Cathal, stood dumbstruck and rooted to the spot in complete surprise, mouth opened wide and eyes even wider.

The staff soared free like it was on the wings of an eagle, taking flight into the air to join the Echidna flame and the Star of Sciran, starting to form a triangle of light above. The three weapons assembled a portal forming below them, dropping from the centre of the triangle a map, slowly falling to the floor, floating down to the ground like a feather.

The map was written in ancient Apprite. The gorge was not on it—the parchment untarnished, seemingly brand new.

The towns and cities of Sciran and Ocard were not displayed. Only ancient cities. Nothing but rubble now, only part of ancient history. "It's Apprite but of old, Legend old", remarked Zenith, recognising the city names from books and papers he had read exploring the Occardian Grasslands.

There was a land many leagues away from the continent that nobody knew or had even known existed. That it even existed was news to all gathered; Lemma, thinking all along, *I've never seen it on any map before in Sciran or the Occardian Grasslands.*

This map was strange. It looked almost freshly drawn, made of parchment that wasn't discoloured in any way, as though time had never passed for it. It had a magical aura; its edges tinged with light. It seemed to have highlighted, drawing their eyes to a place on the unknown island.

It was named in ancient Apprite, the place of jade, which puzzled them all.

Zenith and Lemma looked closer than Cathal.

Both remembered the legend, knowing this could mean two things. *Where the sword was hidden, or, as the play said, did it mean a seal?* Neither knew for sure what to make of it.

What is this? Cathal thought, eyes wide as he stared above. Weapons playing and dancing like children at a carnival, *why do they do this? Magic? Legends? And how on Apprite did I end up a part of it?*

Like thunder, it dawned on him, letting the thought escape his lips in but a whisper. "Was this about the weapons? True!? Was his weapon part of the Rysendar? A weapon of good? A protector of the people?" "I'm pretty sure this display says it all." Zenith jumped in, hearing the latter end of Cathal's mutterings. Cathal had started to believe all Zenith and Lemma had told him. His own eyes could even see the connection between the weapons.

Suddenly, storm clouds gathered overhead, casting the remaining light into darkness. The rain drizzled, moistening the air —a release after days of drought. Crashes became abundant, thunderous sounds filled the silence around them.

"Into the tent", behind Tripas's screaming voice, horse and raw like he'd screamed unheard many times before. "Grab the map." Called Zenith, Hands fumbling in the air, trying to grab the weapons still dancing in the air around them. "We won't be back out in this," glancing at the map in her tight grip, Lemma ran to the glowing embers of the fire, smouldering, fighting against the onslaught from above.

"God's it is coming down like devils go to war," one of the others muttered between blazing bolts of blue and silver glazing the sky, flaunting their power over the ground. "Shift your arses", Cathal screeched from the entrance of the tent.

"It's like the heavens decided the moment had to end." Zenith turned back, looking outside the tent, soaked to the bone. "That sky was perfect moments ago, now look at it, dark, gutted like it's been cursed." Between breaths, Lemma asked, "Was this Storm the doing of Rycore?", a low fear in her voice at the realisation. "That or we've just annoyed nature itself", Zenith answered.

Where a blue-black sky flourished, now dreary and colourless, full of grey clouds, seeming haunted by an evil that wished them unwell. "Let's just dry off and get some sleep, if we can," Lemma muttered, tossing yet another wet towel to one side. The group pushed further inside the tent to dry and sleep; much travelling befell them in the morning.

The rain poured, the wind howled around the tent unrelentingly, poles bending and cracking under the bombardment. Tripas, through chattering teeth, whispered, "It's not natural, it's like the storm has a mind of its own." None inside dared to answer. Never closing their eyes for the fear in their hearts would swallow them up and toss their bodies to the devil haunting this place.

Wailing and cries for blood seemed to flood the air. *Were there demons around them waiting to strike?* They dared not think. *Would this be another wave of disaster for them to face?* There had already been enough blood spilt this day. A guard that was what they needed, *but who?*

Sat in silence, almost sure he could hear his armour rusting, Cathal made the choice, deciding that even though he was the man in charge. Thinking to himself, *I'll take the first watch, I can't ask them, they're lucky to be alive. Tripas the lad hasn't got the eye for detail, so best last I recon.* Then, explaining the rotation for guarding, they agreed that it was probably the best option available.

As the night continued, the cries and wails turned to

chants. Cathal sat at the tent opening listening, watching and thinking. *Gods, why are they the same as before? Too many times, I've heard them too many times to count.* They were Slither war cries, but who was their target? *is it us, or could they be preparing to attack Rockwall?* For fear's sake, he shouted to the others, "Awaken, you fools, you need to make ready, we head for Rockwall now. "Those vile beasts can try and catch us!" At the very least, the others had rested a little and could move more freely.

Startled, the group sprang into action, charging around, loading the Tri-glorgs, readying themselves for anything. Each holding a weapon in one hand, bags and goods in the other. Should they be attacked, they would not go down without leaving a trail of blood in their wake.

Readied, they ran, moving as quickly as they could, the rocky slope sinuously underfoot, slipping this way and that; their footing was almost lost with every step.

This did not seem the wisest of choices after all. If they had been attacked at their campsite, at least it was flat and steady underfoot. Now, if they had to fight, they would have to be more cunning and stealthy in their attacks. Especially to win whilst trying to avoid a drop over the edge into the dark descent of the abyss, not ten steps away from where they walked.

Behind them, the sounds of a bloodthirsty carried on the air. "In all that is holy, what are those sounds?" Zenith shouted to Cathal and Tripas. Neither he nor Lemma had ever heard the like anywhere they had been before. "Just keep moving, they are normal for these parts, but we don't want to be caught unaware by the creatures creating them," Cathal said, seemingly unconcerned in his reply. "These sounds are a seasonal occurrence. Just not usually this early in the season or even this loud, must be a big group."

Their pace, unchanged, the group saw a clearance amongst

the worn and threadbare rocks. Now, not a league away from Rockwall, they rested for a while. Sounds of marching starting to haunt the rise. Weary from their sleepless night and unready for any battle, they peered around for any place that could conceal them from harm.

Even slightly rested, their effort to whittle the enemy line would not be wasted. In their current states, they were more use to the dead than the living.

"There, just ahead, we can get behind it." Tripas signalled spotting a place to hide

Watching and waiting for any sign of their foes, they lay hidden behind a hefty, oversized boulder. Concealed, they saw a party of Slither scouts come over the brow to the clearing.

"They aren't here for us, scouts always go ahead to test a town's defences just like they did with Vastuk." Whispered Cathal to the others a sense of longing hanging in those whispered tones. The scouts passed, and they could breathe again. At least, they knew for now that they were safe to hide where they were.

The day broke, the sun pushing the darkness from their eyes. Now that they had rested and slept, they dared to continue. Cathal hoped they could blindside the scouts and remove them for the sake of Rockwall, giving them a fair chance to warn the others of the oncoming attack.

Cathal spoke to the group, "I believe we will best serve Rockwall if we seek to remove the Slither scouts." Tripas nodded in agreement, knowing it was truly the best course of action. Lemma wasn't overly sure, with a quizzical look at Zenith prompting him to speak.

"Say we do this as you ask, what gains are there to us or Rockwall?" his question hung in the air as Cathal contemplated how to justify his suggestion to them. Finally, he spoke, "Slither scouts, such as those, recon the town and report back to their main force. If we can eliminate their threat, it will reduce the likelihood of a full-scale attack." Zenith could see in Cathal's eyes that much more was behind his immovable stance on killing off the Slither.

He probed further, wanting to understand why. It turned out to be the whole reason: Cathal was the one going to Rockwall, stemming from his feeling responsible for missing the scouts, which had led to Vastuk being devastated by a full-scale raid only weeks ago. This was more than enough to justify the actions Cathal wanted to take.

That was it; they had decided to stalk the darkness for the Slither scouts, the staff of Angelus, potentially able to light up the darkness hiding them. They had an advantage. This was the time for Tripas to shine.

Living with the Slithers always in mind, his father had taught him how to hunt, track and dispatch them most swiftly.

Quickly moving on from behind the boulder, weapons drawn, they went slowly, Tripas leading the way. The scent of Slither in the air now, Tripas had them; he knew they could not be far. The ground covered with leaves yielded his next clue: footprints leading up into a concealed cave in the rock face. Its entrance, hidden from view by boulders jutting out at its base and sides. Perfectly camouflaged from the path.

Climbing onto the lower ledge, "fresh claw marks, we are definitely close", Tripas quietly muttered to the others. The cave entrance was wide, and light barely able to pierce the darkness at the doorway open to them.

Walking in the light had gone; all hoping that Cathal could activate the staff was the least of their problems. The Slithers were awake and readying to move; they had to do this now if they wanted to stand a chance.

Cathal, aware of the situation, concentration bare upon his

face, had managed to light the way with his staff, bright silver rays illuminating the moist rock face all around. Walking deeper and deeper inside, they could hear their common enemy. Their view was clear of obstruction, as they saw the scouts prowling around a pit of blazing fire, dancing, waving, holding weapons aloft; they were unafraid, unaware of their impending fate.

Tripas made the first shot, a clean hit to the face of the largest Slither, slicing clean through brains oozing from the wound mixed in with the globular blue blood. The other Slither, now aware of their plight, gathered in a storm of bodies heading in their direction. Many of the numbers fell within seconds at the hands of the star, bolts of light flashing as it sliced them limb from limb, blood hissing on the fire pooling at the feet of those left standing.

Still, the remaining Slithers charged. Cathal and Zenith stood between the others and the oncoming Slither advance. Ready for the onslaught, they drove forward into the now ravenous group. Cathal was the first to draw blood, crowning a Slither from above. Their skull crushed, falling lifeless at his feet, its body still twitching at the last pains of death.

Zenith met his first opponent head-on, driving the Echidna flame deep into its chest, granting an almost instant death. In its last throes of life, the Slither nicked Zenith's shoulder, drawing blood to the surface—an ungodly rage overtook Zenith deep inside his mind.

The pit of fire started to grow flames, sawed into the air, swirling into a vortex. Cathal and Tripas both asking "What is happening? Who summoned this unearthly power?"

As Zenith slashed and dodged, the others watched with fear in their eyes. While Zenith moved, so did the vortex, swaying and dancing, searing flesh from bone, all the Slither it touched, howling ungodly screams of anguish. Unaware of all around him, Zenith was wild and feral in his movements, twisting, turning, and moving from opponent to opponent.

The bodies were stacked at his feet, blood soaking into the souls of his boots—the flames of the vortex enclosing around him. Unmanageable rage in his eyes, the vortex surrounding him, joining with the Echidna flame, flames leap from the sword, the power in his hands, relentless in its attacks.

Distressed at his movements, Lemma ran to him, grasping his arm in her grip. she screamed at him. "Zenith, get control of yourself." Words going unheard, Zenith slung Lemma to the ground—landing amongst the bodies of Slither, screaming in agony. "Tripas, I'll hold the Slither, you check on her", Cathal ordered

The Battle was raging inside Zenith's head. Unconcerned with the relentless attacks on his body, his mind locked in combat with the Echidna flame for supremacy over its powers, his strength of mind was being tested beyond that of a normal man.

The powers of which he had never heard or felt before, building against him, pushing him back into his subconsciousness. His resolve was swift in its ability to control the Echidna flame, unwavering. Inside Zenith's head, the word rang strong and harsh, battering him, forcing him to listen.

To control my power, you must be one with me, fight as
*   equals.*
I will give you my power and knowledge once you can
Tell me my proper name
Your sword is forged from my body.
Your powers are linked to mine.
Search your memories for the answer you need.

· · ·

Tripas, seizing the moment, springing into action, darting over the slain Slither, trying to get within arm's reach of Lemma. "God Damit, I can't get there, the vortex keeps shifting," he shouted as he withdrew. Lemma, speaking through the pain, squeezing her eyes shut and clenched jaw, "It's ok, my ankle hurts, but I feel no heat from the vortex. I'm more concerned for Zenith"

Inside his head, the voice echoed with a familiarity. *I know the voice. But where from? I can't even see a person or even a silhouette. Who does it belong to?* Memories raced in front of his eyes. Searching deep within them, he heard that voice again, but this was one of the first things he could ever remember. In his father's arms, he cried, his father singing him a lullaby he had not heard in years.

The voice? It wasn't there before. What's That? A shadow, does the voice come from it?

Wielder of the Echidna flame, you shall be.
    My brother, you are.
    Our powers shared throughout all eternity.
    When the time comes, you shall know me as thy brother.
    Call to me with words only you shall know.
    Synergy shall be my name.
    Heed these words, my brethren, do not forget,
    As a test will come to
    Join Us.

His torment over and the battle on the outside won, his senses returned in an instant as he roared the name from his memories out into the cave, "Synergy is thy name, my Brother, you are from berth" At this, the chaos in his mind fell silent, only the voice of Synergy remained.

Now you call my name.
    My powers.
    You shall possess.
    Control will not be yours.
    We shall meet soon.
    Control will be yours upon your test.

"What did this mean? Whom shall he meet?" Zenith asked, his voice silent. All he could remember was a shadow of something high above him. Looking around to see the carnage about him. Confusion filled his head as he surveyed the area. "What power has done this?"

Lemma, slouched amongst the bodies of the dead, Slither lifeless all around her. Hand outstretched, waiting for aid from those around her, Zenith approached her, pulling her to her feet, wincing in anguish, her face clear as she rose to her feet, her ankle more than sizeably swollen, maybe even broken—the look of utter distaste on her face. Perplexed, Zenith looked at her. He guessed it was the pain, not him directly. His eyes showed nothing, blank and unaware of what he had done. Lemma couldn't bring herself to chastise him. Zenith just looked concerned for her. Zenith offered his back to Lemma, lifted her, and carried her towards the cave's exit.

All Zenith knew was that she needed a healer sooner rather than later, strolling with Lemma around his throat, clinging on for dear life so that her ankle didn't touch the floor, a pain so great that she felt like she could pass out at any moment. Lemma dug her hands into Zenith's chest partially to help with the pain, also to extract a small amount of revenge at the man who threw her to the ground, injuring her; *he was only trying to help.* What she now realised between the jolts of pain in her ankle, joined with what she had seen, made more sense; Zenith wasn't even in the cave when it happened. What she and the others witnessed while she lay there was a mystery, obviously something even Zenith had yet to understand.

Stride by stride, Zenith carried her, not knowing he had caused his friend such a heinous injury. Zenith felt her weight increase, her chest and body pressing down hard onto his spine. Her breathing slowed; her pain had whisked her into the dark of her mind. Zenith thought, *Perhaps this is best, at least now the pain will not drag on; we will not be held back.* Cathal seemed to echo his thoughts with words, "We can make good time if she doesn't get any worse than this; the healers will be in sight soon enough."

Reaching the wide mouth of the cave, their eyes burned as the light of the Sun became visible. Cathal could easily guess now why the Slithers liked the dark and why they hunted at night. It must have been something to do with their eyes. Slithers would squint in the sun and hide in shadows. The sting to his eye at this second was nasty enough. Imagining being a creature of the night, the pain of daylight would cause them, made him feel the slightest bit sorry for the Slither.

Their eyes watering, irritated by the change in colour and contrast of the cave they had left, the world opened before them. Once their eyes had adjusted, they could all see plain as day the lake of blood held in Zenith's clothes and the blood dripping from the Echidna flame slowly pooling at his feet.

Cathal and Tripas were amazed at the sight that now stood before them, a river of blood draining from Zenith's clothes onto the smooth, bleached surface of the path to Rockwall.

Lemma's body, now dormant and lame upon Zenith's back,

began to weigh him down. The tri-glorg, already fully laden and unable to carry any more, forced his hand; he would bring her to the healers, even if needing one himself by the time he got there.

Walking away from their last battle, worn and weary, they slowly climbed the gorge, etching their way towards Rockwall. Cathal, fearful of his companion after the waste he had made in the cave, dared not speak or glance in Zenith's direction for fear that some unholy power might remove his very skin from his body.

3
HEAL WELL, MY NEW FRIEND

Tripas had deep compassion for others, which wasn't unnoticed: *They've barely spoken with him.* Cathal thought as he helped steady Lemma on Zenith's back. *And yet he acts like he's known them forever; it may be that's his youth.* Quietly stating to himself, "Life hasn't hardened him yet."

Tripas watched as his companion struggled with each laborious step. Offering to share Zenith's load, but it was rejected. Taking it upon himself to begin explaining what the group had witnessed within the darkness of the cave, and how Zenith had struck Lemma to the ground. Describing how he probably caused her injuries. It was evident that he had borne witness to the birth of a warrior's insanity. In Tripas's eyes, he knew that Zenith was not any different and was no danger to them.

It had strangely reminded him of a legend he had read about in a book from his adolescent years. Reading was relative, as most words were garbled to him.

The book spoke of legend, about an ancient warrior who

had gone insane during an intense battle, described as wielding a staff. However, the warrior he watched did not wield the staff; instead, it was Zenith who wielded a sword. But a warrior was a warrior, vexed though his mind was. Tripas listened intently as Zenith began to recount his ordeal, one that those standing on the outside had not witnessed, while Zenith fought within his subconscious mind. However, it felt genuine to him; it seemed almost fictitious to the others.

Zenith Struggling internally whilst dragging his feet, *It doesn't make sense, none of it did. How could I not see her?* Nothing seemed to make sense. *Tripas is right. I injured her, gods, what have I done?* Having no idea how he fought the Slither and how a vortex of flame formed, disintegrating them. Tripas had told him as much. What he didn't understand was how any of this related to the visions.

A trail marker along the rough edge of the beaten path lay before them; they had reached the outskirts of Rockwall. At last, they could rest safe in the knowledge that the healers and the markets were not too far away.

Cathal could do his duty to the village by selling the goods and returning with building materials and food they so badly needed.

Lemma could get the help she needed and be back on her feet, able to travel home to Sciran. That was the plan, but they would need to find a way out of the gorge first.

Zenith stopped, placing Lemma down carefully so that she could continue to rest; he needed to stop, drink and catch his breath. A smooth rock providing a place to sit, giving him a moment to recover, even the smallest amount of the energy that he'd lost back in the cave and the consequential walk with Lemma, draped around his shoulders.

Tripas offered him a bladder full of mead to quench his thirst. It had been so long since a drink felt this good sliding down his throat, chasing away the dryness and fatigue. Once he had regained some energy, Zenith lifted Lemma from the ground and placed her back on his back with the aid of the others, ready to continue into Rockwall.

Approaching the stone archway, intricate in its design, made by a veteran stone smith, yet built to withstand the onslaught of ten thousand men. The town of Rockwall opened to them, with the path splitting. "Markets that way ", said Cathal, pointing south, "but you both need a healer. They're in the east, up the stairs over there." All acknowledged that a separation was needed. They arranged to meet at the Dancing Queen, the small inn that Cathal had already planned to stay at as soon as their business was concluded. Each agreed they would wait for the other should they return first. It was just as easy to do this as to try to find another place to board them.

Selling in the market was not going to be as easy as they had first thought. Streets bursting with the movement. Carriages lined the road edges. Dozens of traders were confined to one area. Cathal wondered. *How are we to sell this iron?*

There were already many established traders selling metals of all kinds to a wide range of people: Blacksmiths, labourers, weapon smiths, and Armourers. Tripas looked to Cathal, asking, "Who's going to be willing to buy from a weary traveller? Let alone sell us the equipment they required and enough food till the new crop had grown." Cathal snapped back, "Be positive, boy, someone will."

Setting up in a nearby alley. They were quickly surrounded by many people pondering what offers these travellers had brought.

Much to the dismay of the locals, they found that there were no novel items to speak of. Only iron, of no use to most of them, they walked away sour-faced and unhappy.

Only two men remained behind, watching each other hard-faced. They questioned Cathal on the price of the iron. He had planned to ask only for a maximum of five coins per ingot. Each of the men was constantly outwagering the other, and an unspoken bitterness clearly lay between them.

Eager to buy the whole stock from them. "Do they know something I don't?" questioned Cathal. *The mine back in Vastuk did tell me before I left that iron from the Station mine most of the time contained elemental magic. Enhancing and increasing the value of the items made with it. Was this why the two pushed each other to buy it all?* Each of the two men trying to outbid the other constantly calling new values. "Ten coins an ingot, fifteen an ingot, twenty an ingot."

"No thirty gold per ingot", came a rambunctious call from across the crowded marketplace. A slender, more feminine man approached them.

Cathal's word died in his throat as he spoke in absolute silent astonishment, "Does he really mean it? Thirty coins a piece, there are five hundred ingots here, and I only expected to gain three coins per one once I'd bartered with whomever to agree the final purchase."

All they needed for the items they required was twelve hundred coins, and at three coins each, they had some left over for the return trip—a carriage to haul their goods. At thirty, they stood to make fifteen thousand coins. Enough to purchase extra supplies to ensure everyone could fully rebuild.

Cathal resided to sell to this man. Another overly exuberant call from one of the more rugged men who had been bidding previously, announcing "Forty-five coins per ingot."

A bidding war had begun over iron. Indeed, Vastukian iron was strong and easily worked. It possessed the elemental properties and was used for all types of weapons, incorporated into a wide range of objects in Vastuk, from general utensils to building frames and tri-glorg storage containers, like the ones it had been carried here in large flat topless boxes that were easily loaded.

Making this announcement forced his original rival to leave; this was much too rich for his blood. Slumping away deflated. The skinny man, looking on unconcerned, announced at the top of his voice so that all the market could hear: "One hundred coins per ingot." They would make fifty thousand. Tripas could not believe his ears.

At that, Cathal leapt to his feet and shouted. "Sold!" Echoing across the market. The rugged man defeated wimped away to find a stall with more items he could purchase.

Cathal, bewildered by the events, stood tall, awaiting the man who was now approaching. "How do you wish to receive your payment?"

The gent paused for an answer, but could see the confusion upon Cathal's face, so he spoke again. "Coins or goods, I can arrange both for you, you're from Vastuk, are you not?"

Cathal, hearing the town's name, snapped back to reality, his senses frazzled. A pleasant tone left his mouth as her spoke.

"That we are, sir, and we would appreciate it if it would be paid for in cash, apart from a few cartloads of food and building materials."

The man did some calculation in his head before answering.

"Say, around four thousand in goods, including two carriages and the other forty-six thousand in coins, would that satisfy you, sir?"

The unbelievable figures were more than Cathal could have ever imagined; mustering his words, he spoke with a slight hesitation.

"Indeed, that would more than suffice our need." Hearing this, the man gleefully asked, "Shall we meet later when you have made your arrangements?" Cathal had finally got his complete composure back and spoke with a degree of purpose.

"May I ask your name, sir?"

The gentleman looked a little shocked, as if he realised he hadn't already given his name, quite the faux pas.

"I am Remi, owner of the finest weapon and household smithery in these parts. we shall meet there, who shall I be expecting?"

Cathal held himself proud and spoke with a decorum not often heard from a man of his more diminutive stature.

"Sir Cathal of Vastuk." Nodding in return, Remi turned his attentions to the next stall. As he left, Cathal could only breathe in disbelief at the ruckus the sale of his iron had caused.

Approaching the healer's quarters, Zenith knew that somehow, he was destined to meet Synergy soon. *How can I prepare, and what should I bring?* This creature in his mind, and now feeling kindred to it, brother-like. *What type of creature could speak fluent Appritian? One I've never encountered before.* In his memories, he could see the shadow of the beast, but still, he had no answers.

Vexed by so many of his thoughts, his body had been unnoticed; the strain of carrying Lemma all this way had finally taken its toll on him. Thinking to himself. *The final steps, thank god I made it,* then silence, fatigue had taken over, forcing his body to collapse. Skin torn from his knees as he slid down the steps, holding fast to Lemma, still unconscious, just slow, shallow breaths confirming life on his back, the darkness had taken over, leaving him defenceless to all around. "There are two people face down on the steps, Grap stretchers", the old man alerted others who stood about the healers' quarters after discovering Zenith and Lemma unconscious. "Bandages to me, I see blood", the more urgent cry as the stretchers arrived.

Arriving at the Remo workshop, Remi's place of work and home. Tripas and Cathal were stunned and astounded at the building that stood before them. This building could not be a metal smith's workshop or a weapons maker; its grandeur was fit for a Queen. Stained glass windows on all floors depicted the War of Creation, each surrounded by a malevolent sandstone arch within the walls of granite that still shone as if they were fresh from the quarry.

A massive double-arched doorway, set dead centre of the building, was made of oak inlaid with intricate slivers of silver and gold. It revealed a picture of Rysand himself, the Jade Pandora clasped in his hand, below him three figures brandishing the Rysendar in all its glory.

In the picture, there was also a creature standing side by side with the wielder of the Echidna flame, not a dragon but a half-lion, half-eagle, giant dragon wings and Flames leaping from its feet. Tripas, noticing this, beginning to look more closely, wondering. *Could this be a depiction of the creature that Zenith had described? It certainly appears strong, mighty, and capable of controlling flames like the Echidna flame. I must show this to Zenith before we leave to return to Vastuk.*

Grabbing the massive iron knocker of the door, lifting and releasing it, a shock of sound reverberated through the door. Seconds later, the door pulled open to reveal Remi, who was there to greet them. Noticing Tripas's keen interest in the doors, he beckoned them in to complete their deal from earlier that day.

Remi talked as they moved through the building towards its centre. "I see you like the look of my door. I made it myself.

It depicts the generals of Rysand's army and the beast that granted the general of fire his abilities. I believe it's called a Manticore, or something similar. It's part of a tapestry they have hung in the town hall. They say the creature will return to the general of fire when he is needed again. It also mentioned other animals, but not who or what"

In the inner sanctum of the house, they sat whilst they waited for their payment to be made ready. Talking amongst themselves, they discovered that Remi was once a member of the Vastuk mining community in his youth. He left many years ago to seek his fortune here in Rockwall. Remi informed them he wished them to contact his brother, Twain, for him, to give him a message. "Tell him I am now one of the wealthiest men in Rockwall, that I would like for him and my mother to join me here. So that she can spend her remaining days with the two of us in comfort, wanting for nothing. Perhaps they can arrive in time for his wedding to the mayor's daughter."

Cathal and Tripas promised to deliver his message for him and to even send a guard detail with them to ensure their safe arrival; it was the least they could do for such a genuinely considerate man of his heritage and calibre.

Awakening in bed, Zenith lay under white sheets that felt light and airy, with no idea as to where he was. The last thing he remembered was the sight of the healer's quarters, then nothing until now. "Where is Lemma!?" Zenith tossed from side to side, trying to find her. Panicking, his last memory had her on his back. A figure entered his chamber, through the stone arch at the far side of the room, pushing the sheet hanging over it to one side. A short person dressed in pure white robes, matched only by his extensive, untainted grey beard, and gold-coloured sandals on his feet. Silently, he approached, no malice in his eyes or movements, only concern for his charge and their well-being.

"Ah, my friend, you're awake! This is good. I had feared the worst for you. It's been two full days since I found you and your companion on our steps. You had left this plane, your body exhausted. I did not know if your mind would revive with you or stay locked in its own detrimental asylum, leaving you in our permanent care."

Aiding Zenith from his bed and setting him on his feet, leading him from his chamber along a white stone corridor. They passed other chambers like the one he had been in, where he could see other men inside. Other rooms unoccupied, still smelling of their last occupier or of something pure and clean.

Ahead of them stood a mighty opening into a wide-open courtyard. At the other side stood another just as impressive building, this one tinged with indigo, as the building behind them was tinged with aqua. *It's a clear divide and difference between them, but for what?*

Concerns tingled in his mind. *What of Lemma was she awake? Has she healed or passed on to be with Rysand? No, that isn't possible. She had only broken her ankle and been unconscious when I last saw her.* Bought from his thoughts, hearing the healer speak, "You must stay here awhile. I shall go and see to your friend now. If she is able, I shall bring her here to you as only recognised healers may enter both of the dorms"

This gave him a little more clarity; now he understood a bit more about the difference between the buildings. One appeared to be for men, and the other for women. Indeed, a strange custom to him; he had never been to a healer's house where they separated the sexes. Maybe this was just their way of offering privacy and comfort to women who had suffered at the hands of a man, and the same for the men he had seen. Some places took in those women back in Errant and protected them; it seemed possible that they did the same here, albeit in a roundabout way.

Zenith examined the courtyard and the surrounding buildings. Encased in a beautifully tended garden of shrubs and flowers of all colours, none being species that he had seen before. The garden beds periodically interrupted the cobbles, breaking up the solid mass and forming paths that weaved between them. Sensing the goodness in this place, his attention was drawn to the centre of it. At the very centre stood a grandiose site. The finest fountain built of pure white marble, in the shape of a nine-tailed wraith. He had only ever seen one more like this in Grissam; it was meant to be a representation of a Rysander general's warbird and closest pet, Krilos.

Krilos was there to protect and heal all who worshipped Rysand, so it fitted in well here. This one, though, held his gaze, pulling at him, calling him to approach it; the power emanating from it was pure and supportive. He could see now that at the base of the statue was a large, rounded, red stone, from which the power emanated. It seemed likely that the calm and serene feeling of the courtyard was a result of it. Yet again, something new and foreign which he couldn't explain.

From across the courtyard, a voice familiar and kind called to him, coming from the archway of the indigo building, distracting him from the fountain's majesty. Seeing the man who brought him here with a woman, it couldn't be Lemma. She had broken her ankle only three days ago, and this woman was able to walk on her own. The voice calling to him was like a mother, a child, or lovers who had been separated. Lemma would not call to him like this, although somewhere deep down, he wished she would.

Zenith's thoughts shifted to the time they spent at the inn above Rysand gorge. Lemma was the most beautiful woman he had ever met. Long flowing locks of auburn and gold spread wide and down the side of her face, skin golden, browned by the Sun, body lean, muscles toned and firm, her chest surrounded in its fullness covered by her clothes, her shape one he could only describe as that of a goddess.

The voice was now next to him; it was indeed Lemma, and she was fully well. He stared at her in surprise. The clothes she wore now were even more regal than the ones she had been wearing up until now, and her beauty shone even more than usual in the light of the courtyard. Her soothing voice was like music to his ears.

"From what I understand, Zenith, you carried me all the way here, only to finally collapse at the doorway. Why did you do it? You could have left me there" Silence fell over them. His inner voice challenging him. *I can't tell her the truth, can I? She sees me as a friend and brother in arms... but I feel more.* He took a moment to breathe before looking at her to speak. As he opened his mouth, he was interrupted by the healer.

"Now you are both well, I am assured that you will be able to return to whence you came and tell others of our work." That was for sure, they would tell anyone who needed help.

They needed to get back to the Dancing Queen. If Zenith could remember the way back there, *would Cathal and Tripas have honestly waited for them, two complete days?* The stone gate of the healer's yard opened wide before them, beckoning them to leave the haven that had made them well. Lemma and Zenith thanked the healer for his aid as they walked away from the fountain.

Outside the gate seemed familiar; perhaps there was a chance they could get back to the Dancing Queen without aid. If Zenith's mind served him right. *There were some stairs ahead that led down to the road. I carried Lemma along.*

· · ·

Back at the Dancing Queen, Cathal waited, tending to his new animals and their loads. He was wondering. *How long will I need to wait for them? Two days have passed. They still have not returned. Was I wrong to leave Zenith to carry Lemma alone?* Having seen Zenith struggling over the days before they arrived, thinking again on it. *He never complained or asked for help; needless to say, help should always be offered even if not asked for.* That was it; he would go to the healers and check on their care, using some of his new wealth to pay for their treatment should the need arise.

Cathal had become increasingly irate as he contemplated Zenith and Lemma, screaming to summon Tripas.

"Tripas here, lad, you insolent boy, where are you when..." Tripas cut him off, answering mid-sentence. "I'm here, sir. What do you need?" Cathal informed him, "I'm leaving for a while. Stay here with the carts and animals to assure their safety "

Tripas questioned in return, "Where are you heading, Sir?" No less irritated, Cathal scoffed. "To the healers. I have a growing concern for our companions. It's been two days since they left us, and now I must see that their well-being is kept in good hands." Leaving the well-kept stable yard of the Dancing Queen. Cathal headed for the fork in the road where he had last been with his companions. "Should I have taken the path to the right with them?" He could not decide if he had done his friends an injustice or made a judgment error.

Climbing down the steps, Zenith and Lemma walked side by side in silence, neither knowing what to say to each other. Passing glances showed they knew that each other kept their thoughts to themselves.

The uneasy silence between them was palpable. Broken up

by only the sound of birds sitting atop the buildings that lined the stairs. The path now turned into a well-paved road of white stone slabs; luckily for Zenith, the Dancing Queen was signposted; it truly must be a local landmark, he remarked to himself, passing the sign. He didn't need to remember the way.

Turning to walk the way the sign directed, they saw a figure on the horizon, and both recognised it. It was Cathal. His short, stocky build in that battered old armour made him stand out anywhere. "They waited!" The silence broke the seal of contempt surrounding them, erased as both raised a hand to wave and shout to him. They still had their guide and companion in this unfamiliar land.

Reunited, they embraced as brothers in arms. Cathal's face and mind eased at the sight and well-being of his friends. Walking back to the Dancing Queen was easy; they reached their abode in no time. They met with Tripas, who was more than delighted to see Zenith had not forgotten them and that he would be able to show him Remi's depiction of the Rysendar and the three generals of legend.

4
DARKNESS ARISES

The evening drew in fast, the Sun turning dark amber in its descent—the lamplighters were busy lighting the streets. Zenith sat aside his inn room window, watching the citadel become bright as the sun lit up the day. The lamps forced out the darkness of the gorge, making him feel safe here.

On the walls not too far from the Dancing Queen, the guards were changing shifts, and the approach to it all relaxed. On the horizon, he saw a light far above him, drawing him to think about the lands above. *If I'm right, it could be Sciran; it would be faint but plausible for me to see from here, even though we travelled away from it after the bridge.*

Curiosity got the better of him, and he left his room and headed down the well-lit and highly decorated corridor of the inn to Cathal's room. Stood at Cathal's door, hand raised to knock, then heard Cathal talking on the other side of the door. Listening, a second voice, a woman's laugh, came from inside. Averting his attention from the door, Zenith walked away, not wanting to disturb Cathal. It certainly sounded like a bad idea.

Tripas would be able to answer his question. Turning away from the door, the sounds from the room changed; he felt his face brighten and burn as he realised, to his amusement, that the laughter had turned to erotic moans of pleasure.

Pace quickening to escape the sounds now resonating loudly and clearly from the room, he knocked loudly at Tripas's door; awake or not, he was going to answer now.

The door opened to reveal Tripas's eyes half open, hair a mess, straggly and ravaged from a restless sleep. No sooner had he opened the door than Zenith spoke.

"Tripas, I have a question for you."

The door closed as if he had not been heard, a hand raised to knock. Again, the door swung open with some force, strong enough to knock Zenith a few paces back. Tripas was now alert and ready, as if the horns of war had sounded.

"There is no time for questions. I have something I must show you." Pulling Zenith along and out of the inn at quite a pace, leaving by the main doors.

Streets, glowing a burnt orange from the lamps shining above them, with so many lights around, multiple shadows lay at their feet, pushing away from them in different directions. The silence in the air forbade any interaction or conversation they could have held.

Ahead lay a large stone bridge. Zenith didn't know where he was. This place was already strange to him, and even though he had lost his fear of the dark as a child, a strong foreboding sense of unease told him to be wary of his surroundings. The darkness held a terror, his hands reaching to his waist and gathering a firm grip on the hilt of the Echidna flame.

Turning slowly to Tripas, his eyes fixated on all around him, he broke the silence.

"Ready your blade, there is something ungodly creeping in

the shadows following us." Attention diverted to the shadow that lay all around, scanning each corner and building base, even at the several shadows surrounding him, caused by the streetlamps. At the base of the buildings behind him, a strangely shaped shadow looked solid and not part of the building. "There", pointing to show Tripas, he saw his assailant, a lean figure firmly pressed against the building in hopes of concealing itself, hiding its form.

A Slither had made it into the city unnoticed, hidden within the dark. A quick thought struck Zenith. *I can barely see it; no wonder the guards missed it, and now it skulks after us.*

Tripas, paying attention, whispered, "It's different from the ones in the cave, I mean, look at it, it's blacker, almost as if made of shadow." Zenith nodded and replied in a hushed tone, "It's not just its colour. Its size and shape aren't like the others."

So grossly had its body twisted that only its facial features remained the same, where its arms should be, now, blades. Sharpened bone protruded. Its body was layered, covered in an armour of scales and sinew. Its head was covered with a solid, off-white material; the helmet's only gaps showed where its eyes should have been, yet it still retained its facial structure. A product of pure evil now stalked them. The Echidna flame glowed an intense red. It knew this was the work of Rycore.

Zenith felt it deep down; he would have to fight, perhaps for his life and the life of his friend. This would be the first time he would face a minion of Rycore in its truest, grotesque form, his most brutal battle yet.

Advancing from the shadows, the creature came, the shadows following its every move as it slunk its way towards them, weapons ready to attack. *Can I truly control the new powers I have gained to help me defeat this foe?* Dread filled his mind. Only a few seconds remained until the Slither would be upon them.

Lurching forward, the Slither sprang to life, its attack fierce and zealous. The shadows dragged behind, growing away from the wall as it surged forward. Constantly supplying its strength. The first blow deflected away in a daze of sparking red light. The sound of metal and bone scraping against each other resonated off all the surrounding surfaces. Dodging to one side, Zenith prepared for the next assault. This time, he would strike back. The pinch of bone grinding on the ground as the Slither came at him again, this time both arms in a pincer flying up from the ground, aiming directly for his throat, ducking below the blade, a small nick to his forehead as the blade grazed by, a small amount of blood bubbled to the surface..

Zenith struck hard and fast, unthinking and uncontrolled. Flames leapt from his sword, searing the Slither's armour and melting what skin remained attached to its disfigured body.

The Slither, unfazed, slashed downwards towards his chest, bare and wide open, pushing away from the Slither, his torso caught by the point of one blade, slicing clean through his leather shirt, missing by less than a hair's breadth the soft, clean skin that lay underneath. Rolling away, reeling from the last attack, he summoned all his courage, placing all his emotion and faith into his blade, diving around the back of the enemy. Flashes of brilliant red flame wrapped through the shadows, severing them. The shadows, leading to the Slither, shrivelled and recoiled back to where they should have naturally lain.

Howls of pure, unrelenting agony filled the air all around. The Slither cut from its dark power source began to thrash around uncontrollably, striking at all that moved and at all that did not. Now that the field of battle was on a more equal footing. Hoping that dispelling its power source would make the battle easier. Swinging wildly, the Slither's blades struck a cast iron lamp post, tumbling down, it came down, but a few feet from Zenith. Casting an upward stroke toward the creature, slicing through its disfigured body, the crack of bones so loud the sky shuddered, blue blood spurting from the wound, covering him head to toe, his foe still wild and unstoppable.

Gazing on in disbelief at the battle that now raged on, not more than ten feet away. *I can't let him fight alone, can I? I've got to help, screw your head on, Tripas help him!* Realising he must help, pulling his trusty bow free of its bindings, firing his first arrow, a direct hit, if he had been aiming for Zenith.

Zenith's anguish was undeniable as the arrow passed clean through his left shoulder, screaming, "What in all the benevolence are you doing, Tripas?" Watching the arrow sailing away into the darkness beyond them, towards a small light. The course of the arrow drew both of their attention to a bright dot. A friendly, yet sociable, yellowish-gold light

Only one thing they knew emitted such a radiance, Zenith was sure in his head. *It's the star, but how?* They had left without notice or making a sound. Lemma had not seen them go, yet there she was, the star in hand, ready to aid them.

The sound of pain echoed in their ears as the star struck the beast's head, lightning shooting to the ground at its feet. Scorched earth, a smell Zenith did not want to smell again. Filling his nose. "Good god, the stream!" vivid in his memory. Where the star had slain so many so easily, yet somehow this time it acted differently.

No repeat attack as before, just the single blow and return. "Wow", Zenith let slip, thinking. *Has Lemma mastered a new power?* The beast stood stunned; the star's momentum had shoved the beast clear of Zenith, gagging on its bodily fluids as its helmet shattered in two, falling to the ground. A brilliant flash of flames leapt out from the Echidna flame. The blood from his forehead seeping into his eye, the vortex encircled the hideous Slither just as they had in the cave. The flame grew into a twisted inferno, engulfing the beast in a vast, furious tower of blazing, pure orange flame, the true, uncontrolled breath of the sword rereleased.

Trapped within the vortex, the Slithers' armour exploding open, skin inside bursting into flames, in agony so immense, soundless remorse abundant upon its ember-ridden face. Regrets for his loyalty to Rycore were evident in the realisation of the evils it had committed since becoming Rycore's minion and those it could commit, showing as the skin on the beast's face melted away under the heat of the flames.

Drawing its final breath, a heaviness lifted in the air around all of them. A ray of light cascaded from above, surrounding the Slither, extinguishing all of the sword's flames in an instant. A meaningful sense of blissful divine intervention swept across Zenith, Tripas and Lemma as they watched the hideous disfigurement of the Slither revert to its normal state as its injuries pushed the Slither onto its eternal rest.

The bright light stung them as they made ready for their next attack. Watching on, disbelief took hold of them. The sight before them, so pure, so heavenly; their hearts filled with love for their fallen enemy.

Orbs of yellow light flowed up from the Slither's body, following the white light back into the sky. Its spirit free, the body fell to the ground in a heap, what looked like a smile broad and wide across its face. Spirit free and cleansed of all its sins, it had died a valiant death fighting the influence of Rycore, freeing it to join Rysand as all creatures deserved.

Slumping to his knees, exhausted from the battle, panting, his dark, flowing hair matted with blue blood and sweat. Wiping the sweat from his forehead and pushing hair away from his face in one smooth motion. The realisation of the pain in his shoulder crossing his moist and dirt-ridden brow, no anguish evident in his deep claret eyes, revealing no secret to Lemma as she looked down at Zenith. Shirt torn and soaked, clinging to him, showing his naturally toned and shaped muscles like they had been forged by Rysand himself. Firm and tort every movement rippling across them as if there was no shirt at all, her eyes fixated upon him. She had never noticed his body before tonight. Her heart pounded inside her chest, lips moistening at the sight of Zenith there, exciting all her senses. *How did I not notice him before?*

Her feelings were unusual and out of place for the moment. His nature was as clear and beautiful as his body. Calling to her, his voice exasperated from his exhaustion, "Lemma, are you ok?" Only concern for her resounded from him.

Lemma fixated on him; she couldn't help but think, *How could he care about me above himself, injured and all?* Zenith's eyes met hers in a fleeting glance, and she felt her heart sore as his eyes softened. Opening wide, showing her that he felt something for her. *Oh lord, why? Why does his body taunt me so? I want to take him in my arms and never let go. What are these feelings? It's not right, I barely know him.* Lemma pushed back the thought's reddening in her cheeks, turning away from him

Tripas ran to him, pulling him to his feet and helping him stand. Anxiously speaking to Lemma, "We must make our way back to the Dancing Queen to bandage his injuries, allowing him to rest." Feeling this was partly his fault, Tripas hoisted Zenith up, pulling his good arm around his neck and began to walk with him. Struggle emanating from his face, Tripas carried Zenith unwavering, Zenith's physical strength not enough to hold his feet steady, his mental anguish too much to bear. Lemma, seeing this, pushed under Zenith's bad arm, taking half his weight onto her shoulder, carrying him, his body battered and bruised. His muscles pressed firmly onto her shoulders, shivers descending up and down her spine as his hot, moist breath touched the nape of her neck. His arm was strong and tender, wrapping around her as they walked, pulling her closer.

Strength slowly returning to his limbs, regaining his feet, Zenith pulled Lemma close to his chest and whispered in her ear.

"I don't know why, but I would have died to make sure you remained uninjured; protecting you is all I wanted to do. I took an arrow to the shoulder and still fought. I am fond of you, dare I say it could be more?" A cheeky grin appeared for a fleeting second.

Her heart faltered as her face turned a wine red with embarrassment, and her soft green eyes widened. *What did he say? Why would he say such things? Is he delirious? I'm no one special; he doesn't even know my true origin yet.* Panicked, her heart beating out of her chest still, she somehow sensed that his words were of pure truth, and her mind reflected his feelings, but she dared not say such things out loud.

———

Dragging himself into his room, Zenith slunk onto his bed, the pain in his shoulder dulling as Lemma wrapped it with a dressing made from her dress and a poultice the innkeeper had given to them; something smelled faintly of Byzantine crystal roses, a flower that only grew near Isanhal. *Is it Lemma? Or the poultice? How did I never notice?* Zenith's mind fighting through his delirium.

The smell made him think of the city far west of his own home, where he had only been once. The city's beauty was equal to the kindness and quality of its people. Isanhal was famous for its crystal roses, which they grew. Unlike any other rose, the petals were a deep red, with a glass-like appearance. Its smell was that of ambrosia. Relaxing more as the scent filtered into his nostrils.

Downstairs, inside the halls of the inn, a soft lullaby was being played on a fiddle. As he listened, the scent and sound drew him in, helping soothe him off into a deep sleep.

Rysand must have granted this place powers, as the air and poultice seemed to heal his injuries quickly. The next morning, he was fit and well, and not even a scar remained. Only the blood on the bandage proved that he had been injured at all.

Zenith felt ready to attempt the trip that Tripas had tried to take him on again; such an intense battle must have left its scars on the city. He could not admit it was him, as that would book him a place in the stockade; fighting within the walls was forbidden; there was a coliseum for that. All problems that needed sorting by blood and sweat would be fought there; only the city guards were allowed to raise a weapon inside the walls.

Lemma walked in silence beside Zenith. Deep in thought, her mind lost in the grasp of Zenith's words from the night before. *Is he truly in love with me, or was he delusional from the blood loss and exhaustion?*

She knew she felt strongly lustful towards him, his muscles, oh, how his muscles played and danced within her imagination. Her eyes must have betrayed her as Zenith leaned in close to her quietly so only Lemma could hear. He spoke, "I meant every word last night. I thank you for your tenderness in dressing my wound"

Her cheeks flushed red again, her mind bursting to admit to him her feelings for him. She had to hide her emotions. Feelings of lust, not love. It was wrong to play with his emotions, but she now knew he truly held her in his heart.

A resounding and excited shout came from Tripas. "It's just the other side of the bridge. We will see the Muriel from there" The silence broke, and a gap forming between them, Lemma stopped her mind racing, her heart pounding. *Am I just lustful, or do I love him? Lemma, stop being such a Mud muncher, you barely know him.* Only time would give her this answer.

Crossing the bridge, Remi's Workshop came into view. Sure enough, the Archway doors stood there in all their glory, and the picture Tripas had seen was still clear: a creature stood side by side with the wielder of the Echidna flame, not a dragon but a half-lion, half-eagle, with giant Dragon wings, Flames leaping from its feet still clearly visible.

Running ahead, Tripas was eager to show Zenith. Bewildered by this, Zenith stood in shock. The whole picture revealed that Rysand's previous generals had been two men and a woman, like himself, and the others. The current holders.

But the creature was not how he had imagined Synergy. Synergy was a dragon, or so he thought. This was a more beautiful sight: a manticore, the beast kings of the sky, known as dragons to many, as the legends described them. Now he saw what his beast of war and what his most fantastic companion would look like, next to his friends in all of its glory. His mind is asking him. *Does this prove Synergy is real?*

No one knew where the Manticore resided; some said the mighty mountains that lined the coast of the salt flats, some said they lived at the furthest point to the ocean, in the gorge, the place of the last battle, warding against Rycore's return, hoping to find out soon and wanting to learn more about Synergy. Tripas explained this to both. The door was a perfect copy of the Town Hall's tapestry. Moving from the workshop, looking towards the centre of town, eager to reach the town hall as soon as they possibly could, they got lost a couple of times along the way. Eventually, making it after a kind older gentleman gave Lemma directions that neither Tripas nor Zenith wanted to admit they needed.

———

The frontage of the town hall stood in all its golden glory, seamless, smooth marble stood flat against the grey granite of the gorge walls, there seemed only to be a front to this building, no walls at its side, large, aged, wooden doors sat to the left of the structure, leading the way in.

The expanse of the cave that lay behind the doors explained the reasoning for the flat front of the building as it opened into a colossal chamber lit by candles and torches placed high up on the chamber walls. There, in all its majesty, hung the tapestry, larger than they had expected. It started where they entered and finished on the opposite wall. It told the whole story of creation, from its beginning to the end of the creation war, embroidered in the most incredible detail the creators could manage. Gazing along and around its length, you could see where the style of stitching changed as new people replaced those who passed on, revealing decades of continuous work being woven into the fabric.

From across the room, a clerk approached them, his approach nervous and timid, an obvious sign that he was new here, reinforced by the pristine and untarnished clothing he wore. "Salutations, travellers. I had heard some from the world above had survived the fall, but I had not thought I would be so lucky as to meet them. What do you wish to know? What do you wish to find? Allow me the pleasure of being your guide. At the time of your visit to our hallowed halls"

Zenith, taken aback by the clerk's pleasantries, responded in kind to the best of his abilities. "I wish to see Synergy, the manticore. The creature of legend and the part he plays in the story of the twin gods, sir." The clerk smiled and led the way, "Ha-ha, follow me then, sir. It is not until halfway through the legend that the creature you speak of joins the battle"

Leading the way, the clerk headed for the nearest corner away from the entrance. There, upon the wall, Synergy and many other creatures of myth stood side by side with man and Rysand, each man heavily laden with armour and weapons, preparing for battle. Upon closer inspection, they could see a ghostly figure dressed in black robes hidden behind their lines. A black wolf pack lay at his feet like the one that he and Lemma had seen following them on their approach to the inn at the Rycliff bridge.

"Who is that man? What does he have to do with Rysand?" Lemma exclaimed out of nowhere. "Which figure do you mean, madam? You have the generals and the manticore with Rysand himself, nobody else I would know of," said the clerk. Lemma insisted, pointing with frustration in her voice.

"Behind them, the figure in the black cloak, with the wolf lying at his feet." Bemused, the clerk looked intuitively at the tapestry. There was indeed a separate figure clad in black leather armour and a black cape. Never had he seen this person before; perhaps the myth scribe would know more.

Scuttling off with a spring in his step, the clerk disappeared into a small, rough-edged doorway on the eastern wall, beyond the wooden council auditorium that stood at the centre of the hall, studying the figure that had now called all their attention. No one noticed the clerk and a hunched-over, drawn man approaching them.

"That is the legendary Vermont, the wolf tamer, who records all that happens in this world through the eyes of his black wolves"

Startled, all the party turned with great surprise. This

slight hunch of a man held such command in his voice, such resonance that it echoed all around the chamber, ensuring that all heard all he had to say.

"So why does he appear here, sir?" Lemma asked, "Vermont is depicted all around these hallowed halls in some form or another; he has been here since creation itself. Older than the gods but younger than man, he never ages, never forgets." Zenith piped up, "How do we find him? We need to know the truth of the creation war, what happened" The myth scribe ushered them to follow him to his own more comfortable room adjoining the cavern.

Leaving the main chamber, they entered a much more refined and highly decorated room, where natural light filled the space through a large crack in the outer wall. The inside of the crack had been framed over and sealed with clear glass to keep the elements at bay, Zenith noted, thinking it rather ingenious. The elderly gent pointed at some stone bench-style seats and spoke, "Sit and I shall tell you more of what I know, my young friends. Vermont is neither man nor beast, a spirit of a time past and a future yet to happen; he fights for both good and evil to push time along its scheduled track, nudging those back to it if they ever deviate."

Losing interest in the story, Zenith's attention was drawn through the crack in the ceiling. Seeing a clear blue sky, it had been days since they had fallen from the bridge. The first time he had seen the sky proper since camping on the side of the gorge. Not a single thing was visible within view. Staring, wondering *how far are we from home now. Is there any way back?*

The old scribe continued the story of Vermont. Speaking eloquently whilst telling the others that if meeting Vermont was in their future, it would happen; otherwise, it would not. Unless they could somehow capture one of his wolves, he would come in search of them for its freedom. This continued for a short while as the old man whittled on about old tales, seemingly lost in his memories.

———

Leaving the town hall, their discussion shifted to their next step, their location, and how to return above the gorge. Tripas had been thinking on this very point, so brought it up. "There is a point way down south that can be used to get above ground but requires passing through the territories of the Ranther bird" The Ranther were one of the apex predators in the gorge, vast in size and faster than most could imagine.

Knowing Cathal needed to return with the carts and gold to Vastuk. Lemma and Zenith needed to reach the apex of the gorge where it met the plains so they could continue to Sciran to ensure the city's well-being and that of its people. Lemma's concerns more personal matters, those of her, her mother, the Queen and her two sisters.

The heads of the royal army. Had she been there, she would still be commanding her own unique unit, the priests' guard. Their units name not really anything to do with priests or the guarding of them more to describe the fact that that they were trained with, fighting the tainted in mind by no means was Lemma a priestess or did she act in that way. In fact, she was much more than any of her companions knew.

Returning to the Dancing Queen, they drank in merriment at their equalled success in trade and fight. The conversation of their current situations turned to more pressing matters. Each had their own objectives that needed to be completed; one had to give in, or all had to go their own way. Neither wanted to leave the other, but both tasks were of great importance in their own right.

5
THE TAMER

As the light of the sun permeated the small hollow that acted as a window to the dank, dark cellar room where Zenith and his companions had opted to stay since none felt able to ascend the two steep and winding staircases to their rented accommodation after an ale and mead-filled night of merriment turned to dissention as to their next move.

Cathal lay flat on his stomach, asleep, still on the mud floor where he had fallen. Tripas slumped against a larger-than-life barrel of wine, Head still firmly wedged under the dry nozzle. Lemma delicate and stirring in the corner on a feather bed. Zenith, wide-eyed, lay under the hollow watching the small circle of the dark sky come to life. He could make out the shape of the morning creatures, somewhat similar to birds, but not quite the same, preparing for the day, full of hope.

Thinking back to the night before, they had all decided that it would not be necessary for all of them to return. The best move that they all collectively agreed on was, honestly, the simplest. Cathal would take some of the extra gold made from

Remi and pay off a considerable force of men for hire to accompany Tripas back to Vastuk.

The morning grew long as Cathal and the others finally awoke from their alcohol induced slumber. Their eyes wretched in the bright light, heavy and unstable as they roused and stumbled into the main bar of the inn. Zenith was already there, eating his fill of meat and bread, laughing wholeheartedly as Cathal stumbled to the table, falling into his seat as he grabbed a chunk of meat. Tearing into it like an animal possessed, chewing loudly and grunting as he did.

Lemma, much daintier in her steps, sat next to Zenith and began to eat the bread slowly, showing signs that it didn't agree with her or the prominent drums that pounded in her head. Tripas was obviously still not back to himself as he weaved his way to them, tripping on several chair legs. Zenith, ready and alert, had already made headway with the potential cart guards. Their captain, but a few feet away, was drinking— a light breakfast of water and wine alongside toasted bread. Captain Green, seeing the arrival of Cathal, joined the table and began to speak.

"The trip to Vastuk will be two gold per sword and three per bow" Cathal looked to Zenith, a little confused as to who the man was. Zenith looked at him reassuringly and nodded. Cathal trusted Zenith's judgement; he had not seen him wrong or given him reason not to. Tossing a sack of gold over, speaking between bites roughly.

"I'm sure you will supply us more than bow and sword for the weight of this bag." Captain Green excitedly picked up the bag, surprised at its weight and size. He opened it up, expecting to see coins to which he could assign his men, but to his disbelief, the sack contained several gold ingots, each easily worth a hundred coins.

Surprise in his voice, Captain Green spoke, "I am honoured

that you would pay us so well, but I do not see why you pay over the odds, for this I shall send a contingent of fifty swords and bows, I'll throw in the wolf handlers too."

Cathal scornfully looked up from his breakfast. "Should hope you send your best and that they stay in Vastuk for a time to guard in my absence, you have there over a thousand gold coins more than enough"

Captain Green replied, "Sir, for this, my men and I are yours until the turning of the sun and your eventual return."

Cathal heard this, admiration in his words, "You have done me a great service in taking the job. Should I return and you remain, I will have you a place within the Vastuk guard, and all your men, should you accept, there will be no expense spared on your equipment and training." This statement was no ordinary thing, and Captain Green knew it. The Vastuk guard held the highest of honours, holding the bastion against the return of Rycore.

Breakfast finished, Tripas and Cathal made one final check of the goods and gold that Tripas and Greens' men would guard homeward toward Vastuk. Satisfied it was all secured and taken care of, they clasped each other's forearms and bid each other a safe journey.

———

Stood atop the steps leading to the western gate of the Rockwall Zenith, and Lemma waited in anticipation of Cathal's arrival, or lack thereof; they were still unsure if he could truly join them, although they saw trust in him, having met him only a few days ago. Staring off into the distant corners of the gorge, the clank of well-worn armour approached behind them. Turning to see Cathal coming, they raised their hand in adulation, knowing that this next part of the journey would be alongside a new friend and brother in arms.

Half a day had passed already as the three unlikeliest of friends, a farmer, a maiden, and a short, rotund warrior, trudging along the slender and slippery, risk-riding path. This path led them further south toward the apex, where they should be able to ascend to the plains of Arathy, not a million days from the plains of Sciran. But far enough to delay them by several days of the sun's cycle. Longer than Lemma had planned for them to arrive in. Knowing her mother and sisters, Sciran would still stand, and if its wall had fallen. The castle would be a stockade and withstand any army that dared attack her home.

As the day grew long, Cathal became weary of his surroundings; they had entered the territory of the Ranther bird. Cathal brought them all to a stop, describing a flightless bird that ran with the speed of a cheetah and the strength of a rhino; worst of all, its feathers were as hard as rocks and sharp.

Scanning the distance, Zenith saw a blur, or at least he thought he did, spinning round to face his friends. Unsure if he had seen anything, but the look on Cathal's face said all he needed to know; whatever he saw, it was real and posed a likely threat to them. Reaching the hilt of the sword, his hand wrapping tightly around it, watching for any movement, he continued forward slowly, unsure if this path they took would lead to battle or safety.

Staff in hand, Cathal pushed forward of the others, sure of foot, knowing the lay of the land had its advantages; he had trained amongst the Ranther as a recruit and had seen his fair share of skirmishes with them. Many of his brothers in arms had lost their lives to these birds.

The best and quickest course to the apex was through their territory; any other way round would delay them by at least three days. He wanted to get there and back to be sure of Vastuk's safety. Pushing on was their only option, but to avoid conflict with Ranther, they would need to hide well if they met a lone bird; the three had a chance, but a flock and their deaths would be almost guaranteed.

Cathal had instructed Lemma and Zenith to follow his path exactly. The path had widened for now; there were plenty of nooks and crannies big enough for them to hide and run to if needed to avoid the Ranther. But ahead, even Lemma could see a wide-open expanse, strangely lush with vegetation and water, a sight she had not seen at any point in the gorge until now. With nowhere they could conceal themselves, they were left open to all foes.

Bursting out from the gorge wall at an immense pace, the three rushed hard to cross the expanse, similar to a desert oasis, but far greener and more verdant, like a farm at harvest time. It was soft underfoot, and it was hard to maintain the pace. Still, each knew they had to run. Hard they pushed and pushed until in the distance, maybe four hundred yards away, they could see the end of the oasis and the path narrowing, allowing them a safer, more protected place to rest and reassess their situation.

Zenith's pace slowed, but his speed of thought increased in panic. *I can't maintain the pace that Lemma and Cathal set. I'm not a trained soldier built for endurance, as they are.* Tired, his muscles aching, he couldn't carry on, stopping momentarily to catch his breath, a pain shot through him. His shoulder was bashed from out of nowhere, stumbling back, legs caving from under him. Zenith slumped to the floor above him, a grand and looming bird, one he had never seen, its feathers sharp as knives, bared down on him, about to strike him with its enormous beak, within which a row of razor-sharp teeth looked like they could tear him limb from limb.

Reflexes dulled, exhausting his stamina from the run, he only just managed to roll out of the way as the massive bird struck at him. Its beak plunged into the ground inches away from him. Pulling the Echidna flame from his belt, his energy suddenly returned. Gaining a second wind, he jumped to his feet and turned, ready to run. Still, it was too late, the Ranther was already at his front, preparing to slash him with its wings. Luckily, now he was able to fight more agile and aware, he ducked under the bird's wing and in the same motion slashed at its leg, slicing deep and fast at it, but it seemed like he didn't cut it at all, the blade just bouncing away.

Still, the Ranther remained standing tall and swung its head, diving deep for his heart, aiming to kill him in one blow. The bird darting towards him, from the ground he leapt high into the air, landing at the base of the Ranther's neck, just above the wing. Dazed, he grabbed on for dear life as he bucked and bounced all over. By pure luck, the bird could not attack while Zenith hung here.

Cathal and Lemma made the narrowing in the path and ducked behind a huge boulder. They lay just on the pinnacle of the cliff, breathing heavily. Neither had noticed Zenith's perils, only two hundred yards behind them. Both resting, catching their breath, they heard the screams of Zenith, clinging to the neck of the Ranther, acting like he was in a rodeo, maybe to their horror, as he tried to tame the menacing bird that stood three men tall.

Zenith's arms ached, but he could not let go. The bird seemed to be slowing its throws and lunges, studying Zenith, even respecting his strength and audacity for holding on so long.

The Ranther stopped thrashing, tired and fed up. Twisting its head and neck towards its own body to study this human. This person, who had but moments ago, should have been its next meal. It had given up. Seeing the human hanging there in a whole new light, a strange and deep cooing permeated the air coming from within the Ranther's throat.

The Ranther turned its head slowly and pushed the edge of its beak close to Zenith and stared at him unblinking for what felt like an eternity, studying him. Zenith stared back, intent on winning this battle of wills. He had tamed many beasts and animals in Grissam being fortunate enough to be born with it. This was one of those techniques you learned to harness, or died trying.

The bird pushed its beak in closer to Zenith and nudged his cheek, a kindness showing in its deep, dark brown eyes. Calmed and content with Zenith on its neck, the cooing slowed and became more friendly in its tone. Zenith placed his hand beside the Ranther's face, stroking it, keeping constant eye contact and muttering soft and reassuring words.

His skills lay in other places than those of Cathal and Lemmas. He was now able to see that he had broken the spirit of the Ranther. A predator that all the gorge feared. He had to name her to tame her completely. The species name lent itself well to the name Rath. It also coincidentally allowed him to name it after his mother, Rathena. He felt sure it was a female. A sense that deep down she was motherly; he felt one with her, connected, if not through thought or the battle of wills, but through a more spiritual means.

Zenith sat astride Rath's shoulders as they walked closer and closer to Cathal and Lemma, who stood not fifty yards ahead, faces covered in disbelief at what they had witnessed here. Lemma stood awestruck by Zenith and Rath. *There is definitely something different about this man.* It made her heartbeat faster. *Could I love him?* Pushing this silly thought from her mind, she looked up at Zenith and smiled to see only a mark to his shoulder, no other injuries. he had indeed proved to be lucky this time.

Zenith asked Rath to kneel, as he did, and she placed her head down, lowering her body to the ground as if almost instinctively to her. Almost as if she had heard his thought, not his words. Beckoning to Lemma and Cathal to climb aboard Rath's back.,

They remained feet away, standing vigil and unsure of Rath. Cathal's warrior bravery failed him as fear was all across his face, not daring to move. Zenith smiled and reassured him. All was safe. He stepped towards Rath, who cooed at him, waiting. Lemma jumped up onto Rath's back, placing her arms at Zenith's waist and squeezing tight as she feared falling from this bird, or worse, being its lunch. Cathal slowly made his way toward the others, still unsteady and wobbling, not knowing how a Toplander could tame the untameable. *If I had not seen it myself, I would never have believed it.* Mounting onto Rath, he gathered himself and gave Zenith a wary nod, not confident in being seated there.

Rath rose from the ground, lifting them easily, Zenith's full height and a half again above the ground. Steadying herself, she began to walk at a slow, steady pace, gauging the weight she carried carefully, seeming as though she knew exactly which way and where they needed to head.

Rath's pace quickened as she approached the narrowing of the path ahead. The oasis soon became a blur and distant memory. Quicker and quicker, she flew across the ground like an eagle of the land. Dodging this way and that with lightning speed around all obstacles. Cathal held on tight, grimacing and whispering. "This speed is unnatural; no man should move this fast." Cathal's life flashed before his eyes. Sure, he would fall from Rath. Somehow, Rath moved with ease through the winding gorge path at speed, keeping them all steady and safe on her back.

Zenith, adept at riding horses and all manner of farm animals, felt most at ease on the back of Rath. Not flinching or flailing at any of her movements. His mind was cold and calculating, linked with Rath, both attuned, knowing which way to move at any moment; it was as if their two minds had joined in a single thought.

As the greyness of the gorge passed in a whirl of speed, mist seemed to be gathering at the edge of the precipice, beckoning them to fall as they clung to Rath. Rath's speed and strides were perfect, not teetering or fluctuating like the gorge didn't exist. All knowing that their three-day hike by some stroke of luck had become less than half that. Lemma had the thought occur to her whilst holding on to Zenith, *I'll be home sooner rather than later, all thanks to this farmer and his ability to tame wild beasts.*

The sun waned in the distant sky, setting with intense orange hues cast deep into the sides of the gorge. Rath had run nearly half of the distance to the apex this day. From her heavy breathing, she had felt it coming. Pulling to a standstill atop a minor rise in the path, which opened wide enough for them to make camp for the night. The evening drew in eerily fast here, and none felt the courage to push on, on foot or upon Rath's back.

Zenith and Cathal strolled side by side, gathering what dry wood they could find on this desolate rocky outcrop, leaving Lemma cuddled up under Rath's wing. Surprisingly, they had become close in a short time; it was as though Rath protected a clutch of eggs, the way she positioned herself, as if she wrapped around a nest. Rath listened to Zenith's every command; she seemed protective and motherly towards

Lemma, and since stopping here, actively guarded her. Scanning the horizon for any threat to her like a mother cheetah to her cubs, on edge but being caring to her charge, nonetheless.

As Cathal and Zenith collected more wood, they turned to return to Lemma and set their fire. On the way back, they talked. Cathal asked Zenith about his home, his farm and what the Toplands were like, wanting to have some small understanding of what he was going to see. They continued this conversation whilst they started a roaring fire. The heat blazing in their faces. Finally, they felt the chill of the gorge leave their bones. Reaching into his bag, Zenith pulled out several pieces of dried meat.

He handed Cathal and Lemma some chunks and chucked a larger piece towards Rath. She snapped it down in one swoop, looking eagerly at Zenith, waiting for more. Zenith was more than happy to give it to her, throwing three more pieces her way. They landed inches from her open beak, her eyes wide and smiling at him, thankful to him for the food, since he was so close to being her latest meal and had escaped.

He chuckled at himself, thinking how he had hung on despite everything telling him to stop; his shoulder still hurt, but oh well, he thought, a lesson learned. Don't fight a creature three times your size again. Lemma unfurled from beneath Rath and ate with glee, pulling Rath's wing around her again like a winter blanket.

The night came upon them as they ate, darkness surrounding them, making it almost impossible to see beyond twenty yards, even by the light of the fire. The darkness set them all on edge. Rath seemed to sense something in the night and peered deeply into it, watching for anything.

Cathal stood with her on the first watch whilst Zenith and Lemma slept under the cover of the tent. All he could hear was the whirling and whipping of the wind and the occasional snort from within the tent, making him jump. This would be a long watch, even more so with Rath there at his side; "I still don't trust you, bird. A tamed Ranther has never been heard of, and I doubt that it will be again. You and Zenith will probably have bard tales written, from here on out, after others find out how Zenith tamed you."

As Zenith stood tired at the side of Rath in the first amber rays of the sun, having not woken Lemma for her watch. He preferred to let her sleep; it was simply the way he had been brought up. He could not bring himself to wake her from her slumber. She lay there, aside Cathal curled up in her furs, her auburn hair covering her face. A more picturesque image could not have met his eye when he looked upon her. Sound filled his ears, his own heartbeat thumping away, feelings welling up inside him of love and caring.

So refined and beautiful, it would have been unfair to wake her. Turning away and resuming the watch, Zenith's eyes were drawn into the low light of the gorge ahead. "A black wolf!" Do my eyes deceive me? Is it Vermont's wolf watching us again?" spoken in a hushed tone. Rath had seen it too and gained her feet, ready to give chase. Zenith placed a hand on her chest, calming her. He had sensed no aggression from the wolf, just curiosity.

Staring at them, the wolf stood proud and lean, its eye fixed upon Zenith and the encampment, taking it all in as if it relayed the view to someone else in a far-off place. Zenith decided, *I need to capture this wolf and lure it to master here.* Zenith made a step forward, and the wolf sprang to life, leaving nothing but a trail of dust in its wake.

6

WELCOME TO THE TOP LANDS

Morning came at him fresh, with the sounds of waking coming from the tent, as the sun's light burned off the mist that lay close to the rock shelf they camped on. The sun had truly risen, and if they were to make the apex, they would need to leave. Soon, fully packed, their camp stowed upon Cathal's back. Rushed as they felt they made sure all the signs of their camp were gone, the fire tipped over the edge. The ground was swept in case anything or anyone followed their trail.

Zenith was first to climb onto Rath; she would not have it any other way. Lemma clutched less tightly at Zenith's waist. The evening wrapped in her wings had built her trust more with Rath, and Cathal just sat there, slumped half asleep, clamping his legs tightly, his distrust still palatable. Rising to her feet. Rath began at a steady pace toward the apex at Arathy.

It would be a hard day's ride; if all went well, they would reach the apex by mid-afternoon. Hoping to make the ascent to the Arathy plains before nightfall. Cathal assured them it was entirely possible and that it would possibly see them much further along with their current pace.

Cathal, although confident in his analysis of their journey, was apprehensive of the destination. Not having ever been to the top land, nor had he ever wanted to. *"This seems like fate is at work. Destiny has its plans for me, a destiny with new friends outside of my home, my haven within the Rysand gorge."*

The gorge in all its damp, misty glory whizzed by as Rath gained pace, picking up speed as if she wanted to get there, more eager than any of the people she carried on her back. Zenith had been imaging the plains. He had seen them as a boy when his father travelled all over them selling the produce from the farm. It was akin to Rath seeing them as well. Out of the blue, Rath's speed increased. A sense of longing and excitement came from her as if knowing she would be able to run and run to her heart's content.

Has she seen my memories? Did I truly link with her in that most special of ways? Am I truly that attuned to her that our thoughts act as one? It seemed unmistakable that they had formed a full pact with each other, something that Zenith had not truly experienced in the past, feelings close to it, but not the same.

The morning passed in a blink, and the afternoon was on them, the apex looming closer and closer as they approached. They had begun a long ascent upward, drawing closer to the ridge at the top of the gorge. Daylight finally. So bright that their eyes burned as they adjusted to it. It had been almost a whole week since the sun had touched their eyes this brightly, and never for some of their party, as their eyes winced and turned, the darkness of the gorge was driven away from them.

Cathal gasped at the sight ahead of him, a vast expanse of greens, golds, browns, blues, all colours he had only seen in the bigger cities of the gorge. Here they were plentiful, bountiful as far as the eye could see. It made him shudder to think that *I had never dared come here; the tales of grizzly and inhuman creatures in the top land were always too vivid for me and my friends in Vastuk. It always seemed truly horrifying.*

This was nothing like the tales. Now, the gorge seemed scarier than ever. The ever-present darkness and the creatures that stalked it were now more nightmarish than he had ever known. Up here, above the gorge, his imagination exploded. *It's so peaceful, idyllic and serene, not a barren rock or cliff in sight, just fields and rivers stretching all the way to the hills and mountains of the horizon.*

The sun beamed down on the Arathy plains, burning the ground at their feet, the heat unbearable as they rode slowly northeast towards the border of the Scirainian Plains, making good time as they went. The distance never seemed to lessen, and the evening soon encroached on them, the low-hanging sun turning red as it set behind the horizon.

The red rays lay on the plains, making them look like a field of flames as they approached a small, isolated village in the middle of nowhere. It looked like a desolate and foreboding place, the small stone and wooden cottages surrounding a dirt courtyard at its centre in which stood a solitary guard tower. A pointless relic of a bygone era in complete disrepair. In its arched landing above, rickety stairs stood a boy no older than fourteen, watching the horizon for any threats. Suddenly, the ancient tower's bell began to ring, signalling Zenith and his friends' approach.

From the few dozen cottages emerged several ragged and weathered older men, brandishing all manner of weapons, from pitchforks and swords; none looked as though they had ever seen battle, let alone any combat, in the last hundred years.

Zenith pulled Rath to a stop, dismounting. Forethought said this would seem less of a threat to the town since Rath, although soft as muck, looked menacing standing over all and sundry, the buildings of the village were barely as tall as she. Lemma stood forward of Zenith, taking the lead as they approached the village. A lone old man, accompanied by two younger gentlemen, approached them slowly, eyes fixed on Rath in terror.

"We are here in peace." Lemma announced in her most confident and royal voice, "I am Princess Lemma of the Sciran. We are only seeking shelter on our journey to my home and represent no threat" Zenith stood there flabbergasted; he had never heard her speak this way.

Her voice was so confident and smooth that it struck him the woman he had grown close to, loved, and would die for was not at all who she seemed; *she's a princess! What on Apprite? How could she not tell us? I couldn't be more unworthy of her.* Turning to Cathal, he saw the same shock on his face at Lemma's proclamation.

Lemma had never even mentioned her noble birth, and Cathal did not quite know how to take it, sinking to one knee with a shock and fear in his voice. "Your highness, why did you never tell me of your stature? I would never have been so plain of word or manner had I known." Lemma ignored him, waving her hand as if to rise to his feet and bare her no heed, she didn't tell him for her, own reasons one she cared not to explain at this moment in time.

A gruff, old, and tired voice continued on the wind, offering Lemma a welcome of words; the older man's face lit up with enthusiasm and happiness at the realisation. The village had nothing to fear from the travellers; he beckoned them on towards the village. Raising his cane in the air, as he did, the men inside lowered their weapons, returned to their homes and reappeared with women and children of all ages. Stood there, eyes wide in wonder, as the party approached, all staring hard at Rath, a beast never seen in these parts before.

They reached the old man, who stood proudly, examining the group with a look of displaced fear in his eyes as he came to terms with the enormity of Rath. Shuddering, losing his balance as quickly as light, Rath moved around, catching the old man in the middle of her neck, holding him until he gained his balance one more time. His expression changed to one of harmony at this.

This beast not only meant no harm but had saved him from a fall, a minor thing, but still, he had not expected a kindness from her. His voice full of delight, he spoke, "Welcome to the village of Tome. Your presence humbles us, M'lady. We are but a humble farming village and have nothing of any grandeur to offer you. I am Thyme, the village elder"

Lemma looked at this man, old and tired in front of her and waved him down, not wanting a fuss made of her. Just wanting a soft, warm bed to lie in, a decent meal in her stomach, and no grand feast or celebration. She was humbled by his efforts, though. Dropping the royal tone, Lemma spoke to him. "No fuss need be made, treat me as you would a traveller, a bed and a meal for me and my friend will be all I ask" At this, the old man slowly turned and called them on to enter the village where its folk awaited their arrival.

The village buzzed with excitement as the group entered. The children, all giddy and laughing as they walked past, some daring to reach out and stroke Rath as she passed, she cooed and let them. From the main building, a table and many chairs were brought, a fire was lit a few feet away, and a roaster was erected.

Some of the men busied themselves building a makeshift stable at the side of the watch tower for Rath, but none could see how to roof it for her. Zenith led Rath over, speaking as he approached. "We will help with the roof, bring planks over me, and Rath will lift them. You place them in position from your ladders."

The men scurried away to fetch the wood; soon enough, they brought several long and wide wooden beams, laying them near Rath's feet. One by one, she bit into them. At Zenith's instruction, she lifted them effortlessly, high atop the stable frame. As she did, the village men guided them into place, tying them down tight. No sooner had they started than it seemed they finished; straw was placed inside for Rath to lie on, and as she did, they all smiled. Lying on the straw content, a thankful look filled her eyes as she peered out at them.

The fire burned brightly, a fresh boar hung over it, roasting, causing a snap every so often as fat dripped down, splashing on the white-hot coals. Zenith and Cathal sat amongst the villagers, who had managed to prepare such a small but ample feast in a short time, laughing and talking with merriment. Lemma sat amongst them, enjoying the festivities, feeling she had spoken too much on arrival; this village had very little. Yet they had gone to such efforts even though they didn't need to.

Children played games around them or hung out at Rath's stable, stroking and cuddling up to her as they all now realised she was tame, friendly, and seemed to enjoy the fuss they made of her. She cooed lowly as one boy dared to sit on her back and hug her neck. Even going so far as to play peek-a-boo in a fashion, hiding behind her own wing and popping out unexpectedly to the children's delight.

Soon, enough time had passed that the children headed home to sleep. The sound of music struck up from flutes and drums. These people seemed to need a reason to celebrate. The group's arrival had given them that. A royal visit, something Lemma thought about. *I get the feeling this never happens here, being out in the sticks, miles from the nearest urban centre.* She ventured that the nearest would most likely be Arath, the capital city, on this side of the mountains.

Looking out over the festivities, wondering how Sciran was faring and whether she would arrive in time. Suddenly, her hand was grabbed, pulled from her seat. Her reactions were lightning-fast, grabbing for the dagger at her waist as she turned; she saw Zenith had her, and she placed it back in her belt.

His most charismatic and theatrical voice came to the fore. "Dance with me, twirl with me, my fair lady. Your beauty should be on full display for all to see, that I may observe it and lust after thee." Gladdened with wine, he seemed to have forgotten all niceties as he pulled her out to the front and joined the village folk dancing around the fire, twirling Lemma this way and that. Pulling her close enough that his warm breath touched the nape of her neck, sending a shiver of excitement down her spine. Smiling back at Zenith, her feelings flooded with love or lust again.

Not knowing which was which. As they danced, emboldened by the consumption of alcohol, she resolved that only a kiss would solve her doubts over her feelings. *The next time he is close enough, I'll kiss him and see how he reacts.*

Zenith pulled her in close again, and as he did, she pulled herself round to face him. Placing her lips upon his, kissing him. Zenith's face reddened, but he did not pull away. He pulled her closer and kissed her back even deeper. As they kissed, she felt like all of time around them stopped; her heart thudded in her chest, ready to burst. Emotions alight her very essence, dancing, her mind flooded. It was love; she didn't know how to put it into words. *I need to be with him; he's infec-*

tious. I've never felt like this. I don't want it to end. Like a drug that she couldn't be without. His lips on hers, their bodies touching, mind racing, all she could see was a future by his side.

Their kiss seemed to last forever. Finally, she broke free from him, breathing heavily, their eyes locked with each other's, her heart pounding again as she saw his claret eyes fill with love and an overwhelming lust for her. His face was bright red, but a smile from ear to ear filled his Handsome features.

Zenith leaned into her, "I told you in Rockwall and confessed my love for you. No delirium was present, only my unbridled love for you" At such words, Lemma grew a rosy shade of red and bowed, giggling, she didn't understand. *By the god's Zenith, you've got me feeling like a teenage girl. I'll never forget your words.*

She had not felt this way since her first kiss many moons ago, but that was the throes of youthful desire, and it had felt like nothing like love, like all the girls experience it, didn't give her hope of a future or make time stop. This was different. Zenith had suddenly become all she could think of, and she didn't want to stop.

The party had slowly begun to die around Zenith and Lemma. They sat a foot away from the last glowing, flickering flames of the fire. Lemma leaned into Zenith's chest, enjoying the sound of his heart as he gently caressed her hair, lulling her to sleep. She felt safe, protected in his arms, like no foul play could befall her again.

Thyme approached them, speaking in a suggestive tone that was ever present. "Your beds are ready in the village hall. It seems that my presumption of two being needed may have been wrong. Seeing how this night has played out between you," Zenith raised Lemma's head, fast asleep at his chest and lifted her as he gained his feet. He would not wake her unless he had to. Carrying her a step at a time, following Thyme to the village hall, the grandest building in the village, well-maintained and beautiful even in the darkness.

Thyme opened the door for them. As Zenith walked in, he saw Cathal on one side of the room, already deep in slumber, loud, obnoxious snores emanating from deep within his throat, giving the impression that he had been there for hours already. Two beds lay close to the window of the room. He carefully placed Lemma down on the straw bed that had been made for her, covering her over in the firs that lay next to the bed. Observing her face brighten up with a smile that could light the room, his heart fluttered at the very sight of it. Confirming to him that he would marry her, protect her and die for her at any given moment.

Turning to Thyme, who waited at the door, he approached him, held out his hand to shake Thyme's. Nodding and thanking him in the same breath, they had not done anything to deserve such kindness from them. He vowed to return one day and repay them.

Lying there in his own bed of straw, his mind full of the kiss, not able to shift it from his mind, it had lifted him. His spirits flew in ways he'd never known were possible. It left his body in peace, a sense of tranquillity washing over it, yet his mind thrashed in the chaos of such strong emotions, truly confusing him. Hoping that this wasn't dream, Falling fast asleep, knowing this would be the best sleep he had had in months or even years.

7
THE ARATHY DARK

Cathal awoke before dawn, his dreams filled with the wonder of the Arathy plains, a place he had never thought could exist. His world had expanded unbelievably in a matter of hours, and he knew within the next few days it would expand evermore.

Stood taking in the room they had slept in, grand in its design, it just didn't fit in the village; maybe it was just a relic cared for from a bygone era when the village held some significance—donning his armour and making ready for the day. Starting across the room, he strode confidently, his metal boot clunking on the floor, and with a hard shove, he pushed the hall's large wooden door wide open, letting him step out into the darkness. "Well," he said, chuntering to himself. "I thought it was night; the gorge is darker than this on a good day." Stars shone brightly in the sky, lighting up the village and the night, something profoundly beautiful in his eyes, never having seen them before. Across the yard, within easy view, lay Rath sleeping contentedly in the make-shift stable, the tables and chairs strung about, not tidied from the night before.

A brisk walk in the open air should ensure he was fully awake and give him a chance to gauge the surroundings, committing the beauty and sounds of this place to memory so he could recount it to his family and friends on his return to Vastuk, whenever that would be; he did not know.

As Cathal crossed the yard, silent but for the snores of the night watchmen in the tower, asleep after several too many drinks at the feast, Rath opened one eye, looked at him, saw who it was, and closed her eye—falling back to sleep. *She must be exhausted,* he thought, *two full days of hard riding to get here and not sleeping in between helping us to guard the camp.*

Still, he did not truly trust her. He vowed that should she turn on them, he would be the one to extinguish her life as vengeance for all his fallen friends from youth. Also, to spare Zenith and Lemma the fate, having seen how close they had all become, but somehow, he knew that this day would most likely never come.

Skirting the outside of the village as he walked, taking in all the views around him in wonder, trying his hardest to commit them to memory, he caught a glimpse of something approaching from a distance, its form blocking the light, leaving a black smudge in this otherwise picturesque landscape.

A beast of some sort, grotesque in its appearance, several feet high with four arms all ending in large club-like hands, it paced, gathering speed towards him and the village. A sense of horror came over him. He knew this creature was here for the village. His staff gleamed silver in the darkness on his back, lighting up around him for twenty feet or more.

Cathal reached behind, quickly reaching for the staff on his back and made ready for battle. The beast was upon him faster than expected, delivering a mighty blow to the side of his helmet. Cathal faltered, flying through the air several yards and rolling to his feet.

Gathered again, ready to fight, he dodged the creature's next blow aimed at his legs. In an instant, another blow came down from his left, just missing his shoulder, leaving the beast undefended. Leaping into the air, sweeping the staff hard into the beast's torso, the point of the staff piercing deep into the skin.

Blood oozed as the creature screamed an unearthly howl and began a crazed myriad of blows down at Cathal. Watching the beast's movements, more like flashes of thought as he predicted each attack. *Left jab, left jab again, right hook, left jab, right jab, right hammer blow.* Easily reading most of the creatures' onslaught, blocking or moving before the blow impacted, escaping most blows with nary a scratch. The beast's pace slowed. Taking full advantage and skidding under the nearest arm, Cathal smashed the staff deep into its arm, hearing the splintering of the bones under the skin, seeing the Bones tear out from beneath its pus-filled, slime-ridden skin. The creature screeched, its sound echoing in the space surrounding them, pain emanating from the noise it made.

Black oozing from its wounds, still, it maintained its constant attack. Cathal looked onward, searching all around, thinking how to dispatch the beast. *Where does its strength come from? How does it stand against me? Any other foe would have run if not dead and bloody under my feet.* Locked in thought, leaving himself vulnerable, caught unaware, another blow smashed hard and fast into his ribs, and he heard a cracking sound. *This is going to hurt. At least three or four ribs are cracked.* The pain forced the thought through his mind whilst flying in the air, catching just a glimpse. "There on the ground," He exclaimed, then hushing his voice. "That's its power. The shadow must feed it"

Without a second glance, he guessed. "It's one of Rycore's creatures." Screaming in the direction of his enemy. "I will win or I'll lay down my life to end you." Coming to land a few feet away, he rolled to a stop. Hurting, slowly rising to his feet, the beast was upon him again in seconds. This time, though, he slid below its first attack, dodged over the second, and made it safely behind the creature. Screaming a mighty battle cry, "My Light will set you free." Thrusting the staff deep into the ground and shadows at the creature's rear.

Light emanated from the staff, severing the link. Removing the fuel, Rycore fed it. The beast writhing backwards, becoming incensed with anger, thrashing all ways, not aiming for anything. A battle, it seemed, waged within the beast. Cathal knew that he must end the creatures' suffering swiftly. *I'll free you from the forced servitude of Rycore; you will meet Rysand on even footing, free of sin.*

Springing into action, leaping high into the air, landing upon the beast's back as it thrashed and wailed, fighting its unknown assailant. Clambering ever higher, he saw a weakness in this creature's armour; its head was bereft of armour. *Why would a beast this size need it?* He thought. It was immense. All four arms defended just as well as they attacked.

In one final jump, Cathal lifted the staff high, aiming the point down for the rear of the beast's open neck, a perfect strike. The point pierced through and out of the other side, severing the beast's spine and several major arteries as its black, thick blood spurted from the wound. The creature's thrashing slowed, becoming muggy and minimal until it collapsed to the ground dead.

A heavenly light struck deep through the night, lifting the creature from the ground, its body morphing back into its original form. It was a villager, one that had seemed all too eager with his sword the day before; now his corpse lay there, lifeless, regret and guilt-ridden, covering his face, at last granted peace, ascending within the light to join with Rysand.

In the distance, the tower's bell rang long and loud. The creature's screams must have awoken the watch. The village folk and his friend raced towards him. The heavenly light faded into the night, his staff's glow dimming as the blood of the man dripped from it to the ground.

Reaching him, Lemma and Zenith both laid their arms around him, catching him as he fell, exhausted with the pain taking over, now that the battle was won. They dragged him back toward the village. Thyme called to them, "Bring him this way, M'lady," as Cathal passed in and out of consciousness, just about making out several stone buildings pass by.

Zenith and Lemma followed quickly behind Thyme, who led them to a white, slender building. A building without windows, its whitewashed walls thick and cold to the touch. Thyme tapped his cane on the wooden door. A young woman's voice answered, "Bring him in." Inside the cottage, it was larger than expected, lit by a half-dozen torches. They could see slaves and herbs all over. The woman, not more than thirty herself, indicated to a bed, "lay him over there."

They laid him down, well, truthfully, slumped there still unconscious. The woman, laying her hand upon his forehead and chest, closed her eyes, the torches flaring, emanating a calming green light as she did. "What in all the land was that?" Lemma exclaimed, looking at Thyme for the answer. "She has a gift with the elements, the land tells her the afflicted's ailments," Thyme spoke, using a chuffed, proud voice, and returned the answer.

The girl removed her hand, ran to the far end of the cottage, gathered several blackened leaves and herbs, crushed them, then mixed them into a paste with water and golden syrup. Zenith recognised its smell and colour. Smugly saying,

"Honey, well known for its healing properties." To all those around, Lemma just shrugged, "If you say so."

Returning to Cathal's side, she removed his chest plate and shirt with Zenith's aid. "Lift him," she ordered. Smothering his ribs in the paste and bandaging them in a soft, clean white linen sheet from above Cathal's head. She turned to the others and spoke in a soft voice. "He shall sleep for a while, and once awake, he will not feel his injuries. The black root and sage leaves will dull his pain. The honey will see the relief deep into his skin and aid its healing"

Lemma and Zenith nodded and left the cottage, checking that Cathal lay comfortably inside as they did.

8

THE PAST

Taking the time available to them, Lemma persuaded Zenith to recount his journey before meeting on his way to the Rycliff bridge.

Zenith began to recount his journey. "Well, like I said, I left Grissam just over three years ago. I went hours after meeting Thaddeus, the monk of Ayr Rose. Once I had ensured I had enough coin and provisions. Meaning I could get a room in Lehoi, I intended to spend a week or two gathering information. My priority and first port of call was securing lodgings at the inn, so that I had a place to gather my information." "Seems sensible enough", Lemma uttered in approval. "Soon enough, I had settled in. A few days passed, and I gained very little information; nobody seemed to have any clue about the Rysendar or those who wield them. Well, that and the usual things about Hagan and the rebuilding of Ocard." Zenith paused, needing to take a breath.

Lemma looked on smiling, listening intently, nodding before she spoke. "Quite surprised a busy town like Lehoi had no information." Zenith took it that Lemma wished him to continue.

"Errant's teaching certainly showed itself here. Luck shone on me after almost a fortnight; a merchant from the south had come to the Farmers' market. He knew of a temple far to the south. The temple lay within the hamlet of Tree's Edge, south of Lehoi and west of the gorge, bordering the feral forest." "Not one I've heard of?" questioned Lemma quietly. He also recalled one that was supposedly east of Errent, but had never been there himself, so could offer no directions or assurances that it even existed.

Lemma sat under the tree, a sigh dropping from her lips, thinking to herself. *I wish you would speed up the story*, then interjected to offer a few words. "Even the smallest bit of information can change the course of battle or the minds of men."

Still thinking, *watching a Scammel horn foraging amongst the grass had more appeal*. Either way, she let him continue.

All this time, he had been continuous, save for a slight pause in his speech, as far as she could ascertain. Zenith had left Lehoi after a two-month stay.

Lemma continued listening as Zenith droned on, "I made my way south following the trader's advice, stick to the gorge's edge until you have no path left to travel further, then turn, put my back to the gorge and follow the feral forests' tree line until a hamlet came into view. It sits a little way north of the forest."

Checking that Lemma still listened, jokingly saying, "pink, purple polka dots," "was that the horse's name?" Lemma laughed, catching him off guard. he began again. "Erm... Erm... yeah, sure enough it was. Anyway, I followed the gorge, stopping at many smaller settlements along the way for food and water. At each one, a new face would greet me or turn their backs on me; some didn't seem so fond of strangers. Or it could have just been seeing my face." Sure, he would catch her out this time. "I can see why it is rather rugged and eye-catching." Lemma retorted with a sincere cheek in her tone. Zenith blushed and did his best to continue. "I rode daily, making the most of the daylight, and occasionally broke my journey to hunt. Soon enough, I was face-to-face with the Feral Forest. I'd been riding for almost two weeks by this point, beginning to wonder if I'd been misinformed back in Lehoi, and I had been chasing ghosts." Lemma jumped in, teasing him, "What are you, A man or a field mouse? Ghosts only live in big, dark buildings."

Zenith ignored her. The feral forest stood tall and ominous, blackness filling all the air between the ground and canopy, light intermittently piercing it to reveal the greens and yellow hues of the leaves. Each tree seemed to be fighting, twisting its way higher to reach the sun. Low down seemed dead, no noise to speak of, only the occasional rustling of dead leaves and branches lay about the forest floor, moving as tiny creatures scurried about looking for fallen fruit and berries." Zenith stopped speaking, noting that Lemma was slowly becoming disinterested; indeed, she was, and her face revealed the thoughts swirling through her mind. *Good god, man, this is one long, boring story.*

So, with a degree of sarcasm, he started up again. "Anyway, I digress, the forest was a wondrous sight, such as I'd never seen, but not why I was there. I must have travelled west for several days before Trees Edge came into view on the horizon." "Finally, the story gets somewhere." Lemma grinned, mocking Zenith's storytelling ability. "You tell a long, tall tale, don't you?"

Clearing his throat, trying to seem unbothered. "Long and tall it may be, but I assure you it is all relevant", then stuck out his tongue before speaking. "Sure enough, it was north of where I currently stood. The buildings were nothing more than wood and straw-built round houses, all but one structure that stood proud and strong among them, built of a slate grey rock, it towered over the outlying buildings by at least a second height, it bore the symbols of Rysand on its walls and another, less prominent symbol, a Helmet and a small bat type object."

Lemma piqued an interest in the second symbol. Knowing the weapons. She knew the third was a staff of purity. He described a small bat-type object. *Could this have been something similar? Or even just an eroded reference to the staff.* "So the temple was for Angelus?" she asked.

"Yes, it was." Between Coughing and taking a swig of water to parch his dry throat after all this talking. "I entered Tree's edge, tattered and torn from the long journey. There was no inn to speak of; fortunately, a local welcomed me into her home after a discussion with the scholars at the temple. She would provide me lodging for as long as I stayed in Trees Edge studying. They had many ancient parchments and scrolls, these even dated back as far as the birth of Errent under Hagan, also a brief history of Angelus, the temple's name, the Rysand Temple of Angelus threw me, since there was so little of it." Pausing again for breath, Zenith looked to Lemma, who sat deep in thought, it seemed

I know who Angelus is. I've never heard of any general keeping his history. Odd. Lemma piped up, confused like she thought out loud. "Hagan and Sciran, yes, they have a detailed history, accounts are stored all over Apprite, but a history even in short form of Angelus? It's unheard of. No one had records since his disappearance."

Content with Lemma's voiced thoughts, Zenith returned to the story. "I spent almost all of my days in the temple reading and studying the scrolls and questioning the Scholars. The days I didn't study were spent in my host's fields, where I maintained them, showed them how to improve their harvests and yields, and helped them over almost two years. I did this, even introducing them to the simplest of ploughs pulled by Mullocks." Lemma just blurted out in surprise. "You must be messing with me; they didn't even know about a plough."

Zenith chuckled. "That was the best reaction yet. All the village had used them for before me was milk. Not a soul in the village considered using them as working animals. The capital must never have ventured this far, as they barely had even basic knowledge on how to produce a crop, let alone farm the land to its fullest."

Realising he was digressing further, he refocused his words. "I read of the Rysendar and of Angelus, how he had left his weapon in a place no one would find it unless fate deemed it so. This offered no clue to its location at the time. Seeing passages covering his journey here on his final pilgrimage. Angelus had hoped that he would be able to rest in the place of Rysand's birth and eventual assent to the benevolence at the western cliffs of the Orcadian Grasslands."

Lemma interrupted him, "I've never heard any of this before!" She had spent many years studying back home. "The teaching of Rysand in the Occardian Grassland seems more masculine than what I learned back home." Falling silent, she thought about the teaching she knew. *Birthplace of Rysand, never heard mention of it, pretty sure it isn't in the book of Sciran either.* Asking Zenith to give her a moment, she continued to think it over, feeling befuddled and lost. *The city's namesake wrote that book for every star holder after; surely it should have been in there, it's essential. No, I definitely can't remember any mention of it. I wonder why?*

Giving Lemma the moment she needed to think came at the right time; it allowed Zenith to breathe and enjoy the moment for a few minutes before Lemma prompted him to continue. She had finally taken full interest, putting on his best scholarly voice to sound like he had something to teach.

"Once I'd done all the reading I could. Understanding was only natural. The legends told of three, but never where to find them. Their descriptions and information were mostly scrubbed away by time, leaving the history broken and marred. I thought perhaps that one may lie with Angelus to the west. It seemed that he had taken his weapon to the grave. No one in their right mind would leave such a weapon unprotected and lost to time. At least that's what I thought"

Lemma lent in closer. This seemed to be getting interesting, all this new information that even she had never been able to find. She listened as Zenith carried on speaking. "Once I had paid my dues for the kindness shown to me by my host and the scholars. I planned my next step. The scrolls describe Angelus passing close to Tree's Edge, making his way to the most westerly point of the grasslands, where Rysand had first stepped onto the land with Rycore, his place of birth at the western cliffs and ultimately where Rysand left it as well."

Thyme had put together a small selection of foodstuffs with water skins. "Young ones these days forget to look after themselves." His old voice trailing off, telling a young village girl to take it over to them. After noticing Lemma and Zenith, they had been sitting under that tree all morning, talking.

Diner had come and gone, and he felt he needed to ensure they were fed. The small girl scurried quickly over to them, passing the tray to Lemma, and darted back towards the village.

· · ·

Lemma, tucked straight into the fruits, bread, and cheese, chuckling at the action of her hand and how her mind saw it, causing her cheeks to flush rose. *Oh lord, when did I get domesticated? It's like I'm making lunch for my husband.* Zenith drank, parched from recounting his journey for nearly the whole morning, yet he was so obviously not finished.

Lemma happened to feel at ease, though sitting here listening to him. Laughing, if he got animated, feeling content to watch him and listen, it just felt right. Then her mind wandered to something her sister once said. *Suppose you are ever invited alone by a gentleman to eat and drink. That would be a date, especially if you enjoy his company.* A sudden rush of heat filled her face as she realised she was on a date with Zenith, hiding her face behind the waterskin to avoid further embarrassment. *How did I forget that?* Once they had finished the picnic-type meal they had been brought, she beckoned him to finish his tale.

Zenith obliged and settled back into his story, "Setting out from Tree's Edge, I headed West, days of travel, loneliness, and boredom, as all that stretched before me was grass and the ever-moving horizon. I had been alone for I think three days when I bumped into a group of ten roving bandits." "Bandits, what happened?" Lemma just blurted out.

"Let me get there, I promise it's worth it." Just the sign of a grin appearing above his top lip as he said this. "They blocked the path ahead, insisting I hand over all my coin along with my horse. I had to laugh at them. Each one of them looked destitute, all wearing similar clothing that was tattered and torn, except for one man. The man who spoke was, in a sense, their commander, I think. His clothes looked newer, his weapons shiny and well-kept.

Once I had dismounted and refused, they attacked me, showing no real skill with the sword, just poking and thrashing at me. I hadn't realised at the time how the Echidna flame enhanced my abilities, so I managed to maim all his subordinates. He chose this moment to advance at a run; he came at me sword in hand, then fell flat on his face, arms stretched out over his head, sword forced clear of him from the impact." Lemma looked at him like he was joking, *Ok, he's got to be kidding me, hasn't he? Those eyes say it's no lie,"* so she probed *further.*

A smirk formed over Zenith's face. This was his favourite memory from that journey, laughing as he spoke. "No, he hadn't given up. The idiot hadn't watched his footing while running. Must have misstepped onto a small rock or something that slid from under his boot, causing him to lose his balance and face-plant the floor. It looked like he had just slammed into water stomach first as he hit the deck." Lemma couldn't help herself as she imagined it; she burst out laughing, falling to her back and curling up. She hadn't heard anything this funny in years; it sounded so surreal. "I can't stop laughing. Help me, my stomach hurts."

Zenith interrupted, trying his hardest to continue and ignore Lemma's barrel laughing and rolling about the floor. "Well, as you might have guessed, he truly embarrassed himself, or at least I expect he would have if he hadn't only gone and knocked himself out in the process. His own men, even though they were in pain, laughed. Once I got over the humour of the situation, I found myself hopping back on my horse and leaving them there."

Lemma, still unable to control her laughter, lay flat on her back, trying to catch her breath, admiring the white clouds that floated overhead. "I haven't laughed like that in so long. Thank you." Zenith, though he may as well finish his story, so on he went.

"Eventually, I came upon a view that astounded me. The

world just stopped meeting the ocean. There stood an ancient monument, weathered and torn, and time had not been kind. It seemed forgotten by all. Its pillars, eroded to the point of collapse. The roof was barely visible, only aloft atop the three pillars that had not collapsed. No seeable entrance, obviously buried in rubble, meaning I would need to dig my way in if I wished to see if the weapon resided here.

It took me many days, but eventually I uncovered a staircase leading into the earth. Taking a torch from my mount, I headed inside a burial chamber of granite and obsidian. Opening before me as I reached the bottom of the stairs, in the centre, a sarcophagus of white marble gleaming as if it had only just been carved. I searched the chamber and all the areas surrounding the sarcophagus to no avail; nothing, not even the remnants of the burial gifts.

All that remained was the sarcophagus. I approached it, examining it, looking for any clue it could provide, truly wishing I wouldn't need to disturb the resident. Fortunately, at the foot, a plaque was inscribed The staff does not lie within. I left it for the people who followed me to hold for the next time it is needed." It made complete sense to Lemma that the weapon wouldn't be there, but Zenith still hadn't finished.

"Considering who this chamber belonged to and all that I had learned, I decided I would trust these words of the man closest to God in all the legends. Good job, I did since I wouldn't have found it." Pausing, Zenith took a deep breath, a slight chuckle loosening from his lips. "Lemma, you know well the rest of this story, you're in it." Staring straight at her and adding. "My head still hurts from the fall"

With his story up to date, Zenith spent the rest of the afternoon just content in Lemma's company, waiting for Cathal to wake. It didn't seem likely to be today, so they asked Thyme if they could stay again that night.

9
FROM HERE TO HOME

Daylight descended upon the village, sparking instant small-scale pandemonium. Men heading off to the fields and workshops, women to the river to wash the clothes and cleaning the village centre. Children played in the water just in sight of their mothers. Zenith decided he would help the locals as best he could. Missing the days of hard graft, tilling his farm, tending the crops, so this seemed an opportune time to get back to his roots.

Lemma leaned against the frontier fencing that lined the field where Zenith had set to work with a Mullock tethered to a makeshift plough. He walked up and down the field, hard at work in the midday sun, shirtless, his muscular body glistening with sweat. Watching him work hard made her love him more.

Stood here watching him, letting her imagination play out the long term, glimpsing a future where their strengths could rival one another, emotions and skills guiding a new generation. The future held many unknowns, ones that she could face alongside this unskilled fighter, but the most skilled provider and caretaker to secure a place for their legacy. It brought back Rockwall to her memory, where he first confessed his love to her, the injury to his shoulder now nothing but a scar. *Well, that's one memory I'll keep to myself until I want to tease him.* Words passed through thought, reflecting in Lemma's mind.

She didn't know how she could love him so dearly, but she did. Nothing could keep her from him, not even death. Now, she wanted to be by his side forever. Proven to be a fine man, she hoped and knew her mother would approve of him, since her eldest sister had married nothing more than a furniture salesman; Zenith was one of the Rysendar generals, certainly a cut above that.

One question remained, though. All she knew of his past was his brother, nothing more. She resolved to question him later that day to find out more about the mystery of this man.

As the afternoon made its way deeper towards dusk, Zenith finished the field. Fully tilled and cropped for the planters to arrive. A lone woman, the healer, made her way to them across the fields, a gleeful expression on her face. Bearing tremendous news, "Your friend is finally awake and awaits you at your giant bird's temporary home. He was so Eager to move on, I couldn't stop him. He just pushed on past me." Cathal couldn't wait to leave the village and his most brutal battle to date behind him.

Lemma grasped Zenith's hand as they walked, with a slight swing in her arm movements. A small sense of Whimsy washed over her, a feeling of youth breaking through the surface of her warrior's face, bringing a glint of sparkle to her eyes, as she wished she could let herself be free and dance or skip alongside him. Yet, she held back her feelings all over the place. Thinking to herself, *How am I so blessed? I never even considered I'd find love, especially one that leaves me so defenceless.*

Lemma joyfully and bouncing spoke up. "Cathal's over

there." Ahead, a dear and new friend, safe and well. Most of all, this would be Lemma's day to return home even more triumphant than she had ever wanted or imagined possible. *I only sought the Echidna flame, but somehow found both of the other generals' and weapons. I must admit one of them is pretty cute as well.* Destiny seemed to be shining over all of them.

In Rath's stable stood Cathal, proud and tall, patiently stroking Rath. The day must have allowed the two to bond as they now seemed closer. Rath was even loaded with multiple bags of food and skins of water for their journey to Sciran. Finally, all stood together, greeting each other like old friends, making ready to leave.

Thyme approached slowly, his cane cracking the dry earth beneath it "I see you are all ready, and everything is in order. Ready for you to leave. Tome will surly miss you you've been here a day saved our village from a giant beast and done the work of several of our men, within a day tilling that one field" a laugh burst from him as he said the last words " now they all feel like useless little boys and are working into the night to catch up" Zenith grew a pale shade of red it was no effort for him but had he known the others didn't fare so well he would of taken it much slower he had meant no offence.

Thyme handed Lemma a small bag of coins and told them that the mountain pass had become a refuge of bandits who charged a toll to all travellers to Sciran. It was the smallest thing he could do to help at the moment. The feeling that they had done the village a grand service left him holding a far larger debt.

. . .

All sat atop Rath; they were led from Tome by a small parade of women and children, all throwing flowers at their feet and cheering them on, some of them with faces full of happiness, others of sorrow, not wanting their village's saviour to leave.

Their direction set, they continued north northeast towards the ever-looming mountain pass that stretched from Arathy to Siran's sovereign land. The village was a distant sight now that Rath had taken off at full speed, the surroundings a blur to them. After all, she was free to run, and they were aware of it. She didn't slow down or dodge; she just ran. Her speed was gaining all the time. The hours flew, and the sun started to settle, casting a giant shadow across the arid plains of Arathy. They neared the Drakes' mountains.

Cathal looked ahead; he felt like he was back in the gorge. These mountains, taller than the gorge, were somehow more intimidating. It could have been the fact that they rose above the setting sun or that he had never seen their likes before.

Either way, he wished to pass them soon as the night drew in; there ahead was the pass, the only way through unless you climbed up and over a natural choke point where a few could hold the many. Lemma sat there thinking, *No wonder Sciran lays claim to all on the other side; it has the perfect natural defences, these mountains, North, East, and South of it.' The gorge touching its Western border. It's almost impenetrable.* Lemma had read of many a distant land trying to invade, though here the heads of ten thousand men's armies were destroyed by but a few hundred Sciran bowmen.

Zenith pulled Rath to a stop a hundred yards from the entrance to the pass. A massive, newly built palisade stood there, atop its wooden walls and walkways, and a few ragged archers stood staring at them, bows pulled, ready to loose their arrows.

Jumping down from Rath, Zenith strolled to the gates alone. Cathal and Lemma waited behind with Rath.

The gate creaked and shuddered as it opened wide, revealing a man clad in a full suit of brass coloured armour bearing the Scirainian insignia. Slowly, he walked, hand on the hilt of his long sword, primed and ready, approaching. Zenith's hand was on the hilt of the Echidna flame, unsure whether a fight was coming or if the man was being cautious. Stopping easily ten feet from Zenith, the man bellowed, "This pass is subject to a toll of seven gold coins for passage and safety; the mountain men control it now."

Zenith raised his voice, shouting in response, "All we seek is passage, no fighting necessary, we will gladly pay when your archers lay down their arms" With a mighty wave from the man in armour, the archers lowered their bows and unstrung their arrows, easing their postures.

Rath walked slowly and carefully up to Zenith's side, carrying Lemma and Cathal, both of them apprehensive and ready for battle. Lemma peered hard down at the man who wore her home's armour. She knew him; his face was familiar, but his name escaped her, all the same.

Zenith helped Lemma dismount. His arms held her firmly and aided her to the ground. From her waist, she pulled the bag of coins. Approaching this man had her on edge. *I know him. I'm sure I recognise that scar?* His face was scarred on the left side of his jaw. Now, she knew who he was as she screamed at him indignantly, "Brent, how dare you challenge me?".

The man looking upon Lemma dropped to his knees and laid his head at her feet. "I'm sorry, princess, I did not recognise you. The kingdom thought you lost, as you never returned," he said, his voice filled with regret. Lemma became even more indignant, kicking Brent on the side of his head. "Get on your feet, you imbecile." She boomed at him. "You know better than to bow at my feet, maybe my sisters or my mother, the Queen. I have never made anyone bow"

Brent rose to his feet and waved to his men, who came from within the confines of the pass, all stopping and gathering up behind him, laying down their arms and bowing their heads. "Men, a tremendous honour has befallen us this day. Princess Lemma has returned to us with friends and a fearsome creature built for war. We shall escort her to Sciran forthwith. The pass will be free passage once again, for I am sure that now the siege will be broken for good"

At these words, Lemma grimaced. A siege at Sciran's walls, not what she had hoped to hear, but it at least meant the city and its people still stood and were fighting for freedom from the forces that assailed them.

The men all gathered their arms and formed into tidy, neat lines at Brent's command. There were no bandits; they were soldiers, lost and alone, outside of their beloved city. They had secured the pass to prevent any more intruders. Greed had set in after days of waiting; they charged all comers as a deterrent or used a show of force when necessary. Now they had hope renewed, their faith restored.

Zenith walked, guiding Rath with Lemma atop, proud of her people as they walked headlong into the pass heading towards her home. Cathal, at their side, was talking with Brent as one General to another. He gathered all the information he could about the forces they would face upon arrival in this short walk, wanting to start formulating a plan. They were but a few hundred men, most skilled archers, not many swords to speak of. The odds did not stand with them at all on arms alone; the army they marched to face was dark ranks filled with all manner of Monsters and disfigured men, at least five thousand strong. The saving grace was that they seemed to have no leadership and attacked sporadically, mainly at night.

The contingent was ready to leave the pass; they would have a day's journey before reaching the scarred remains of the once formidable Draklow Fort, which guarded the mountain pass from its northern side.

Brent talked with Cathal as they guided the men from the palisades, explaining that he had been stationed at Draklow heading a force of five hundred men split two to one, archer to sword, and how the fort had fallen weeks before, of how he and this rag tag unit had ran for the mountains but two hundred heads and the rest running north for Sciran.

Narey, a single man, was able to grab a horse or even a weapon when the monstrous army fell on them, bent on blood and destruction of all who lay there. The creatures had seemed uninterested in the fort's stables and its large horse herd. He hoped that the fort stood and that even if scattered, the horse saddles and supplies would remain; if not, this march would take nearly a week. On horseback, and it would be halved.

Heavy in the sky, the sun had begun to wane as Draklow came into view, a magnificent structure built from the grey, speckled granite mined from the mountain range. Its walls stood fourteen men tall, each of the compass points marked by an impressive tower almost a third taller than the walls.

Approaching the main gate that lay in ruins, the party could see horses milling all about the stables and barracks within the wall, grazing on scrawny, well-trodden grass. The barracks hadn't survived the monsters' wrath; large parts lay in ruins, and the roof was nothing but burnt beams. On the other side, the stable stood without much but a scratch or mark.

The food stores were perfect, doors sealed shut as if the Nightwatch had forgotten to unlock them that morning, a welcoming sight indeed. Brent called out orders for his men to find sacks to carry food for five days, and to prepare every horse that was not already assigned to a man to bring food or weapons.

With the slightest of hesitation, fearing there may still be beasts dwelling within, the Scirainian soldier at his command sprang into action, readying everything within three bell chimes, allowing all to rest a whole night before their three-day march to the aid of their beloved city, Sciran.

Those three days of marching soon passed. The days whistling past as each man grew bolder and braver on the approach, each day of triumphant march had them ever closer to loved ones and home.

Newly armed and full of grit, the unit made camp around an hour's walk from Sciran. Brent knew to attack now would guarantee there slaughter the monsters gained strength in the dark for some ungodly reason in the day they became more sluggish and easier to kill that is how Sciran has survived these past weeks picking them off in the day and defending during the night slowly their numbers dwindled but the city surly had depleted most of its reserves by now and soon would be over run.

The night drew in thick, the fire blazed, and all the men slept except a few who were posted on guard. Zenith lay near the fire, head resting on a log. Lemma, asleep on his chest, cuddled into him. Feeling reassured knowing she was safe with him, no issues would stop him from guarding her. Staring into the night sky, stars twinkled and shone, unable to sleep, the battle ahead playing with him, trepidation on his brow as to whether they could make a difference.

In the distance, there came a tremendous roar. The night

sky above the mountains lit up all ablaze. There stood a creature that was neither quite a lion nor quite an eagle. *Is that Synergy? Has he finally awoken, ready to join me?"* Zenith felt perplexed, looking around.

It must have been an apparition, as not another soul stirred. The guards didn't move from their posts, still staring straight out into the darkness. *Am I the only one seeing this? I'm sure I'm not dreaming, am I?* he hoped not. Maybe it was an omen of the days to come.

10

BATTLE TO FREE A CITY

Cathal and Brent walked silently and sombrely next to each other back to camp as the first almost violet rays of the sun broke over the horizon. Awakening early to assess the best strategies for the battle ahead, neither had anticipated quite what they saw: an army of monsters stretching around the outer walls of Sciran, fires burning brightly, giving them an excellent and terrifying view of the field.

One hope had come through on the near side of the siege: a hill tall enough to hide on and place Taxophite and bowman upon to fire down onto their enemy. Still, the vast numbers meant they would be overrun quickly. All their hope was placed in the fact that the limited number of swordsmen with Zenith and Cathal could hold them back long enough for the archers to slow the army's ranks and dent them enough so that whatever remained of the main military stationed in Sciran could flank them and cut them down quickly.

From the moment Brent left Sciran to secure the pass at

Dralow, he knew there were roughly one thousand archers and double that number of pikes and swords within the walls. Even if half that number remained, they would still have a chance. The element of surprise was on their side. The Scirainians were a proud people, all of whom followed the code of honour, and would set their lives on the line to save their beloved city.

The camp woke early, the sun barely risen into view, providing the clouds with a pure halo of light —a good omen in the eyes of all the camp. A fever ran through every man here; their spirits soared as they readied for battle, each willing to die a warrior's death to free their city, their senses and hope restored by Lemma, their princess, feared lost in unknown lands.

Lemma stood in front of them, proud, looking into each of their eyes one by one. Zenith, Cathal, and Brent standing aside, Lemma addressed them, briefing them on the battle plan that had been devised. She knew a speech was needed to bolster their spirits even more, as some, although ready, seemed unsure of their chances.

"Each and every one who stands here now is a free man to do with their life as they wish. All I ask is that you take arms to free a brother trapped within the city wall by this horrendous army that lays them siege."

The men cheered and chanted, "For our princess, for our princess." Lemma cast her hand through the air to silence them.

"They are the ones we fight for, not me or the crown. We fight for the freedoms of all Scirainians. The Rysendar will be your guiding light, standing ready to aid you and fight alongside you. Without this war, peace cannot be gained. Peace will enshrine these lands by day's end; the mead will flow to the victors."

The speech echoed around the camp, "one for the history books," Brent thought, as all his men raised their weapons high and cheered Lemma's name. "Surely even the benevolence could hear their words and, in the coming battle, perhaps even provide its aid to them; after all, the three generals of Rysand stood with them." Every man had similar thoughts.

The camp moved as one marching on through the plains to the rear side of the hill, and archers stationed themselves just out of view behind the brow. The swordsmen and Brent followed after Lemma and Cathal, ready to charge into the field below. Rath stayed hidden at the back, Zenith would make use of her height, weight and razor-sharp feathers.

The horns sounded, and instantly, the sky was filled with arrows above them, landing square and true into the masses below, most striking an enemy combatant. Several of the enemy were killed by the barrage, which caused hysteria in the monster's army—spinning, looking for the location of the archers. The next flight was just as accurate, cutting through. Fifty to a hundred more, dropping dead in the chaos. Unfortunately, the second volley alerted the bulk of them; they had seen the arrow's flight direction and trampled over there dead as they raced towards the mound.

Several more flights of arrows flew all true, dropping hundreds of the advancing horde, but still they came thundering, a mass of hideous creatures, screaming, guttural roars and all manner of sounds, now close enough for them to see the men stationed at the top of the hill.

A great screech filled the air as the horde shifted its gears, charging faster and faster towards them. Rath raced full speed around the slope, Zenith on her back, focused, casting orders wordlessly. *Rath, we run, take them,* wings at full stretch, feathers sharp and strong, darting through them, slicing the army down this way and that. She cleared them, not one of the horde able to see where the foe lay or went. *Turn* the next order, he thought. The next instance saw many monsters slain. Their death throes rising into the air, permeating the cries of war and the sounds of swords crashing against shields. Cathal watched in amazement and regret. *No wonder I lost so many brothers to those birds over the years I spent training; she's an army by herself.*

Those who didn't fall spun in Horror, trying to track the devastation being spread to their ranks. *Keep moving, don't stop circling them.* Zenith's unheard words followed in less than a second.

The others had their chance while Rath did her thing and confused the monsters; that's when they chose to strike, Cathal and Brent at each other's side, both eager to kill and maim these beasts, screaming out at the top of their lungs. "Charge!" headlong into their ranks, all the men plunged. Brent, caught unaware and surprised, was swept cleanly from his feet by a large beast. It's Warhammer then coming down towards his head, in a flash, Brent rolled left just as the hammer dug into the ground beside him.

Without warning, the beast fell beside him. Blackened

blood stained the earth. Atop this beast stood Cathal, his staff piercing the skull without a second glance. Brent tried to warn him. "Behind", Cathal had already pulled back, catching a second beast off guard. The staff smashed hard into the bridge of its nose, breaking it. Bent winching at the sound, screaming. "Good lord, that's one powerful blow."

Having tried to attack his rear, the beast screamed and made another attempt. This time, Brent, leaping to his feet, cut deep into the enraged beast with a gleaming blade, severing its head at the same time whilst it raised its arms to strike at Cathal. The beast's body hung there, staggering about until it slumped to the ground. Cathal's eyes went wide with shock, thinking. *Glad his blade is on our side.* Then nodding in congratulations.

Lemma stood higher than them all, the star gleaming as it soared into the air, slicing and dicing their rear ranks as it flew. Streams of lightning cut down those who dodged, weaving its way within the ranks, circling and swerving to the areas Rath had yet to arrive, following the movements as she flicked her wrist, directing it.

Brent and Cathal stood observing the battlefield as the beasts' ranks thinned, both having the same thought: *Maybe they could win.* Around them, thousands of the beasts' army lay dead or injured, and only a few of their men were hurt or worse. Still, a vast amount remained, easily two thousand or more. Brent had seen no movement made from within Sciran's walls. "Where are they? Why haven't they come out yet?" asking the question into the air at the centre of the carnage.

. . .

Lemma watched the battlefield, the star swooping and curling through the air, attacking the beasts not within her control; typically, it would have returned to her hand by now. As she watched the unusual movements of the star, though the corner of her eye, she glimpsed Cathal swinging his staff, striking at enemies. She noticed the star emulating the motions of the staff's pinnacle. The staff and Stars glow brighter and pulsate in unison with each foe they lay to waste.

Rath became tired at the rear of the beast's ranks, soaked in the black blood of the enemy ranks. Zenith dismounted, signalling through thought for her to return to the base of the hill and remain there in defence of the Taxophite and bowmen still raining their arrows into the advancing hordes over the tops of the men who defended the base of the hill.

Now, alone at the rear of the creature's army, Zenith drew the Echidna flame from its sheath; "God, sorry sword, where were you waiting to join the battle? Your dim light looks angry. Well, let's fight." In Front of him stood at least two hundred of the beasts. At the rearward flank, an insidious armoured beast, its body covered in ragged spikes protruding from the very bone itself. *This one looks like fun, not*" Thought Zenith. The Echidna flames light, bursting bright in agreement, so he thought.

Readying himself, blade in hand, as the first of the beasts approached, swinging its club high. Zenith took his chance, sliding under the beast's body and carving the Echidna flame deep into its gut, felling it swiftly. "One down, Oh crap!" he screamed as two more approached, attacking in tandem, one sword aimed for his chest, another swinging upwards, arching towards his stomach.

Stepping back swiftly, the beast's swords met crashing into

each other, deflecting them away from Zenith, seizing his chance, jumping high, swooping the Echidna flame downward in the air, arching his strike into the first beast, slicing bone and sinew alike. Landing and switching his stance, he drove his sword forward into the second beast's chest, piercing the beast's still human heart. The beast's screams curdled the air as it hung dead on the tip of the Echidna flame. *Is your anger slaked now, I wonder?* looking at the tip of the sword.

The ground echoed as the spiked beast charged through his ranks, tossing his lesser beasts asunder, impaling and cutting them with his spikes. Driving headlong at Zenith, a rage in its eyes, still dealing with several beasts, Zenith had not noticed the encroaching danger. In one swoop, he was lifted clean into the air, A long spike carving deep into his calf, blood streaming out.

Landing in a heap several feet away, the agony of the injury dragging his mind into the darkness, Zenith lay there, lifeless. The Echidna flame erupting into flames, the energy of the blade pushing him to his feet. His mind turned to a blood rage, the blade swung wildly and without reason, scorching enemies that approached. He had lost control again.

The Echidna flame ablaze, and Zenith's body stood in a ring of death carved by the Echidna flame guiding his movements, each body scorched with fire and brimstone as it made his body artfully duck and dive, blow after blow, he cut and stabbed his way through more and more of their bodies, piling high at his feet their blackened blood soaking into the green grass of the Sciran plains staining the earth with the malice they left behind.

The insidious beast plunged in again, throwing its humongous mass of a body at him. The Flames of the Echidna grew large, forming a vortex that twisted and curled up from the ground around them. Burning all other beasts to ash in its onslaught, at its centre, Zenith's body moved quickly to the side, avoiding a swipe from the giant beast's arm, the spikes missing by mere inches. Rolling away, regaining his feet, he ran at the beast, almost throwing the Echidna flame ahead of him, sending the blades' flames forward like an arrow, piercing the beast's shoulder and rendering its arm useless and floppy.

Stance shifting to his off foot, curling the flames around himself, sending flares outward, pushing the beast away, causing it to stumble over its own clubbed feet. Falling hard to the ground, the beast's own lame arm stabbed deep into its side, blackened blood spewing out from the wound. Pulling the spike out, dragging its own guts from its side, spewing out to the floor, screaming and retching, the beast lay there unable to move. The Echidna flame plunged deep into its chest; flames burst through its body.

Surrounded by a glorious light, the beast's skin began to melt away, revealing its human form once more. Remorse and pity abounded on its face as it realised its spirit, cleansed of Rycore's influence. Rysand's grace had been granted.

Collapsing from pure fatigue, Zenith's mind empty and dark, hearing a voice. Synergy's voice, "My brother, again the blade controls you, but less and less each time. I shall join you when you truly control your power. Until then, use my strength and forge your path."

At this, Zenith began to doubt his mind and regressed further and further. The black city in the fog appeared, and an ominous green glow now lit the centre of the mist. *I can hear the battle in full swing, but I see neither man nor beast.*

Outside of his mind, a great roar resounded above the field of battle, A giant shadow blocking the sun. Both sides stopped and stared up into the sky as the Echidna flame came to life; a vortex sprang from earth to heaven, enveloping the entire field of battle, closing in on the fighting armies, burning Zenith's enemies to ash but leaving all of the Scirainian men unburnt. The fight would be won as Lemma had promised, but not in the way they had expected. Zenith had again unknowingly summoned the full might of the Echidna flame. Cathal watched, scared to move. "It's the cave again, but this time I know it's safe."

Lemma stood on the hill in the distance, as the sounds of a hundred horns filled the air. The Scirainians' army was bursting through the Clad iron gates on the south and east of the city, encircling the battlefield. They had come to help their brethren fight, but they stood in awe. Ranked and filled, watching the vortex close in on the centre of the field, and the Ashes of the dead float to the ground, forming a blanket of death over it. Brent slyly commented. "About time, better late than never, I suppose." Cathal looked at him, "Well, you aren't wrong."

Lemma scoured the entire field. "Where is he?" Nearly all the beasts were gone. Seeing him at the centre of the field finally. "God, he had better be alive, or I'll murder him myself." The death and blood screams of an entire army filled the air and hung there, haunting this land for how long no one knew. Lemma could feel it in the air and sensed it in her thoughts. "These men are going to need time to get past this. The priests can help ease their minds with prayer."

The vortex had dissipated, and only a few meagre groups of their adversary remained, starting to panic, running straight into the waiting pikes and arrows of the Scirainians' army, who maimed and killed each one with glee, knowing that by the grace of Rysand there city was free and because of these few and that one man lay amongst all the ash especially.

Cheers rose all around as the final screams of the beasts

dissipated from the air. The day had been won, hours had passed, and yet the sun hung low as if disdainful of the violence below. The bulk of the Scirainians' army began to run the boots of their collective thundering as they sprinted to greet the few hundred that had surprised even them, with bravery against their odds of victory.

Halfway up the hill stood Lemma, the star in hand, covered in black blood but shining golden in its victory. The whole army stopped and dropped to their knees at the sight of her; no one from within the city knew she was there until the battle had ended. Now in her homeland, recognised by all, she smiled, her city, her people, free, happy and at peace. Thinking, *for how long though?* Before summoning her most confident and royal voice and booming across the field,

"Do you people never learn? I ask none of you to bow!" Across the field, Zenith had begun to wake, unaware the battle had ended. he clasped the hilt of the Echidna flame and stood, examining the field of battle. He saw Lemma standing on the hill, meandering forward. He worked his way towards her. Still in a delirious state, pace slow and cumbrous. His injury was steeped with blood, still oozing, soaking his leg.

On the wind, Lemma's voice, sweet to his ears yet harsh in tone, calling him onward. "I will get to her, I need to see she is ok", repeating with each step in his head.

"I have a title, not a royal complex; none of you are lesser than me now, stand!" shouted Lemma. In seconds, the hundreds of men stood as one. They cheered her name as she ran down the hill towards Zenith, embracing him and kissing his cheek, whispering in his ear, "Thank you, my love, you have honoured me this day." These words brought Zenith back from his delirium, smiling as he looked at her. Lemma turned to her mother's army, who all now waited silently in trepidation over her next words. Cathal and Brent came to her side. "Zenith, you mud muncher, why did you have to go and scratch yourself?" Cathal made light of his wounds, Brent also took the mickey: "On ya feet, farmer boy, the princess didn't say you could sleep." Both hooked under his shoulders, supporting him, keeping him on his feet as Lemma spoke.

"Your praise, my compatriots, is misplaced
  I am not the one to praise this day, my husband-to-be
  Zenith and these men who followed me to battle are the
  ones you sing of in the streets as the mead flows to the
  victorious"

Zenith hung there, face almost purple. *Did she... tell these thousands of men she's going to marry me?* He wanted it but hadn't dared to say anything. His heart flooded with emotions; pride beamed from his face. His faithful love truly loved him. She had decided he was to be her husband. Grimacing in thoughts hidden by pain, *she doesn't know the truth. Uncle Quinten sits on the throne that governs the eastern side of the gorge —Sciran's sworn enemies.*

He always knew he must tell her and hoped that she felt no differently towards him. That it didn't matter. Hate was not the way he thought about his uncle; perhaps disdain was a better word. Hatred for what the man did, everything about how he treated the people of Errant, making them pay inordinate taxes for what seemed to have no benefit to the populace.

Just lining his own pockets and punishing anyone who dared to question him so harshly that death was preferable. Just before he left Grissam, he heard of one poor fellow who had been fired from the wall javelins for saying that Quinten would get no more from him, not even his blood. Then there was the fact that somehow, Quinten convinced his grandfather he was the better choice, which made no sense at all, but he honoured it.

The Rumours still circulated that he had infected Grissam with the plague that killed his mother and father. *How can she love me, knowing nothing about my real background? Just the man she met.* The thoughts weighed heavily on him, and almost certainly added weight to Brent and Cathal's arms

The army, elated, now led by Brent, paraded the gathered ranks around the triumphant few and escorted them back to the city, with the heroes locked in a circle of honour, the customary way to greet returning heroes. Zenith and Lemma had hung back from the fuss and hullabaloo of the main army, deafening them.

Just wanting to be alone, to talk and be together, gather their thoughts together. It was obvious that Lemma had caught Zenith off guard by saying she intended to marry him. His face was distorted. Lemma watched him deep in thought. *I need to know if I have scared him with my love or if something more is playing with his mind.* Cathal waited alongside, unused to this type of event, not knowing what to do.

Held by Cathal, Zenith limped slowly, stirring in thought about his heritage. *I need to tell her about who I am, where I come from, and the truth about my past. Now more than ever, she needs to know it's the least she deserves.* He could tell by her face that she held concern and knew something was wrong with him. *It must be showing all over my face, she can't not have seen it.*

Stopping mid-step, he took both of her hands, staring intensely into her brown eyes.

"My love, I must confess a most desperate sin and secret; they may cause you disgust and have me exiled from your kingdom, but you must know this truth now more than ever, as we now seem to be betrothed in front of your army"

Lemmas' heart sank. *What sin and secret could he tell me that could be so bad I'd go from love to hate in a heartbeat? This could not be true, not him, not now.* Her mind whizzed in fear, still listening to his words, "As you know, I hail from Grissam. I am one of two brothers. My parents died from plague many moons ago."

She was puzzled by him as he paused in confusion, asking, "I know this. It's not a sin in any way."

"It's my family where my deepest sin lies. I am the son of the late crown prince of the Eastern continent, my uncle sits on the throne, your detested enemy, and I am his blood"

His word rang clear in her ears. He was of royal blood, her mother's enemy's blood. His words, spoken with malice, convinced her that he harboured great disdain for his uncle. If he was truly who he said he was, she didn't care; she had heard the rumours around the plague that killed the actual crowned prince.

So, no matter where he hailed from, he hated his king with more passion than even her mother, the Queen. As her mind whizzed and whirled, her face sombre and silent, she remembered something that may ease or intensify his hate for his uncle. Her mum held captive in the dungeons a man who had confessed to striking Grissam with the plague at the new king's orders, a coincidence, she thought, but best not to say and delay their arrival much longer.

She thought about how to present him. *A prince of the true Eastern king, not her mother's enemy, but a future son-in-law who could take the throne from Quinten and depose him justly and end the years of war between their nations.* She considered this to be the best answer.

Summoning the sweetest voice she could, she replied to him with a small tear in the corner of her eye. "My love, although you are his family, you are not his blood. You carry the blood of a true king and of those before him. I could not love you less; in fact, now that I know you more, I love you more."

Lemma's words lifted his heart, making it sore; even the cloud did not seem high enough. It was not a want but a need to make the engagement official right this moment.

Taking one knee in a very ungraceful way to avoid the injury already on his leg, almost toppling over once or twice, he took her by the left hand and gazed into her brown eyes. Reaching inside his shirt, pulling from within its secure pocket an oval ruby ring. The same ring his father had given his mother, Ake and Rathena had left it to him, carrying it with him at all times to keep it close at hand for this moment, this person, the one he intended to give it to his true love.

Though the pain, he summoned the words firm and sure, "Lemma, in such a short time, I have grown without doubt to love you more than my life. As you have shown, you hold me deep in your heart. I ask if you will do me the greatest honour of giving me your hand in marriage. As a sign of our union, I offer this simple ring, one used to wed my mother and father."

Silence, her voice held inside like the vocal cords had stopped dead; not a word could escape, save for an almost unheard whisper of a laugh, a smile just peering at the edges of her mouth. Inside her mind, thoughts chastised yet commended him. *I just said I would marry him, moments ago. Now he proposes to me in this blood-stained field. How romantic?* Diving into his arms, sending them both rolling over and over across the only non-blood-stained part of the battlefield. Cathal sent skuttling rearward, landing firmly on his rear end by the force of the leap. *They're just like kids at the playground.* He thought to himself as he watched. As they rolled together, kissing him passionately, any romance lost, Lemma screamed out for all to hear, answering him. "Yes, yes! I will marry you."

11

A LIE WITHIN A TRUTH

The giant iron gates slammed shut behind them, locking out the world as the last remnant of the army wandered back into the city. Lemma and Zenith hand in hand. Still aided by Cathal, walked through the street towards the castle, tall and regal at the city's centre.

Rath strode along, surrounded by men-at-arms led by Brent. They had all seen just how dangerous a warbird she was. None dared let the citizens near, even though Lemma and Zenith said they could. Brent piped up to them, "For benevolence's sake, you two, she's covered in beast blood for one, and for two, we have to keep her safe." Brent forgot to let them know he would have her stabled at the hall of arms until they called for her, and that she would have a squad of Junior knights seeing to her every need, before Lemma dragged Zenith off alone in another direction.

As they walked, citizens appeared from doors, hung out of windows, and lined the streets, cheering and laughing with excitement. Their city was free. The lost princess returned to them. Zenith couldn't help but think. *How much of a fuss they make, Lemma must truly be loved.* This was indeed the best time to celebrate, even if Lemma's wedding had not been made official by the Queen, the battle and her return held cause enough.

The streets, growing larger the further they walked, buildings becoming more spaced out, roads paved with golden sandstone. The buildings looked magnificent, taller, reaching high into the sky with each new street they passed through.

Lemma led Zenith off from the main road, the usual route that headed to the castle, "We are not walking the normal route. I want you to see Sciran the way I do and greet the people. I will show you my favourite places when I get the chance." A smile covering her face and a sense of joy in her voice. Walking with his hand in hers, hung softly at her waist. Pulling her close to him, he smiled, beaming as she pointed out the buildings of friends and nobility, each more lavish and decorated than the last. All in the same royal colours of deep purple and emerald green. Flags hung on poles positioned outside the upper windows, flapping in the breeze. Zenith couldn't help but comment on the display. "Your home is amazing; you truly are blessed by the people. Unlike me, I work in the dirt; I'm not suited to it the way you are." Lemma snapped back. "I don't ask for it, I'll work the mud with you if needed."

The streets gave way to a high inner wall as they approached the council chambers. Before the council members who milled about could interrupt, Lemma hid her face soundlessly in thought. *I hope they don't see us. I don't need the hassle.* The gate cracked and growled. It gave way to the force of several attendants as they approached, all present bowing their heads as they passed through. Lemma met each of them with a broad smile and sarcastic thanks. "By the gods, will they ever stop being formal with me?" Lemma muttered under her breath to Zenith. It was clear that these people adored her;

every single person they had passed, seen, or made conversation with on their way here had become lighter in step, large smiles crossing their faces, eager to see her home.

Rumours had begun to spread all over the place. Her announcement over Zenith, and now bearing his ring, they all saw it was true: she had chosen to marry. Nobody in this city had ever tempted or come close to her enough for this to happen; many of the people believed that destiny had decided years ago that the one she should have married was dead. Although they did not seem to care in the slightest, they appeared happy and content for her, overly excited about the evening's festivities to come, especially over their newfound freedom.

Weaving in and out of the arched covered pathways around the council chambers, Lemma nuzzled her head into Zenith's shoulders, her breathing content and slowed. She whispered into his ear, "I love you, and I'm sure my mother will, too. No matter your family, you are a hero to her people now." Zenith turned his head away, embarrassed to reply. "I hope so."

The archways opened out into a beautiful garden filled with a vast array of colours: blues, reds, greens, purples, pinks, yellows, all leading them slowly through to the solid white granite steps of the Queen's castle. Frozen in his step, Zenith stared upwards at the spectacle of the palace that lay before him. *There are so many colours, erm...* his thoughts cutting off in distraction.

The highest parapets coiled their way to the sky, the walls lined in deep purple and emerald-green banners, soldiers standing every ten steps on its walls, mounted trebuchets made from fine oak between them, twin arrow ballistae all loaded and ready for use. Zenith couldn't voice what he saw, thinking, *This is no common city, the walls are heavily fortified even though the city is at peace. They must be constantly ready for war. Lemma's mum must be a wise ruler. Its walls show no fear of being breached.*

Already standing on the white granite step awaiting their arrival. At the top, in her royal gown, was Lemma's mother, Catherine; several steps lower, her eldest sister, Isis, the carpenter's wife; and below her, Faith, the middle sister, still unmarried and uninterested in it, some suspected other proclivities based on lies and rumour about the company she kept.

Faith and Isis rushed forward to their sister, hands flung around her, spinning her there, joy plain to see. Their steps were light as air; you could see they were close and had feared her lost, "Where on Apprite have you been, Lemma?" Isis asked, interrupted by Faith. "You should have been back weeks ago. We feared you gorge food. When the bridge collapsed again." Lemma somehow managed to keep a straight face, but internally, she was gripped by fear, thinking. *I won't be telling you that story for a while.* But her voice just said. "Oh, I got way laid in Lehoi, having too much fun toying with a local boy." Isis and Faith looked at each other, shaking their heads in tandem "Lemma, what are you like? Is that the local boy you taunted?" Once the sisters had finished this whimsical greeting dance, Lemma stood proudly and introduced them to Zenith with his full title: "Zenith, Prince of Errant, and the wielder of the Echidna flame."

The sister's face dropped, her words stung them and angered them. Smiling Lemma spoke with a sweet, angelic voice, one that had twisted them around her little finger since she was just a wee bairn, trying to win them over.

"Sisters, you need not fear Zenith; he is a prince by blood to the truest heir of the Eastern continent, nephew of Quinten, and he hates him with a passion not even our mother could hope to match."

Lowering his face, Zenith nodded a look of sorrow clear across him. "I am he, but I have always wished never to have been." His words and sorrow pierced deep into Isis, and faith, their hearts swelled with a deep empathy, knowing of his father's demise, they understood and smiled. Both were speaking in perfect unison.

"We will welcome any who Lemma chooses with open arms." The words were somehow soothing to his core, brightening his drooping heart.

Isis, the oldest of the sisters, linked arms with Zenith. Faith linked up with Lemma and proceeded to pull them up the granite steps at a reasonably rapid pace toward Catherine. Zenith's head hung low; the shame of his heritage now plagued his thoughts. *I know it. I'm off to the gallows, surely, she will despise me just for bearing blood similar to his. I really hope Lemma's heart doesn't break too much.*

Low and afraid, almost dragging on his knees, slowly lifted his head to see Catherine, in all her majesty. She seemed kind of face, true of heart, and most of all held in her gaze years of wisdom. An older lady in her late forties to early fifties, she still stood firm; the intrusive thoughts got in for a second. *I can certainly see where Lemma got her gorgeous looks and how men would fall at her feet.*

Yet her face seemed familiar; he knew her face, his memories were trifling, stuck and vague. *Catherine? Older, yes, but I know her. How? I met her years ago when I was like five or six? How did I forget them? I knew them all as a child; they visited his grandfather, the king, in Errant, as foreign dignitaries.* Still, he remembered her differently. *She was far younger, carrying a child; could that have been Lemma?* As he searched deeply, he saw the childlike faces of Isis and Faith, who had barely aged, but Lemma was nowhere to be found.

The next memory struck like Rath cascading through the battlefield. His mind sent itself into a frenzy, withdrawing as he saw the memory play out: his grandfather standing with Catherine, him and the baby—a moving picture that played out in an instant. A treaty was signed as a promise of peace and the betrothal of Zenith to the baby girl at her coming-of-age ceremony.

On her sixteenth birthday, they would wed and unite the two kingdoms, their royal lines to be joined, creating a great empire. They would together rule East and West. His mind locked in on self-reflection. Holding him. *My uncle is behind them, holding a blade? towards dad?* His legs were going weak and losing all feeling, and he slid deeper into the memory, forcing his mind to go blank.

Isis struggled to hold on to Zenith as he fell at her mother's feet, his eyes vacant and disturbed as his face smashed hard into the granite. He screamed his uncle's name, malice permeated all around him to their core as he passed into blackness.

Lying slumped over a soft bed inside a castle chamber, Zenith slumbered, his mind racing at the image of his uncle threatening his father's life. In the memories that played on repeat, his grandfather took on the role of a diligent ruler and politician, securing the future of both his country and his family line.

The image ingrained in his mind. *Is the rumour of the plague being one of Quinten's creations true? Who killed my mother and father?* Repeating, Ringing in his ears, not one ounce of truth had he considered giving to this before. Still, it was now clear that the various images proved his uncle's betrayal and showed him for the evil man he was.

Lemma lay beside Zenith, holding him in her arms as he tossed from side to side, obviously in internal torment. The nightmares were tormenting him, making her pray silently, "Rysand, grant me the strength to help him through this". Still, she couldn't; all she could do was comfort his body, and in doing so, pray harder, wish harder, "Open your eye, Zenith, let me see into those deep claret eyes, I want you to see the love in mine."

The doors to the chamber swung wide, and in marched Cathal and Brent side by side, concern for Zenith written across their combined faces as one. They knelt by his side, staring at him, a slight tear grazing Cathal's face at the sight of his newest brother in arms, tormented as he was. Strife mixed Cathal's thoughts. *Zenith, you have been by my side for only a few days, and you are already like a brother to me. Stay strong and awake.*

Both had been in the hall of arms when they heard of Zenith's collapse—no sooner had the message arrived than both sprinted with all their might to him. He had saved both their lives on the field of battle, and they owed him a great deal.

The hours passed as Zenith still lay there in his torment. Well-wishers from the army and the families of those he had saved came by hundreds, laying gifts and flowers around his chamber. A shrine encircled him, candles burning, the fragrance filling the air. Lemma still lay with him, mopping his sweat-soaked brow, refreshing the towel and cooling it down now and then, her arms throbbing as she still held her love deep in a loving embrace, hoping her feelings could reach deep enough that they would help. *Zenith, feel me, hear me, know I'm here, come back to me, how can I marry you if you don't?* Anger came from nowhere. "Zenith, dam, you stop toying with me, wake up."

The midnight bells tolled. Lemma had finally fallen into a deep sleep next to Zenith. Cathal and Brent slumped up against either side of the doorway like two guards asleep at their post. None of them had eaten since that morning. None felt hungry. The confusion and pain they all felt over Zenith's condition had held them each determined to be here when he finally awoke.

The last candle flickered in the night breeze, fighting to stay alight, a beacon of hope in this sombre room, its strength slowly waning as the wax around its core dissipated. With its final flicker, a huge flame filled the room so bright that the whole castle woke, and a booming roar came from within the flame.

"Zenith, my brother, you dwindle in your mind, wake now and reclaim what is truly yours when you do, my truest home will be freed."

The room fell instantly dark and silent. Lemma, Cathal, and Brent all stood, shocked, taken aback, and lost for words, their glances fleeting from one to the other, until all their eyes fixed firmly on Zenith. Cathal, first to speak. "Who or what was that?" Lemma had jumped from the bed, dropping Zenith on the bed. "I have no idea, but the voice sounded like the roar that came through in the battle." Brent swiftly moved to the bedside, lifting Zenith back into bed properly, his body still, a deep groan coming from his throat. "Zenith? Zenith? Are you trying to speak?" Zenith's eyelids flushed with blood, his eyes underneath brushing from side to side—Lemma back at his side, cold cloth to his forehead. "I'm here, Cathal and

Brent are here. Come back, please." Pleading with all her worth.

They all stood waiting with bated breath, watching Zenith's life slowly returning. His hands curled, feeling the bed under him, his legs stretching, feeling returning to them with a sudden startled bounce, his eyes flew open, his voice split the air, "My father was murdered by his own brother". Shock and terror filled the silence at his words.

Lemma sat aside, Zenith awake, waiting for him to speak to her. He had woken but not completely returned. His senses were dulled, and his surroundings were unfamiliar. Soothingly, she talked to him.

"Zenith, my love, you are safe, you are here among friends, calm yourself." Hearing her words penetrated deep inside his heart. He turned to her, his eyes full of grief and anger. "My mum... My dad shouldn't be dead." Lemma knew these eyes; her mother had them when they lost her father. She knew Zenith would need her more than ever. "For now, Zenith, we must rest. You need to settle your mind, put things in order yourself. Once that is done, we can focus on Quinten and his crimes." Cathal and Brent both bid Lemma and Zenith a goodnight and returned to the Hall of Arms, where they found themselves a bunk. Lemma and Zenith lay beside each other, Zenith's head tucked under Lemma's chin, tears rolling from his eyes, Lemma stroking the back of his head until both drifted off to sleep.

The morning rays touched the sill of the balcony as Zenith stood there looking out over Sciran at its glory and embedded strength. *Do my memories play with me? Creating illusions to torment me into submission to become tainted and weak to Rycore's will, or are they true?* His silent thought slipping into spoken word, "I should have been king over here and Errant. Overall, the East and West. Who is my true betrothed? My only wish and strongest hope, to which I pledge with all my might, that the baby in my dream was Lemma." Still, his imagination played and toyed with him, choosing the solidity of thought, *I know it must be Lemma, it's too much of a coincidence not to be. But why had the union never come to pass? Has my uncle defiled my father's honour once more and my grandfather's will and promise?*

———

Zenith had spent the morning walking around the city joyfully with Lemma, greeting the people and her family. It seemed surreal in its entirety, a blur to him, with so many names and faces; in time, they would become clear. The only thing left to do was visit his future mother-in-law; he alone had been summoned to Catherine's throne room.

As he ascended the steps, he grew fearful, thinking about the worst case. *Is this my trial and death sentence I walk to?* The guards at the massive oak doors saw him approach, beginning to open the doors before he got to them. As he reached them, peering through the ever-growing gap between the doors into the room. There, sitting high on her ivory throne, was Catherine in all her royal regalia. Walking in tentatively, eyeing each escape route just in case, as the doors slammed shut behind him, his mind raced, *Oh lord, I'm stuck, there isn't another way out.* Pulling the bright light of the sun from view. The room was suddenly filled with a light of many colours from the stained-glass windows stationed above him and directly behind the ivory throne, giving Catherine an aura that made her seem angelic, dare he say it, almost godlike in appearance. Before him, the threshold of the throne, he took a knee and bowed his head.

Catherine stared down at him, intensely scrutinising him. She was no fool; he could see that. She said nothing. Arising from her throne, she strolled down the marble steps to Zenith. Placing a hand on him, she pulled him to his feet, reached around his shoulders, and embraced him tightly against her chest, pulling him so close that he could hear the beat of her heart. It was almost as if his mother was holding him.

Stood there, not flinching or moving, as she released him and stared deeply into his eyes.

"Before you speak, my boy, yes, you know me, I have known you since birth." Ears burning, these words, making his dream ring true, at least in part; he did know her. "The words I speak here today are for your ears only; No one, not even my daughters, must hear it, at least for now. Although they may know my secret, they need not know I share it with you."

Staring in wonder at her, he dared still not speak; the thoughts raced about his active mind. *What could she know about? That Lemma and her sisters could not hear her say to me, How do I fit into the picture?* Catherine began her tale twenty years ago at the birth of Lemma. Telling him of his grandfather's wishes that he should take the throne on his Eighteenth birthday. The same year, he should have wed her daughter, not telling him which it was, but blatantly hinting that it was Lemma.

Hearing this tale, his heart rose and fluttered. The memory of the treaty was all actual truth. He was betrothed to her daughter, and now he felt more than ever that his love, Lemma, should already be his wife.

At this point, though the tale turned sour, she told him, within three seasons, his grandfather had become gravely ill, unable to rule to his fullest until on his deathbed some years later, as he knew Quinten was his named successor over his father Ake. Zenith knew in his heart that his uncle had forced his grandfather's hand to this.

This brought a great and seething anger out of her as the tail moved forward, jumping a year or so nearer. She explained that his father, the true heir, had been working in secret with her to reclaim the throne from Quinten and to honour his grandfather's wishes. Before their plan had been used or brought to the fore, Ake had become infected with plague, as had Zenith's mother and many of the townspeople. She paused here, dwelling on the next turn of phrase. She was unsure if Zenith could handle it.

Catherine took a deep breath, steeling herself, preparing to deliver the worst news Zenith would possibly ever receive. "Now, Zenith, this much of the story you knew most of it is commonplace in Grissam that your father Ake died of plague" Zenith looked at her quizzically, asking the obvious. "Why do you tell me what I already know, expecting it to hurt me?" Catherine sighed, not happy to be interrupted, and continued.

"We had all been told that you and your elder brother were buried with your parents, dead from the plague. It's now plain to see Quinten never made sure of this in his hubris, assuming and notifying all of it".

Zenith froze in place, his brow sodden. "I was supposed to have died with my parents." The thoughts ran wild again. *It all fit the rumours and lies that had circulated. My uncle killed my father, the only one capable of claiming the throne from him—no wonder the villagers had always kept Merik and me hidden from the officials in our younger years.*

Trepidations filled the air. He wanted to enact his father's plan and regain his throne. "I've never wanted the throne, and still don't, but I don't want my murdering uncle there either. How, though?" Catherine cleared her throat, bringing Zenith's attention to her.

"Now for the worst of it, I hate to tell you this, but all those years ago, your father was murdered. I have proof of it, sworn testimony of his agent, and now this person, a prisoner of mine for nearly seven years, will be the one to fell a king and regain your father's throne should you want it".

His mind didn't register her words entirely, just proof of murder and father "What man? Where and how did he kill my mother and father?" Anger held strong in his voice

Catherine stumbled backwards, falling to the floor, shocked at how angry her words made Zenith. She sat there on the floor watching as the sweet boy she knew, a man in his own right, smashed away with bare knuckles at the floor, his blood staining the white stone increasingly with each throw of his hands. *How could their murderer be alive? How did I not know? I will see Quinten removed from the throne.* Screaming seemed to help, but it also gained attention from the guards who rushed into the throne room. Catherine waved them off. She knew to expect it, but not to this magnitude and with such resentment.

Slowly, Zenith calmed his thoughts and turned to Catherine. Now, she would tell him, his father's and her plan to oust that petty, immoral excuse for a king, no longer his uncle, just another person who would bleed at his hand on the tip of the Echidna flame.

All he needed was proof and a plan.

12

A PRISONER'S PROOF AND PROMISE

Catherine led the way across the vast courtyard out into the city, marching with intent. All bowed their heads as she passed. Silence fell at each step, her walk imposing, showing that she was in no mood to be trifled with. Zenith hobbled along, doing his best to keep pace, several steps behind her, Catherine's face brimming with rage. They marched to the prison where he would meet his father's killer.

The air grew thicker, muddied, even poisonous. The closer they got to the prison, the resentment of those inside filled it, tarring deep into the soul of the city. The worst of the worst were held here. Zenith imagined the man he was about to meet. The image envisioned that of a scrawny, older man covered in dirt and wasting away, a shell of the man he had been before, kept alive by only Catherine's grace, closer to death than life.

The prison guards lurched to attention; they seemed bemused at Catherine's arrival as if she were a stranger and never frequented this place. Why should she? She was Queen.

These Nair do wells held no value to her; the mere fact that they lived was proof enough that she was benevolent in her rule, unlike most kings or Queens who would just exile or hang all criminals.

The iron door to the prison wall opened, scraping the floor as they did, revealing a dim, long corridor lit by sporadically placed torches along each side, where they were not lined with iron bars. Some cells contained one prisoner, while others contained many. Inside, jeers started up as Catherine and Zenith entered. It was truly clear that everyone here hated their Queen; all the more reason to keep them here, Zenith thought.

The guards walked in, closing the doors behind them, which slammed shut with a crash as the metal of the doors collided against each other. They moved in unison to the front of Catherine, smashing their maces into the iron bars, screaming for quiet. A few prisoners who were caught unaware, losing fingers to the mace, and others falling backwards to the floor, clutching what remained of the broken fingers and bloody stubs of their hands. Silence soon fell after.

They proceeded to the far end of the corridor. Here stood another iron door, which looked inches thick and was barred in several places. What lay beyond was all the rapist murderers and such like, the worst criminals anyone could imagine, those set for the gallows or to be torn apart by ballista bolt flight eventually. Hurriedly, the guards removed the giant iron bars holding the door closed, unlocking it for the Queen.

Elsewhere, Lemma looked too busy herself; her mother had instructed her and her sister to ready the wedding she had planned many years ago. She wanted the whole kingdom there, so she had chosen the palace courtyard for the ceremony

and the feasting halls to celebrate. Sitting in a room filled with
attendants, Isis and Faith trawled through pages of ancient
books, all devoted to royal weddings. A genuine who's who
had written these over hundreds of years on how to plan,
engage and effectively pull together a royal wedding.

None, however, even came close to what Lemma sisters
looked to create for their baby sister. Each promised to stand at
her side from now on and through the ceremony. The flowers
were easy; she picked roses and lilies of all colours, as well as
the national flower of the country.

The one flower she loved most shone with purples and
greens, emanating its light, looking ready to burst into song
and dance. Lemma only wanted a small affair, but her mum
was never one to disappoint her people; they wanted a
wedding that would last in the city's memories for a lifetime.
For some reason, it seemed that her mother had another
underlying plan in the works. Not one to pry, she went along
with it, guessing the intention was to endear the people to
Zenith. She loved her sisters and mother dearly and would go
with their choices as long as she wed Zenith; it didn't matter.

Isis and Faith gazed deeply into books, wondering how to
seat the thousands that would come. Most of all, they
pondered how they would retrieve Zenith's brother from the
East; the bridge being down was problem number one. The
second was that he lived within enemy territory.

Attendants stood about the room, each eager to gain their
orders so they could set forth into the city and gain the
sequestered items the sisters needed. As soon as one attendant
left, another returned, handing the complete orders to the
sisters.

The wedding banners were being made by the finest of the
silk smiths in the city. Lo and behold, no charge; the people
had fallen in behind Lemma, all wanting to partake in her

wedding in any way they could. Again, another attendant returned, this time bearing an invitation to the royal dress makers for Lemma. Having been prepared for this day, they kept stock of the finest fabrics from all over the world, stored ready for any of the princesses' weddings.

Lemma was in disbelief over how viral and centred her sisters were over the wedding, sitting away from the busy centre of the room, gazing through the opening onto the room's balcony, her mind wandering over why her mother had summoned Zenith alone. *I hope she has no dastardly plans for him. She welcomed him and gave her blessing for them to wed as soon as possible, but then why did she not invite her?"*

This vexed her, leaving her unable to focus on any of the tasks at hand. *What has my mother shared with him? That could not be shared with me.*

Back at the prison, Zenith and Catherine had made their way along the next corridor past all of the worst the city could offer, coming to a set of stairs leading high up into a tower situated within the city's inner wall. It stood for defence, but connected to the prison, it must hold a second purpose, he thought.

At the top of the stairs, there ahead lay a thick old oak door, lines of iron running through it. Catherine stopped and pointed at the door, sternly speaking.

"Compose yourself, Zenith. The man we seek lies inside" Zenith's face hardened. He was about to meet the one man he had never imagined he would meet. The one who killed his parents and so many of his village. He felt even more hate build deep inside and reached for the Echidna flame, his face solid as steel, he knew this man should die at his hand somehow, at the same time knowing now was not the time. Pulling the blade from its sheath, placing the grip in the guard's hand, he dared not take it in.

The guard struggled to hold the blade, hunching over it; its weight seemed enormous in his hand, so heavy that he had to have the second guard help him. Zenith thought his eye played tricks. In his hands, the Echidna flame was but a feather.

Peering through the bared opening in the door, Zenith was shocked at what he saw — a forty-something, plump, well-kept man, noble-looking, and not at all what he thought he would see. Catherine had kept him alive for nearly a decade, hoping to utilise him during this time. She had cared correctly for him, using this opportunity to sway him and gain his loyalty, so that should the chance arise, he would not falter.

Catherine produced a key from within her dress and turned the lock to the cell. The man turned inside, smiling to greet her like an old friend.

"Your majesty it is a very long time since you last visited I see you bring a friend" Catherine snapped back at him "Vex quiet! less you wish his anger bare down on you" her voice callus and straight Vex shocked at this, dared not retort her and stared at Zenith his eyes darting ablaze had his death finally come was Catherine finally having rid of him. He sank low into the corner of his cell, his face begging to live.

Catherine lowered her tone and spoke again. "Vex, you have told me your truths and the lie that led to it many times now. I ask you to repeat them for the penultimate time to your true king, the son of the crown prince Ake. Dare not lie, he has laid his weapon aside at his own choice. Wishing to know the truth about his parents and how you became their executioner"

Zenith stood tall, watching Vex squirm and dodge eye contact with him. Deep inside his stomach, the anger boiled. Still, in his heart, pity for this man scarred by him beyond belief, fear coursing through his very veins, as he hunched over, cowering in the corner. Evident in his face were the sins that perturbed him, and he wished he had never committed them; he was genuinely remorseful.

Zenith mustered himself, trying to speak with an air of magnanimity "Vex, I will not harm you. I see in your eyes the remorse you carry, and for that, I can forgive you a little. I know Quinten, my uncle, ordered this and that, in no way absolves you, but grants you a stay of arms at least. Your life is not worth taking, as it will not return to my parents."

Zenith paused, Vex's eyes looking at him in admiration. He seemed, to him, wise beyond his years and so different from his uncle, in fact, his opposite in every way, nothing of what Quinten stood for.

Vex stood moving to the barred window of his cell, breathing deep the air of the city, trepidation clear on his lips as he began to reiterate the story he told Catherine many times, fresh in his mind as if it occurred yesterday.

Lemma lurched from her chair amidst the wedding planning, startling everyone in the room, storming to the arched doors and shoving them open wide. Her stomach and heart had dropped, and anger washed over her body and soul without warning. In the back of her mind, she asked herself, *Is this Zenith's anger? I need to find him and ensure his safety.*

Isis and Faith stood, shocked and aghast, at their sister's abrupt exit, unsure whether to follow, stay, or leave for now and return later with Lemma. Faith chased Lemma down hallways, turning this way and that, Lemma fast and fleeting of foot, her face tortured with concern. *I must find out what's wrong.*

Faith knew something was wrong. Her sister only went like

this when someone she loved was in trouble or if a great darkness approached. It seemed like an extra sense that she felt in her very core, an extreme empathy. Feeling their feeling as her own.

She had to help her calm, see senses, as last time Lemma had been like this, it took days and countless injuries to armed guards and attendants who stood in her way. *Fine, she did find the culprits who had dared bear a blade at our cousins in the outer ring of the city and had them arrested by her priest guard then taken away to the stocks, but still, the carnage in her wake took longer to clear than the event itself.*

Storming through the city street, tearing her path of destruction, people dived for cover as any man who stood before her was sent sailing through the air with a flail of her arm. Faith still on her tail screamed her name. "Lemma." Unblinking, she continued her path, weaving this way and that, heading in the direction of the prison, her course set.

Lemma was guided by a sense that she didn't recognise the anger she felt, not her own. She walked, not knowing where she headed, not caring. She reached the alleyway to the prison, it lay down the path, clear, with no guards in sight. Only the great iron door blocking the path stood locked.

Throwing her arm down, reaching for her belt, grabbing the star, aiming it precisely, and throwing it. Set sailing for the door, it hung in the air, buzzing sparks flying as it cut deep into the centre mass of the doors, wearing its way through the lock. Only then did it return to her hand once the doors flew open, smashing to the sides, sending bricks from the arch above crashing to the floor.

Without hesitation, Lemma walked into the torchlight corridor, marching deeper and deeper. A man caged alone on her left made a move to grab her. As he did, her elbow raised squarely, smashing it into the base of his nose. The sound of bone breaking, blood sprayed over her, covering her white dress. Undeterred, she continued repeating the same motions as before with the second and stronger iron gate.

The prisoners reeled away as she entered the star, glowing golden in their presence; they all knew it sensed their evil and dared not come closer. She stormed closer to the stairs, climbing them two and three at a time, reaching the top, the guards turned, fear crossing their brows, as she let out a blood-curdling scream. "ZENITH"

The scream rattled the whole prison. The guards in front of her went pale. The blood drained from their faces. One dropped his hold on the Echidna flame as it swung, making a deep gash in the wall, carving through it like nothing was even there.

Zenith flew from the room; he hadn't even stopped for Catherine. She stood there, fear-stricken and afraid to move from her spot. She knew that voice all too well from the last time. Lemma's senses had driven her to this type of behaviour, and she didn't feel like facing that.

Leaving the Room, Zenith stopped aghast at the sight of Lemma there, her flowing white gown stained with blood. *What's happened? Has she been hurt?* He ran to her, worried, no concern for those around him. Grasping her hands, he examined them; her hand was covered, but there was no cut. *Whose blood is it? Has someone dared attack her?*

Staring intensely into her eyes, he didn't see hers; he saw his own looking back, full of anger and spite. Lemma seemed possessed by his anger, the very same anger he squashed deep down, so he didn't strike Vex down at the very sight of him. Zenith's core chilled. *How did this happen? What has happened?* This coursing through his mind, he had not noticed Lemma slip from his grip, heading for Vex's cell.

Lemma reached the cell, withdrawing the star from her belt, taking aim, wanting to take Vex's life. Somewhere deep inside the real Lemma, the one who knew of this man's true treachery and who loved Zenith with all of her being, fought back, staying her arm. Praying that someone could take control of her body, the emotions in a screaming match, kill *him*. *No, I can't*, trying to stop Zenith's anger from overrunning her; she needed someone to prevent her from committing cold-blooded murder.

Zenith snatched the Echidna flame from the guard left with it in hand, pale in shock, not moving from their spot. Pushing hard, he made the cell, placing the Echidna flame against the star and holding them both there. All his strength was needed; he was fighting himself, as well as the woman he loved.

Slowly, he realised he would need to face his fear here and now; if he didn't truly forgive Vex, he didn't know if he could hold Lemma's arm much longer. Screaming, he spoke, "Vex, I need to see your true remorse. I need to hear it in your voice and see it in your actions. "This is not Lemma she is held captive by my anger, how I do not know, but if you value your life, then show me"

Vex, frightened to his core, rose, his head hung low, and approached Catherine, seizing the dagger that lay hidden in her belt. Rushing over, he knelt between Zenith and Lemma, placed the dagger to his throat.

Vex's voice, panicked and afraid, filled the void between the three of them. "I will gladly end my own life as you truly showed me mercy, and for that I will always be grateful. I mourn the loss of your family, friends, and all those who died by my hand; this is the only sacrifice I have left. I was never worthy of Catherine's mercy, let alone yours. The years have allowed me to reflect, caged here alone. I now see the only true way to make amends for what I have done is to save at least one life, even if that means my death"

Lemmas' eyes slowly glazed, becoming her own again, the anger leaving her. Zenith had become more stable, his mind free of it, too. Vex's words sang true into their hearts, piercing the vale, freeing them both. Vex, still holding the blade against his throat, began to slice deeper, blood trickling from the blade as the first droplets coalesced on the cell floor. Lemma lurched forward, grabbed the blade from him, his sins absolved and threw it, lodging so deep in the cell wall that it would never come free. A reminder to him of this day, the day he spared not only their lives but also his.

Catherine, still motionless, reeled at the throw. It sailed past her, the breeze moving aside her hair. Now she dared to breathe. *What powers my daughter does possess*, which seemed even more magnificent in her eyes than ever. In all these years, Vex had not once done such a brave and selfless thing.

Catherine looked down at Vex, still kneeling, his throat slowly dripping with blood, and she spoke. "Vex, your actions show that you truly feel the loss of every soul you have taken. In an instant, you drove out the evil. I believe you now have earned the right to be free of this cell. The city will be your prison; its streets are open to you. A guard always at your side, but that will be the best I may offer"

Vex stared up at Catherine. *Does her mercy know no bounds? For so many years, I have been alone, and now she has granted me half freedom. Able to walk among the people, breathe the air, and work to salvage myself.* He felt there were still significant amounts of good he could do.

Zenith and Lemma both stood there, embracing and looking at Catherine, their faces alight at her words, for they had never truly known her as this magnanimous person.

13

TO STEAL A BROTHER AWAY

News reached Sciran. The bridge at Rycliff was rebuilt. Isis and Faith, within moments of receiving the news, dispatched their regent to Grissam to seek Zenith's brother.

———

Stood in the field of his farm, Merik worked with a scythe in hand, swinging it from right to left as he moved in horizontal lines across the expansive ground. He would usually share this workload with his brother. *Zenith, where did you go? Why did you go? With no warning and no goodbyes.* Not knowing why or what preceded his upheaval from their farm and lives.

The sun shone high in the sky; *It must be midday by now.* He thought, glancing up before, slowing his scythe to a halt, A quick look toward the gate, *Good, nobody stole my lunch today or my water. I still need to figure out who keeps doing that.* Dropping the scythe where he stood, he turned, stretched and walked to the entrance gate. Opening his lunch, biting deep into the ham leg, tearing the flesh from the bone, complimenting himself, "Tasty and well earned."

A call came on the wind from one of his farm hands, "Merik, where are you? You've a visitor," booming back "Oh, by Rysander, can I not break in peace? I'm at the gate trying to eat." From his seated position, he saw two figures clad in strange garments, one regal and bright, the other a swordsman, with an insignia across his breast that he didn't recognise.

What foolishness was this, another pompous fool who had heard of Zenith's supposed demise, cross thoughts passed over his sweaty forehead. *Not another goody two-shoes trying to buy my farm to help me.* Already, Merik's anger showed, his mouth grimacing and turning down, his eyes scowling and spreading daggers at the two who approached him.

"Are you Merik? Brother of Zenith?" spoken softly from the lips of the regal lady. Who now stood by him. "Whatever you meant to say, don't." Merik snarled at the lady, "The farm is not for sale! Zenith will return. Besides that, this land is my family's legacy, I would never sell it, not for all the coin in Apprite" His harsh words took the lady by surprise, stalling her advance. The Swordsman with her stepped in front, hand shooting to the grip of his sword, ready.

Gathering herself, she spoke softly. "You mistake me for someone else. I come not to barter or trade. I've travelled three days and nights to get here, at the behest of Isis and Faith, princesses of Sciran. I must know if I address Merik?"

The robed woman's words confused him, as the anger on his face gave way to dipped eyebrows and the O-shaped lips of confusion. The thoughts moved through his head in squiggly lines, not making any sense at all. *Sciran, Isis, Faith? What do these people know of my brother? Why do they seek him? What does it have to do with me?*

Continuing to speak, she addressed him further. "I am Amabel, a regent of The Scirainian Princesses. I've been sent to Grissam to find Merik, to bring him a message and escort him as soon as found to Sciran, where his brother Zenith waits."

His ears perked at his brother's name. Questions flooded his mind again, yet a moving, squirming thought tore through his mind. *Zenith? Sciran, do I need to be there? Why? What could have befallen my brother? More to the point, how do I get to Sciran?*

A short, near-angry voice deep from his belly spoke up, "I'm Merik now, speak, regent, what news do you bear of Zenith?" Amabel spoke in hushed tones. "It is nothing we can talk about in the open air, sir. Do you know of a place where we can talk freely in secret?" Perturbed, Merik rose to his feet, still being short with Amabel, "Follow me." He walked ahead of Amabel and her guard, a strong purpose in each step, heading for the farmhouse.

At the end of the lane stood a small building, not grand but well-maintained, its exterior whitewashed with black framing, the roof a lush, golden thatch, its door large and heavy. Merik pushed hard on the door, creaking open with age. The door moved slowly, revealing a large room with a stone chimney at its centre. A fire blazed, filling the room with the smell of roasting mutton as it hung on the spit.

Beckoning Amabel and the guard in. Merik placed a metal jug on a stove top attached to the left of the chimney, "I'll make Tea once the water boils, then we can talk" Acknowledging Merik's intent, Amabel and her guard took a seat under the larger window that looked out into the farmyard.

Slamming shut the door, smashing the rusted bolt shut, securing it, Merik turned and walked to the kitchen, taking tea and goblets from the side. He placed three goblets on the table, mixing leaves with water in the jug over the fire. He spoke, "What message do you bring?" Amabel stared at Merik and said in a soft, unfaltering tone. "I bring news that Zenith is safe and well, but" "But What!" Merik interrupted. He didn't have the patience for pleasantries.

Thrown off, Amabel coughed and stuttered, words stuck in her throat. Merik had surprised her. He had been pleasant up to this point; she didn't know where to look or what to say. Regaining her capacity, as Merik placed a goblet next to her, she smiled and thanked him. Speaking again, "All I can say at this time is that Zenith is well, he is in Sciran, and I am to bring you by hidden means to the city"

Her word hung in the air, and in his mind, *hidden means. Why the subterfuge? I can travel freely, and why should I trust her? All this woman does is confuse me.*

Her words and sentiment seemed pure of intent. Pleading with him, Amabel spoke, "Please, Merik, we must leave by nightfall. Those who mean you unwell may already know I'm here, and of your continued life, I shall tell you more as we travel" Shook to the core. Merik nodded. Amabel sat waiting, her Guard taking leave from her side for a break until they were to take their leave.

Upstairs in the house, Merik gathered his leather travel sack, filling it with clothes and rations. "A week or more of food should do." Thinking of the stuff he would need.

"Continued existence" resonated around his head as he prepped to leave the farm. *What did this mean?* Still, he had More questions than answers. *Hopeful Amabel can help me understand as we travel. If not, perhaps Zenith when I finally get to see him.* Many questions remained unanswered, and it seemed they would have to wait.

Walking back into the main room of the house, Merik peered out of the window. Coming down the lane was the tax collector and his guards. Tax was due; *Damnit, it's Tax Day. I knew that, so leaving tonight won't work; the watch will be on high alert*. Luckily, he had time to tell Amabel of this and concocted a sensible yet straightforward plan, which he put into place. Hastily, telling Amabel. "You will leave. Thank me for the corn, and make payment, which will then cover the tax collector's expenses and hopefully make him forget seeing you here."

Amabel, after leaving and taking her guard with her, would agree to a delivery in Lehoi the next day. A loud thud, thud, thud shook the farmhouse door. Merik had already begun a conversation about the corn as he pulled back the bolt and opened the door, taking a payment of several silver coins from Amabel as the door fully opened, in full sight of the tax collector.

Amabel thanked Merik and stated the location for delivery in Lehoi, passing by the tax collector, the swordsman's insignia clearly showed him where they had come from. The tax collector, no fool, noticed and commented indignantly, "Far from home, my lady?" Amabel retorted, "Indeed, we have been told the corn here in Grissam is of a quality above ours back home, so we've sought to purchase it." The tax collector accepted this for now and turned to Merik, who waited with payment in hand. The tax collector spoke with a hoity-toity attitude. "A glorious day, sir, and a fortuitous sale it would seem." Merik spoke with a degree of malice." Take your money and go, I'm rather busy, I need to load the cart before dark"

The tax collector marked his paperwork, turned, and left the way he came. Merik summoned two of his most trusted farmhands, and they began to load the cart for the morning. Taking his gathered food and clothes and hiding them under the corn, then returned to the house and made himself ready for bed, his mind still buzzing.

The morning soon came round, and the sounds of birds pierced the air. The sun still hadn't peeked over the horizon. Only the moon shone, still providing some light to work by.

Waking Merik, gaining his feet, he dressed, placing a hooked dagger under his shirt just in case, and a blade at his ankle. *Will that be enough to defend myself? Actually, can I protect myself?* A little stroke of fear tugged the side of his brow before he pulled the farm door open, thinking about it. Outside stood the farmhands ready to leave for Lehoi.

Merik instructed the farmhands. "I'll be taking the corn this time, lads, you mind the farm for me, it may take a day or so there and back" The lads nodded and hooked the horse to its harness and the cart. Merik took his seat at the helm of the cart, slapping the leather reins onto the horses ' hindquarters. The cart pulled away up the lane.

Passing into the Village, he took a prolonged look over his shoulder. *That place is my home, I will be back, that I promise myself.* Ahead, he saw the guards. Luckily, they were in the midst of a changeover, so getting past would be easier. The guards waved him on, paying little to no attention. A sigh left him as he passed. He was on his way, speaking to himself under his breath. "Zenith here I come." Still, he considers Amabel's words, thinking about them. *What could she tell me that required such cloak and dagger?*

The first rays of day highlighted the outskirts of Lehoi as they came into view—Lehoi, already abuzz with the market setting up. Merik pulled the cart up in the large, cobbled marketplace. Tying the horse to the tethering post, glancing around, eyeing the town's guards, *God, these guards look like they may do a proper job, unlike those back home. I'll need to be careful."* He pulled a solid wooden till box from under the driver's seat and began to set up his stall, aiming to seem like a normal trader.

The day drew on, and he had made many a sale. The swordsman approached, a bag of coins in hand. Their interaction, brief; a sale was made. A coin sack was exchanged. Inside the sack was a letter giving him further instructions, detailing where to meet Amabel later that day.

The letter read very ominously, provoking a crack of fear to manifest as he read it, hearing Amabel's sweet yet tender but still assertive voice.

Merik, you must make it to the Rysand gorge. Once there, we can meet and cross to the Sciran plains together. When we are on the bridge, I can tell you the truth as to why I was sent to fetch you. The reason why your life is in danger. Signed Amabel.

Finally, the market had died down to a low rumble, just people scanning the remaining stalls, none particularly interested in making a purchase. Merik, observing this, said, "Time to pack up." He closed the till box, then closed the rear of the cart, and finalised his sales for the day. Whilst untying his horse, a guard approached him, scowling and grumbling.

"Have you paid your fees yet?" Merik exchanged a confused look with the guard.

"What fee, sir? I have been told of none. This is my first trip to the Lehoi market. Who do I need to pay?" The guard accepted his plea of ignorance, took the payment, and left. Taking a deep breath, sighing in relief, he jumped into his seat behind the horse and pulled the cart out of the marketplace.

The cart pulled easily, containing less than half the corn he started with at first light. Substantially more than triple the coin, just the thought, *A good day's business.* Bought an unexpected smile to his face as he asked himself silently, "Why have I not been to Lehoi market before?" After this trip, it made sense to bring his wares here again in the future.

Merik's cart plodded along the dirt road from Lehoi

heading towards the Rysand gorge. Beginning to wonder how Zenith had gotten to Sciran, *did he walk this same road?* pondering further, *was it shortly after he disappeared from the farm, or later in his journey?* The silence of the road and the rhythmic click of the wheels left him with only one thought. *How has my younger sibling changed? Is he the same man as before he left? Surely not, as the past three years must have taken their toll on him.*

The evening arrived, the sun beginning to dive beyond the furthest mountains as he passed a watering hole, a short way from the road. Stopping briefly, observing blackened rings dotted about the earth, like many fires had been lit here some time ago.

Amabel waited for Merik at the gorge. The Rysand bridge has been fully repaired again since its rope fixings failed a few weeks ago. Not a soul knew how, but bloody marks indicated something foul had been at play when it had collapsed this time. These repairs were done far quicker than last time, thanks to a new rope type.

A blacksmith's apprentice had come to the bridge builders with an ingenious idea. He had developed with the aid of the senior smiths. Strong and durable rope containing metal strands that were woven through the regular ropes. Using these had increased the bridge's strength tenfold, allowing larger, heavier loads to cross. In turn, it had increased the amount of trade, making the Crossing more profitable to all who used it. A small trader's hub had sprung up near the bridge's entrance, also providing extra trade to the Inn that lay along the gorge edge. Amabel waited there with bated breath for Merik.

Time passed so slowly as she waited, the horizon closing in

as the sun set. Yet, there was no sign of Merik. Worried, she turned to her guard, ordering him.

"Please go and search the road for Merik; he should have arrived by now."

In no time, the guard had set off on horseback following the road back to Lehoi. He had ridden for half an hour when he met Merik, his cart moving slowly. His horse had slowed down after being in the sun and working all day. He would arrive soon, but to speed him up, they swapped the horses over.

A fresher horse in front of him, Meriks' speed doubled. Soon arriving at the trading hub and inn, he was greeted with a smile by Amabel as he jumped to the ground. Fleeting glances from all around at the new arrival, like all small villages, a new person is soon noticed. Unfortunately, this wasn't such a good thing, as the watch here paid attention to any small detail and change, especially where Scirainians were concerned.

The night had drawn in; crossing now would be hard, even with fresh horses and lanterns, but it was what they needed to do. The bridge could take the cart's weight, and Merik had the coin to rent a well-rested horse. Amabel insisted that she sit with him on the cart so they could talk; he eagerly accepted. Merik wanted his questions answered.

The cart was unloaded, and a passing baker traded the remainder of the corn for a horse, a good deal since it meant that no coin was spent. Moving off to the bridge, the swordsman and Merik both paid notice to the fact that a single member of the watch had followed them. Soon enough, they were on the bridge, moving well, the watch guard still at their rear, seeming of little threat, just following at a distance.

The swordman made sure to remain between the guard and his Charges, meaning that Merik and Amabel could speak quite freely. Amabel started the conversation. "Now Merik, I promised to tell you more once we were here so I shall, your brother arrived a month or so ago in Sciran with princess Lemma, without him Sciran would of fallen to an evil army, he has slowly healed from his injuries but is perfectly fine now, that is the good news" Merik's heart began to sink that was the good news he thought to himself. *The good news is. That my brother fought in a war; how bad must the bad news be?*

Panic in his voice, Merik spoke. "Please, Amabel, hurry and speak, for I need to know what truths you have for me" Amabel took a deep breath and swallowed hard. "Now the next part I need you to listen to, but please, I'm only the messenger" Irritated, Merik spat his words at her ", Speak, Damit messenger, or do not tell me." Her voice broke as she began to retch with sadness and fear.

"It in truth relates to your late mother and stepfather; their deaths were not as natural as everyone believed. The plague that took them from you was an evil machination of your uncle, King Quinten of Errant. It was supposed to have killed you and Zenith, too." Merik reeled at this, dropping the straps that controlled the horse. "That is not true. How dare you say such things?"

Amabel's eyes welled with fear, tears rolling down the side of her face, as she heard the anguished tones in Merik's voice, guilt-ridden as she continued. "That is not all the thief that your uncle used to deliver the plague still lives and is jailed in Sciran, Fortunately he never revealed to Quinten that you and Zenith lived, but surely now with my arrival no doubt Quinten will of heard I arrived and spoke with you and knows that Queen Catherine of Sciran knows the truth, at this moment likely plots to finish what he started. If you didn't realise your brother is the true king of Errant"

Merik, now stunned to silence, sat there unmoving, almost

unbreathing, staring into the darkness ahead. "My Mum and Dad murdered? The rumours weren't just rumours. *Does Zenith know?* his eyes screwed up, holding back floods of tears, then suddenly blurting out. "Zenith is King?" Amabel jumped visibly, leaving her seat, then had to grab the reins and control the horse that was verbalising its fear, neighing and thrashing its head around. Amabel spoke calmly to the horse before tapping the reins slightly to increase its speed. She knew too well that the longer it took, the worse the journey would be for Merik.

The hour had gotten extremely late as the torches of the Scirainian bridge port came into view. Amabel pushed the horse a little harder, wanting solid ground under her again. The guard from the trading hub had long since turned and stopped following them; that was one less worry. Merik still sat motionless beside her, his mind in tatters, trying to process what he had heard from Amabel. She only hoped that Zenith could explain it further.

As the Cart left the bridge, the Scirainian guards greeted them with open arms, asking how Amabel and their brother in arms had fared with their mission. Once they had all caught up, fresh horses were prepared; no need for a cart. Amabel turned to Merik. "We will reach Sciran after passing through the valley of Solus, so named after some long-forgotten bandit prince, and then across the plains."

The three pressed on hard; the Scirainian mares ran like the wind through the verdant green valleys of Solus, whisking them past fields of wildflowers and small groves of trees that stood against the harsh rocks of the crags that lined the valley. It was too easy to see why a bandit prince would have liked this place, with numerous vantage points and almost double the number of hiding spots, making it a perfect place to ambush unsuspecting people.

Luckily, that didn't happen here anymore, but along the

valley walls, many teams of Toxites and archers watched and guarded the borders of Sciran. Riding had become tiresome as the first ambling rays of the sun lifted the veil of night, bringing with them views of lush, green, fertile plains. In the distance, a gleaming white city stood proud, shining bright as the sun hit the marble walls and towers of its outer ring.

"We are nearly there, Merik. You can rest soon. Then your brother will meet with you." Merik, silently looking at Amabel, dreary-eyed, more asleep at this point than awake, mustering a small but meaningful smile, acknowledging her. A few minutes later, they passed through a large iron gate, and the city unfolded before them. Its white and golden stone roads paved the way to the castle.

Amabel rode ahead and signalled the guards, who opened the gated entrance to the inner castle, allowing them to pass freely. Within, Amabel dismounted, she waved and spoke for Merik to do the same. "Merik, dismount, we are nearly there, I promise." She led him to a small wooden door, opened it wide and slowly moved inside, calling him on. Once inside, she showed him to a small bedchamber, where the swordsman placed Merik's travel pack and left them. "Merik sleep now I'll wake you later and take you to your brother." Her parting comment was delivered with an air of ease and a soothing tone.

Merik exhaustedly collapsed on the soft mattress of the bed, asleep before his head hit the soft feather down pillow. Amabel smiled, pulled the door shut, and left him to sleep, heading to her chamber, a few doors away.

14
PREPARING FOR A ROYAL WEDDING

S tanding above the flowing and busy Courtyard, Zenith stared as the venue became filled with chairs and all manner of flowers, servants darting this way and that, readying it for his wedding. Behind him stood a great altar made of silver, carved with the words of Rysand and the Sciran crest in gold filigree; atop it were several candles, one for each member of the wedding party, to light and give their blessing to the union.

Between them lay an empty bowl; on the day of the wedding, it would be filled with his and Lemma's blood to form the true blood bond between them. This custom had long since died out in his homeland, deemed unnecessary and pointless. The same applied here in Sciran to the people, but the royals observed it still as a way of showing the masses that the actual values they held so dear in the royal family still flowed strongly in each member of it.

There was also great symbolism in it, showing that the people were all linked to the royals, as one commoner would be chosen to join them in their blood oath. The binder would then entwine the blood of royals with that of the humble, making it common.

Zenith, having chosen Vex for some strange and unfathomable reason. Asked Lemma and Catherine's permission for him to be the binder, not knowing why, only sensing it deep down inside his very being that somehow it was what Rysand and fate wanted. This made him think, *Maybe Vex has a larger part to play than just helping remove my uncle from my stolen throne.*

In the merchant district at the dress fitters, Lemma stood on a podium. Below, several attendants busied themselves around her, taking measurements, testing colours against her skin, and asking which she would like. Already having made the choice that would be the base from which the design would grow and change, a fantastic lace in ivory and rose. This would make up the bodice and skirt of the dress, showcasing the tanned colours of her skin flawlessly. Isis and Faith had both been left awestruck by the choice and by how beautiful it made their sister look. It was as though the fabric had been designed with her in mind.

Lemma stood there, looking at three colours: a white, a gold, and a pure ivory fabric, all of which matched perfectly with the bodice colour. "They all fit so well, which do I choose? Isis? Faith?"

"My lady", came a whisper at her feet. A young, peaceful girl, not more than sixteen, spoke to her, "Yes." Lemma nodded at her, whispering. The young girl spoke unconfidently. "If I may be so bold as to suggest an idea, as I sense your inability to choose between them. That you make use of them both," the girl paused as Lemma looked down, confused at the notion. "Speak, girl, how would this be done?"

The girls stood making moves around the room, taking all the samples from the others, and taking them to the window. She placed the ivory over the gold and white in the window's light. Lemma stared in interest as the ivory became translucent to a point where the Gold of the fabric below showed, though not in all places, but enough for the ivory to look like it held starlight in its folds.

Lemma leapt from the podium, shocking all the attendants around her. Some fell to the floor, jumping out of the way. Lemma rushed over to the servant girl. She grasped her arms and swung her round. "It's perfect, how did you know that would happen?" It turned out the servant girl had spent many nights alone in the dressmaker's store under torchlight, playing with fabrics, combining them and joining them together in her designs. It just so happened that some of the designs were now dresses that nobles wore.

Still, she had kept the ivory starlight a secret until she saw Lemma holding those two same fabrics. "Young girl, I see now that the true talent in this store is not the master dress makers but lies within you. I ask that you become my soul dress maker," the girl blushed and turned shy, lowering her head to the floor "I wish only that I could be M'lady, but my master would never allow it." Lemma looked scornfully over at her sisters, who knew precisely what Lemma wished them to do.

Isis and Faith left the fitting room, entering the shop at the counter, where the girls' master, the royal dressmaker, stood. A slothful, cowardly man, but a cunning, devious businessman, he may have offered the dress for free, but he was charging double the rate to all other comers to make up for it. The sisters knew this; some of their cousins had already paid for dresses.

Approaching him, they smiled and spoke in unison, "Our sister has requested the soul service of your young, servant girl, for her to be released to her, to make the wedding dress. I should think no issues will arise, good sir, in doing this." The dressmaker's face hardened as he turned to the sisters, his raspy voice cutting like a rusty blade through the air as he responded to their request.

"I shall not release the girl, nor will I allow her to make the dress; she is my property, and I will do with her as I wish; that is not a request I can fulfil. I'm afraid. The girl will need to be removed from here; her boldness is too much, and a newer cruller master will suit her better. Perhaps the laundry quarter will break her spirit enough for her to return."

Lemma stood in the shadow of the fitting room door, her temper reaching its limit, cursing through thought alone. *How dare he devalue the life of this girl so much. The indecency in his voice is making my blood curdle. I wish I could end his life. That is no way for a citizen of Sciran to speak, let alone to my sisters. They are princesses, royalty. He is the royal dressmaker. Because mother allows him to be.*

Lemma turned to the girl. "Can you prove the designs are of your hand, not the dressmaker's?" With barely a sound leaving her mouth, the girl spoke back. "Indeed, M'lady, I have sketches hidden that he does not know of, and I can sew a dress as proof. Why do you ask?" Lemma had already formed a plan. She summoned the royal messenger, instructing him to find the Queen and pass on a message that asked her to come to the dressmakers and assist with the dress choices.

Catherine arrived soon after at the dressmakers. The man's whole speech changed suddenly, shifting from the cruel and devious man they had heard but moments ago to a polite, civilised, and regal man, a complete mask worn only for the Queen; he didn't dare show his true colours around her. He valued his neck too much. "Leave us, Dressmaker. I wish to speak with my mother and sisters alone" Whilst she Cast a scornful look at the man.. "The girl may stay to attend to my needs." Lemma's voice sounded unusually commanding to those around her.

Speaking in a sweet yet devious tone, Lemma discussed her findings and plan. "Mother, I am sorry to bring you here, but that man whom you appointed to be the one who adorns you with clothes is but a false apostle. He did not make the very dress you wear. He could not if you asked him to repeat it" Catherine stood there, face frozen in anger.

"These are grave accusations, Lemma. I hope you have proof that you can show me. To lie to a royal is punishable by death immediately at the gallows" Lemma paused, turned to the girl, whom she had already sent to fetch the drawing, reaching into the pile, she pulled the design for the dress Catherine wore, shoving it into her mother's hand.

Lemma smirk grew "This is the design for your dress penned in the whole by this young servant girl he has her make them and sells them as his own" Catherine stance switched she needed to tread carefully, even it was only a slight chance Lemma was wrong "Lemma my angel these drawing are not proof enough any hand could pen them but if what you say is true then I shall set him a challenge I shall tare this dress and ask that another be made. To secure the girl, I will have her arrested so that he cannot use her to do it"

At that, Lemma smiled naturally. The girl, apprehensive and scared, being dragged from the shop, held by two guards who took her in the direction of the prison, instructed to circle to the castle so the dressmaker would not see where they truly went. Catherine then took the dagger at her waist and sliced the dress from the base to the waist.

The dressmaker, dumbfounded, gasped at the girl being dragged from the shop, his face crumpling like his dreams had just been crushed. Running to the fitting room as he entered, falling to his knees, asking why the girl had been taken. Catherine faked anger as she spoke. "She fell and cut through my dress with a blade whilst cutting a swatch of fabric for me. The blade drew blood, a heinous crime." Catherine had been wise; she had nicked her leg enough to cause blood to trail down onto the torn fabric around her ankle.

The dressmaker bowed and begged for the girl to be returned; he would ensure her punishment fit the crime. Catherine didn't budge and instructed him to have an exact duplicate of her dress made in two days. She wanted it for her daughter's wedding, at that, She turned, grabbed a fantastic sky and night blue gown from the stand, one she had ordered the week before and left the room, returning changed, tossing the torn dress to the floor without a word or a blink.

Cathal and Brent walked side by side there strides matching they had become fast friend since their arrival in Sciran not spending not a minute apart Cathal telling stories of the gorge, Brent speaking of his many adventures in the Toplands now though their purpose was set by the Queen herself they were to take Zenith to the armourer and get him an armour fit for a prince to wear in battle and one other more showy set he could wear on his wedding day.

Cathal and Brent stormed into Zenith's chamber, catching him by surprise, both grabbing Zenith under an arm, lifting him into the air. This time, he wouldn't evade them; he would go kicking and screaming if necessary. Managing to waylay them a couple of times, he didn't want the fuss to be made about him. Both agreed, however, that he deserved it, and this time they wouldn't let him have a choice in the matter.

They knew his true identity, and of course, he wielded the Echidna flame. That in itself was worthy of great armour, but he was a prince, the true heir to a throne, and he needed to look the part.

Dragging Zenith, who struggled hard against them, was a great deal of work. He was taller than both of them. Still, there were two of them fighting him, holding fast. "I'll smack you up the side of the head if you carry on fighting me." Cathal threatened. "Even if you get a smack on the side of the head, you still need to look your best. Do you want to disappoint Lemma? Do you truly dare to anger Catherine?" Brent's words said less aggressively.

They released him after promising to go with them willingly. No hints as to which one had persuaded him, His thoughts did just as much. *I don't want to deal with Lemma. If I turned up in my tired, worn farmer clothing.* Imagining, *she would gut me at the altar, or worse, refuse to marry me, that would hurt more than death itself.*

Looking ahead, they neared the forge, its chimneys taller than the city walls, almost level with the castle parapet. Around it lay many smaller smiths producing general everyday items, but this forge was grand; *Wow, and I thought Remi's place was grand.* Jumped to the forefront of Cathal's mind. The door opened on its own as they entered. There stood a man, his body haggard from the years, yet his eyes looked younger than his body showed.

Around him hung a great aura, filling the very air they breathed with magic, most definitely a master of the elements. The forge produced no heat, yet it glowed white, hotter than a volcano. The man's tools lay next to it on top of the anvil, ready to work, made from a metal none of them recognised.

Cathal and Brent stepped back, shoving Zenith forward. The forge master stared at him, looking him up and down, then suddenly pointed to a doorway on their right. The three passed through the door into the armour room. Before them stood many suits, all colours and metals gleaming in the light, with not a single tarnish on any of them.

Each piece was made for a person of noble birth. "I'm not worthy of any", Zenith whispered, pointing at the most basic armour he could see, and dared not ask for more.

The forge master walked in behind them, a scornful face on him, staring at Zenith. He shook his head "These are not for you your highness." Clapped his hands and in the blink of an eye, all the suits of armour disappeared, their place now nothing but air.

The forge master stood there, gazing at Zenith again. He clapped his hands, a suit of armour appearing on Zenith, a pure silver suit made of trident metal that seemed to have been tailored to fit his body perfectly. Yet the forge master seemed unhappy at it. "This is too much already." Zenith complaints went unheard.

The forge master approached him, laying a single finger on the armour, drawing with it. Ruby red flame of meridian metal, following his every move, engraving into the trident metal surface. The forge master stopped. His face still unsettled, he placed the palm of his hand firmly in the centre of the breast-plate and chanted in ancient Appritian; the insignia of the royal court of Errant appeared.

Not satisfied, still the forge master began to draw more flames, intricate and foreboding like a tribal tattoo, from the base of Zenith's boots up his legs to the chest plate. This time, the fire burned orange with a flicker of meridian, made from a metal Zenith didn't know.

Finally the master seemed pleased with the armour now and clicked his fingers; a helmet and gauntlets appeared on Zenith. The trident metal, inlaid with meridian flames, mixed with flickers of a deeper silver metal.

A gleaming golden sheath appeared at his waist, holding

the Echidna flame inside, a golden short sword on the opposite hip held in a black leather casing.

The forge master spoke in a low, droll voice, struggling to say the words as if he barely ever spoke. "The sword is my gift. It was your grandfather's. I made it for him and retained it upon his death. May it serve you well."

A grand mirror appeared before Zenith. He stared in wonder. The armour was so beautiful that he could not speak. It fitted perfectly and felt like he had worn it for years. Staring deeper into the mirrors glass, he saw his friends Cathal and Brent behind him, their armours changing before his very eyes. Cathal's a splendid black inlayed with gold and his family crest on both shoulders, Brent's brass armour disappeared, replaced by a fabulous Meriden armour. At the brow of his helmet, a grand sash of green and purple feathers protruded. Holding a meridian shield, the insignia of Sciran was inscribed so large that it filled the whole thing.

The forge master beamed with pride, "These are my finest works to date, and I shall not repeat them. No one shall ever wear this armour but your bloodline. They are your family's lineage and my gift to you all. Your quest will lead you far, but this armour will never break."

15
AN ACCIDENTAL DATE AND A HANGING

The wedding lay but a few days away, and the castle gleamed in the sunlight; the courtyard looked magnificent, better than either Faith or Isis imagined it would be.

They had also succeeded in getting Zenith's older brother, Merik, here, utilising subterfuge; they had placed their faith in Amabel, and she hadn't let them down; she had the right amount of wit to match her confidence.

A couple of days had passed since Catherine and Lemma had issued the challenge to make a copy of the gown. Through the wooden doors of the shop, they burst, followed by the royal guard. Lemma's face contorted and trembling with anticipation, her thoughts all over the place.

I know the dress was the girl's, but what if he managed, I'll have sent an innocent child to the gallows on a whim. Shaking her head. *No, no, I must have faith in my decisions; he cannot make it again, he has no designs or ability.* Still, she couldn't settle for speaking in hushed tones to Catherine. "Mother, if he has completed the task, what will happen to the girl?"

Catherine looked at her with the eyes of a mother and years of experience. "Lemma, my dear, do not worry. I honestly doubt his abilities myself, and anyway, Isis told me of how he dared speak to her and Faith, for that alone, he will lose station." Lemma understood now that the Grumpy condescending man was done either way, but realised Catherine hadn't mentioned the servant girl. "Mother, about the girl?" Catherine let a slight chuckle escape her royal façade. "Lemma, I said, don't worry, but I see you still do, even if he completes the task. The girl is safe, a castle job already in place." A weight dropped from Lemma's eyes and face, a smile growing in its place, lighting the room for all present.

"Your majesties, welcome, welcome. Please come to the fitting room." The old man spoke with decorum and grace, totally different to how he talked to Isis the other day. "Yes, Dressmaker, I hope you are not going to disappoint me." Catherine's words spoke with immovable authority. Lemma watched the dressmaker, talking to herself, voiceless. *Yes, that's it. I see you, I see the fear fill your eyes. I knew I was right.*

The dressmaker led them into the rear fitting room, which was still full of grand and beautiful dresses, many of them unfinished. "Your majesty, please excuse the mess. I have solely focused on your dress these past two days." "Stop with the niceties. Where is my dress? My new dress and old so that I may compare!"

The dressmaker looked like he wished for the ground to open up where he stood. Lemma kept the callous thoughts in her mind. *Oh, I see you failed, exactly as expected.* "Your majesty, what do you mean, both? You asked me to repair your dress?" Fear filled the room as the dressmaker spoke. "I most certainly did not say repair. I said I wanted a duplicate made for Princess

Lemma's wedding." Catherine's face filled with scorn at her words, her mind reflecting it. *How dare you try to treat me as a fool? I don't need to see the dress now; I know the truth, but I will play your little game.*

The dressmaker scurried slowly away, fetching the dress Catherine had discarded. "Here, your highness, it is better than new. The rip has been disguised. I added a slit to the gown's skirt to allow your legs freedom of movement." Lemma stepped forward, her words full of malice and anger. "You dare present an inferior dress, not a new dress as your Queen asked of you. Tell us the truth, you did not make the original dress. Did you?"

The dressmaker dropped backwards, falling to his back, the dress flying into the air, released from his hand, coming to rest, wrapping around Catherine's head and face. "I made the dress, I promise I have lost the designs, so could not repeat them, your majesty, please believe me," he pleaded, before seeing Lemma holding the design in her hands and Catherine's face full of destructive anger, feeling overly insulted and offended with the dress hanging about her. "You did not make this dress. You dare to lie about it, and then you insult me by throwing the dress you failed to repair at me. I am done with you. Guards take him!" The guards lunged forward past Catherine and Lemma,

The old dressmaker scrambled backwards on his hands and rear, trying to get away until he was forced to stop by a wall a few steps behind him. "Your majesty, mercy, I beg of you, mercy." His voice was full of fear and terror. "Mercy, you beg of mercy after you dare threaten the life of another citizen, talk to princesses in a manner unbecoming. Then you insult me and attack me, you will see no mercy from me. The law is the law; you shall hang immediately."

Clapped in iron chains, his arms and legs bound, dragged

to his feet and from the shop, the chains scraping the cobbles, screaming. The dressmaker still pleaded, tears streaming from his eyes. "Your majesty, who will look after my family, my fortune if you do this?" Lemma heard his phrasing, Catherine didn't, and all she could think was. *You miser, all you think of is gold and riches; your words betray you. It's goodbye to you, a prime example of everything Sciran is not.*

The royal guard dragged the Dressmaker kicking and screaming through the high town, followed by Catherine, Lemma and the rest of their unit. Before them stood the city gallows, at the centre of a large communal square, solid wood and two stories tall, under it, several sets of stocks were filled with a mixture of men and women, all petty criminals, mid-sentence.

The dressmaker, making one last attempt to stop his imminent end, dropped to the floor, deadweight, taking the two guards who held him to the floor with him. "I would pity you if I didn't hold you in such contempt. Your futile attempts amuse me," Catherine spoke, looking through him. Two more of the guards moved forward, taking hold of the dressmaker's feet. The two guards had stood up, grabbing his arms and shoulders, lifting him, keeping his face to the floor.

The square had become silent, the air full of anticipation as it flooded with people wishing to witness the hanging and to hear the dressmaker's crimes. His daughter looked on, embarrassed by his attempts to squirm free. She just stood quietly thinking. *Dad, your crimes and machinations have finally caught up to you. I am so glad I married and left your home.* Carried to the platform of the gallows, held standing in front of the trapdoor and noose, Catherine recited his crimes to the people.

"Citizens of Sciran, I see you gathered here. I will now list this man's crimes worthy of death." The crowd fell into a deadly silence, not even a bird chirped, awaiting her proclamation.

"This man, the appointed Royal Dressmaker, is a fraud and a fake. Not only did he lie to all of your precious Princess, he dared to lie to my face, as if that was not enough, he dared to claim another's work as his own. Talk to two princesses like they were mud munchers. Place a price upon a young, talented girl and threaten the girl's life to protect his own." The crowd's outrage grew palpable, murmurs rife, as some people recognised his daughter, dragging her forward to the front of the gallows. Screams erupted from the crowd. "His daughter stands before you, does she deny his crimes?" The Dressmaker screamed at the top of his voice, making use of his final time to commit one good deed. "She knew nothing of my crimes; she was unaware."

Catherine looked down at the girl, staring straight into her eyes, seeing nothing but contempt for her father in them. "This girl is not guilty. Leave her be. Let me finish his list of crimes." She waited for silence. Catherine finished listing the crimes and then made the official guilty decree. "You have been found guilty of the listed crimes; you will now be weighed and measured. Then you will hang until you are dead. Do you wish to speak any final words?" The dressmaker tried to speak through sobs. "I am sorry for my crimes. I will go to Rysand, admitting my sins. My daughter, I leave you my fortune should the Queen not see it forfeit."

Pulled back and placed on large scales, his weight taken, the length of the hemp rope adjusted, the loop checked, the knot lubricated, all to aid a humane execution. Dragged over, he stood on the trapdoor, with the noose placed around his neck, the knot secured at the side of his face. The Dressmaker prayed, eyes closed. Catherine, seeing his remorse in the final moment, felt she would deal him one small mercy more for his child than for him. "Do not cheer, do not boo this man, he repents. Anyone who does will spend a week in the stocks and face daily stoning. His remorse deserves notice and respect."

The guard stepped to the lever that released the trapdoor, awaiting instructions. Catherine turned to face the Dressmaker, Her Arm raised skyward. "At the end of my speech, you will hang, go to Rysand in peace, for your repentance has been heard." At that, her arm dropped, and the Trap door opened. The dressmaker fell. The snap of his spine echoed across the square. Lemma stood and cringed at her thoughts with the man. *I heard your repentance. I'm glad it was instant and painless. Go in peace.*

Catherine returned to the castle, calling the Servant girl to her throne room, bequeathing the servant girl the dress shop. Lemma returned to the shop daily until the dress was done, seeing that the girl took pride in her new role. The shop shone with all its colours, ready for the wedding. Lemmas' dress was the most beautiful and gracious the girls had ever sewn. Her very heart pouring from its seams, the brightness of her eyes, prideful and trailing from each carefully placed stitch, swearing never to repeat it, having the designs burned at the dress's completion. Much to Lemma's disappointment, the drawing had been magnificent, leaping from the parchment. Not wanting to disrespect the girl's vision and feelings, letting the pattern burn, but thinking. *I was unwilling to let the drawings burn. I wish I could have saved it, but this was her magnum opus. I had to respect her wishes wholly.*

Back in the castle, Merik had not long woken up. The cacophony of sounds outside his room made sleep impossible. A low monotone voice seemed to be barking orders at many people, rushing them to prepare for a large banquet and a wedding. Gaining his bearings, Merik stood at the side of the bed, examining the room in which he had slept. After being shown to the room on arrival by Amabel. Merik only noted the room layout and aimed his fall in the general direction of the bed, paying no attention to any other areas before the exhaustion had taken over.

Now, having slept and feeling more refreshed, he turned around, examining his surroundings. *Oh, this room is small; my room in the farmhouse is bigger. That tiny window, I'll be surprised if I can even see the city from it. Ah, there's my bag. The guard put it under the table, personally, on top would have made more sense, but oh well, I've found it.* Nothing else in the room caught his attention.

Quickly diverted to the door by a soft, low tap tap tap, and a lady's voice that came from the other side. "Merik?, Merik?" A voice he knew. Sure, it was Amabel. "I am awake, Amabel, come in." Entering the room, smiling. "Glad to see you rested." Merik became sheepish as he looked at Amabel, who stood there in an above-knee-length royal navy dress with a white pinafore tied at her waist.

Merik had only seen her up to now in a cloak, and most of that time, her head was covered. Indeed, she appeared to be in her early twenties, having already shown him her kindness, which gave him a much fuller, more complete, and rounded view of her, not significantly younger than him. More beautiful than any girl in Grissam, except perhaps his mother. Amabel spoke to inform him, "We have informed Zenith of your arrival. He's Eager to greet you, but still unable to stray too far from the main castle." Concern lingered in his words. "Let us go to him, please. Will you accompany me? I know not the way"

Out into the corridor, Amabel moved from the room, Merik in tow. They were greeted with a long, white stone corridor, longer than his entire house, with a ceiling low enough that he could reach it with ease. It seemed that other servants rushed this way and that, carrying all manner of foods and drinks. Then he heard it echo; the whole castle must have heard it, as all the servants stopped looking at one another, wondering where the loudest of grumbles came from. Merik froze in place, his face turning a deep shade of red with embarrassment. *Oh no, it's my stomach, I haven't eaten since yesterday morning.*

"I do believe we should feed that monster, you're carrying first", Amabel chuckled, seeing the embarrassment on Merik's face. "This way to the kitchen, we needed to stop there anyway", Amabel indicated its direction with a pointed hand. Moving along the corridor, Merik's face seemed to get redder and redder as his stomach kept growling, catching many of the servants by surprise, one or two dropping what they were carrying.

Oh, how I wish the ground could swallow me up. I'm in a royal castle of all places. This was not the greatest of first impressions, and it was not one Merik had expected. Amabel kept chuckling to herself, skipping and chanting ahead of Merik, becoming more carefree with each movement. "Got to run, got to run, there's a growling monster, looking for its mum." Merik didn't want to be here right now. Amabel wasn't helping at all. She was indeed innocent and full of life, so it was easy to forgive her.

Soon arriving at the castle kitchen, the corridor opened into a massive room with ovens and spits all around. Preparation areas filled the centre of the room. The most wonderful scents wafted to Merik's nose, making it challenging to decide what they all were. *Venison, beef, Lamb, and vegetables.* That was without all manner of foods he didn't recognise. Amabel skipped over to one of the chefs, grabbed a plate and filled it with meats and pulses.

From out of nowhere, a chair and table appeared at Merik's

side, along with cutlery and a giant goblet. Then Amabel placed the overflowing plate onto the table. "Sit and eat, I'll fetch you a drink, can't have that monster eating the kitchen staff, can we?" and off she skipped, returning seconds later to fill the goblet.

Sitting, staring at the plate. This was a week's food back home on the farm; in no way could he ever eat all of it by himself. Waving, calling Ambel over. "Sit with me, my lady, and partake of my meal; it's too much for me alone." Now it was Amabel's turn to blush. No one ever asked her to eat with them; it just wasn't done. Although this time there was a reason to indulge, having been instructed to cater to Meriks every need and comfort. She still felt awkward, her mind racing with excitement as she thought. *Oh my lord, this is just like a date, does Merik not know that?*

Zenith had returned to his chair, placing his wounded leg on a stool in front of him. Lemma came and sat on the rug next to him, cuddling up to his legs, smiling up at him, seeing that he waited with baited breath for his brother to arrive, after all, they had not seen or heard from each other in more than three years.

As the castle bells tolled outside his chamber window, Zenith started to get fidgety, wanting to know where Merik was. It was already past noon. "Does Merik not want to see me?" Noticing his agitation, Lemma made her best attempt to calm him "Calm, my dear, I'm sure, he will be here soon. Perhaps he has not long woken." This only calmed his nerves slightly and held them for a smaller time; "the way it's going, I'm going to be old and grey before Merik gets here."

Sitting by the fire was taking its toll on both Lemma and Zenith; it was beginning to lull them both to sleep. The heat soothed them, while the crackling of the logs brought a sense of relaxation. Slowly, they both began to drift off as a loud knock came at the chamber door.

Both sat upright, jumping to attention as the knock came again. From behind the door came a strong voice calling them. "Your highnesses, are you there?"

The castle steward was at the door, wanting entry. Lemma never really liked the old man, his voice rough and coarse, his face pitted with age, a dark shade of grey. He had always been very critical of her as a child and still was now, but he had her mother's ear, which made it almost impossible to stand up to him.

A slight indignation in the tone Lemma spoke, "Yes, Barret, we're here, where else would we be? Zenith still cannot move around without aid. Come in, then. What's the issue?" Pushing the door open, Barret entered the room, hunched over as always. "Prince Zenith, your brother Merik will be here very soon. Is there anything you require before his arrival? Would you like me to get an aide to take you to the terrace rather than receive him in your chamber?"

Zenith's mouth turned down at being called prince rife in his thought, chastising it; *I hate that term, don't want it used, or to be called that even if I am a bloody prince.* It was not his chosen title—just an ordinary man in his soul. Irritation sets in after repeating this for likely the twentieth time. "Barrett, I've asked you and asked you, please call me Zenith. I don't ask for a title, but I agree my chamber is not the place to meet my brother."

"Your highness, no matter how much you ask, this old soul cannot change his ways. A prince is a prince, and I will call him as such." Not budging on his stance, Barrett stared at them. "Well, you know I ask you not to, that will have to be enough," Zenith sighed, his point yet again unheard. Barrett just carried on regardless "I'll go now and fetch a servant for you. Would you like food and wine placed on the terrace?" Lemma piping up to break the tension. "Yes, please, Barret, if you would kindly see to that." With that, Barret left the chamber, closing the door behind him.

Amabel sat beside Merik as he ate, staring intently at him, thinking. *He looks similar to Zenith; his eyes and brow are the same, but the rest of his face is different. More feminine? Likely due to his mother's influence and the lack of Zenith's father.*

Merik waved a slice of venison in front of Amabel, snapping her from her gaze. "I asked you to join me and eat with me, M'lady, yet you sit in silence?" Flustered and blushing, Ambel took the venison from Merik, biting into it; her mouth watered. She had never tasted the royal chef's food; servants were not permitted to do so.

The food soon left the plate and filled Meriks and Amabel's bellies, leaving no room. Stretching upward, Merik yawned. "Haven't eaten that well in years." Rising to his feet, he clasped Amabel's hand and aided her to her feet. "Shall we go to my brother's now?" Amabel politely replied. "Indeed, sir, please follow me."

Leaving the kitchen via the farthest exit, they emerged into a multi-doored hall. Merik wondered where they all led as they walked. Stopping at the last but one door, Amabel pushed it open. The sunlight flooded their eyes, and the white stone and golden cobbles of the courtyard shone bright.

Barret approached from the Resident quarters, heading straight for Merik and Amabel, His pace slow but full of Haste. "Amabel Girl, what has taken so long?" Taken aback, Amabel whispered back to him. "Merik wished to eat, so the chefs fed him." Congenially, Barret replied. "Ahh, I see no problems then, young lady. Their Highnesses will be on the upper terrace. Please take Sir Merik there, then return to your usual duties" With that, Barret scuttled on past them.

Zenith, helped to his feet by Lemma, leaned on his crutch and hobbled to the door, where a young servant boy was ready and able to take him to the Terrace. Lemma observed that with each step, Zenith was walking far better now than after the battle. He would be running again before the wedding. A smile beamed across her face. *The wedding planning is well underway, being dutifully handled by Isis and Faith. It would cause numerous issues at the altar and beforehand if he were not healed.*

Merik was in awe at the pure size of the castle as they crossed the courtyard his eyes could not take it all in, statues of marble, stone and metal sat above a prominent ornate water feature in the centre, The tops of the walls surrounding them adorned in gargoyles and stone scrolls, all meticulously carved into the very stones of the wall its self almost as if they had once lived before freezing in place.

16

AWAITING A BROTHER

Zenith sat alone on the upper terrace, awaiting Merik's arrival, his impatience evident as he scuffed his seat on the terracotta tiles. Lemma had left him alone, going off to see how the wedding plans fared. His thoughts were full of questions. *How is he? Will he be in good spirits? On second thought, he's likely going to want to kill me. Where do I start, with leaving, Lemma, or my adventures?*

Peering from the archway onto the terrace, Merik saw Zenith sitting at the opposite end. Feelings of anger and rage filled him, but at the same time, love and worry; *I don't know whether to slap him upside his head or to hug him, that brother of mine, what a mud muncher.* Walking onto the terrace, staring at Zenith, Merik ran, stopping short of Zenith.

Grasping Zenith's forearm, lifting him clear from the seat, pulling him in close and embracing him too tightly. Zenith stunted his wail as his leg struck Meriks. "Merik, what on Apprite, that smarts, ok, ok, I get it, you want a hug." Releasing

Zenith, smacking him hard in the chest, slamming him back into his seat, watching it topple over, Zenith with it, a heap on the ground. "That's for leaving without telling me!"

Leaping into a tirade of questions, Merik unleashed on Zenith, "Why did you not come to me? Tell me before you left? Where did you go? Where have you been?" The questions just flooded from Merik's mouth to Zenith's ears. "Slow down, I get it, you want answers, you have concerns. I'll answer them all, take a breath."

Zenith grappled with the chair, up-righting it, using it to aid him back to his feet. "Merik, brother, calm down. I'll answer all your questions and more. Please sit, speak to me as your brother, not a mud muncher's boot."

Merik stepped back, taking a deep breath to settle himself. His attention, drawn to Zenith's Leg bandage. *Oh, Wheat sacks. Mullock dung, I didn't see his leg.* A quick nod and apology before taking the seat opposite him. Now that the situation had calmed, Merik felt a release of tension in his stomach; his anger toward Zenith dissipated, leaving both of them feeling more at ease and able to speak. "Merik, we have much to discuss, so you tell me where you wish to start." Merik retorted. "Start, START! At the start, not the end or middle! For God's sake, you know how to carry a Wheat sack, so I'm sure you can tell a story"

Zenith, seeing Merik confused and angry at him. He tried to calm him, apologising numerous times for the wrongs he had done. This only pushed Merik deeper into his resurfacing anger. "Why did you leave?" Zenith began recounting the beginning, telling Merik of Thaddeus, the monk from the Ayre Rose, and his journey to bring the Echidna flame to him. Zenith's mind flashed back to the day he received the Echidna Flame, telling the story as if he were Thaddeus himself, even going so far as to imitate Thaddeus's voice.

17
A VISION AND A THEFT

S itting at his solid oak writing desk, gold and silver vines and leaves weaving their way from leg to shelf, Thaddeus stared strong and hard at the brown leather papyrus-bound book that lay silent, dreary and lifeless in front of him. The history of his cloister protruding deeply into the pages, not leaving the page, no room for intrigue.

Thaddeus had been reading the histories of the Echidna flame and the Ayr Rose Brotherhood for an eternity, or so it seemed. He had only joined the order a couple of years ago, after his uncle passed away; he had been left alone once again. His longing for a family had brought him here. The long days of training in the skills of craft and defence drained him; the nights, well, seemed to be longer, stretched and agonising as he had but another full year to finish this tarnished, well-thumbed book.

He knew by heart that the Echidna flame had been handed to Kastow, the first brother of the Ayr rose, by one of the generals, as he lay blood-stained and gasping at the end of the creation wars. The general's name, long forgotten and his name unreadable within the pages, as so many had touched the book since it was written, the only clear words seemed etched into the page, shining bright and silver as if made of metal. Simply reading 'protect,' the blade until Rysand needs his generals again, and shows one of your distant ancestors the blade's true keeper. From there, the Ayr rose had grown into an army ready to fight, with the new general when he called.

Thaddeus sat trying to read, the darkness shrouding his eyes, his head falling forward, forehead and oak desk slamming together with an almighty crash. Dazed, Thaddeus regains his posture, the darkness reclaiming him once again. He fell into a half-aware sleep, almost a sedative trance, his eyes flickering side to side, reacting and frantic, as he saw without truly seeing.

His body was stationary, seated in front of his oak desk, yet he could see himself as though he weren't the person in the room. Slipping away, his body becoming but a glimmer in the distance, he felt an overwhelming presence behind him. Turning to see, he found a giant of a man standing there, his head balding and his body wide, aged beyond his years, wise and courageous in his stance, carrying a sword. This sword shone with a deep red hue.

The man spoke with order and strength in his voice. "Son of my sons, it is time, time for you to do your duty, return the Echidna flame, take this sword to the new general, the true king of Ocard, the rejuvenated general." These words hung in the air as he whisked across the sky, not able to control the speed or direction, dragged by a force he had never felt before.

Seconds later, he came to a stop, his body left to float over fields of golden grass swaying in the breeze, the river babbling and rolling along its edge. A small village was just in view on the brow of his sight, His focus drawn, as if forced, guided, to a Farmhand, in the field, a man with jet black hair matted to his forehead as he drank deep, an average stature no real body mass to him, yet muscular, proof that the man spent many a day working these fields of gold by himself.

A familiar voice drifted in the air as a man in Ayr Rose robes crossed the field, calling to the farmhand. In one hand, he held a flame-emblazoned staff, and in the other, a sword, its deep red glow now a bright, intense light, becoming more brilliant the closer he came to the farmhand. The voice danced on the wind as he listened, the Ayr rose monk removed his hood. It was him, Thaddeus. *But how is it me?*

In a blink, he was back in his body, his eyes flaring open just as his head met the desk again, ringing clear in his ears the giant's voice. "Son of Kastow, monk of Ayr, rose, you have seen and been shown that which you must carry, who you must seek." The voice carried on in his ear as if the man stood at his shoulder. "Lastly, you must know where to head. Go to Grissam and find the flowing fields of gold, pass the Echidna flame to its true general."

Racing down the tarnished stone halls, his boot nails cracking the stones under his feet, the screech echoing ahead of him. *I must reach the master chamber; the elder needs to know of my otherworldly experience.* Sure, he had been summoned by Kastow to deliver the Echidna flame to the general.

Before Thaddeus knew it, the master hall doors stood tall, grand, and menacing, made of wrought iron and hardwood, adorned with brass embellishments, built for defence, heavy and strong. Using all his strength, Thaddeus heaved at the door, pulling it open enough to squeeze his body through. He understood more now why they trained so much; *it seems that door would take three or more to open fully.*

Entering the master hall. The darkness of the room loomed, only lit by a small flame that rested on rocky outcroppings above Thaddeus. The room was large and dimly lit, where the elders stayed. The chamber housed a grossly exaggerated statue of Kastow, depicting him as a muscular, lean warrior clad in the finest knight's armour, nothing like the man in his vision. The opposite. *How can the depictions be so different?* At the base of the statue, a rigid, strong and Bold stone plinth.

Upon the plinth cushions of red and gold sat the elder. An elderly wise man in the later days of his life, his body still lean and strong, seeming agile, trained and ready. Thaddeus raced across the expanse of the room, his boots scraping the floor as he ran, puffing and panting, until he fell to his knees at the base of the plinth, gasping and calling out to the master, gaining his attention.

Looking down from his seated position, querying why Thaddeus had come, the elder spoke. "Young brother, why such haste? Why do you come to me at this hour?" Thaddeus, regaining his breath and composure, spoke firmly and honestly. "Kastow has shown me the new general; he lives and works in Grissam's fields of gold. I must take the Echidna flame to him. Leaving the cloister is the only way." Glaring, the elder stared at him, furious, his face twisted in disgust. "You child are not a child of Kastow you are nowt but a common mud muncher, we welcomed you here to fill our ranks only, I am the true heir of Kastow and I will be the one to whom the vision will come, Leave this hall continue your studies and stop having such ludicrous dreams of grandeur, you will never be more than a foot soldier."

His pride diminished and in tatters, Thaddeus slunk, his shoulders hanging low to the ground, almost walking on his knees, making his way to the hall door, his mind rife and restless. *What am I to do?* The master behind belittling him with each step; here he was nothing, less than nothing, but he knew from his vision he was so much more. *I am the true heir of*

Kastow. Kastow had come to him, told him so and given him this quest. *"What am I to do? Who should I turn to now? Where can I go?"*

Slowly walking back along those very same stone corridors, he had so adeptly run along less than an hour ago, his mind deep in agonising thoughts of what to do. His eye was drawn to a dim red light emanating from behind the stone wall. There were no torches, candles, or even windows in this particular area of the cloister. There was just solid rock behind this wall, which butted up against the rock face of Mount Vallen.

Back in the confines of his chambers, staring at his oak desk and the book still lying there, he began to understand the predictions in the later pages. Within its aged pages, within the aeons of dust, grim and layers of smudges, it said that only sons of Kastow could see the actual Echidna flame. He already knew that the sword within the cloister vaults was a fake, a lie, a recreation to throw those with ill intent off. The real sword was hidden even from the brotherhood; only their faith kept them all here, solid in their joint commission.

Knowing that the elder had dismissed him, taken him for a liar and a fool, called his vision a dream of grandeur. Knowledge that only he could do this and that only he could find the general, to visit upon the man in his vision his true destiny. Donning his robes and taking up his flame staff, he turned to his chamber door. A scratch echoed in the air. Someone was at the door, attempting to gain attention. Another brother would use a firm knock.

Thaddeus's staff clapped against the stone floor of his chamber as he strode towards the door, his mind stretched in deep thought over the red glow he saw permeating the cloister wall. Tenderly, he pushed his chamber door open, first a fraction, and nervously peeked through the gap to see if he could see anyone there; nobody appeared. The corridor outside the door had a strange, reddish glow; *perhaps the torches have burned down to embers and needed to be replaced.*

Pushing the door wider, he stepped out, looking left and right, not a person in sight. The red glow was shifting waxing and waning, like the spikes of a flame, nobody was in the corridor, *so who scratched and scuffed my door,* returning inside his chamber door, pulling the heavy door a glint of red caught his eye, there above the ever diminishing gap of the door an orb, Thaddeus dismissed it as a trick of the light.

Red floating and angered at Thaddeus' ignorance, the orb struck across his septum, wrapping itself up in his robe, dragging him back through his chamber door, releasing its grasp on him and poking Thaddeus. It beckoned him, streaking away, calling him to follow. The little orb spoke in Kastow's voice. "Follow, my son, I will show you the way."

He followed the orb down these familiar darkened corridors, approaching the section of wall where he had seen the red glow earlier. The orb stopped and danced about from the ceiling to the floor. It darted, "Where is it?" the voice echoed. "It must be here." Thaddeus stood eyes fixed, watching as the orb argued with itself over whatever it couldn't find. A silver glint fixed his gaze. The orb, witnessing his stare, flew to that spot. "It's here, it's here," it seemed to say, burying itself into the wall, its glow dimming and then disappearing.

"Oi! mud muncher!" came the shout, "What are you doing there? Explain yourself." Twisted with anger, the marshal walked towards Thaddeus. Thaddeus, fixed in his position, did not hear the shouts or the clonking of metal on stone, but he certainly felt the pain of a brass knuckled glove striking the rear of his head. Crumbling to the floor, his staff smashing into the stone of the corridor wall, the wall exploding, crumbling down as he sank to his knees.

Where the wall should be now, a great crevasse into Mount Vallen, a vast chamber opened before him and the marshal, the brass knuckle struck again, this time gouging his shoulder, drawing blood. The orb, enraged, grew twice its size, its light blazing out of control, searing and burning deep into the marshal's eyes, blinding and burning away his sight. Screams and retches of pain and anguish leapt from the marshal's throat as he spun and grabbed at all around him. Sightless, he screamed "Thaddeus!" out loud and crumpled to the ground, his hand clutched to the burning embers where his eyes once were.

Grabbing at his hood, the orb pulled at Thaddeus, forcing him to his feet, dragging him into the mountain, into the dark and cold of the unexplored. Behind him, the marshal lay still, writhing to and fro, grunts, leaving his crumpled form. In the distance, the crash of many sets of boots striking stone came closer. There was no way he could explain it to the others, thinking. *I don't even understand it myself.* Blood dripping from under his robe pooled at his feet. Pulled forward, he followed the orb once again.

The channel narrowed as he moved deeper into the bowels of the mountain, the only light the orb sitting just above his shoulder, tending his wound, the bleeding now stopped. Aching, he stooped low, ducking under a stalactite protruding down from the roof of the crevice. He saw it —a fire-emblazoned blade emitting a roaring red light that called to him. Tentatively, he crawled his way to the sword, the orb circling. "Pick it up, take it, do your duty," The orb whispered repetitively in his ear.

Clasping the grip of the Echidna flame, his vision flashed through his mind once again—the orb dictating instructions directly to his mind. "Take the sword, cross the salt flats, traverse the snaking pass, trudge, and follow the river to the fields of gold and the village of Grissam." Then, in a flash, the giant man appeared to him, speaking in his firm, orderly voice. "My son, now is the time to prove your grit, show your faith, relieve the brotherhood of their burden, return the Echidna flame."

18

TRIAL OF SALT

Slipping from the cloister, through the large, fortified stone wall, Thaddeus began his descent down Mount Vallen. Its steep rock slope, with interlocking pathways and rugged, jagged-edged rocks, made the journey slow and arduous, making the walk uneven and unsteady underfoot. Eventually, it passed under the waterfall and out into the final path to the base of the mountain. Sneaking into view after what seemed to be hours of slow, energy-draining, misleading, foot-scoring torment. A trail that many of the Ayr Rose failed when attempting the climb to the Cloister.

Laid bare before him, looking upon the arid, thirst-inducing salt plains. The very air seemed to rip the moisture from his skin; the first of his trials was to begin, one that would test his strength of mind and body. The distant horizon showed no end to the flats, just a smooth creamy white mass without an end, even though his studies told him that the horizon at best only gave him a clear view of the next thirty to forty miles. In his mind, speaking, *I swear that the horizon shifted further away the longer I spent looking at it.*

Taking stock Thaddeus secured the Echidna flame at his waist, covering it with his robe, his attention turned to his pack, rechecking its contents he reassured himself that the few days of food he had grabbed in his escape when rationed would stretch to six days at most, his water skin laid atop them making sure to bring at least seven full days' worth, this should sustain him until he arrived at the Hatena oasis which at a normal pace, was a five days walk across the flats should he maintain the correct path. Once there, he could restock his bags and pursue the next step of his journey, the last stretch of the flats.

There lay the gorge and the snake's way, a narrow land bridge that curved back and forth on itself until it reached the other side, out of view from most other places, given its isolated location and position relative to the Mountains— pulling his sack up over his left shoulder, securing its waist ties, readying himself. Behind him, the only home he had ever been accepted in, in front, the unknown.

Staff in hand, pushing forward, knowing this first step would see him walk long into the night after already burning too much daylight. The extremes of the salt flats caused each step to suck the moisture from his body, seemingly eager to drain the very essence of his being entirely. A small gulp from his water skin barely quenched his thirst, enabling him to continue.

Walking alone, he gazed up to the night sky drawing in over him, stars shining, hanging there, small crystals emitting enough light to make out a short distance ahead. Time had already become lost on his body, feeling like he had walked for days, his head knowing he had only walked for meagre hours. A salt crystal jutted from the ground a few steps ahead of him; its edges had been carved away into a place to lie and escape the beating sun's rays by many brothers and nomads who had passed this way before him.

Thaddeus knew this was the best place to stop, sleep, and regain his energy. Untying his sack from his waist, he dropped it from his shoulder at the foot of the salt crystal. Finding and pulling together the small amounts of previously burnt logs and fresh tinder that had been left behind by those who had been here previously. Able to take the time to slowly prepare, finally managing to create a small but rambunctious fire within a few moments the area around him was lit and warming, this was more than enough for him to sleep until the first light of day, slowly he turned away from the fire pulling himself into the carved salt ledge that was to be his rough but welcome bed.

It seemed as though morning had arrived before his eyes had even fully closed, still feeling the exhaustion of the prior day's rough and seedless hike. Thaddeus pushed up on his heavy arms, feeling his body's weight, which was lagging and struggling to move.

His eyes adjusting to the morning sun, twisting on his ledge, legs hung over arms reaching down to pull some dry bread from his sack, suckling at it, swapping from bread to water, using the water in his mouth to soften the bread as it passed through his chapping and sore lips, the salt in the air had already torn and ravaged them.

His rations eaten, he came to his feet, pulling his sack on his back and tying it at his waist, knowing that he still had at least 4 days of this torturous heat and thirst-inducing salted air to outlast.

The salt flat lay quiet and still all around him, his only guidance his sense of direction and the sun in the sky, walking hour upon hour, only stopping to drink small amounts here or there, the lifeless flats only changing slightly a salt crystals rising or sinking, shifting salt bed bring the only differences he could see in the ever growing white horizon.

Three heated, arid days passed, his lips completely burned and blistered. The only way to manage his thirst was to wipe water over the less painful spots on his lips. Catching any burn or blistered section would nearly reduce him to tears, not that he could shed a single tear due to the lack of hydration. Doubt had set in deep within his mind, beginning to believe he would never leave these flats alive. Almost sure that he hadn't changed direction, but who could tell, north to south, east to west? It was white, with the occasional shimmer that produced a pearl-like essence in the salt.

Still, Thaddeus stumbled on pushing himself as hard as possible, his legs aching from the constant march. Then, upon the horizon, a tall, twisted salt palm stood, shimmering and swaying, almost fading into the background, then solidifying back into the foreground. *Is my mind tricking me? Have I finally gotten close enough to the Hatena oasis to see it?* Nearly sure that it was an apparition of the mind. Begging his body to make the first step forward, picking up a relatively rapid foot pace, striving and hoping that the salt palm was genuine.

Progressing at a speed he hadn't since he descended Mount Vallen, solidifying his view of the salt palm, the shimmer had lifted further beyond it, causing a translucent yellowy brown tented settlement to appear, off to its left and slightly further away.

It was clear that although his mind faltered, his faith had not. This was indeed Hatena Oasis, and by pure chance, the nomadic tribe that moved from Oasis to Oasis was also here. "People!" An opportunity to rest and heal, indeed, even the slightest glimmer of a chance, they could be convinced to give him a salt weasel.

To gain the use of a salt weasel would dispel the need to

carry his pack; indeed, it could double, if not triple, his water and food.

Moving from the palm, approaching the nomad settlement, rough fencing penned in the weasels, and surrounding the tents, warding off feral weasels and any other of the local wildlife. At half the height of a horse, body round and stocky, legs thick and stumpy, furless and surprisingly agile. They could still injure a person with great ease if provoked. They just stood alert, watching anxiously and sizing up the human who approached them.

The nomads used them to carry the mobile settlements from place to place, breeding them for this and meat, surprising the meat of the Salt weasel was tender and juicy, one of his more learned brothers had hypothesised this was because they could retain several days' water within the very muscle and fats that made them so strong and that the onslaught of the salt flats tenderised them even while they lived. Thaddeus oddly remembered eating a salt weasel quite a while ago, and agreed that the salt flat made some difference to its taste.

Finding the improvised gate that allowed him entrance to the settlement, Thaddeus made his way toward the centremost tent, an impressive feature as prominent as some of the buildings in the cloister courtyard. At the threshold of the tent, his body suddenly failed him, his knees buckling under his weight.

Falling forward, his mind exhausted and his body battered, falling through the tent's closed cloth flap that formed its entrance, blinking as the rough ground approached his face, his body hitting the ground with a thud, limply bouncing before finally coming to a rest, feet remaining outside the tent, the rest of him face-first upon the ground within.

Awaking in a silk hammock hung between two thick tent

posts, his body sore and stiff, his lips feeling ashen and drained. Thaddeus didn't know where he was. The last thing he remembered was approaching the settlement. On a table beside him, a drinking cup and jug of water, reaching eagerly, forgetting the cup, pouring directly from the jug, satisfying his thirst, looking about, noting his pack and other items placed neatly against the post, at the foot end of his hammock.

Twisting to the side, he tried to right himself, but failed and tumbled from the hammock. Thud! He hit the floor hard, having been higher up than expected. Crawling to the pack and using the post to aid him to his feet. Behind him, one of the nomads entered the tent, making a coarse sound to alert Thaddeus to his arrival.

Caught by surprise, Thaddeus jumped from his skin, gasping for breath, speaking slowly between gasps. "Hello... Where... am I?. Were you the one who aided me?" The nomad nodded in acknowledgement and pulled his hands to the tent's door, beckoning Thaddeus to follow him out. Placing his pack on his back and other items around his waist, Thaddeus moved outside the tent. The nomads' settlement before him, people moving about, packing down tents, loading salt weasels with supplies of all types, ready to move to the next oasis.

Another much older member of the nomadic tribe approached, a gruff smile pushing its way through the gent's elongated beard, which twisted down from his chin to a point midway down his chest. Covered in a blueish thobe, and on his head, a matching ghutra. Following behind this nomad, a salt weasel harnessed and saddled up, overflowing with supplies. Speaking clearly, the nomad told him they had recognised his robes and prepared the weasel for him to continue his journey as he slept.

Thaddeus was quite surprised that he did not know that the nomads knew of the Ayr rose. Accepting the fully stocked weasel with glee, his journey time would be reduced and his survival assured with these supplies. Taking the weasels' harness, he thanked the older nomad, who returned to breaking the settlement. Pulling the map from his backpack, he looked at his next steps. Now having the weasel in hand, the snake's pass would be only a day ahead, once across the land bridge to where it would meet the river, then on to his destination.

A fond farewell from the nomads saw him on his way, the salt flats endless white ahead but less daunting than before. Sat in the fur saddle of the salt Weasel, he trudged on each hour, passing the horizon not changing, the manometry of it causing him to drift in and out of sleep, fighting against it, slapping his cheeks to shock himself awake. It must have been the fourteenth time, cheeks braised purple from the increasing force of each slap, but it had all been worth it. In the distance, the greens and greys of the gorge edge and hopefully the start of the snake's path.

———

The snake's pass was only just wide enough for the weasel to cross, drooping low inside the gorge. It's drop into blackness and doom on either side, slow and steady movements where called for. Slowing the weasel down to a tender step so that each step could be sure and steady. This pace would still be faster than if he had tried to traverse it himself; the nomads had perfectly balanced the load the weasel carried. If they hadn't done it, or if he had walked it alone, no doubt he would have been fighting to keep his balance, or even worse, fallen over the edge.

Slowly, they navigated their way up and down the path, never quite sure which direction they would be forced to turn next, stopping once the sun had nearly set. Thaddeus secured himself to the weasel's back so that he could sleep in some safety. The weasel lay down flat on its belly, snoring after it drifted off.

The next day came and went, the pure boredom of blackness and weaving beginning to play with Thaddeus's imagination after removing most of his sense of sight. Wandering to things he had never known, reminiscing over the last moments in the compound and how the orb or Kostow's spirit had reacted to the very suggestion he was not the one who should receive the visions—burning out a man's eyes for disbelief.

Several days had soon passed as the far edge of the gorge came into view. A river falling over the gorge's edge, cascading down the sheer cliffs on either side of the snake's pass into the darkness. The path joined the mainland via a natural rock formation that bridged the river, which flowed south from his position into the Occardian grasslands.

The map Infront of him tracing the river south calculating the days to reach the field where the man he sort would be, reconning on a minimum of two days solid travel without stops or a max of four if he took it easy and aloud the weasel plenty of rest, no matter the choice he would be at least two day ahead of himself and the original arrival, *Would the man be there waiting?*

Unfortunately, on his first day of travel following the river, Thaddeus was visited by great misfortune. The river's bank had given way under the weasel, seeing it fall and be swept away in the current, the only fortunate thing being that he walked alongside the weasel as it happened, able to leap away, landing in the brush, watching his mount disappear.

Longing for rest, he stopped, sitting propped against his pack, as the river led slightly inland. The grass swayed in the wind, its long, unkempt blades of green and sporadic wildflowers granting it patches of different colour now and then. The loss had slowed him substantially, at least by an extra day. Staring down the map blurred through tired eyes, two days of trudging onward by his working out would see him there.

Zenith came back from wherever his mind had gone while he told the story, looking at Merik. "I hope that explains at least some of what happens."

19
A BROTHER'S CATCH-UP

Merik was not happy with the story; it made no sense, and it still left him wanting to know more. "Why didn't you tell me before you left?"

Zenith was unable to provide a proper answer. "I honestly can't give you an answer, Merik. It was just an uncontrollable need. Before I knew it, days had passed, and I still didn't know where I was going or who I was looking for."

What was this mystic force that could change his will? Merik knew all too well that Zenith always had a strong will all of his own, the same strength of will as their father; w*hat could overpower him so much that he lost his sense of self?*

This was getting nowhere; the answers were producing more questions. Encouraging Zenith to give him more answers. "Why did you not send messages to me to let me know you were well at the very least?" Zenith sat there silently, unsure of the best answer. "I did try to send you letters dozens of times, I sat down most days at a table, desk, even just a log on the floor, quill in hand. I would pen to parchment and sit watching the ink drip from the quill and form a puddle on the page, my mind blank, no words forming even to express the guilt." Truly, it must have shown all over his face.

Merik, looking at his brother, could see with ease that he held something back, so snapped at him and pushed harder for the answers. "Damnit, Zenith, answer me. Did you not care at all how I felt? It's always been me and you since we lost mom and dad" Tears pouring, worry replacing his anger. Zenith struggled to speak, clearing his throat several times. "I tried, I did, I just couldn't explain all I needed to on paper, even though I didn't understand it myself. I wished to, but I could not return."

The glances passed between them, seeing the remorse and guilt on his brother's face, made him leave it there and move on to his next question. Anger still smouldering, moving to lighter things to calm the mood that hung around them. "When and where did you get to Sciran?" This question elicited the longest answer. Zenith began in Lehoi, driven by his need to cross the Rysand Gorge. Then, watching and cowering at Lemma's prowess with the Star at the stream and how she had cut down so many men, leaving the ground scorched.

Merik jumped back in his seat, almost toppling over in shock, "Scorched the ground?!" Puzzled, Zenith asked. "Yes, why?"

"The ground still holds the marks from that. I stopped there. Now I'm glad you made it here, more so than before" Zenith looked blank, thinking out loud, "surprised that the ground is still black weeks later."

Reasserting his senses, Zenith continued explaining how the Echidna flame had saved him from the star, thus bringing him to meet Lemma. The bridge came next again. Merik, astounded at how he had lived. A fall from that high should have taken his brother. On and on describing his journey through the gorge, Zenith went, Merik hanging on his words, bemused at the strife his brother had endured, thanks to a sword.

Then came the explanation of the Echidna flame's habit of acting on its own, and how he kept seeing Synergy in his mind. Describing the blackened city in the fog, the green lights and the unseen battle, trying to describe Synergy was harder. A lion with eagle's head, dragon wings and flames at its feet, fitted but didn't express the size of the shadow Synergy always cast inside his head.

Thinking about it made him realise now that he had said it out loud, just how crazy it sounded; barmier than a court jester came to mind. Merik's face conveyed the same sentiment, but with concern for his brother's mental state.

Merik questioned how and when Zenith had seen Synergy, pushing to find out why he hadn't told his companions. Zenith, in truth, had not considered this or indeed spoken to anyone of Synergy until his brother, since talking to Tripas in the gorge, for fear that they would think him out of his mind and untrustworthy. "You must tell your companions, they can help if the weapons are kin, then so are they to you," Merik advised Zenith.

Merik now sat there, a solemn look upon his face, scared for his brother, but still needing more answers. Bringing up the plague and their families' demise was going to be hard. *Does Zenith even know yet, or have his injuries prevented him from discovering the truth?*

A sudden surge of anguish crossed Merik's Brow as he blurted out his next question. "What truths do you know, brother, that I need to hear from your tongue?" This was the conversation Zenith had dreaded; the only truths he had to reveal to Merik were that of their mothers and fathers' creative murder at the hands of Quinten.

Steadying his voice and body, Zenith braced himself. He

knew that what he needed to tell would sting Meriks' very soul, possibly destroy it. He knew that Amabel had given him the basics, but nothing of Vex or his incarceration in Sciran. He began to speak in a whisper, daring not to raise his voice to more than a low moan.

Starting with the prison, Zenith recounted Vex's admissions, describing how Vex had explained Quinten's plan and how he had executed it.

"It was years earlier, nearing the end of Quinten's first year as king. Quinten had summoned Vex, a vagabond and bandit willing to commit all atrocities for the correct weight of gold. Speaking within a darkened room, Quinten gave Vex his instructions to eliminate Ake, his wife and their two sons in Grissam but to hide their deaths within multiple." Merik's face turned sour, his face turning grey, trying not to stop Zenith speaking.

"Vex sort out an apothecary that sold the sorts of things that didn't need to see the light of day—purchasing a glassed vial of blighters' plague. He then travelled to Grissam, where Ake and his family worked the land. He sat making his plans on the outskirts of the village, away from the farm, so that he was not seen or in the view of any property." Merik's tongue slipped. "You mean it wasn't a natural plague? A man-made illness?"

Zenith nodded to let Merik know he had heard him "Let me continue, it will all become clear." Merik accepted that and returned to silence, listening. "The day he set his trap. He snuck into the Grissam village hall, pouring the vial into the mead for the night's festivities, making sure not to be seen. He then made his way back out. Walking to the farthest point within Grissam from the hall, far enough away that he would remain unnoticed for the longest time possible, but still able to see the goings on." Merik's jaw was hanging low. "I really can't believe this, it all sounds too fake." Zenith still droned on not noticing Merik being dubious of the story.

"He spent the dusk hours observing Ake and us children in our home; he loved to see the faces of his victims before their death. As the full dark of the night set in, Ake and his wife left their home, Headed for the Village Hall, along with many others from Grissam, adult and child alike. Once those at the festivities became infected, they would infect those close to them, resulting in the deaths of our family among many others." Merik again interrupted. "So, he aimed to kill the entire village?" Zenith wasn't sure how to answer, so they just avoided it and carried on.

"Leaving the Town, passing dad in the street, stumbling over a misplaced wooden Tankard from the Village Hall, he fell, splitting his head open upon a rough stone protruding from the earth, knocking himself unconscious." Merik burst out laughing, "Vex got his just deserts, I'd say." Zenith shook his head. *How did I know you would laugh at that?"*

Merik stopped laughing. "What, it's funny, oh, whatever, Zenith, you've no sense of humour. Carry on." "Well, Vex awoke sometime later at the local inn, well, a room in a farmhouse that took visitors on occasion, you know, the one on the far side of town. Vex then spoke with the innkeeper. He was astounded to be told that Dad had carried him there, paid for his room, and had even taken the time to dress his wounds. Vex had never experienced this type of kindness; it was something he was not accustomed to. Instantly, he began to feel something strange, he said, a feeling not familiar to him. It was guilt, although he didn't know what it was. It was too late once he realised. That was when he ran from the inn, knowing he could not stay now, or he would die with the rest."

Merik overspoke him. "That sounds just like dad, kind to a fault, always thought about others first." Zenith smiled. He couldn't have agreed more; it was so Ake. Still, he needed to finish, so he shushed Merik.

"Vex couldn't return to Errent; his guilt meant Quinten would probably put him to death. His only choice was to seek Asylum with a neighbouring Country, offering his guilt and knowledge as collateral for his own life. Knowing prison was in his future, but the feeling of guilt drove him; he felt he had to do the right thing somehow."

Merik struggled with all this information. *This is utter nonsense. How am I supposed to process all of that?* Anger and hatred surfaced inside him. *God, you still haven't told me about Mum and Dad's murderer living.* Not knowing Amabel had already informed Merik of Vex's continued existence, Zenith prepared himself to deliver the worst part, his upper lip trembling. "Now for the most challenging part, Merik, I must ask that you forgive Vex as I have. he placed everything, including that of his own life, on the line to save mine and Lemmas, not two days ago. His remorse and guilt were evident in his actions."

Merik flew into a frenzy, jumping from his chair and scuttling it across the terrace. "You let him live, why did you not end his life there and then? You besmirch our parents' memory" Merik's anger burst violently in a crashing wave from deep inside his soul. His screaming could be heard from even the castle kitchens.

Zenith remained calm, explaining about what had happened in the prison when meeting Vex, recounting how Lemma had become entangled within his anger, blinded by it, and that she had attempted to take Vex's life. Vex, in turn, saved her with his self-sacrifice.

Merik dared not speak his anger in full flow. *I can understand the decision to spare the man's life now, but can I forgive in the same way? If Zenith could, for his sake, I can try though.*

Fetching his seat from across the terrace where it had landed on its side, seeing scratch marks on the tiles from the force of the throw, placing it back on its feet by Zenith and sitting silently, the brothers bound in each other's stares, filling the air with stagnation.

Lemma broke the silence, running onto the Terrace, flinging her arms around Merik, smiling at him. "Please say he has told you?" Merik Startled pushed Lemma back towards Zenith. Bemused, "Who are you? told me what?" "Forgive me, Merik, I presumed you would know by now" Embarrassed, Lemma skulked to Zenith's side.

"Merik, this is Lemma. Now, how do I put it?" Looking sternly and speaking in the same tone, "Put what? Zenith, please tell me no more unwelcome news." Zenith looked at Lemma, her face betraying her, like a small child, she smiled from ear to ear, swaying from left to right, her whole demeanour ready to burst.

Zenith began to speak, a lively tone coming from him, his face beaming like Lemmas. "Merik", interrupted by Lemma, Zenith stopped speaking. "I'm going to be your sister" Lemma had not been able to hold her tongue any longer. She had just burst out with it. Merik, so taken aback by her proclamation and outburst, sprang from his seat, tripping over his own feet, falling on his face, and head-butting Zenith's uninjured leg.

"You got married when?" came the groan of pain in word format from the floor. "Get up, Merik, you fool, I'm not married yet. I will be in the next few days. That's why you're here."

The conversation turned to more jovial things, such as the fun Merik would have in a suit of armour, as he had never worn one. Still, he would soon be couped up inside one, standing by Zenith, also a new sister-in-law, a princess. *I had better take a bath soon.* He thought. *I already smell. I know it, and some of those servants made a right old show of it earlier.* The instant realisation that he was about to meet a royal family reinforced his decision. *Better put my best foot forward, or is it headfirst into the tub?* He chortled to himself, the mental image of it bouncing about his head.

Laughter could be heard all around the castle now that the Three had finally spoken. Merik had settled and calmed, talking about how Amabel had joked that his belly was a monster, which made them all laugh and ease the air. It just so happened that Amabel had been listening from the entrance, and she was chuckling to herself when Lemma spotted her.

"Amabel, come on over here," Lemma shouted, noticing how Merik blushed when he saw her, thinking to herself. *Hum, I believe Merik still needs a date for the wedding. His eyes betray him; he has a fancy for Amabel, now to set them up.* Unfortunately, Subtlety was not in Lemma's Vocabulary; pushing Amabel onto Merik's Knee.

Amabel dared not move. *Oh, Wheat sacks, what do I do? Princess, you mud muncher, why on earth did you sit me here?* Red-faced, watching Merik blush too as her mind blasphemed at Lemma. "Now, Zenith, my love, do you see what I see?" Still stunned, Zenith answered, "See what?" "A perfect lady to accompany your brother to the wedding, his eyes say he likes her" Squealing, Amabel ran from the terrace. Merik followed his embarrassed plan to see.

Lemma laughed as did Zenith. He could see Lemma was right. Merik liked Amabel. *Many times, I've seen that look on his face whenever he found a lady to be attractive and provoking his interest."*

20

PERFECT DAY FOR A WEDDING

The royal guards had all spent the last few days preparing by polishing their armour and grooming all the castle animals. One had dared to attempt to groom Rath and had lost his hand for it, so Zenith dealt with Rath from that point on. The Queen had had a golden leather saddle built for her. It fitted perfectly, and she loved the way it made her look in the daylight. It made her feathers simply luminescent, and the forge master had crafted cuffs that sat just above her foot and guards that covered her talons; then she donned a neck and head brace that matched Zenith's armour immaculately. Rath's eye twinkled with delight; she felt so special and loved by Zenith and Lemma, especially.

Lemma had chosen Rath as her way to enter the grand courtyard before her final walk to the altar; besides, Zenith and Rath knew just how special an honour this was for her, sensing it from the very fibres of Lemmas body.

. . .

Standing again, watching in wonder at the courtyard, Zenith's body stricken with nerves at his impending nuptials, his mind rife with worry over anything that could go wrong. Standing there so long that night drew in the torches lit, and the hustle and bustle around him faded into silence. Now, in less than two days, it struck him that he would truly have his whole world around him celebrating his love for and marriage to Lemma. He couldn't wait for it to arrive.

Lemma paced her chamber, strife with the same nerves that Zenith carried. Still, she also had to contend with the impending wedding night. She had never been close enough to any man to let them share her bed. Yet, she knew Zenith would be there beside her in a short time, and custom dictated she had to give her body and all to him that night or curse her marriage.

She had always toyed with the idea of motherhood, but in this place, at this time, her mind became solid. *Rysand, I wish to be a mother, I wish to be the best wife. Please let this happen, but not before Zenith has seen his country free.*

The day of the Wedding arrived. The whole country seemed to be trawling its way through the city gate, winding its way to the gangways of the city wall, all hoping for a magnificent view of the wedding. Those of nobility made their way to the courtyard, directed by the guards. Their armour shining in the light, holding their heads high, all glad and rejoicing in the day's revelries.

The courtyard stood open. Grand decorations hung everywhere. The seats, all decorated in gold fabric with bouquets, turned from their sides. Everything was beautiful.

The day could not have shown more promise. The skies were seamless, with not a cloud in sight; the sun sat high, glowing and fresh. The sky looked renewed, as if the sky itself were almost rejoicing at the wedding festivities.

Stood in his chambers on a pedestal, attendants busied around him, placing his armour on him, spraying all manner of fragrances and sticking decorations and charms all over their way of giving the wedding a commoner's blessing. Zenith could not wait, just thinking. *Come on, speed up, would you, I want to be at that altar, seeing Lemma in her dress. That dress has got my interest; the rumours have been rife.*

Lemma stood in her borrowed chamber within her uncle's mansion, much the same as Zenith, her dress hanging from her. Draped from her shoulder, the bodice hung low-cut, revealing her tanned skin below it and accentuating her chest. The ivory and white gown glowed in the light, hugging her body and showcasing her hourglass figure. The dress transformed her into a real princess, not the warrior everyone else knew. Catherines's eyes swelled with tears of pride watching Lemma's transformation. "My baby girl, you look perfect. I could not be prouder than I am in this moment."

Lemma was already struggling to hold back tears of joy; Catherine's words certainly didn't help, so she joked back. "Mother, would you stop? You'll have me crying, ruining my makeup. Do you want to explain the delay to Zenith? Because I'll have to get it redone."

The ivory starlight fabric, draped over her legs, was twinkling like the stars in the night sky. Delicately grazing her thighs and calves, the cut was made to accentuate her legs, hiding the muscles gained from a rigorous life. The dress slowly widened to the bottom, becoming an immense train that layered up in this room, too long to be contained.

A grand tiara, placed on her forehead, made from platinum. Diamonds, emeralds, and amethysts set in the main band on the pinnacle of the five spikes that adorned a representation of the star of Sciran, large multi-faceted purple sapphires representing the durability of royalty and green emeralds to convey the compassion and vitality of life.

It was previously Catherine's wedding tiara, passed down through the succession line, adapted and reset for each new heir. Ringlets of hair curled up and around the band; the gems reflected light through her auburn hair. The colours of the stones dance along the rose-gold coloured veil of delicate lace attached to its back, trailing over the back of her head down through the nape of her neck into the mid-back. So fragile was the lace that the slightest breeze had it floating in the air, waving around lighter than a feather.

Walking through the castle side by side, matching his strides to those of Merik, Cathal and Brent. Zenith was unable to take in all the actions around him, feeling wholly unworthy of all the fuss, thinking to himself. *I wish this pompous show didn't need to happen. I would marry Lemma in a den of thieves or even in the middle of a rat-infested sewer.*

Every servant they passed stopped dead and bowed to Zenith in turn—Zenith scowling and telling them not to bow. The same as Lemma would, the royals led the people, not demanded of the people. His mind reeling, *For Rysand's sake, I'm a farmer, not a royal.*

Yet now that his world had been lifted to such lofty

heights, making it dizzying, his view had changed in the blink of an eye.

The courtyard was bursting at the seams with guests. Walls seething as they all overlooked the wedding venue, waiting in bated breath, low mumbled chatter amongst them as they stood awaiting the ceremony start, looking around for the arrival of both sides of the wedding party. The Marble Arch stretched high and wide on Zenith's approach, adorned in all manner of banners and decorations. It looked magnificent, ready waiting for a king.

The expanse of the arch seemed larger than usual as he passed under it, shaking in his armour as the nerves became clearer, making the feeling of running a viable option. Cold feet were something he had never experienced, and it wasn't nice. Soon, he would hold Lemma in his arms forever. The light pierced his eyes as he exited the arch on the courtyard side. The entire crowd of waiting guests fell silent in a gasp that cut the air like a knife.

All the nobility and common folk who had made it inside the venue stared at him from their chairs in the courtyard or from above. His armour was so unique, they had never seen anything like it before; the trident reflected the rays of the sun, casting spots of light on the granite walls. The flames glowed brighter than the sun, almost as if a phoenix was living within the very fire engraved on the armour as it captured the light and released it in oranges, yellows, and reds all around.

Merik, Cathal and Brent waited several steps behind. This walk was Zenith's; he was to become the people's new prince. They did not feel worthy to bask in his moment, his light. Each in procession stepped into the courtyard, following Zenith, all their armours shining in the sun, most of all their heads held high; they could not be prouder of this moment.

The base of the granite step loomed in front of Zenith, the

altar standing waiting for him with Vex and the high priest behind it in his best robes, sashes of green and purple draped over his shoulders, lying on top of a cream robe, they proudly displayed symbols of faith. A golden rope secured the robe closed around his rotund stomach.

Stopped at the base of the Granite steps looking up at them, Zenith lifted his helmet from his head; his curly locks of deep black hair fell gracefully around his shoulders, framing his face. Placing the helmet under one arm as he ascended the granite steps, one at a time, his brethren a step behind him, removed their helmets in much the same way before beginning to climb.

Zenith reached the top of the steps, stood at the altar, and placed his helmet at his feet, moving to greet the priest. Then, in a smooth motion, turning to the crowds below, greeting them with an unwavering smile, and his right arm over his chest.

Lemma descended the grand staircase from her chambers, arm in arm with Catherine. Isis and Faith, light of foot behind them, her uncle's home was the place she had chosen to dress in secret for the wedding, so Zenith had no chance to see her or the dress before the wedding. She didn't want any foul omens to show on this day, her day.

Outside the grand door, waiting for them was Rath, who knelt, all of her splendorous adornments ringing. A proud look in her eyes. Behind her, a procession of grand white horses pulling golden open-topped carriages.

At the threshold of the door, Catherine turned to Lemma, her eyes filled with joy. "My dear Lemma, now you can know the real truth." Lemma's eyes were puzzled. "What?" A royal messenger stepped forward, holding an aged parchment, and handed it to her.

"Read this, my daughter, your marriage to Zenith is long past due. You should have been in his arms many moons before you met." Unrolling the parchment, Lemma stared down, holding the seals of Sciran and Errant. Her mother's name and Zenith's grandfathers were listed at the top of a treaty in royal Appritian writing. Under them, the knot of union remained almost fresh, placed aside. It displayed Zenith's full given royal name, Zenith Ake Ocard, and Lemmas' name, Lemma Catherin Sarah Sciranton. She hadn't considered his given name yet. *Ocard wouldn't be so bad.* Considering it, she decided. *Sciranton-Ocard works better; Zenith will have no option but to accept it, and he will learn that a happy wife is an easy life.* Then, realising that she was to be Mrs Z Sciranton-Ocard, future Queen of an empire and current Princess Royal.

Lemma fumbled and dropped the scroll to the floor. Isis caught the tears flooding her eyes in a soft tissue pulled from her sleeve. "Now, sister, this won't do. We can't redo your makeup now." On her knees, head hanging out over the Parchment, the tears missing the tissue, pooling next to their names. A wet line of joy, soaking in and spreading across the parchment, connecting their names. She knew now more than ever that she was meant to be with Zenith. Here on the ground just in front of her knees, the proof that they were arranged to be married on her sixteenth birthday, years before they met, but the fates, or some other force for yet unknown reason, pushed this aside. Their actual meeting was postponed until the fateful moment she had almost ended his life at the riverbank.

Somehow influenced by Rysand, perhaps or just by a stroke of luck. Love had blossomed true from their meeting; no paper was needed to unite them. Cruel the faiths had been, but only to further the kindness they bestowed on this day. Springing up from her knees, smiling, gleaming in every sense, she could not hold back. The emotions, overflowing.

Flinging her arms around Catherine, she wept so many more tears of joy. Releasing her grip, she turned and strode up next to Rath, aided by many attendants, mounting her. The dress was too long to stay entirely on Rath's back. Attendants had to stand behind and hold the train at whole arm's length above their heads; many others would swap in as they progressed towards the castle courtyard to prevent it from falling to the ground.

Lemma looked back at the rows of carriages that lined the road, each one slowly filling her wedding party. Catherine and her sisters sat in the royal carriage directly behind. Its flowing sides looked reminiscent of clouds intermittently broken with flecks of gold, green, and purple—luscious purple velvet seats, wide enough for three people on either side. Behind a regiment of six strong and willing mares all adorned in golden harnesses and feathers of the city's colours, their mains braded with ribbons to match.

Beaming with pride at her uncle, who stood below her, waiting for his moment to speak. He promised her father on his deathbed that he would be the one to vet the man Lemma married—the one to give her away on the day of her marriage. "Lemma, my precious niece, your father smiles upon you this day. I sense his pride in the fact that you have found your perfect match. I don't think he would have wished for a better man, one royal by blood, yet more humble than most of the city's people."

Wishing her well as he turned, walking tall, to his carriage behind Catherine's.

In the air, trumpets sounded, signalling for the procession to commence. Lemma gestured to Rath to move on slowly, her dress trailing high behind her. As the wedding procession wound its way through the city streets, people flew flags high in the air, hung them out of windows, and all smiled whilst shouting joyous well-wishes to her.

Children ran alongside, gleefully throwing confetti in the air and watching it land around their feet, each one meeting Lemma in a fleeting glance. Their pure souls filled with joy, filling her heart to bursting, she began to feel unworthy of such treatment. And uttered "I'm not worthy of this," under her breath.

The people all listened out for the bells, the signal that the princess had arrived. Rath came to a stop outside the marble arch that led to the great courtyard beyond. Rath lowered herself to the ground, helping Lemma dismount and land gently on her feet. There at her side, ready to hold her arm and give her away, her uncle, a great smile fully encompassing the fullness of his face.

Everyone inside or out of the courtyard now held their breath. Silent, waiting for Lemma to emerge on the far side into the glory of the sun, where she would look up to the castle and see the man she was to wed. Most of all, the ones in the courtyard wished to see the dress she wore. Rumours had been circulating about its design and maker since the hanging of the previous dressmaker; no one knew what they would be greeted with. All the rumours made the dress sound heavenly.

Her rose-gold veil fluttered gently in the breeze, brushing against her cheeks. Their pace, guided by the Sciran national anthem being played, would soon give way to the wedding march.

Zenith stood by the altar, his eyes fixed on the exit of the marble arch, his breath silent and heavy on his chest, his fears creeping in. *What if Lemma had turned and run? What is taking so long? The tunnel never seemed this long before.* Glancing over at Merik, he saw a face that was elated and confident, a reassurance that it was his mind playing tricks on him.

From the darkness, the glimmer of stars, twinkling and swirling, as they drew closer to the light. Knowing then that Lemma was about to pass into view. Forcing his heart to rise high in his throat, feeling as if it might burst at any moment.

Into the glory of the sun, she stepped, her dress casting rays of light all around, as gasps and cries were heard from all around, leaving them stunned by the beauty of her dress. The wedding march began. The gasps gave way to cheers and shouts. Raining from above was golden confetti, and at her feet, parchment lay. Placed there by guests on arrival, with blessings and well wishes. In front of her ran two young girls, cousins dressed in rose, scattering petals of all colours before her feet.

She gazed through her veil up at Zenith. Looking magnificent, his armour shining like it was made by the right hand of God. A smile filled his face, his eyes locked on her, his love pouring down the steps to greet her and lift her spirits.

As Lemma carefully placed her first foot up onto the granite steps, the courtyard and city fell into silence. The only sound left was the wedding march playing, aided by her uncle stepping beside her, helping her take one step, then another, each step closer to him —the one man she loved and had been destined to be with, even from birth.

Finally, Lemma ascended the last step. Her uncle turned, faced her, and placed his hand gently on her cheek, whispering in her ear how proud he was. He then placed a small kiss on her forehead and stepped back, revealing her to Zenith.

Her veil lifted, allowing Zenith to see her face, his eyes not once wandering. A tear rolled down his cheek, crying tears of joy. The priest stepped forward, booming to the crowd,

"Let it be known that I stand here witness to this union, the eyes of Rysand himself pass through me if you doubt the purity of the love they share. Speak now!" The silence became deeper, so deep that not even a lone ant dared to move.

His face became calm as he looked between Zenith and Lemma. Vex was called forth as the priest boomed again. "The binder is summoned here to fortify the blood oath of the royals with his common blood. He shall humble them and temper them, but by their will set aflame their love for all to see." With that, he placed a Religious dagger into Vex's hand, without a second thought Vex sliced deeply into his palm letting his blood drip into the golden bowl at the centre of the alter, speaking the binders oath "My blood will bond this union lend it my strength and valour, weed out any guilt or evil, free the pure love to flow."

Stepping back down one step, Vex sank to one knee, his head bowed, wrapping his palm in his shirt to staunch the bleeding. The pain was nothing compared to the honour he felt being asked to bind the union of his victim's son.

The priest began a holy chant as he lifted two more daggers high above his head, each as beautiful and as highly decorative as the other, rubies, emeralds, and diamonds inside the blade centre, making the light dance as they caught the sun. As the priest continued his chant, Zenith and Lemma became lost in each other's eyes, their love pouring forth, outstretched hands neither in control, drawn to the priest and the golden bowl. With a simultaneous cut in both palms, their blood began to drip slowly into the bowl, Zenith's vows spoken.

"With each drop of my blood, the bond is formed, my bond will hold until my death, and into the heavens themselves, I shall never forsake you, always protect you, share in your joys and comfort your sorrows." The words rang from him into the crowd, each word hanging in the air as if spoken truly from his heart, his eyes never leaving Lemmas.

As Zenith finished, Lemma began to speak, "With each drop that falls into the bowl, my oath is fulfilled to you. I will love you until death and the heavens above, give my body and soul to you and allow fate to see me bear your child, no man will tempt me nor separate us, I will celebrate you in your victories, and console you in loss, my heart is yours to hold."

These words echoed around the courtyard, the bowl becoming luminescent. Droplets of blood mingling together, forming a ring at the centre, small parts flowing up the sides and over the edge. Evaporating before it touched the altar, as the last drop fell from the bowl, the remaining blood changed, and a pure light filled the air around them.

"The binders' work is done; it has purged the guilt and evil from their blood, humbled it and shown it the way to unite in true love." A great cheer arose from all around at the priest's word; they all knew somehow that this was the purest and most blessed binding any had ever witnessed in this lifetime. In the bowl, only a small amount of blood remained, yet it emitted such power that they expected the bowl to be full to the brim.

The priest struck up his choral chants again, each member of the wedding party placing a hand on either Zenith or Lemma. They smiled as they lit their candles on the altar, signifying their blessings and honouring the union. The final candle lay waiting unlit at the centre of the table, situated just behind the bowl. Between them, in their clasped hands, they lit a wick, moving forward, lighting the candle. It burned brighter than the others, blinding all those who stood near momentarily as it flashed to life, then settled into an intense, steady burn.

Once the candle burned steadily, the priest stopped his chant and placed a golden rope around their wrists, tying them together, and uttered one final blessing as he did. The priest bellowed out to all as the bells began to strike, confirming the union.

Lemma and Zenith turned to the crowd, each smiling, their hands clasped tightly. Their union, complete. They felt connected, their Feelings on full display for all to see; slowly, they began to walk down the granite steps to cheers and blessings from all sides. The wedding party filed in behind them, linking arms with their appropriate partner, each heading back through the marble arch out into the city where the carriages waited to take them to the feasting hall.

Rath waited, her eyes shining with excitement, to carry Lemma and Zenith around the city to meet the people and to receive the city's many blessings.

21

WE ARE A MAN AND WIFE

They had walked all the city streets, greeting every subject of Sciran. Turning back, Rath strode along, almost skipping, as the centre of the city came back into view.

There before them, the noble row, the most important people in the city, the people who lived here thought so anyway. Lemma and Zenith disagreed with their assumption, "These nobles, we just need to show them decorum for mother's sake." Lemma cursed them under her breath, "Do they not realise that without the street sweeper or the litter men, this city wouldn't run." Zenith spoke firmly. Lemma agreed with him wholeheartedly. "You are not wrong without those at the bottom; the top would fall. In some respects, those are the people you need to care for most." Zenith smiled back, echoing the sentiment.

Rath moved along the white cobbled roads proudly, strutting and cooing as she passed well-wishers. Most stood to the side, one person stood at the centre of the row, blocking them from passing. A tall, muscular man, dressed in fine white cloth glittering in the waning sun, a heavenly aura surrounding him.

"Zenith of Errant!" the man shouted, hitting them like a vast storm, halting Raths' movements. "Kneel before me and receive my blessing." Zenith turned to Lemma, his face a mask of questions, the same face she saw reflected in him. *Who is this man? Who dared assail a prince and princess in such a way?*

"Who are you, may I ask?" his voice stern and vicious as he addressed the man. "It matters not who I am but who I am to you. Feel in your heart and know the truth of who I am." The aura around him intensified and enveloped the noble row; all that stood there gone, dissipated into nothingness. Left alone, only they stood there face to face with the man. Even Rath had gone.

Their stares intensified, fixed, each unmoving and untrusting, unsure of where the situation would lead. Lemma felt a strange sensation; her happiness intensified as she looked upon this man, and she somehow sensed a strange youthful energy from him. She thought she knew him. Zenith relaxed and felt his heart slow, breathing calmly as he stared. Desperately wanting to remember him, the memories just weren't there. *I don't know him yet, but the feeling is so familiar, like I should know him.*

Slowly, the light surrounding them gave way. Floating high above the city, *standing on a cloud? Clouds are but water in the sky. How are we standing on it?* Lemma wanted to ask, but was interrupted before she could. "You will remember me; I will show our history." Said the man in white. Far below, spread out as far as the eye could see, were the plains and the gorge. They looked on, fear gripping them as the man spoke again. "Zenith, you know me from another time and place, one you will not remember, but I remember all too well." As the man spoke these words, the world below became a blur, carried away on the wind far into the distance.

They stopped hanging in the sky above a city that neither he nor Lemma could recognise. Zenith recognised the fields and hills he was in, his homeland, but below was not the city he knew. Below stood a magnificent city built from ruby-red sandstone. Its towers and spires touched the very sky itself.

"Below you is your true city of birth, Ocard, the place your soul clung to for millennia until your new form came to be." It was like an arrow to the heart at the mention of Ocard whilst he looked down at the red city. Visions flashed throughout his head. Ocard taking pride of place, its magnificence not even portrayed by pen or paper—flashes of another childhood running through red city streets and chasing down a manticore.

"Zenith, you were once the general of light. You gave your pet to your closest friend as his protector, now you are reborn in this age, ready to fight not as you did but as you wished, to see my brother vanquished finally."

Lemma's eyes widened as she slowly realised who stood before them. "Only one being could do such things, show us history and times past, know so much. It must be Rysand himself." Her voice cracked as the gasp ripped from her lungs.

Falling to her knees and praying, begging Rysand for forgiveness as she felt she had wronged him by not knowing him. Zenith listened as he heard the words she spoke, falling to the floor, joining Lemma in prayer. Both knew him and knew what he said to be true; the very essence of his body resonated with this truth.

"Rise, my children, I do not ask you to kneel, nor do you need forgiveness. You are my chosen, and I am the one who needs to beg forgiveness for leaving you for so long, but I seek it not. I wish you to forgive in your own time. I bless your marriage and future, your children and children's children. I will hold my gaze until I am seen fit to hold theirs in full faith. I will protect you and your lineage through all, until the line comes to an end." Lemma's mind raced with images of multiple futures rushing, bombarding her; all she could think about was one thing.

Did god say I'll be a mother to more than one, a grandmother and a great-grandmother to many?

A bright flash without any warning surrounded them. Suddenly, the city street was back in front of them, the people around them looking at them in silence, questions running over all their faces. Lost for words, one spoke,

"You disappeared hours ago!" Indeed, hours had passed, and the dead of night had set in. The people were no longer dressed for a wedding; now they wore formal attire, the attire of morning. Their eyes blinded and dazed, they reasserted themselves in their surroundings. At last, Zenith and Lemma saw each other, still dressed as though the wedding had just taken place.

A shout in the distance caught their attention; the guards were calling throughout the city, "Rejoice, they've returned to whence they left." Thunder echoed from the feasting halls as all within ran into the streets, falling over each other, the stampede of bodies too much for the road to hold.

The guards were doing their best to restore order to the crowds as they all came to see their princess safe and her husband well. Joyous shouts boomed through the city as the people began to hear of their return.

———

There, out in front of the feasting hall, stood Catherine and Cathal waiting for them to arrive. The smell of food was enchanting to them, realising they hadn't eaten since morning, stomachs beginning to growl like a murder of crows. Catherine and Cathal, laughing at them like the court jester had just fallen on his face, called down to them. "Come on, you impetuous pair, go and change to evening wear, then join us, eat, be merry and celebrate your misgivings. The stories can wait till the wine and ale flow free, and the embellishments seem true."

The feasting hall opened wide, and the space filled their nostrils with the smell of a royal feast. Venison, roast pig and apple, threaded fowl, and all manner of fruits and pastries adorned each table.

At the far end of the room, a grand mahogany table, twelve persons long, sat, empty and frozen in time. Food untouched, jugs of ale still full and unused. They were waiting for them to sit and celebrate. A glance between Cathal and Zenith. Both sensed it. Lemma pulled into Zenith's embrace and heard the whispers. "Something is in the air, do you feel it?" Lemma placed her lips close to Zenith's ear, almost silently speaking. "Yes, something dark, evil."

———

Smiles all around watching them walk, float across the hall to their table, the two grandest seats saved for Lemma and Zenith. Giant oak thrones carved with intricate tree designs, their branches flowing and swaying like a spring breeze had blown on them. Their names engraved in gold and silver lettering.

Lemma sat first in a most magnificent evening gown, Zenith next to her, having shed his armour and returned to more comfortable clothes, these even had a royal twist, having been made for him by the dressmaker. His eye sparkled as the reflection of the ale danced on them. Gazing deeply into them, Lemma's heart filled with love and devotion, yet she wondered over Rysand and how he had come to them. *Rysand's prediction, if indeed it was one, what do I say to Zenith?*

Sensing a devious, unruly tone in the air. The uneasiness was slowly digging into her chest, and she was hurting emotionally. Not having the star left her feeling uneasy. Zenith had the Echidna flame emblazoned on his hip as always, and even it seemed twitchy. Cathal's staff sat there, a faint but stiffening glow coming from it; even the weapons felt the darkness in the room rising.

Sat amongst friends and family, Zenith tore deep into the meat, affronting him, the fats dripping from his jawline. The flavours were something he had never dreamed he would taste, so robust, succulent, divine. This was beyond anything he had ever seen or eaten, Lemma next to him, eyes looking like stars, smile shining bright.

Something isn't right, he felt it as the others did. The Echidna flame sensed it. Encroaching darkness pushing its way into Sciran, skirting its borders, probing for its weak spots. Eluding them all, they questioned silently. *Is it man or beast, demon or monster?* Seeing it reflected in Lemma's face, he spoke. "For now, we are safe. Celebrating our marriage."

The celebrations ran until the early hours, even without the happy couple's presence; they had taken their leave early, retiring to their wing of the castle, which Catherine had gifted for their residence. Zenith helped attentively remove Lemmas' dress, his eyes dancing over each curve and line of her, as if enthralled and enticed by her form.

Once free of the dress, Lemma's girlish spirit crept in, the embarrassment of having Zenith see her almost naked body causing her to flush a deep red, sweat moistening her forehead.

This moment was the one she had prepared for. All that preparation failed; now that she stood alone with him.

Zenith saw the discomfort present on Lemma's face. Offering her a robe to cover up, thinking. *I'll take the lead and put her at ease, Cathal mentioned, dancing for women worked, I'll give it a go.* Then, taking to the chair at the edge of the room, spinning it around, sitting legs spread on either side of the backrest. "Sit on the bed, Lemma, this is for your eyes only."

Leaning back, one arm remained fixed in place on the chair's back, twisting his body upward and dropping back, tearing his fine shirt from its collar down to the chest, showing off his firm pecks, the rip of fabric echoing throughout the room. Pushing the chair forward, letting it fall under him, he placed both hands to his chest at the rip, pulling vigorously, exposing and flexing his defined biceps to complete the task. Across the room sat Lemma, cross-legged on the four-poster bed, stunned and fixated, biting down on her bottom lip, a slight giggle of excitement on the tip of her tongue.

A visceral red flush spread across his face as sweat dripped over his muscles from the discomfort he felt, portraying himself this way as he slowly walked around the chair, maintaining constant eye contact with Lemma, using his right foot to right the chair, quickly spinning it to face directly at his new wife. Sitting down, back arched up over the chair, pulling his belt loose and hooking his hands on each side of his waist, tugging downward, revealing the V line of his pelvis.

That was enough. Lemma had forgotten the embarrassment. Something primal had started to stir inside, watching Zenith's movements. *God, what am I doing? I want him.* The night soon became a blur of their bodies moving in a battle only ever fought in the bedroom.

22

A WATCHER AND A SPOT

S at aloft in the wooden watchtower, Fenno looked out over the northern borders of the plains. Having been here for many months with nothing but the local flora and fauna to keep him company. The current posting and solitude were entirely his fault; *what did I expect? After all, falling asleep guarding the treasury could have resulted in a punishment much fouler. This is preferable to the alternative. A dark, dank cell within the Sciran jail, forgotten about. No, thank you.*

The sun hung low in the sky, protruding loosely above the horizon, offering a pleasant enough vista for the early morning. Yet, it was somewhat strange; a darkness was creeping in each day, taking slightly longer to shift the shadows. It could just be the time of year, after all; they were approaching the end of summer.

Days repeating on a loop, consisting of the mundane: waking up at dawn, cooking breakfast, doing morning exercises, and then spending the first watch until mid-afternoon watching the blank horizon, checking the hunters' traps, cooking and eating his afternoon meal if the traps had been successful. Often, he would go without a meal if they hadn't. Then, reset the traps and return to his post to survey until all the light faded.

Totally mastering this routine over the last few months, becoming faster each day and more accustomed to the terrain, mapping it in his mind and even paying attention to the most minor changes. Today felt strange; a heaviness hung in the air.

Near the end of the first watch, gazing off into the distance where the plains met the mountains, at the end of the Sciranian lands. There, on the windward side of the most prominent peak, a black spot, big enough to see with the naked eye, but not abundant enough to gain any accurate detail. Taking his quill, he made a slight note of this difference on his trusty pad. A huge gurgle, shaking his entire body, told him it was time for his next meal; he would review the spot later. For now, he needed to check his traps.

Fenno searched all the traps. They had been empty repeatedly for several days. Only one had successfully caught anything today —a gangly squirrel. Slim pickings indeed, since he had been lucky enough to have caught rabbit, hare, wild fowl, and many more meat-bearing creatures before. It seemed odd. To catch a squirrel meant he could at least eat.

Putting the kindling into the fire pit, striking his flint and steel twice before the kindling caught, protecting the small flame, and adding several small sticks to aid its growth. The flame caught them quickly, burning fast—a larger log needed to be added. Once burning well, the fire was left to reduce, waiting for the coals to be ready for roasting the squirrel.

Squirrel gutted and cleaned of the internals and pelt, fastened to a large stick, hanging it over the fire to cook. Fenno enjoyed the breeze that flowed towards him from the mountains, the faint smell of meadow flowers, refreshing his senses. Over the top of the flowery scent, the wind carried with it a more potent scent; it smelled like the barracks back in Sciran, polished metal and tanned leather, with a hint of horse. Maybe his mind was playing tricks on him; *It's just me, I'm homesick, missing my bunk and brothers in arms.*

Having eaten what little meat the squirrel had to offer, Fenno began to climb the ladder back to his perch for the remaining watch. Back atop the tower, he sat eyes fixed once again, the northern border surveying all he could see. The black spot on the mountain had grown wider, now a smudge with specks of red appearing within its borders.

Sure, it had also moved closer, as now he could hear horses: no wild horses called here their home, or any herd animals for that matter, apart from his tower; it was green grass as far as the eye could see. Maybe tiredness was getting to him, and was his solitude finally driving him to insanity? Scribbling a note on a small piece of parchment, he reached into the hawk aviary attached to the tower's viewing deck, selecting a lean and strong bird. Hessian wrap used to secure the note to the bird's leg.

Speaking directly, staring into the eyes of the bird, making his feelings and point precise, "Fly straight and true, my friend." The hawk released a pitched squawk before flying upward into the air, turning in the direction of Sciran. A mighty flap of its wings, darting off at high speed away from him.

Such unusual occurrences were surely to be reported back to the officers in Sciran. *For now, I'd best monitor the black spot, make notes of its size, growth, and distance from my post, and hope that help or at least orders arrive soon.*

The officer's mess was a hustle and bustle, Brent and Cathal at its head, preparing for a royal inspection later that day. Brent had taken Cathal into his ranks, requesting a position similar to his from Catherine. Lemma had persuaded Catherine to grant it, wanting Cathal to feel welcomed.

In the far corner of the yard, slumped against the wall, Merik, deep in thought over the truths Zenith had revealed to him, about grandfather's demise and their parents' subsequent murders, paid for by their uncle Quinten. He had no claim to the throne of Errant, nor did he want one; after all, he was only a stepchild, although he was never treated as such, all his father's relatives had taken him in as a true son of Errant. Zenith was an actual blood prince and should have been king.

Sitting in contemplation in silence, his mind perplexed by the news and jubilation of the past few days, he longed to return to Grissam. Still, he had been warned not to, as surely by now Quinten had heard that he and Zenith were alive and had not succumbed to the plague as everyone thought.

A screech came from above as a Hawk descended, crashing into Merik, its body bloodied from some aerial attack, perhaps by another bird. Screaming in pain, the bird stabbed its beak into Merik's hand, dragging it to its feet, where a small parchment was attached. Merik grasped the bird, pulling it close to his chest, panicking, jumping up quickly to his feet.

Racing across the yard, bashing and barging past men-at-arms and squires alike, the skin of his hand, being torn by the pain the bird felt, passed to him with each scratch. Merik finally reached Brent and Cathal. Breathless, he thrust the bird into Cathal's arms, pulling the parchment from its leg and handing it to Brent before finally catching his breath and feeling the searing pain in his bloodied hands.

Cathal handed the wounded hawk over to a squire with instructions to head for the healers, then turned to Brent and Merik, asking. "What does the note contain?" Peering at the note, struggling to decipher the scrawled note, Brent spoke in perplexity. "It's from the Northern border. A strange black mass has appeared on the mountainside, moving and growing the closer it is to crossing the border. Carrying a scent of metal and animal?"

Looking more puzzled than informed, Cathal spoke. "A black spot if we were in the gorge. I would suspect a Slither army moving to attack, but they don't do well in the light," Merik, still breathing heavily, spoke. "Black is the main colour of the Errant army, but they're to the east over the gorge. How would they be at the Northern borders of Sciran?" Shaking his head. *It can't be them?*

Brent stared at Merik, knowing all too well that the enemy's armies always came clad in Black. Still, they hadn't been able to attack in a long time, thanks to the bridge being out, and it always came from there, through the valley of Solus. All he could consider was. *Is this a new enemy, or has Quinten found a new way to attack Sciran? If so, how and where?* Cathal and Merik looked befuddled, both shuffling about where they stood, looking clueless.

Summoning a squire from the rear of the yard, Brent handed a letter over, ordering him to take it straight to the Queen. Sounding his Horn, Brent summoned his chief at arms, "Form a small contingent straight away. You leave for the northern border, ahead of the main force, go now." The chief at arms scurried away, grabbing swords, men and bows alike, indicating to follow him.

No sooner had he gathered a hundred or so men than Brent ordered them to take to the road. All one hundred grabbed their arms, and those with horses loaded them; the others found space within carts, leaving via the main gate, with a three-day journey ahead. The squawk of hawks sounding from the rearmost cart, the foot soldiers behind that marching in formation, five abreast.

23
CALL TO THE NORTHERN FRONT

The squire reached the gates of the castle, where the guard halted him in his haste. "Boy, why do you hurry so?" the guard asked, showing him the note. "Sir Brent sent me with a message for the Queen." Quickly, they ushered him on, sending him to the main castle door, shouting ahead to the next set of guards, "Let the Squire past, he is to see the Queen", before arriving at the castle door, already wide open, freeing his path. Each guard called out to the next set of guards. The doors opened, ready, allowing him to maintain a continuous pace until he reached the throne room, passing through each of the four sets with ease until the throne room door.

Halberds clapped together, barring the door. The guards, not moving, halted the squire, not letting the boy pass without the Queen's permission. "What do you want, Squire?" The Squire again showed Brent's Note. "Sir Brent sends this for the Queen." Rapping his fist on the door, one of the guards waited until a hatch in the large mahogany door pulled open, revealing the eyes of an attendant, iron bars overlapping his face, sealing the room from view. The Queen's guard then spoke sternly with authority.

"Brent has sent a squire with news of the Northern border. Can her highness receive him?" The hatch slammed shut, and the only sound heard was the clonking of hard-court shoe heels as they crossed the marble floor behind the doors.

Minutes later, the Hatch flew open, again revealing a man's eyes appearing through the opening. "Send the boy in!" he commanded, then slammed the hatch shut. The halberds pulled back, the door swung open, and the boy was shoved inside, doors slamming closed behind him.

Pulled by the attendant across the throne room floor towards Catherine, seated on her ivory throne, his legs visibly wobbling beneath him, he dropped into a low bow, presenting Brent's note with arms outstretched. A single lady-in-waiting moved to him, took the note from his hand, turned, walked up the steps, and placed it in Catherine's open palm. The attendant, seeing the squire's job complete, grabbed the boy by the scruff of the neck, dragging him away, forcing him out of the throne room. Job done, Petrified, he sprinted from the castle, returning to the barracks, hiding in the haystacks among the horses, trying to recover from the ordeal.

Catherine unrolled Brent's note. Peering at it, she read, taking her time to understand its essential contents, letting its words form Questions in her mind. "A Black spot on the northern front, what on Apprite?" Catherine rose from her throne. All present in the room instantly bowed their heads to the floor, taking multiple steps backwards, clearing the way for Catherine.

Striking out across the room, she passed through an archway into the residential area of the castle. Ladies in waiting followed in tow, briskly making her way upstairs, winding up and around, appearing out onto the floor that she had bestowed on Zenith and Lemma as their own home. Private and secluded from the rest of the castle.

A guard stationed at the entrance leaned against the wall next to the domicile's door, springing to alert, hearing Catherine's approach before seeing her. *I know the sound of those footsteps, every guard worth his salt does.* The Queen is here." He wrapped his armoured gloves, hard on the metal-studded door. *Open the mud munching door, someone, anyone.* Cursing his luck, thinking. *I'm for it now. Where is Amabel or anyone?* Dropping into a bow just before Catherine arrived. Catherine came to a stop in front of him. "Guard, why does no one answer?"

Catherine's patience was wearing thin as she tapped her foot, staring blackly at the guard, who was unable to provide an answer. Annoyed that Lemma and Zenith had not answered, not even Amabel, who had become Lemma's favourite, making her head maid over all others in the new household. Not a sound came from inside, and no servants opened the door. Catherine spoke to the guard once more, who didn't know the correct response. "Has that impudent girl of mine sent the servants home again?"

Catherine knew all too well that Lemma and Zenith both hated being waited on and had a habit of sending their household staff home fully paid. Catherine, enraged, said, "Open the door." The guard turned quickly, "At once, your majesty, pushing the door hard and forcing it open, crashing and colliding with the wall behind it.

Striding through the door, Catherine's shoes echoed loudly with each step. A wave of her hand indicated to the ladies-in-waiting to stay at the entrance. All of them immediately stopped dead at her glance and signal, not daring to move. "Lemma! Zenith!" Catherine called in her most regal yet angered voice, summoning them.

Panicked Lemma leapt from the bed. "Mothers here, get your rear moving. She has the worst possible timing. Oh, Mullocks' dung, we gave the staff the day off as well." Cringing heavily, quickly grabbing a dress from the floor, throwing it on over her head, pulling her hair up into a hastily tied ponytail, running from the bed chamber, still panting and covered with sweat. Zenith, meanwhile, hopped around the room struggling to dress, pulling his leather pants on inside out, his ankle getting tangled in the base of the left leg, rushing to pull on his shirt and getting knotted up inside, fighting to find the head hole, tumbling over, hitting his head on the edge of the bed, "urg, ouch. Wheat sacks I've not time to moan" pulling himself up then following from the room with urgency.

Entering their day room, Lemma and Zenith found Catherine next to the fireplace, her face stern and absolute, fingers tapping with annoyance on the mantle, Brent's letter in her hand. Rereading it, she turned to them. "Finally, you two arrive. Where were you?" A sudden pinkish shade of red crossed Catherine's face; she knew all too well where they had been and the actions that had been taking place, spotting Zenith's misguided attempt at putting on his leather pants.

Catherine couldn't help but burst out laughing. Zenith and Lemma looked at each other, confused and discombobulated, until Lemma looked down, her face flushing, a shyness and childlike state taking hold of her. Squealing, "Oh my Rysand, Zenith, can you not dress yourself?"

Zenith ran from the room, utterly embarrassed, quickly

redressing himself. Upon returning to the room, Zenith entered to find Catherine and Lemma embracing each other. "Lemma, my child, you are truly a woman now." The words hit his ears as he moved closer. He knew Catherine was no one's fool; she was very astute—what a way to greet his mother-in-law, let alone the Queen, only days after the wedding.

Soon enough, the conversation turned to more strenuous subjects. Catherine showed them both Brent's letter, its contents detailed the Northern border watch post and the black spot. It also provided information regarding its size and scope. At Catherine's description, Zenith knew there could only be one kingdom this army hailed from "That must be Errant, but how? That black march I know it to many times have I seen it march through Grissam, a constant black line moving like a snake, I know it is, I feel it in my gut." Catherine shook her head, unsure herself if it could be Errant, but knowing all too well that it wasn't a coincidence.

"Brent has sent a small contingent ahead. He has requested that the generals of Rysand join the main force, not to fight but to spur morale within the army."

"I will go without Question, Your Highness, it will be the first step to removing my uncle from *my* Throne. Lemma, my angel, I see the guilt in your eyes. Do not worry, I know you will fight with me, but I must go for my own country, not for Sciran. I do not ask you to join me, although should you stay behind, my heart will weigh heavily"

Lemma turned, raising her hand, slapping him square across the jaw. "How dare you try to leave me behind? I promised to remain by your side through all." Zenith clasped his cheek, the sting of the slap leaving a perfect handprint embedded in his skin, fiery and red. Soon, he realised this was his first mistake as her husband. Lemma was a warrior before meeting him, and she still was; he should have known she would never have taken up the mantle of a delicate flower.

The scorn on Lemmas' face ran deep; even Catherine dared not speak. "Zenith, I will go. If anyone stays behind, it will be you." Indeed, she intended to accompany her husband, stay by his side, and fight for his country, just as she would protect her own. Catherine summoned one of the ladies who still stood patiently at the entrance. "Find Sir Brent and Sir Cathal, tell them to meet us in the throne room; we must plan."

Catherine, accompanied by Zenith and Lemma, made their way to the throne room. Back through the castle, they walked deep in conversation. Lemma raised concerns, "Mother, I worry this black spot will be just men, no beasts or creations of Rycore." Zenith shared Lemmas' sentiment, "I feel the Same. Your highness, we must not use the Rysander if they are only men; I will only wield my grandfather's sword. Besides, with Rath at our side, we should be able to match several hundred men alone." Lemma interjected, "We will only unsheathe the Rysander weapons in dire circumstances. Hearing this vow, Zenith made the same promise. Catherine, impressed by them both, spoke. "You two may yet be young and inexperienced, but you care enough for any man to know the true value of life that will stand you well in the future."

These people did not know their true king was alive, so they would not bow to him, yet he would show them mercy, even in the way he fought them.

Brent and Cathal awaited them in the throne room, eager to leave for the Northern front. Brent paced the marble floor, aged boot leather tracking his steps; the leather of his aged boots scuffing the marble, leaving a lustreless path in his wake.

Entering the throne room, Catherine smiled at Brent.

Lemma ran to Cathal, throwing her arms around him, greeting her friend. They hadn't been together since the wedding, days ago. She and Zenith hadn't left their home since. Zenith marched to Brent, clasped his hand, and smirked. he proceeded to do the same to Cathal, but this time pulled him close, slapping his hand on Cathal's back as Cathal did him.

Seated in her throne, Catherine coughed loudly to gain the parties' attention. They soon turned to her. "Brent, what plans have you made up to yet?" Brent looked solid in his determination as he spoke. "I propose that we lead two armies, one to take the longer path, allowing them to circle to the rear of this black spot. The second to draw their attention from the front, as to who will lead each, that is for you to decide, my Queen."

Catherine knew all too well that Brent was a brilliant tactician, and even without the generals of Rysand, this was a solid strategy. Zenith was listening intently and spoke out of turn, "If I take Rath to the rear, I can deal with a larger force, the same as a thousand men could." Brent scoffed at this, not having thought to use Rath and feeling that a Scirainian commander should lead the army, posting themselves at the front and speaking with malice. "Given the chance, I will protect Sciran. The prince and Princess do not have the experience of command." Choking on his words, quickly adding. "I mean no offence, your majesties, I only wish for your safety and the best outcome."

Catherine found Zenith's idea good, coupled with the fact that he had promised not to use his powers to fight as a man for the good of Errant and Sciran, she agreed but made sure, after seeing Brent's face, to add that he was to follow Brent's lead and to stay by Lemma's side. Zenith bowed and spoke, "I will do your highness's bidding, I will protect Lemma with my life, but if I may, we all know she will probably be the one saving my behind." Catherine just looked at him, then Lemma winked at her. Lemma got her mother's message loud and clear, clipping Zenith around the back of the head. "Do you want to get out of this castle? You are cruising, my dear husband."

Cathal, meanwhile, stood aside from the group, listening, unsure that he could fight well in the open fields of the plains; "If I may speak your highnesses?" Catherine nodded, "Speak, Cathal, you are an honoured guest. Clearing his throat. "I worry that I may not be much use. I am used to the crags of the gorge, not the open field." Brent jumped in, "If you fight half as well as you did outside this city's walls, we need not worry, nor do you." The others all nodded in agreement.

The discussion continued into the early hours. Finally, they agreed on a plan. Brent, with Cathal, would lead the main force and march down the throat of the intruders, while Lemma and Zenith, with a few hundred swords alongside Rath, swept from the rear. All agreed that attacking from both sides would surprise and disorient the enemy.

Lemma had also tried to convince her mother and the others that the battle could be avoided if they could convince the Errant army, if it were indeed them, that Zenith was truly who he claimed to be. If only the way to do this did not elude them, their current idea would probably not be enough; Zenith would enter battle armoured, bearing the sigil of his grandfather.

Zenith's grandfather had always worn a chest plate that displayed Errant's insignia and a sigil. The shape of a strange key. A wide bar that more than one man would need to twist, a bar descending from it, a key-like bit on the end. Zenith knew that Quinten had abolished this sigil once he took the throne, so they hoped that his knowledge of it could aid them.

Brent's anger subsided when Catherine gave him battle-field command, suspecting that Lemma or Zenith would have been in command; to him, their lack of experience commanding an army seemed the wrong choice, even as the prince and princess. Experience of battlefield command would still be needed. Perhaps Catherine realised this.

Indeed, their lack of experience was one of the reasons, but Catherine, being Lemma's mother, had first done this to keep her from the battle as best she could; protecting her child was natural after all.

The group left the castle and hurried to the barracks. On their arrival, they were greeted by thousands of men waiting for orders. Brent sent Lemma and Zenith to the Smiths to have Zenith's Errant-style armour made while he addressed the men and told his commanders of the plan. Firstly, he sent several of the taller and stronger Squires to Raths' stable, with orders to tack her up, making sure that she was ready for the forthcoming battle.

Brent then climbed up to a podium so that he was above the heads of all the men that he marched with, speaking to them he gave them the lay of the land, the information they had about the army that invaded and made it clear that, Lemma and Zenith where to be protected, their lives were the life of Sciran, he made sure that he stated to each man their lives meant no less than that of the Rysander, And that the Rysander had pledged to lay their lives on the line for the sake of Sciran.

The entire army cheered and chanted Brent's and the Rysander's names, elated to fight alongside them, unaware that the Rysander generals had all agreed only to use their powers in dire circumstances, as each one of them was an army to themselves, and this victory belonged to the men and women of Sciran.

Not long after, Zenith and Lemma returned to join the army, each adorned in new armour. Lemma wore a golden vest of mesh and a plated skirt; her legs were covered in thick leather trousers wrapped in golden metal thread. Her helmet covered the rear of her neck, and a giant feather plume erupted from its top. The star adorned her hip, held in place by a quick-release clip. Zenith's new armour, a combination of blackened metal and red flame —the Errant insignia, his grandfather's sigil —placed at the centre of the chest plate, shone silver. The Echidna flame was clad in a silver plate scabbard on his left, and Barathor's golden sword was in a silver mesh sheath on his right. His whole face helmet was ablaze with roaring flames that seemed to leap off it in the form of red feathers bursting from the top.

The armies of Sciran made ready, filing out of the citadel's grand gate, led by Brent and Cathal, both on giant black horses tacked up in gold armoured plate. Six abreast, men on horse-back, some with attack dogs bounding along beside them, others armoured to the teeth, multiple weapons filling satchels thrown over their horse's rump, carts full of supplies, bows, swords, and all manner of extra weapons brought up the rear. All the armour shone bright in the sun. The people of Sciran cheered and wept, bidding a goodbye to husband, wife, and child alike, knowing that it may be the last time they saw them.

Zenith and Lemma, mounted on Rath, a double-seated saddle of toughened leather and silver studs. Covering her head was a rounded metal helm. Leading a smaller contingent of a few hundred men, all on horseback, each carrying their weapons and supplies, they would soon splinter from the main army and take the longer road in hopes of rounding to the rear of the enemy. The cheers grew to a fever pitch as Lemma and Zenith passed through the gate, each person in Sciran still elated at her return and wedding, wishing them well and a safe return.

———

Making camp at the end of the first day's march, the army settled in, choosing to sleep under the stars by their fires, as setting up tents would expend unnecessary energy. Brent and Cathal walked the camp, setting watches, seeking Zenith and Lemma, who sat by a fire in each other's company, Rath sleeping behind their bodies, curled around them as if guarding them.

Finding Zenith sat with Lemma. They settled down with them. Cathal and Brent struck up a conversation about the upcoming battle. Zenith and Lemma felt uneasy. "Let's not talk of blood, I need to turn my mind away from it." Zenith insisted on changing the conversation. Cathal took the opportunity to speak. "I have grown to love the sights and Sounds of the Toplands over the past few days. I've lost count of how many times I got lost, becoming accustomed to the bright days in the sun. It got all too common most days, I'd be lost four or five times, even once I ended up in the back of a baker's shop lifting and shifting bags of flour the same size as me. I quickly learned to take Brent or a Squire with me."

Brent chimed in, "Now, Cathal, that isn't the best story to tell, is it?" Zenith's curiosity got the better of him. "Brent, do tell, I need to know," so Brent happily obliged. "Cathal had wandered into one of the less desirable bars of Sciran, rife with temptation and vagabonds." Shot dagger eyes by Cathal, Brent chuckled and continued. "He'd been fleeced of all his coin by men and women alike. I had to attend with the city watch. I finally arrived to find many of the patrons in less-than-ideal conditions. Then his accuser was somehow hung upside down from the stair bannister. Oddly, Cathal wasn't culpable for the lout outside who had been defenestrated."

Lemma leaned forward, egging Brent on to continue. "The bar brawl broke out after someone dared to accuse him of cheating at a card game he had never played before. I couldn't keep a straight face. Cathal stood there stomping his feet like a child, cursing out the poor innkeeper who could barely see him hidden behind the bar."

Cathal, somewhat embarrassed, said, "Well, I must admit I had been drinking most of the day, I may well have been more than a little drunk. This Topland Ale hits different. It made me angrier. I just wanted to fight; the guy gave me an excuse. Not my fault, he was lighter than a long sword. One punch sent him flipping over and landing on the stairs. In my defence, I only fought hand to hand"

Lemma and Zenith fell back off their log laughing as Brent spoke, "Then that's not to mention finding you in a male brothel, surrounded by scantily clad men rubbing themselves up and down on you. Unfortunately, Cathal only wanted a bath. One of the local Nare do wells directed him there. I do wonder if he got a commission for sending people?"

The night seemed long as the group chatted and laughed in their merriment, carrying on long past that of the army. All around them, the soldiers slept, taking this as a sign. Brent and Cathal retired to join their forces. Lemma and Zenith lay down, snuggled into Rath, using the bulk of her body as a shelter and cover.

The morning broke, so did the silence of the camp. Many soldiers awoke, using the remnants of their fire to cook, boil, and prepare food for more than just themselves. A squire had taken it upon himself to cook for Lemma and Zenith, leaving them to sleep a little longer. Over the fire hanging a rabbit roasting it, placing Crusty bread on a stick at the side of the fire on sticks setting it to toast, spreading the embers of the fire to put a pot of water to boil.

Once breakfast was set to cook, working away making a large breakfast of meats and cereal for rath, Rath moaned, opening one eye to the smell of food cooing at the Squire in excitement, stretching her neck moving to eat without knowing that Zenith and Lemma still slept cooped up inside her wing, awoken with a thud after they dropped to the floor, each panicked and panting at their shock awakening. Rolling over, jumping to their feet, squabbling with belts and trouser folds to grab their weapon, thinking they had been attacked.

Rath emitted a squeak that resembled a laugh as the squire's shock turned to rambunctious laughter, watching the two heroes act like fools at the carnival. Realising they were safe, Lemma launched into a tirade of words, questioning the squire about what had happened, letting the squire speak through strong throws of laughter, knowing this might be their last chance to enjoy any humour or peace.

Once all in view had eaten and risen to life, the army made ready for the day's march. The main force would arrive by nightfall, the second contingent by the early morn. All hoped that the battle would be staved off for the next day or later, part of the reason for nighttime arrival was so they could rest for at least several hours.

The march moved along most sensibly, making up time as they went, meaning they would gain even a few extra moments once they arrived. The point at which they would need to leave soon came into view.

Splitting from the leading group, Lemma, Zenith, and their few hundred horseback warriors diverted west around the greenwood, A giant forest that separated this part of the plains.

Using their path, they could reach the mountains by a late hour and conceal themselves until Brent, Cathal, and the main forces made their first attack on the black spot. They had all agreed that it was Quinten who was invading again. They didn't know how his army had circumvented the gorge north of Sciran.

24

THE FIRST STEPS TO A THRONE

Arriving at the mountain range, making camp for the night, all checked weapons, shields and bows. Tending to horses for those who carried lances, this was essential. Zenith stood, his eyes drawn up to a rocky outcropping above him, where a black wolf sat, again staring down on them all. This was his chance, he thought, to capture one of Vermont's wolves, to force a meeting between them or gain his advice.

Staring up at the wolf, Zenith noticed that it stared down, observing the entirety of the camp, not fixed on any one point. This would be to his advantage, he thought. Behind the rocky outcrop stood a small grouping of trees. The trees would provide the most excellent vantage point for him to capture the black wolf. The idea formed that if he could get close enough, he could tame it.

Crouching down to his knees, eye fixed on his target Zenith began to crawl his way around to the wolfs right hand, making small slow movements, edging his way further and further up the mount, moving away from the wolf at first to escape its view, checking that he positioned himself and remained down wind, not letting any scent be smelt as best he could.

The need to prostrate from his crouch to lie flat on his stomach, speed ever decreasing the closer he got to the patch of trees. The wolf's gaze was unalerted, still fixed upon the camp, as the contingent set up camouflage shielding to hide their presence.

One final stretch lay before Zenith, a rocky area that would scrape at him as he slid across on his stomach, gritting his teeth and grimacing as he dragged his body over the rocks. Making the tree patch, he pulled up onto his feet, remaining still, checking the position of the wolf, the direction of the wind, ensuring that the wolf hadn't sensed him.

Taking a little time to catch his breath, settle his mind and steady his body, nerves shaking hoping that he could catch Vermont's pet, the stillness of the air seemed loud he could hear his heart pulsing in his ears, he suspected that the wolf could too as it's ears perked up more attentive than before, its face never moved and soon its ears sunk back down.

Awaiting his chance to strike, hoping the opportunity would let him pause once he had the wolf, able to take it under his control, only relinquishing it once Vermont had taken notice and come to them. His chance had come; the wolf lay down, still watching the camp below it.

Zenith sprang from the trees. Lurching forward and diving for the wolf, arms outstretched, he was sure he had it. His hands touched the body of the wolf, it evaporated into a black mist, wisping off into the air above him. Zenith slammed down onto the rocky outcrop, his chin bouncing hard, knocking his teeth together, and splitting the top layer of skin on his chin.

Rolling over onto his back, grabbing his chin, luckily, not cutting it open, only a stinging pain hung naggingly at him. Looking up to the sky, he spoke words in his mind. "Rysand, I ask for your blessing and fortitude for the forthcoming battle, that the soldiers of Sciran be granted a swift, bloodless victory and that my grandfather's sigil aid in this."

Once back on his feet, making his way back down the mountain, it was much easier walking, ambling his way to Rath and Lemma. Lemma lay curled up, snuggled under Rath's wing. Rath seemed only half asleep, alert to every noise, any loud noise and up her head came scanning the area, checking for anything untoward, then settling back down after making sure Lemma still slept soundly.

Taking a place nearby, lying next to the fire, drifting into a deep sleep, his dreams took him back to when he met Thaddeus all that time ago. It must have been the fact that he was in the mountains that brought it to the forefront of his mind. He recalled that the monks of Ayr rose lived on Mount Valen, the northeastern side of the plains. A ready-built army of a few thousand that swore fealty to him, well, the general that carried the Echidna flame, without even knowing or meeting him.

Again, dreams guided him, telling him that the monks would be of benefit to him; they would aid him in all the battles to come, whether that be to defeat Quinten or to fight Rycore. Still, though in the corner of his mind's eye sat this figure, shadowed and calling him. *It looks to be Synergy. Still, is it just in my head? Is it just a vision?* The Echidna's flames' power manifested as he fought to gain control of them.

The morning arrived, and a mist lay heavy on the ground, covering the camp; all could only see a few feet in front of their faces. The eeriness spooked the soldiers, an omen of misfortune they called it, even Lemma had to agree, "This mist doesn't bode well, the men can feel it, and so do I." Exchanging glances with Zenith, she could see his face read the same.

Both stood calling their men to them. Lemma led them all

in prayer, which seemed to improve the overall morale of the camp. Once the prayer had finished, the camp busied itself. Horses were prepared, swords sharpened, bows tightened, all in readiness for when the sounds of battle pierced the air.

The camp fell silent as the mist finally began to lift, letting the grey skies above spoil their brightened moods. Rain had come; a heavy storm brewed above them, a god's anger hanging over them, so they felt. A great crash of thunder enveloped their ears, deafening them as the sky lit up bright blue, lightning forked as it splintered through the clouds.

The trees that lay over the camp caught in the strike burst into flames, soldiers scattered, trying to calm their mounts and load-bearing animals. Then, on the wind, the sound they waited for, but none wanted to hear, with the heavens seeming in complete defiance of them.

Surveying what was to be the field of battle and the black spot. Brent confirmed it was an army of Errant they faced; five thousand men easily marched towards them. Had the warning not come from the Northern watch tower in time, they may well have overrun Sciran, in its jubilant state, the defences had slacked.

Brent and Cathal led the charge, sword and shield in hand, with all their cohorts alongside them. They pushed forward, colliding with the Errant pikemen, forming an unmoving wall with shields raised and thrusting in front of each man to fend off the pikes' advance. They held them here, neither side giving an inch, each pushing and jostling the other for supremacy. The Toxites and bowmen firing overhead into the masses of Errant Javlineers that in turn threw many javelins at them, both sides held in a stalemate. Brent and Cathal hoped that Lemma and Zenith would arrive soon; they would break the impasse and hopefully swing the battle in their favour. Their ace was Rath; she was an army to herself and could reduce the Errant numbers in seconds. They just needed to hold them off long enough.

The crash of swords and battle pikes smashing against each other came on the wind between thunderous roars from the skies. In haste, all at the camp took to their horses. Lemma and Zenith jumped onto Raths' back and took the lead. All horses, at a gallop, pushed to the field of battle, where the screams of dying soldiers and the sound of metal on metal grew louder and louder. Scirainian battle horns calling for their reinforcements had begun to sound as Lemma, Zenith, and their contingent came into view of the battle.

From their rear vantage point, they could see Brent's Army bravely defying the advances of Errant's foot soldiers, Errant's pikes prodding and skewering the Scirainian front line. The Scirainians' Shields were still raised high, forming a wall that slowed the Errant advance. Javelins flew above the wall, aimed for the Toxites and bowmen.

Screams echoed on the wind from bowmen and javelineers alike, the battle being fought by range as the centre lines held each other in a stalemate. Zenith, watching from his vantage point, looked for the general that commanded Errant. His job was to slay or cajole him; honestly, he hoped it was the latter to save yet more lives.

There at the centre, seated on horse at the rear of the second battalion was the general, aged and battle hardened, giving his men decisive and exact orders. His armour Black and gold carrying the Errant insignia, he looked vaguely familiar to Zenith his face just seeable under his round cap style helmet that covered his brow and bridge of his nose, his face nagging at the forefront of Zeniths mind, the armour even more familiar.

Zenith looked to Lemma "I recognise their General, I think he looks familiar to me." Lemma eager to press on nodded to Zenith, indicating to soldiers stood with them, issuing orders for the horse back lancers to make ready to charge the rear battalion, once clear she ordered the Toxites to release several quick flights of arrows. At the same time, the lancers rounded on themselves for a second charge.

So it began, the lancers charged, cutting down many men before they could react. Then, an aerial barrage of arrows dropped many, many more. This had broken the rear flank. The second charge of lancers came, meeting slight resistance, a lucky hit from one lancer threw the Errant general from his horse.

Now, Lemma with Zenith on Rath charged, cutting down hundreds, wings spread wide, catching so many unaware, dropping them to the floor. Meanwhile, the front line remained deadlocked as the rear guard of the Errant fell without their knowledge.

Zenith leapt from Rath's back, meters away from where the unmounted general stood defiant, surrounded by men-at-arms and swords alike. Lemma and Rath continued onward, heading towards the front lines.

The rain still poured down, making it slow and unsteady underfoot. Zenith moved forward, each step slurred in mud thrown up by his armoured boots. He approached a group of men standing locked, ready for battle.

Zenith, drawing his grandfather's Sword, moved into battle. Many of his contingent, following suit, dismounted and drew swords or pulled pikes from their mounts upon their steeds. Moving in unison with his men, Zenith plunged headlong into the general's main guard.

Parrying and thrusting left and right, dodging blows like a sixth sense guided him, he fought forcibly, with most strokes of his sword aimed to disarm and snatch away their ability to fight, aiming to force them to the ground, injured but still alive. Wanting to show them mercy, they were, after all, his countrymen, even if he fought for the other side. The swordsmen and warriors with him saw his actions and began to follow, disarming, injuring, and committing to the attrition he sought to use.

Errant soldiers began to become bewildered and scatty as the Scirainians didn't go for the kill; some even dropped weapons and yielded, instead of fighting, moving to aid and treat the wounded. The Errant general, in bewilderment at the scenes happening around him, slowed, his attacks less blood thirsty, his malice giving way to mercy in the same way as Zenith had only been wounding and disarming.

Unable to fathom and understand why, watching this man in blackened armour fight had slowed his temper, stayed his hand; this battle had suddenly changed. It had become a compassionate battle, neither side now wanting to kill; the battle could now end when only one man remained standing. The soldiers were injured, but all were able to heal, and fewer deaths and cruelty suited both sides.

Zenith moved slowly, soldiers in blue and black stepping aside, dropping their weapons to tend to the wounded, all their bloodlust extinguished by his philanthropic actions. Moving forward, headed towards the Errant general, who now stood within easy reach just ahead of him, motionless, fixated on his movement.

As Zenith was nearly a step away, the Errant general dropped to his knees, placing his sword on the ground, removing his helmet, bowing his head and showing his neck, prepared for death. Stopping, Zenith looked upon the general, unsure of his actions. "Why do you prostrate to me, sir?"

Looking up from his bowed position, the general replied, "You have bested my army, sir. I offer my life for my men." His satire intensifying as he saw Zenith's chest. "Do my eyes deceive me? "Is that the Sigil of Barathor?" Zenith stumbled back in shock; the general knew his grandfather's name and Sigil.

Overcome by the statement, Zenith mustered a swift, polite reply: "It is indeed Barathor's Sigil." The general, angered, rose to his feet, brandishing his sword once again. "Only a direct descendant of Barathor V, should wear that symbol! Since Quinten, his only remaining son, has banished that sigil. Why are you wearing it?"

Zenith tightened his grip around the handle of his sword. Steadying his voice, he spoke with all the authority placed behind his faith and power, a price both countries could muster. "I am Zenith Ake Ocard, son of Ake Barathor Ocard, son of Barathor Valen Ocard. The true prince and heir of Errant, this is my grandfather's sigil."

The general studied him slowly, assessing this man who stood before him, claiming to be the dead prince of Errant. "Remove your helmet, sir. Prove who you are, as Prince Zenith met his demise sixteen years ago." Zenith sheathed Barathor's sword, using both hands, removed his helmet, placing it under his left arm, stood there, staring, a dire look on his face, hoping the general realised somehow who stood before him.

Shock shuddered through the general's very soul, his knees buckled under him, falling to the floor, lowering his head, and sobbing loudly. "Thank Rysand, near two decades we have suffered under Quinten, his reign has been dark, but the true king lives, I was your guard while you and your step brother stayed with King Barathor, I cannot mistake you, you are your father, and still hold the same innocence in your eyes as all those years ago whence last I saw you."

The General signalled to his men, calling them "sound the surrender, fly the white flag, we fight our true king, we fight our people." The soldiers grabbed their horns and raised the white flags. The sound of surrender filled the battlefield, as it caught the ears of the Errant men. Each one dropped their weapons to the floor, taking a knee and placing their hands on their heads. The Scirainian main army, led by Brent and Cathal, looked on in amazement, confused; neither knew why the enemy suddenly stopped fighting.

Zenith stood over the general, in wonderment at this man's grace and selflessness, moments earlier willing to give his own life for his men. Something his grandfather would have done, undoubtedly one of Barathor's men, not sworn in his entirety to Quinten. "What is your name, General?" The general looked up, "I am Asger, your highness." Zenith felt an iron hammer strike at his brow, and he recognised this man. Far older but definitely the guard that spent more time playing with him than protecting him as a child in the castle of Errant.

Lemma came to a halt at Zenith's side with Rath, her hair soaked and clinging to her armour. Helmet lost amongst the many dead and injured on the battlefield, knocked from her head by a stray arrow that had hooked into the plumage adorning it, she stared down, speaking royally. "General of Errant. I, on behalf of Queen Catherine of Sciran, thank you for your surrender. Also, from myself, not injuring my husband, Zenith, prince of Sciran." Brent and Cathal had made haste to their side, still bewildered at what had just happened.

Brent removed some iron manacles from his waist and approached Asger to place him under arrest.

Zenith stepped in front of Brent, stopping his hand. "Do not place those manacles upon this man. This man surrendered of his own free will, showed many men mercy, you will not treat him as a dog." Brent attempted to push past Zenith, completely ignoring the presence of Lemma, who moved on, Rath, towering above Brent. "Brent, how dare you disobey and place a hand upon a royal of Sciran and Errant! Stay your hand now or those manacles will be used to restrain you!" Brent stopped dead, scared to move, his princess had threatened his very honour, and Rath held a most imposing presence. He had witnessed Rath's strength; should Zenith speak, his head would be severed before he could react to the words.

Meanwhile, still on his knees, the rain lashing at his head, Asger stared up at Zenith and in turn Lemma on Rath in amazement and awe. "By Rysand's fortune favours me this day, not only do I escape death, but I have also found Ake's son." All around the group, men from both nations had begun tending to the wounded, regardless of whether they wore black or blue, treating each other as equals and aiding one another in their time of need.

A fever began to run among the soldiers of Errant as each herd news that the son of Ake lived and had fought alongside Sciran this very day. The majesty of his amour became more exaggerated with each man that passed the message along, his mercy and fighting ability almost becoming that of a legend, before the last man had heard of him.

Those who had not started to tend wounded or identify the dead made their way to the group standing in the centre of the battlefield. The men were all at a loss for words; their general, who until this point had never lost a battle or campaign, knelt before this man who wore an armour that showed their emblem.

Asger rose to his feet, slipping as he did. Zenith caught and steadied him, helping him to stand, making a request of Lemma to stand upon Raths' back to address his men.

Lemma signalled for Rath to kneel, allowing Asger to climb on her back. He stood proud and tall in his defeat, facing his men.

"Men of Errant, I am but a humble soldier of the kingdom as you all are. This day, however, we have been bested by mercy and philanthropic behaviour. I fell to it, and as you have heard in some shape or form, this was at the hands of the prince of Sciran.

His hands stayed my blade, and his, had it not been so, we would be still embattled and more blood spilt for both us and them.

I also bring you news of which celebrations should endure. Not only is he a prince of Sciran, but he is also the true heir to the Errant throne—Son of Ake, and grandson of the previous king of Errant Barathor the Fifth.

I give to you all our true king, Zenith Ocard. I know many of you may not know his name, and if you do, it's a story of loss and betrayal; those stories are proven wrong today.

From this day forward, I ask you all to do as I do, swear allegiance to this man, our true king. I know not his destiny, but I, for one, shall follow him along this path, in hopes that one day we can end the tyrannical rule of the false king Quinten."

Asger's words filled the air reaching to each corner of the now silent battlefield, even those soldiers not nearby stirred their souls at his proclamation, injured or not they all cheered, "Long live the true King of Errant, Long live the true king of Errant", so infectious the chant that even the bemused soldiers of Sciran began chanting along "Prince Zenith the merciful." Zenith, so brushed with emotion, stood silent, a single tear forming at the corner of his eye. Lemma, dropping down to him, pulling him close, hiding his tears, concealing it to retain his honour, whispered in his ear. "My husband, you began the day a prince of my city, you end this day a king of men, and the head of two great armies. Each man here will now fight to place you upon the Errant throne, your rightful seat."

The day closed with both armies helping each other, making good the transports to return all injured to Sciran for treatment. The dead's tags collected, and their bodies prepared for the pyre. For three days, the healthy attended to the pyre, giving each soul a send-off they deserved, loading the injured into cart after cart, a continuous train going to and returning from Sciran.

Asger had already taken a knee and sworn his sword to Zenith, as so many had from the Errant army, each one of them scoring their chest plates with the sigil of Barathor to show their fidelity to him. Lemma, Cathal, and Brent had all taken to their knees as well in recognition of the future king of Errant. However, Zenith had told them not to swear their lives to his cause. In turn, they had scored the Barathor sigil upon their armour. Many men of Sciran did the same, but as a sign of respect, they kept their fidelity and swords for the protection of Sciran.

25

A HIDDEN TOWN AMONG
THE MOUNTAINS

The last of the dead were placed on the ceremonial pyre, and commemoration rites to Rysand were performed. Lemma led most of them, as head of the priest guard, she had the most familiarity with them. All the injured Scirainian or otherwise had left the battlefield to heal in Sciran; those that remained were soldiers who had joined Zenith under the Barathor Sigel. The four thousand-strong army, made up of mostly men of Errant and some five hundred Scirainians who had remained as Lemmas' battalion. The rest of the Scirainian army had returned home to rest and ensure the well-being of the men from Errant.

Busy packing up the makeshift tent town that sprang up over the last three days, ready to move off, not a soul knew where to, and no orders had come down from the top. All the soldiers knew they would either head to Sciran, where they would be camped outside but afforded use of the city, or return to Renton, a town that lay in a crater hidden from view behind the mountains, the place where Asger's army had formed in secret.

In deciding where they would all go, Zenith, Lemma, Brent, Cathal, and Asger had spoken at length, learning about the birth of Renton.

Quinten had instructed Asger to establish the town years ago. It seemed a farmer's town, but in truth, the whole place was a massive hidden-in-plain-sight barracks. Quinten had spent years planning it with Asger, sparing no expense on camouflaging it. All the families of the soldiers lived there. The soldiers themselves tended the land by day and trained by night under muffled torches capped to prevent light from cascading into the night sky. It was quite the operation; it had succeeded under Asger's gaze, the ingenuity involved had all been of Asger's creation, just as skilled an engineer as he was a general. The outside world would see a town of farmers, not the full-size army that resided within, ready to invade when the order was given.

Asger, Lemma, Zenith, Cathal, and Brent had closed the gaps between them over the last few days, forging a bond between men of both countries and becoming one congealed unit. Asger had regaled them with tales of Zenith as a child, like the time he had decided the palace koi pond looked to be a suitable swimming pool, becoming tangled in the weaving vines of the lily stems and the subsequent soaking he endured to rescue him. Storied memories recounted of Barathor and how malevolent a king he was.

If Zenith needed to be more convinced, to take back his grandfather's throne, these stories did it, especially after hearing the stories of Quinten's rule. The group eventually fell into conversation over the army, Zenith speaking his concerns. "If we stage the army from Sciran, we can invade from Ryecliff bridge, but that leaves whatever route you used, Asger." Asger still wasn't ready to reveal that secret. "My lord, I do not wish to reveal how we arrived yet for fear there may still be those who will report to Quinten." Zenith understood, Lemma not so much. "So, Asger, you say you are with Zenith, but you hold back. Will you at least take us to your home?" There was no doubt in Asger's answer. "I will take you there straight away if you wish, M'lady. I want to ensure that everything can be trusted."

Lemma was satisfied with the answer and smiled in agreement. "That's a sentiment I can understand." Zenith began to form a plan, but he didn't know if it was good. "I say we move with Asger to his home, keep up appearances while we prepare an army capable of war." Brent and Cathal both piped up. "That works well." Brent's machinations didn't show while he thought. "This works well, I'll know his base should the Queen wish to squash them."

Once there, he would establish himself within the populous. Asger reckoned, "Many of the towns' armed forces would remember you, as well as they do your father; most of them held positions at the Errant Castle estate before Quinten had ascended. We all had a feeling it was to keep us out of the capital."

Their plans slowly formed Zenith, suggesting. "Primarily, my first meet and greet with the people should be as a farmer." Asger liked the idea and added. "I will plant the seeds of rebellion as the town's mayor. That will let us sow dissent and declare Renton independent of Quinten and the rest of Errant."

Lemma jumped in, flabbergasted. "A new country under the sigil of Barathor with Zenith at its head! That's quite the idea." Lemma knew but didn't say. "That probably won't happen easily. Mum would rather see the town put to the flame than let any part of Errant taint her country's lands."

The soldiers received their orders quickly. They had the Tents dismantled, packed away, and loaded onto carts pulled by large mullocks. Marching from the plains that still held a red hue from the blood spilt there, heading for the northern mountain range. They moved as one, a giant black spot with occasional blue dots interspersed by those of Sciran.

Rath, towering above all, carried Lemma and Zenith while pulling several fully loaded carts behind, hitched up and attached by a makeshift harness created from fabrics and the pole of damaged and disused tents, plodding along, cooing happily to herself, content in her lot.

She had grown a lot since Zenith had tamed her, now probably standing the height of a second-floor sill. A noticeable change occurred. A sufficient change without the additional strength increase that equalled her size, likely due to her well-fed state, from the rich and full diet that was now provided for her.

Asger sat on his steed, at the head of the joined forces, with Brent and Cathal at his left and right. These three had become close, swapping war stories and experiences. They realised each had a shared commonality in the leadership of battle. They all led to protect those dear to them, not one had chosen this path; instead, they had been plunged into it as life pushed them to be better men.

Approaching the mountain following Asger's lead, Brent and Cathal looked up at the mountain, Steep and tenuous to traverse, dumbfounded. "What in the Name of Rysand Asger, it's a sheer face, a dead end." Asger seemed unfazed. "Ye of little faith, wait and see. Look on my men, even they are unfazed." After all, Asger and his men knew these mountains well.

As they marched up the mountain, following a well-trodden path that weaved its way up, slinking in and out of rocks, outcrops of stone, and trees until they reached a ridged rock face, flat, broad, and unassailable. Asger stopped, pulled a funny little thing from his saddle bag, a whistle of some type, gave three hefty blows into it, and stopped, waited, staring at the rock face. It broke in the centre, pulling inwards; it was a façade, a camouflaged door built in the very face of the mountain. Opening wide into a large tunnel wide enough for ten men side by side, even on horseback, tall enough for most types of siege engines to pass unhindered.

Several guards hauled each door open, straining as they did. Once open, they stood at attention, greeting Asger as he passed through, their faces showing confusion as much as concern over who these others were who walked alongside him. Their weapons drew as they saw the blue armour of Sciran's men.

Asger quickly dismounted once through the door, taking his time moving to the guards. "Lower those weapons, soldiers, these men are prisoners, they are not to be harmed. The king will see to their punishment."

No sooner had the last man passed into the tunnel than the several guards began the arduous task of closing the behemoth doors.

Zenith was in a fantasy inside the tunnel, amazed at its construction, each tool mark visible in the bedrock of the mountain as Rath pressed forward. A genuinely remarkable marvel of engineering, which had taken years to mine out of the rock. No wonder the army had appeared overnight on the plains side. Zenith looked at Asger, whispering to Lemma. "Asger is indeed a tactical genius, one I'm glad to have on my side. Better than him being my enemy." Lemma could not have echoed that sentiment more, whispering back, "If Asger can create a fake town and construct it without Scirans' knowledge, he will be a valuable resource and friend."

The walk through the tunnel took a couple of hours, and as the end came into sight, the soldiers were elated to be home; most of their loved ones awaited them, hoping their family member would be among them. Thanks to Zenith's merciful way of ending the battle, many more men had returned than expected unharmed, and the injured would follow later; their names had been taken so that their families could be informed.

Those who had lost loved ones would receive the soldier's tags along with their final payments and service decrees. The town would observe a period of mourning for those lost; all would wear black on their bodies somewhere for seven whole days to honour them.

Zenith appeared in the light, blinded slightly by the sun hanging strangely low above the hills and mountains surrounding the town's basin home. The townspeople all ran from Rath. Screeching and wailing, scared that Rath would harm them. Zenith directed Rath off to one side and had her set him and Lemma down. Looking over to the townspeople as an inquisitive child appeared within sight, mesmerised by Rath.

Calling to the boy in a calming tone, Zenith spoke. "You there, boy, don't be scared, she will not harm you. Come closer." The boy walked to Zenith and Lemma, apprehensive and fearful. Taking his hand, Lemma walked with him to Rath's face, placing her hand upon her beak. "Do the same as me, child, she will not harm you." Rath's eyes softened, smiling at the boy as he stroked. Her breathing settled, and she purred, somewhat similar to a cat, only more high-pitched and screechy. The boy giggled and stroked her more, calling over his friends, who all eagerly joined.

Soon enough, the commotion of their arrival ended, and Rath was more than happy to lie there, gaining all this attention. Adults had slowly started to do the very same as the children. All were fascinated; such sights had never been seen here.

The enormity of Rath surprised most once they stood at her side, even lying down, at least two men taller than most.

Leaving the remaining Squires attending to Rath, everyone made their way into the town centre. News had already spread about who Zenith was supposed to be, making his original plan null and void. There were, of course, those who doubted his claim; many of the older townspeople recognised him upon seeing him, seeing an almost exact copy of Ake in his likeness.

So many familiar faces he didn't quite recognise fully, but knew somewhere within his mind that he had met them before. Speaking with Lemma. "This is so strange, so many seem familiar, but none form a full memory." Lemma turned to him, hugging him close so she could speak without being heard. "Take a breath, calm yourself, it will come back in time. You had your childhood ripped from you, so I'm not surprised you struggle." Lemma wished him well. "I'll let you mingle alone, meet your people as you. Not my husband." In actuality, wanting to explore alone, unfortunately, Brent would never let that happen and followed her. Asger called a town meeting for that very evening, summoning everyone who was able-bodied to attend.

Zenith sat inside a small inn-type building after spending time talking to the locals. The building wasn't an inn; it was a fake. It was designed to act as one if the townspeople had ever been discovered. Across the table, Cathal sat silent, waiting to talk. This was the first time they had been without the others in a fair while, so they had a chance to speak.

Lemma had become jubilant with excitement seeing the shops of the town, fine clothes, beautiful jewellery and all types of odds and ends that she had hardly ever seen back at home with embargos and blockades on Errant goods. Without a care, she had become enthralled with them and was spending her time and coins perusing the stores; she, of course, had Brent at her side. "You choose to follow me so you can be the pack horse for my purchases." Chortling to herself as Brent spat out his drink. "Oh, erm, yes, of course, Your Highness."

The conversation between Cathal and Zenith soon became dark, Zenith growing angrier with each turn of phrase. Seething about his home, "Quinten had tried to kill me! He killed Grandad, killed my parents! Now he dares to attempt the assassination of Lemma and my new family! How dare he hide an army inside their country?" Cathal didn't think before speaking. "By Rysand, credit where credit was due, Asger is a genius; not a soul could know that Renton was here. Fully ready to act as intended if people had become aware."

Lemma had already been taken by surprise at the size of the town, without the fact that it lay within Scirans' borders. Asger bumped into her while she shopped, and they spent time together speaking about the town, explaining how he had set it up. "Starting with just a few men, we built the first farm, and from there, more men arrived. The number of farms grew, and soon enough, there was sufficient food to support them." Lemma pretended interest; even her mind did the same. "This is more what Zenith would like to know," Brent, however, hung on every word, nodding. " Yep, yep, what else?" Asger shook his head and continued. "So, the families of the stationed men were sent for. Before long, a town was forming at the centre of the crater, houses were built, shops opened, and the roads went from mud tracks to granite cobbles." Lemma suddenly realised and spoke without thinking. "Wheat sacks, you're a smarty pants." Asger just laughed. "I've been called far worse, I assure you, M'lady."

The conversation carried on for a while with Asger explaining how a self-sufficient industry emerged, producing clothing and goods to supply the people and, to some extent, provide a serviceable trade with the capital, increasing the town's economy. This growth was further enhanced by predictions of the construction of the first town walls within a year, intended to provide defence and safety to the inhabitants.

Asger became a mayor, rather than being just a general. Renton became a home. Families, friends, children, and animals alike had become accustomed to it, still in the back of their minds, they knew one day Renton would be left to rot as a ghost town. Asger ended the explanation with a very joyful tone in his voice. "Luckily, it can be a permanent home, as the bastion of Zenith's fledgling army, as he sought to reclaim what was rightfully his by blood and become part of his country fully."

Zenith moved away from the fury that Quinten brought out of his very soul, speaking to Cathal of the Ayr Rose on Mount Vallen, and how the brotherhood awaited his arrival. Explaining "They are another small army, sworn in allegiance to the bearer of the Echidna flame, thereby extending their allegiance to me by proxy."

Soon, they turned to planning; they had to figure out how Quinten had gotten these men here unnoticed. Catherine's spies had missed it. Zenith spoke in an apprehensive tone as the plan began to form, "I need to ascend Mount Vallen to seek the monks of Ayr Rose." Cathal responded. "Lemma won't like you leaving so soon." Zenith understood his concerns. "I need to go alone as well. I think that's for the best." Cathal's brow bunched up, furrowed lines forming. "Are you a mud muncher's nephew? You already got whacked twice trying to leave her, and now you say you need to." Zenith felt the pain in the back of his head from the earlier slap, grimacing. "I know I'm likely to get whacked again, but I need her to convince her mum, with Brent." Cathal interrupted. "Even without that, what do the rest of us do?" That was the most straightforward answer for Zenith. "You and Asger, I would have you learn his methods from him and start a plan to invade based on it." Cathal nodded his understanding.

Staring out of the inn window, Zenith took note of the marketplace, which had begun to swell with men and women. It seemed most of the townsfolk had opted to leave their young charges at home to sleep since the night had started to set upon the town. In the centre stood a large diorite stage and lectern, with stairs leading up to it. At the top, Asger strode towards the lectern, no longer in his armour, now dressed in rather formal attire, making ready to address those gathered.

Rising from their seat simultaneously, Zenith and Cathal made their exit from the inn. The market had filled up to the point that many of the side streets had become blocked, filling with those unable to filter towards the stage, still stood at the centre, Asger seemed to be scanning the crowd, signalling off to Zenith's left, a figure emerged onto the steps of the stage. It was Lemma with Brent in tow. Asger started to rescan the crowd, unable to see who he was searching for.

Zenith raised his arms high, clearly signalling his location. Asger, spotting him, passed orders down to the first row of people who parted, creating a domino effect of people stepping to the side until a path became accessible for Zenith to approach.

Zenith began to walk to the stage; many of the people started to bow their heads to him—those who didn't still held great mistrust in their eyes. Zenith greeted them all with a smile. Once on the steps, he took Lemma's hand and ascended to the side of Asger.

Asger shouted out over the gathered crowd, bringing them to attention. All gathered perked their ears and began to listen to their leader, who stood before them. "I have gathered you all here for one reason, I'm sure by now you have all heard that, Prince Zenith lives, he was not taken by the plague that took his father Prince Ake" chatter rose in the crowd, speculation rife among those that had yet to see Zenith, many of them still young, only children when Zenith had been thought dead.

Asger stamped his heavy foot, bringing back the attention to him. Continuing to speak, he beckoned Zenith forward, showing the sigil of Barathor to those gathered. All the soldiers still wore their armour, which now bore the sigil etched into the plate metal or leather. Asger began to explain how he knew Zenith was the prince and how he recognised the person he claimed to be, then formally introduced him. Regally, he spoke.

"My precious people, I give you Zenith, the true king of Errant. I have known him since birth, I stood guard over him as he slept, I became his aid as he learned of the world. I could not mistake him. He still carries his father's looks and eyes!" More people started to look accepting. *"He wears the sigil of Barathor V, his late grandfather, our greatest and most joyous king to date. I have questioned him about his lineage, and given my trust, knowing only facts that only the real prince of Errant could know."*

A shout flung out from within the crowd, a young woman questioning Asger. "Prove to us here and now that he speaks the truth?" Lemma stepped forward and spoke.

.   .   .

"People of Renton, I am Lemma, princess of Sciran, yes, I'm your country's sworn enemy, I still know not why? This man is Zenith of Errant. My mother, Queen Catherine, has known him since birth and recognises him just as your General does. If you need more proof, there is no more to offer, even if you believe him a fake, I know in my heart my husband tells no lies."

The woman who asked for proof spoke again. "So, Mayor, you bring us a prince of Sciran and proclaim him the true king of Errant, how can we trust him?"

Asger's rebuttal came straight away, loud and angered at this insolence from a woman of no standing. "If you continue to place trust in me, as you have all these years, then trust that I speak the truth, I have never led you wrong or brought you ill! Have I?"

The woman fell silent at his words; in her eyes, you could see concern yet an uninhibited trust in Asger that held against further speech. Zenith stepped forward, knowing he needed to speak, as his words stuttered and his tongue tied itself, he had never been a public figure. Once sure of himself and confident after a fleeting glance at those around on stage, all with reassuring eyes, showing an unbridled trust in him, A tremendous change came about him. His voice became loud and clear.

People of Renton, I am Zenith Ake Ocard
I am the son of Ake Barathor Ocard
Grandson of Barathor Valen Ocard
I am nothing but a farmer who has had royalty thrust
upon me

I was content with my lot farming in Grissam
Fate did not will this for me, and handed me the
Echidna flame, a weapon of Rysand
It showed me my true love, and my weapons kin
It made me a prince in a new country
Left me to lead an army and face evils you have never
seen
Now it places me at your feet
Asking that you all choose your own path
I am not a king, nor am I a peasant
I do not know who I am in my current state
All I can ask of you is that, as Sciran have
Is place your faith in me and trust that I speak the
truth
All I wish to do is restore the honour of my grandfathers
throne and remove a murderer and tyrant from it

A gasp spread across the crowd, somehow his words lifting and changing the spirits of all present. They all knew of Quinten's evils, but now they heard he was a murderer, this man who stood soul bared to them, only wished to lead them back to the light they had lost so many years ago. In that moment, a town and army fell to their knees swearing or reaffirming an oath pledging allegiance to Zenith.

26

SEPARATION ANXIETY

The sun rose quickly over Renton, pushing the morning gloom away. Everyone had assembled at the table, eating in glee as they downed water, meats and vegetables all grown by the hands of the town's folk. For some reason, this seemed to make them taste better; the flavours, rich and lasting, each bite needing to be savoured. The meat, melting with each bite, tasting fresh, a hint of earth in its flavour, unfettered, evoking notions of free-range animals that live with peace and glee.

Zenith tapped his goblet on the wooden table, gaining the group's attention. he needed to explain his plans to the rest of them. Cathal already knew what he was going to say; he sat in silence awaiting the other reactions. Both had hazarded an educated guess at how each would react on hearing the plan. Not fancying getting the brunt of Lemma's wrath, knowing the force of her slap, and not wanting to feel it again, Cathal had made sure Brent was between them.

There, they all listened intently as Zenith laid out his plan to them. "Friends, we must look to all three fronts; our current situation demands it. I must seek the Ayr rose on Mount Vallen, Cathal and Asger, I wish for you to stay and plan how we get in my hopes ten thousand plus men into Errant under my uncle's nose. That leaves you, Lemma, my love and Brent. Lemma..... I" ...... This was hard; he didn't want to leave Lemma's side, but he knew that he had to.

Lemma locked eyes with him, betrayal and sadness flowing forth, knowing that Zenith's following sentence would hurt deeply. *How could he?* She knew her husband wished for them to be parted. Fixing his gaze, speaking meekly, "Lemma, I need you to return to Sciran with Brent, and convey all that has happened to your mother, also to request her aid by sending as many Toxites and Bowmen as she can spare to aid us in the coming battles."

Gut-wrenched and twisted up, Lemma pounced up to her feet, slamming forcefully downward, hands slamming down on the table, seat flying backwards into the room wall.

"I will not leave your side!" Anger and frustration pierced the air, a proverbial arrow aimed straight at Zenith. Everyone else beat a hasty exit from the table, scarpering out of the nearest door. It certainly seemed breakfast was over. Sat stooping in his chair, receiving an onslaught of garbled and misspoken words and sentences, through Lemma's anger and tears. Calmly, he rose, moving around the table to her side, took her hand, and pulled her into his chest, whispering directly into her ear.

"I truly wish I could take you to Mount Vallen with me, but the Ayr Rose is all men. I feel that they will accept me more alone than if I were to arrive with even one other person. I love you and have not slept since I made my plans, knowing that I would hurt you."

Lemma's sobbing lessened, and spoken words began to make more sense. "I know, but it's too soon, I don't wish to part, but I know we must, I'm angrier at myself for my selfish desire than I am with our plan."

The two sat down at the table, Zenith cradling Lemma in his arms while she calmed herself, understanding and accepting what duties they all must attend to. Separate or apart, they worked together towards one goal. However, the nagging feeling that she would be lost without him plagued her. There was no way she could wait in Sciran for news of his return. Forcing an agreement with Zenith, a compromise that once Catherine had been informed, and arrangements made to send an army that they would return with its ranks to Renton, awaiting his safe return, she could also help with the plans to enter Errant.

The afternoon sun beamed down, flushing Renton with heat, with not a breath of wind, the friends gathered making ready to part ways. Lemma and Brent, along with Rath and the remaining Scirainian army, would head back to Sciran, speak with Catherine, and ensure that those still injured returned. When they did, Cathal and Asger had already made their first strides to setting up an intelligence network and war room in the town hall, and had already included a giant map of Apprite, showing two bridges crossing the gorge. The new bridge indicated on the map, constructed from wood and metal. Sturdy and well concealed from the naked eye. It had been designed to rise and lower on chains from the depths of the gorge.

Zenith had prepared a horse for himself, opting to wear no armour, just regular farming clothes. Not wishing to appear out of the ordinary. Lemma still held out that Zenith would change his mind, but knew in her heart he couldn't; *it will be a bittersweet goodbye*. As the time to depart came, Lemma grabbed hold and embraced Zenith, pulling them into a deep kiss that seemed to last forever, determined to mark her man for all to see. Zenith melted away in the kiss, wishing at that moment that he didn't need to travel alone. Around them in the crowds that gathered to wish them all well, wolf whistles and cheers from the adults. Fits of laughter and giggling from the children.

The two parted, leaving the embrace, both glowing red but smirking at each other. Brent piped up and joked to all gathered, "Absence will make the heart grow fonder, and his sword far stronger." The deviant look on his face certainly portrayed a different meaning to the adults around them, who erupted into fits of laughter, leaving all the children rather confused.

Cathal and Asger stood amongst the gathered crowd, waving Lemma off. The assembled army trailed behind, making their way to the tunnel pass and the road to Sciran, each knowing they had at best two at worst three days' travel ahead.

Zenith stood away from the others, contemplating his coming journey to Mount Vallen. All the expectations said that he would need to cross the desert, like salt flats. Needing to carry double the water, making sure to add extra skins to the already laden horse. Once there, he would have a day or so before the possibility of refilling the water skins. Watching intently, following Lemma with his deep claret eyes clouded with sadness as she rode off, carried on Raths' back, feeling his guts twisting inside.

Lemma made a fleeting glance back in Zenith's direction, locking forlorn hazel eyes with his, mouthing to him, "I love you," turning away, tears beginning to fall.

Zenith was next to make his departure following directions gained from Asger who directed him to head east following the base of the mountain range, he warned that the path was hard, tracking over rocky terrain, progress would be slow taking him several days to wind in and out of all the mountain valleys, before meeting the salt flats, that lead to the base of mount Vallen.

27
UPDATED TOPOGRAPHY

Zenith left Renton not long after Lemma had disappeared from his view, following the path Asger had set him on. A smell in the air, fresh hay, which reminded him of home, causing a daydream, *wondering how the farm was faring; neither he nor Merik were there to oversee the day-to-day running.* Fully trusting Merik's decision to leave the longest-serving hands in charge. The thought begged the Question. *If not for meeting Thaddeus, would they even be in the current situation?*

Pushing the negative thoughts away, focusing solely on all the positives. If he had never met Thaddeus, surely the meeting with Lemma would never have come to be, Cathal, or any of his new friends, for that matter; better than that, never could he have imagined having the most wonderful woman as his wife. Brought back to the present by the horse slowing and swaying as it walked, the path beneath its hooves had become jagged with rocks, points sticking out from the ground.

This horse was smart. It had slowed to almost a stop, head downturned, watching the ground, taking tentative steps, as it weaved its way through the treacherous path. Zenith was watching, intrigued; it was almost as if the horse knew every step like it had ridden this path a thousand times. A small, enchanting chuckle escaped his pursed lips, thinking, *It must be quite the sight to see, almost majestic and just as fascinating.*

No horse could have been trained for this; it was the horse's genius on display, thinking to himself, *I could train one to do it on flat ground?* Considering this, the horse would be an ideal gift to Catherine as a token of appreciation for all she had done.

The path smoothed out after a while, becoming a flat rock surface that led up the side of the mountain. Well-trodden, the rock was scraped and dented, with horseshoe marks and boot prints evident. This must have been the route Asger's army had taken to enter Sciran; no wonder Asger knew of the path. Soon, having climbed up higher than the peaks of several of the other hills in the mountain range. The view became beautiful, a serene and ambient sun casting shadows into the valleys, lighting the tops of the tall hills in amber rays. Clouds catching short and leaving dew to glisten on rich green pastures. Barren rocks thrusting upward defiant of their station, Zenith decided, *one day I'll bring Lemma, maybe even our children.*

As far as the eye could see to the south lay the grassland of the plains. In the far distance, he could just make out the outline of Sciran; it still shone brightly in the sun. Pondering how Lemma and her men fared. Dropping from his mount, pulling a large leather watering bag from his satchel, placing it around the horse's neck, filling it with water, letting the horse drink deeply. Placing the water skin to his lips, gulping the water down, not realising just how thirsty he and his horse had become.

Once the horse had finished with its water. Strapping away the watering bag behind the saddle, then jumping back onto the horse. Slowly at first, they moved off, the rock surface giving way to grass. They traversed a tiny path that carved across the side of the mountain. A plummet of a few hundred feet on their left should the horse even slightly misstep, heading towards the next peak, if memory served, they would cross three peaks, the first one being the highest and coldest, needing to pass it before nightfall. Asger had advised making camp in the next valley over, where a stream ran through it and plenty of critters lived, most of them edible, allowing him to save food for later when he couldn't catch dinner.

Pushing his horse hard they dropped down the side of the current mountain, sizing up the next, forcing the horse to hit the mountain side at a full gallop, hoping the initial burst of speed would carry them up before the horse tired, little did he know, no matter how hard the horse ran, that snow awaited him.

The cold hit like a hammer, freezing him to the very core. The sudden thought smashed into the side of his head. "I left without clothes for these temperatures. Damit, Asger, you mud munching wheat sack, you could have warned me!" Reaching behind, quickly rifling through the satchel bag, pulling the watering sack from it. It was the only large, fabric item available. Using it meant the horse would likely be unable to pass the salt flats. Left with no other choice but to use it. He would need to walk carrying as much water as possible, pulling a knife from his belt, slicing a hole big enough to put his head through in the bottom of the sack.

Pulling the sack over his head, he stabbed holes from the inside to push his arms through. The sack's handles hung at his waist. He cut them loose and tied them together to form a belt. The difference was noticeable straight away, as he felt heat throughout his body.

Slowly he made his way further up the side of the mountain criss-crossing as his did so that the horse could climb easier, a trail appeared in the snow, an animal track, flat enough for the horse to walk on, seemingly heading around the mountain, maybe even aiding making it to the other side, it would be dark soon but at least he could get down the other side into the valley below.

Darkness slowly descended, making his path all the harder to navigate. Slowed down to a pace barely that of a walk, the horse testing every step it wanted to make before moving forward. Some steps were not as sturdy as they could be, the horse dropping down into the snow and shocking itself several times, almost throwing Zenith from its back.

Still, he had to pass here, not wanting to make camp on the side of this mountain. There is no chance of setting a fire if he did, the snow melting would most likely smother it, so he and the horse would likely freeze to death. The only thing keeping them warm was his makeshift top and the horse's resolve to keep moving forward.

Darkness had truly set in as the snow gave way to patches of lush green grass and sporadic jagged rocks; they could finally descend into the valley. The babbling sounds of a stream whispered in the air; nothing else made a sound. It was well into the twelfth hour of the night, and not one animal stirred. Following the sound of the stream, they carefully navigated through the rocks. Finally entering into a lush green Valley, Zenith dismounted. Getting down from his saddle, letting his horse stand at the stream edge to drink and feast on the grass about them. A quick search provided plenty of tinder and kindling to get a fire going. Zenith looked to the clear starry night sky. "I won't need a tent tonight, just the fire."

Sat By the campfire, Zenith's mind drifted back to the Gorge and the time he stood watching the Weapons dance in the sky, when the map fell from the portal they formed. He stretched his arm back, reaching for his backpack, and pulled the Old Parchment from within. Under the light of the Fire, he studied the map. *I can see where I am. I'll need-* his thoughts were interrupted by markings on the map. "There are other trails, Asger didn't mention them, maybe he didn't know. Where do they lead?" Zenith followed them over the parchment with his fingers.

One of the trails seemed to lead from the valley where he made camp. The trail wound its way through the Valley, then skirted the base of the mountain range. Zenith took note of some strange markings along the route. *There are some figures. Monsters?* Zenith couldn't describe what made the path seem ominous, but he certainly felt it. If this part of the map were correct, it would cut his journey time down by at least a day. To the side of the pictures, References and notes saying Slaine and Gone, with arrows pointing to the drawings. Zenith wondered, *Does this indicate that the path is safe to travel. It must be; otherwise, why would someone make the notes?*

Something else hung in the air around Zenith, a strange feeling or perception, nagging at the back of his head, making his thoughts overzealous and mixed. *What is this feeling? It's hitting me on all sides. The brook, I can make out each little ripple on its surface, the swish of- Was that a fish? Oh god, the smells there are ripe, even the dewy smell of the grass. It's so pungent; it's as if all the scents are fighting for my attention, making me more aware of them.* A pause in his thought, whipping around, watching his horse eat the grass at its feet, still, the thoughts whirled about. "Gah, what is this place? Mullocks dung, I haven't named you; I'd better name you. You look like a Drake, what do you think, Drake?" A soothing, nayed, hum of acceptance came over to him, pulling Zenith back to silent contemplation. *God! Even the horses are hypno-tising; there's so much going on, my head hurts, yet why do I feel calmer? I feel like I can see for the first time.* Zenith needed to verbalise it, express the magical feeling. *Drake, I see each blade of grass moving in the wind, the ripples and waves of the current in the brook, the Rising and falling of your chest, I hear the slowed, concentrated breaths from your lungs.* No idea why he did, but Zenith asked Drake, "Is it magic, Drake? Is this place holy, possibly linked with Rysand? It's so serene and pleasant here." Drake just looked at him, snorted and continued munching on the grass.

Checking back to the map, the paper looked different, illuminated in the dark, as changes began to take place. Apprehension pierced Zenith's lips "Drake? What's the map doing? Any ideas?" The Old cities were removed, and the new ones replaced them. The Gorge emerged from the previously flat plains, and the image deepened, revealing depth and height through new lines and routes that formed beneath the gorge. Looking over at Drake, "Yes, I know I'm talking to a horse, Drake, but you're my only company." The new lines included passageways and tunnels, as well as new trails previously unseen. Zenith pupils grew wide-eyed, dancing, watching the magic transform the parchment. "Err, what on Apprite is happening? Is it aiding me? Drake, what do you think, buddy?" No reply came. "Of course you've no opinion, you're a horse, I'm talking to a horse, erm." Dropping silent, paying attention to the newer detail appearing before him.

The map illuminated the route he must follow to gain access to the Ayr rose. An in-depth look at the map revealed one tunnel that seemed to start somewhere in the mountains, then pass under the Gorge, crossing its width, and continuing to move underground, emerging at the far side of the Errant. It also appeared to be large enough for an army to march throughout. Making a mental note, "We can use that, somehow."

Zenith, even in his heightened state, had become relaxed, beginning to drift off to sleep. His dreams betrayed him, visions of the Black City, the jade glow from the centre growing, summoning him. He wasn't a part of it; all of him was there, but not solid, just floating, a whisper on the wind, witnessing it happen.

Pulled and dragged forward towards the glowing Jade light around him, above him, the silhouette of Synergy, soaring high over the Black City, sweeping in, diving, casting vortexes of flames in what seemed to be an ancient Battleground. As he watched, he could see three warriors.

The Warriors stood there, all holding one of the Rysander Weapons; they seemed to be fighting in unison against an unknown enemy. None of them were clear, just shadows in the form of people.

Suddenly woken by the sound of breaking branches cracking on the ground, springing to his feet, the sun hadn't even risen yet, he tried his best to see what the dark held. Fortunately, it was just a night hare. "Well, at least I can catch some breakfast."

Pouncing fast, he caught the hare unaware while it drank from the brook, grabbing its hind leg. The hare struggled, scared for its life, justly so. Zenith reached back to his belt, pulling his dagger free. Swiftly, he plunged it deeply into the rear of the hare's neck, severing its spinal cord and jugular in one, granting it a quick death. Moving back to his fire, Zenith started to skin the hare, pulling its innards out, covering his hands in the creature's blood. Soon, the meat was cut from the bone, skewered and placed over the fire on a makeshift spit. By morning's light, he would of eaten, refilled the water skins, and readied Drake to move on.

Giving him time to think about his dreams. "It's not the first dream I've had like that. I keep seeing it. It's not familiar yet somehow feels like I was there, or at least some part of me was. Synergy is always somewhere in the Black city. Are they linked? Hopefully, those answers will become clear in time. Hopefully."

The map had given him a quicker route to follow, guided by the stream up the valley. Coming to a small lake that was fed by several small springs, from the map's directions, knowing that he needed to climb the hill behind the lake. Once ascended, it looked like there was a natural land bridge that linked with the mountain before the salt flats; this route saved him a day of climbing and descending several hills to reach the same point.

The fact that he could arrive ahead of time lit his heart aflame. "I can get back to Lemma faster, maybe even before she arrives in Renton, so that I can surprise her." The midday sun was high in the sky, and the land bridge was in view. Looking at it, it seemed to stretch from where he stood to past the horizon, weaving around the next mountain and then passing out of sight, hidden.

"One final push up this mountain, Drake, and we can rest," Zenith said to encourage Drake. The plateau coming into view, the land becoming flatter, several rocky outcrops, shaped like giant bowls, popping up all around them, Zenith couldn't help but think. "Perfect natural watering troughs. This will make life easier." Pouring water into the largest of the several natural bowls, showing Drake to it and letting him drink, joking about. "Hey, I led a horse to water, and it chose to drink." The silence and absence of laughter deafened Zenith. "What a waste that was, the perfect joke as well."

28

CAGED AND ALONE

Having passed through the tunnel and descended back down the mountain, Lemma and the consortium of men faced the trek over the Scirainian plains to home. Brent had urged her to let them camp roughly halfway back.

Moving the same pace as the men surrounding her, Lemma sat high over them aboard Rath, contemplating Zenith's journey to the Ayr rose. "Does he stand a chance of recruiting a two-thousand-strong army? They are monks sworn to his very protection, those who had guarded the Echidna flame. So, they should, shouldn't they?" Speaking without realising, "Rath, you agree, don't you?" Rath cocked her head, looking at her as if to say, "Agree with what?"

Lemma continued to think. *How is he doing? The path, as Asger described it, was rough and long, forcing the army to slow down and take extra time as they walked it. Zenith walks it alone. Is he safe? Does he fare well?* Her Mind was a whirling storm of concern and thought, needing to refocus on the task before her.

Ahead of them, the plains opened vast clear skies, grass-lands up to the horizon. The boredom was creeping in on all who walked. Even conversations fell silent as the heat of the day almost became too much to bear. The sound of water splashing caught the attention of Lemma. "What on Apprite was that?" The men had begun pouring water over themselves, attempting to cool down.

Evident that the heat was unusually high, as their actions showed them getting worn down. Some had even fainted and needed to be carried by others, causing their pace to slow further. Lemma spoke with Brent, "We need to rest, let the men recuperate, but there isn't shade anywhere to protect them." Brent, feeling a little bit cocky, wanted to show he could be as creative as Asger. "Your Highness, I see something you may not. Look at what we carry." Lemma didn't have a clue what he was on about. "Make sense, Brent, please," Brent quickly said with a massive grin.

"Your Majesty, look at what and who you ride on, we need shade, make Rath spread her wings, many men can fit there." Lemma got a disgruntled look on her face, thinking. "Not a bad idea, why didn't?" Her thought was cut off by Rath's sudden halt and turn, looking directly at Brent and smashing her beak into the floor at his feet, sending dirt and grass flying in all directions. Rath's face was a picture of anger and malice. Lemma, caught off guard, couldn't help but laugh while speaking. "Brent, I have a feeling I don't quite know why, but Rath doesn't like that idea." Brent stood pale-faced, scared to within an inch of the benevolence, stuttering "I.. I.. I'm... Sor...Sorry... Ra...Rath." Lemma looked down at him "I hope you are. Any other ideas?" Brent replied slowly, still hesitant to anger Rath further. "I do. Using Rath was a joke."

Directing Lemma's gaze, he described what was in his mind. "Take note of the many pikes, most of the carts had been covered with hessian sheets, perhaps we could use them, form some awnings large enough to shade many of the men, those that it doesn't could cycle in as necessary, whilst others moved out, in this way we could potentially keep moving forward."

Hearing Brent explaining his idea, Lemma agreed that it was possible. "Ok, Brent, I'll give you that one, that's actually very smart, issue the order." The men all worked together to fashion the awnings. Soon enough, most of the men could now walk in the shade, which came as a great relief, cooling them down, in turn, boosting their foot speed.

The passing of the midday heat couldn't have come soon enough as a strong cooling wind blew across them, and a huge sigh broke the silence. Unfortunately, the wind also lifted the awnings out of the men's hands, sending them aloft, flying like a kite without a string. Those who could grab reached out to catch them. The awnings hadn't finished their aerial dance, those who grabbed on to them lifted upwards. Men and pikes dangling in mid-air, acting as counterweights. Their ankles caught before they could float ever higher, pulling the sheets back to the ground. Whilst others ran after the men who took a higher flight, eventually cushioning them as they crashed to the ground. Lemma placed her hand to her forehead whilst he laughed at the spectacle. "Maybe next time we cut lines in the fabric so wind can pass through." From the corner of his eye, Brent caught sight of Lemma. *Did she... place her hand on her forehead and shake it at me? Surely not.*

Once the sun began to show its evening colours, Lemma decided that making camp would be a promising idea. Casting Orders to Brent, making him responsible for the camp's erection. Without hesitation, the men gathered wood where they could, set fires, and formed the watch. Brent placed Lemmas' tent at the centre of the ring, posting a personal guard at its doorway—Rath Lay at the rear, where no guard stood keeping her ever-sleepful watch.

Commanders made sure all had eaten, watching as most took to their tents, sleeping soundly, allowing themselves to follow suit; those on guard stood rigid, watching from their vantage point. In her tent, Lemma tossed and turned, sleep evading her; something ominous was growing. She could sense it; the star also shone silver, lighting up the whole tent.

Her mind would not close off finally thinking. "Maybe a nighttime stroll will help." Leaving the tent, her guard stood bolt upright. Lemma scowled, thinking. "When will they learn? This was unnecessary?" Lemma walked to the edge of the camp, with two guards following close behind.

The star began to pulse at her side, sensing evil near, its silver hue intensifying. She walked out into the darkness of the plains. A rumble came on the air from the distance, with each step it gained volume, and its tone changed, sounding more like several different rumbles and growls—guttural roars leaving fear in the guards' hearts.

Unhitching the star from her waist, she carried it. A heavy presence close. The star casting it's light showing a distance all around. Nothing currently made itself known or was within her vision; "I know it's there, just out of sight, hiding in this abyssal dark that surrounds me." Muttered under her breath.

Bloodied, garbled screams filled the air behind. Spinning, catching a glimpse of several creatures, one of which had just bitten clean through the throats of her guards, faces stricken with fear reflecting their sudden violent demise, leaving her alone. Lemma's eyes must have deceived her. Only a second free to think. "What on Apprite their bodies! The darkness swallowed them up; their screams, I didn't even hear them." The next second, the creature was behind her again. The others to her left and right, surrounding her just outside the influence of the star's light, thinking, "I saw at least three."

All of a sudden, she noticed it. "The Camp, where is it, the fires, torches, why can't we see them?" The Darkness swallowed it all, blocking her vision beyond its abyssal edge. An Abrupt thought hit her like a bolt from the blue. "Gods! The darkness has me caged, alone. The camp will be of no aid." On four legs, they ran, their skin blistered, dripping with viscous black liquid, no face to speak of, just a giant jaw full of jagged, gleaming white teeth, bodies heavy-set, muscular, and agile. The creatures circled, growling and snarling, only just hearable.

The first creature launched at her into the light; its skin beginning to burn and spit as it did. Lemma clasped the star in her right hand, pointing one of the Kuni blades to the front. As the creature gained ground, its pain filled the air, the light burning its skin. Grotesque roars pierced the silent veil of night as it jumped high into the air, clearing Lemma's height. It came at her from above, raising the star over her head, thrusting it into the chest of the disfigured hound, pushed forcefully, falling backwards, throwing her legs into the creature's stomach, trying with every ounce of strength in her, launching the beast. Its bones crunching as it hit the ground, the star spitting lightning as it was pulled free, scaring the earth as it penetrated through the creature's torso, its face appearing briefly happy at its death. For but a fleeting moment, Lemma thought she saw the flames of the campsite.

Circling round, seeing that the two remaining hounds had joined with another giant creature. It resembled the Slither that had been dispatched in Rockwall, but this time its face seemed more human, less twisted, yet just as evil. The star pulled at Lemma's arm as if begging to fly. "Ok, I get it!"

Lemma shouted, "You want to attack." She changed her stance, clasping the star, ready to throw it.

Releasing the star, an overhead throw had it carving a straight line in the air, as it approached the creatures, the humanoid one grunted. Lemma heard this while watching the hound's actions. *Did it just order one of the hounds to attack?* she thought, soon getting her answer in the hound's next action. The hound launched into the air, straight for the star, no regard for its life. The star sliced the air under the creature, carving into its chest, sending blood and tissue spewing over the ground below a gaping hole cut through its stomach, intestines hanging out, dragging behind it. The bolt of lightning just missed and burned the creature's hindquarters. Without pause, the star continued its flight, instantly turning on its axis, and arched around the heads of the two beasts, missing them.

The star reacted, a sudden vibration in its movements violently arching back on course for the creature that now rushed across the ground at Lemma. Watching the beast closely, preparing for its assault, she pulled a dagger from her boot top. At the same time, the star dived down towards the ground at the last moment, switching to a horizontal movement. Zipping inches from the floor, it cut through the hounds' legs like a buzz saw, halting its advance, leaving it motionless. This time, the lightning didn't miss, as it struck the body of the hound, causing it to explode into black miasma, a mist of blood and fibre raining down all around the scene of battle. Its spirit hanging in the air, peace on its face, and it floated up into a white light. Again, a fleeting vision of flames through darkness, brighter, clearer than before.

Lemma caught the star in her left hand and made ready for the next assault. But forgetting to guard herself whilst she thought. "Each time a hound dies, the veil weakens, I have a

way out or for aid to reach me. I will keep fighting, I will win."
Not having seen the humanoid creature order the remaining
hound to her flank, it crept slowly, sticking just outside the
dark border where the stars' light couldn't reach. The star
sensed it and yanked hard to turn Lemma around to face it.
Clasped her fist around the centre of the star, splaying its five
points out horizontally below her hand, stood ready, swooping
low, drawing the star in a curve left to right as it connected
with the creature, severing its lower jaw clean from its body.

Reeling back the creature, took to a run, making for her
now exposed rear. Lemma curled round as it jumped at her,
dropping to her knees. The hound sailed overhead, landing
away from her. Seeing her chance, she threw the star, which
cut into the upper jaw of the beast, burying deep into its body,
bursting free out of its back as the heavens struck this hound
dead, freeing its spirit. The light of the camp was more visible,
this time, almost entirely visible. Staying longer, in view,
before it faded back to black. Lemma saw it. Her mind.
Whirled, knowing nearly all of the answer. "Ok, that has the
cage weekend, now how do I break it completely?"

All that remained was the giant human-like creature, its
movements slow and cumbersome. Lemma Thinking there
was time to prepare, an unbecoming burst of speed; had it
upon her fast, its Thick bulbous handless arms descended,
aiming to crush her. The star still circling back flipped onto its
vertical axis, cutting up from the ground, and passed effortlessly through the creature's right stump.

Stunned, the creature flared in agony. Black viscous blood,
raining down from the wound, gave Lemma an opening.
Plunging her small dagger into the creature's shin as she rolled
away, catching the star in her right hand as she rushed to her
feet. Behind it, Lemma saw the answer she needed, its shadow
connected to the darkness. Before she could react, the beast

was on her again, sending her several feet backwards, with a heavy swing from its only remaining arm.

Stars buzzing circling her head in a daze, she tried to regain her footing, but the creature was there again, a giant hammer blow coming at her from above, managing to roll in close to the beast, pulling the dagger from its shin, black blood spurting from the wound, in the same smooth motion, Thrusting upwards, plunging the dagger with every ounce of strength left in her body, up to the handle into the creature's groin. Through its legs she rolled, to its rear flank, digging the blades of the Star into the ground, scarring it, ripping the shadow apart, disconnecting them from the beast.

Falling backwards and toppling over. The creature let out a blood-curdling scream, black blood bursting from its groin like a fountain. Lemma rushed to her feet, pouncing on the beast, plunging the star deep into its left shoulder, smashing bone and ripping muscle as the two-bladed ether side the frontal blade carved into the tendons, rolling forward past the creature's head just before the lightning hit, completely removing the left arm at the shoulder joint. Still dazed, she managed to stand, turning back to the creature. Already running at her, a crazed rage had taken hold of it.

Its remaining stump outstretched, it intended to ram her. From nowhere, an arrow pierced its throat, halting its advance. Lemma stood stunned, looking on, seeing the camp in full, the darkness gone. The screams had woken the slumbering camp. Brent had grabbed the nearest weapon and run to her aid. Fortunately, his arrow had arrived at the right time. Lemma pulled as far back as she could, throwing the star hard in a straight line at the creature. The star buzz sawed its way from the front and out of the beast's back. Its action, more acute than before, pivoting nearly ninety degrees, flying up above the creature's head, stalling at the pinnacle of its flight, each point becoming merged with the lightning.

Its speed doubled as it sped back to earth, entering at the head of the beast and carving it in two as it passed out of the base of its torso, then returning to Lemma's hand as the creature's body split. The two halves falling to the ground in opposite directions, lightning striking and eviscerating the body entirely, leaving nothing but glowing red molten earth.

The creature's spirit, that of a man, older in years, hunched over, floated above the ground, guilt-ridden and remorseful for their actions, clear to see as it floated up into a white light, free to rest with Rysand.

Collapsing to the ground, grasping for breath, energy sapped entirely. Lemma lay there motionless, just staring up into the night sky, now cleared of evil and light, the stars shining bright. Brent, running to her aid, scooping her up in his arms, carrying Lemma back to camp, her body limp. Cursing silently. *For my sake, don't tell Prince Zenith I need my Wheat sacks attached. Thank you very much!*

Brent set Lemma on her bed; she had fallen asleep in his arms. Exiting the tent, closing the door flaps behind him, his own emotions high, ever climbing. He had never witnessed a Rysand general fight; now wishing he hadn't, but he was surely glad that they fought on the same side as him.

29
GRASS TO SALT

Drake had drunk nearly all of a day's water allowance; in truth, Zenith had drunk that much as well. The water from the valley tasted amazing. Something in its taste was magical and special, making him stronger and more perceptive. Looking at Drake, the water had done the same to him, watching him jump about like a pony, playing in the field.

Whinnying and snorting with glee, Drake danced about, waiting to move on. Zenith, barely in the saddle before Drake took off, galloping full speed onto the land bridge, moving faster than he had at any point until now. Before Zenith could blink, the campsite was gone. The horizon didn't stay still, ever changing. "By Rysand, Drake, what's gotten into you? You're almost flying."

The first of the three mountains the bridge skirted passed by before a single hour had gone by, Drake showed no sign of slowing anytime soon. Ahead of them, the next section of the bridge. Zenith spotted the steady incline in the path. "Hey Drake, it's uphill, recon that will slow you down?" The rise in their altitude seemed to depress their speed slightly. "Drake, good job you didn't let it get to you, did ya boy, I can tell you're breathing a little easier. I am as well less wind hitting me in the face, thanks." Mid-afternoon had arrived, and the sun had begun its descent behind the horizon, taking with it slowly the heat and light of day.

"Hey, Drake, looks like the path level's out ahead, we'll take the opportunity to stop. Time to rest and maybe be a little less vigorous."

Drake pulled to a stop on the plateau, a slight pant in his breath. "Looks like I was right, ay Drake, you needed the rest. Give me a second, I'll make a bowl somehow for you to drink from."

Resting with his back against the mountain face, while Drake drank from the crude bowl fashioned from the water sack. Zenith reached into his pack, retrieving the map, tracing the route they had followed with his finger, finding his location easy enough. Working out that the distance he had travelled already, thinking to himself, "that's the better part of a day's travel, I'd say I've got about a quarter of a day's ride till I hit the salt flats." Hearing a scuffing sound coming from Drake's direction. Zenith looked up. "What do you reckon, Drake, make the next camp by early morning? Then we can make for Mount Valen once the sun's up."

Hopping back into the saddle, still Drake ran at an astonishing speed, rounding the side of the mountain, the side of the next mountain came into view, the final amber rays of the sun hitting its side, lighting the polished granite outcrops and pedestals a brilliant amber tone. The grass, green and lush, held a burning hue as it swayed in the wind, imitating a wildfire; the whole mountainside looked as though it were in full flame, magnificent to see.

Driving drake on full pace, thrashing through the grass as

the sun's amber light fades from view. The bright light of the moon brought life to the path again in a silvery retinue of sparkles, dancing about all Zenith could see. The Landbridge dropped from view just ahead of them. "That looks a steep drop, Drake, take it slow, will you?" A quick snort told Zenith Drake had heard him.

The lush green hue of the grass gave way to the brilliant white of salt; Zenith winched the moonlight bouncing up almost enough to blind him. Zenith leaned forward in his saddle, patting Drake on the side of the head, speaking to him, "Drake, we did it, boy, we made brilliant time, well done." Forcing Drake to stop before he overshot the edge of the grass and dived headlong into the salt flat, Zenith hopped from the saddle. "Perfect place to camp, hey boy, you agree?" Drake looked like he nodded in agreement.

Overhead, Zenith heard the sound of squalls and flapping wings as bats took flight from a cave somewhere behind and far above him.

"That sounds like dinner, and it's coming to me for once." Zenith, though, while fashioning a makeshift shelter from his belongings, then gathering dried grasses and the sparse wood available to him. With a single strike of his flint, the fire flared to life, filling the darkness all about with light. Searching one bag, pulling a dry loaf from it, a meagre meal, drinking some stale, tasteless water from one of the skins he had first started with back in Renton, shaking his head, "I wish I'd exchanged this old water for the water back in the valley."

Drake stood close by, munching on the grass, pulling a strange, contorted and oddly amusing face now and then as he got a mouthful of salt. Zenith sat by the fire using its light to see and utilise random items from his pack to fashion a small net. Watching the air above him, whilst remaining still, holding in his breath as several of the bats came into his sight.

Throwing the net up in the air, aiming for just ahead of the bats, the attempt went unfilled, missing them by mere inches.

Steadying and calming himself, he remained motionless, waiting again. This time, a larger group of bats was returning to the cave. They pushed into his eyeline, his net set to soar. Success it clustered around several bats, bringing them to the ground. Quickly to end their suffering, Zenith broke each one's neck in turn. Returning to his seat by the fire, he pushed a sharpened stick through each bat. Crudely fashioned skewers, placed to cook over the open fire, and soon they made a small, nutritious meal, accompanied by the dry bread.

Stomach full, Zenith lay back and settled down to sleep, the sounds of nature all around created a natural lullaby that pulled his consciousness quickly to the point where it shut off, sleep taking over. Throughout his mind, the mountain that looked on fire from the day's journey, circling above its pinnacle, a silhouette of Synergy, feet ablaze. Instantly, his mind shifted, scenes being relived from the journey to this point. All of them smudging into one mass of vibrant colours and a cacophony of sounds, mangled words, and the tears others had shed.

Come morning, he woke delirious and confused. *Is my mind playing tricks on me? I still don't know if Synergy is real or if it's the sword's powers manifesting.* Zenith had finally given in to the thought that Synergy was his mind's way of coping with the powers of the Echidna Flame, but it still nagged at him. The many images of Synergy in his mind, combined with those he saw in Rockwall, sparked a grain of truth that Synergy was real.

The embers of the fire glowed a dim red, almost extinguished, Drake standing to one side, just staring at Zenith scuffing his front hoof on the ground, kicking up dust as if to say get a move on. "Alright already, I can take a hint. Let me get sorted" Pulling himself to a seated position, packing his belongings away, and making ready for a long, arduous day riding across the salt flats.

Taking the reins in hand, beginning the day by walking, leading Drake, after checking the map. Zenith determined the best route to Mount Vallen was heading almost due north. Not wanting to tire Drake quickly, feeling like the extra strength had left him, and guessing Drake would be the same. Forward they walked, white no matter which way Zenith looked; luckily, the sun hadn't risen too high yet, and the salt wasn't reflecting it too harshly, leaving them with the ability to see ahead unencumbered.

Mile after mile dragged on and on as the morning sun rose, its heat becoming greater with each passing hour. The horizon, still filled with white, stretched far ahead of them. Even further behind, the mountain range had faded from view. Moving forward was all Zenith had left.

Body aching and flagging skin burning to the touch, reddening with each passing moment in the midday sun, heat piercing to his very core. Sweat poured from his brow, exhaustion setting in. Pulling himself almost lifeless up onto Drake's back, Drake continued moving forward, trudging slowly on. The horizon finally broke after many slowly won miles. Drake starting to stumble and groan with each new step. Finally, Mount Vallen pierced the vale, standing tall, defying the skyline, creating a break in the horizon.

Zenith renewed in resolve, pushed forward. Striking the hindquarters of Drake, forcing Drake into a canter. Drake's energy was already drained, but somehow Drake managed to boost his speed, aiming at Mount Vallen, as he ran onward with abandon.

Mount Vallen kept growing, overtaking the horizon as they approached. The enormity of the mountain came more and more into view; its peak obscured by clouds as if it pierced the very heavens themselves. As the advance brought him closer, features began to take shape. Mount Vallen stood there defiant, its rock faces hard and unforgiving. Watching as the ground below him, slowly becoming sporadic with brush and thorns of grass.

The salt flats were nearly at an end; salt had begun to fade into rock, rock into grass. The familiar sound of water pouring from somewhere, filled with a thunderous deluge of splashes as it crashed down somewhere hidden from view within the ever-enlarging natural rock monoliths.

The ground under Drake had given way entirely to grass again. Zenith dismounted, looking around for any sign of a path to ascend the mountain. Feeling a need to make the Ayr Rose before night fell. Searching the map, finding a general direction, heading towards the sound of the waterfall. There, finding a place to stow Drake. Under a rocky shelf overhanging a patch of grass next to the waterfall basin.

Once securely tied, Drake moved to the water's edge, drinking, with enough room to eat the grass at leisure, plenty of space to sleep, a perfect stabling area. The rocky outcrop above provides the ideal protection from any weather.

Zenith looked at the map, which showed the ascent to be hidden from view, obscured by the waterfall itself. "You would never know it was there without prior knowledge or a map to guide you." Drake just ignored him and carried on drinking.

Able to navigate a way around the basin, plunging head-first through the waterfall, its waters soaking him, refreshing dried-out skin and breathing a new lease of energy into his aching limbs. The water caused his clothes to tighten around his body, restricting his movements whilst showing each muscle's flex. There, behind the waterfall, a staircase, carved into the rock, buried its way upward, the light of the sun showing its exit several feet above.

Starting his climb up the steps, each one just as slippery as the last, Zenith dropped to his hands and knees, gaining extra grip, pushing his way up one soggy knee at a time, leather trousers squealing with each movement, bursting out of the rocks that surrounded the exit into the baking sun. Steam rising from every millimetre of clothing almost blinding him with a smoke screen of mist. Zenith spotted A healthy, well-trodden path ahead of him, enclosed on both sides by sandy boulders and rocky monoliths alike. A quick check over his shoulder, looking below him, to the basin of the waterfall, and where he had left Drake. Happily chewing on the rich green grass. Muttering to the air, "No wonder the Ayr rose had managed to stay hidden from the rest of Apprite."

Trudging up the path, each step took more strength. The leather of his trousers tightened around his leg, squeezing tighter and stiffening his leg muscles, making them cramp, causing each step to be more painful than the last. Zenith's thoughts on the pain in his lower extremities: "I swear these trousers are tighter than when they were new, they need to stretch, only going to do that by moving. The pain is making it hard to think."

Night had finally fallen; the leather on his legs had finally loosened so that walking was easy again, his inner voice moaning at him. "Maybe next time take the dam trousers off, there's no one about to see anyway."

The moon's light didn't do much to light his path, nothing but blackened earth and rock, no idea which way to head— forced him to stop. "I give up, I'm exhausted, it can wait till morning now," he rested against one of the monoliths that lined the path, just thinking to himself. Examining the surroundings, a flicker of red flame caught his eye. "What's that? A torch? I'll be a mud muncher's uncle, it is. That's got to be the Ayr rose, it's not too much further up the mountain. I can do this, Zenith, get it together, move." Gritting his teeth, legs in pain, pushing hard back against the monolith, forcing his back upward against the rock to steady himself, using almost all his waning strength to get purchase underfoot. Planning how he would get to the Ayr Rose as he did, "If I use the torch as a guide, and keep my arms in front, I should be able to avoid most of the rocks, I hope so anyway."

Bumping into the rocks, grazing knees and elbows, managing to move upwards, cursing to himself each time. "Ouch god dam Mullocks dung that hurt." Still guiding himself with his hands. Not only happy at the pain, but still he thought. *Progress is slow, but at least I make ground.* Roughly an hour passed before the torch's light grew stronger, revealing a sandy-coloured stone wall that stood at least thirty feet high.

The imposing wall halted his advance. A voice, "Who goes there?" resonating and echoing on the rocks, threw Zenith's judgment off, scaring him, *Did that wall just speak? Don't be so stupid, Zenith, it's got to be a person, but I can't see them, let alone locate them, a person all the same. Walls don't speak!*

A quick shake of the head to reassure his common sense would prevail, and he shouted his reply, "I'm here seeking the Ayr rose." Zenith's reply bounced off the rocks, making it sound like there were ten of him standing all over the side of Mount Vallen.

No reply came from above him. Zenith called again, "I am the keeper of the Echidna flame, I come here at Thaddeus's bequest." No sooner had he spoken Thaddeus's name than the earth beneath him began to shake. A massive section of the wall started to move, opening wide. Through the opening, he thought he could see buildings lit with torches. *Is that a church built into the very mountain? It looks like it has arms stretching out, holding on to the rock face.*

. . .

The giant stone door stopped moving, fully open, several monks rushed through it, brandishing their bow staffs. Heading straight for Zenith, their intentions were clear: they were going to attack. Zenith shook his head in dismay *Why on Apprite would they want to fight me? I already said who I am. I don't need this, even with the Echidna flame. I'm just too tired. Wheat sacks, looks like I have no choice!*

Drawing the Echidna flame from his waist, he made his best attempt to be ready for battle. Disillusioned, not wanting to fight, they were human, devout followers of Rysand, and the Echidna flame. They left him no choice but to fight as the first monk struck a mighty blow, his sword raised just in time to deflect, but still heavy enough to send him, in his weakened state, scuttling backwards.

In came another blow and a second monk striking as well, This time Zenith parried the first blow setting the monk of balance, leaving him open to have his leg swept from under him, The second monks blow glancing off the sword and connecting with his ribs, A loud crack echoed all around, a searing pain coursing through his body "AHHH that's at least two or three ribs broke, you absolute Dung eater."

Zenith in agony began to fight harder, parrying blows, landing punches, not once striking with the Echidna flames blade, all the time thinking. *They may injure me, but I will not seriously harm them. These mud munchers don't know who they are attacking. They are just defending their home.* A fleeting glance from a bow staff carved into his brow, scratching deep, his blood began to seep from the wound, only a small cut formed, but it was enough.

His mind blanked, his conscious mind falling into darkness, his unconsciousness linked with the Echidna flame. Bursting from the sword's tip, flames shot, winding and twirling through the gaps between each of the monks, not touching them, just dividing them apart. Each of the monks stood frozen, stunned to silence, mesmerised, as the sword's flames danced around them, protecting Zenith.

Dropping their bow staffs to the floor, they quickly followed, dropping to their knees. The monks' assault stopped as the last monk dipped his head; the flame subsided, retreating into the Echidna flame. Zenith's Consciousness woke, leaving him looking on, questioning. "What did I miss now? What happened? These monks, who had attacked me a moment ago, now bowed to me. I wish this would stop happening."

Shouts and hollers echoed above him, "The General is here, fetch an elder, Thaddeus was right." As the shout moved further away, being echoed by voice after voice from atop the wall. From behind the rock door, a young man in a full robe limped slowly, leaning on a cane, his face bruised and bulbous, cheeks swollen, eyes almost shut, with the injuries around them, one leg looking nearly hobbled.

The disfigured monk made his way with his hobbled leg dragging behind him as he limped. Waiting in place, Zenith looked at the man, confusion crossing his face, "Why do I meet so many people that I know yet can't quite remember names or faces? I must remember Lemma's name; I don't need that issue." The man raised his hand to wave, but it just looked like he waved a wooden club, no clear fingers, just a mass of black swelling.

Finally, the monk was close enough to see who it was. Zenith exclaimed. "By Rysand, what on Apprite happened?" Stood looking at a hideous, disfigured version of Thaddeus hidden under a red hood that draped over the bulk of his battered face, the thought raced. "Had his brethren done it to him?" "Zenith, I'm glad to see you, you look very well," whispered in a low rasp, the swelling placing pressure on his vocals.

Placing his hand on Thaddeus's shoulder, he looked at his acquaintance. Guilt flooded his heart. *Had this happened because of me, because Thaddeus had bought me the Echidna flame? I already knew that Thaddeus took the sword, leaving a great shadow in his wake, his brothers believing him to be a murderer and a liar.*

The hollers continued to echo across the stone courtyard, announcing the emergence from the large stone door. A monk, much more ornately dressed in golden robes. Zenith figured. *That's got to be an elder. Something's wrong with his face. His eyes they're full of rage.*

As he approached, the elder's face had already begun to warp, grimacing and scowling, his body bulging and dipping in areas of his robes, tearing as white spikes burst from his torso. The white spikes of bone twisted and snarled as they wrapped around the elder, forming into an exoskeleton of bone armour. The transformation happening in mere moments, Rycore's influence, explicit and exploding from every pore.

The closer he got to Zenith, the more the pressure pressed down on his chest. The evil emanating from the elder was visible and palatable, driving deep into the surroundings.

The Echidna's flame began to glow with a red light, intensifying with each step closer this monstrous form took.

Zenith stepped back, drawing the Echidna flame up to his front, ready to strike. The elder's monstrous form now complete, it rushed at him with a giant axe made of its bones, swinging it from high above, missing Zenith. Instead, connecting with the ground and rocks, scarring the earth beneath them, dust and stones flying into the air, obscuring the monk's view momentarily. Zenith took the opportunity to strike, smoothly arcing the Echidna flame up from his lower position, smashing the blades length into the chest of his opponent. The blade bounced away, deflected by the thick bone armour that covered this warped creature.

The armour scuffed but took no damage as Zenith righted himself. Another swing from the bone axe cleaved from his right, skimming just above his head, shaving a patch of hair, watching as it floated past his eye and fell at his feet. Zenith blurted out, "Holy Mullock dung, that's one sharp axe." Further enraging the bone-armed elder. His repeated missed strikes drove him deeper into his madness.

Plunging fast at centre mass, the Echidna flame stuck and dug into the bone, wedging itself there. Zenith, unable to pull it out, held on, struggling to avoid the frantic swings of the axe and solid bone off-hand of the elder.

Caught unaware, a slap crashed into Zenith's face, forcing him to release his grip on the Echidna flame. Disarmed and endangered, Zenith called out to the open sky, screaming to Synergy for the power he would need to end this battle quickly, letting him release this tortured soul.

A roar filled the air, booming and echoing as it rebounded from the walls of the cloister and the rocky outcropping, bouncing all around, stunning the elder and forcing him to a standstill. Overwhelmed by the sound, the elder staggered, falling to his knees, the Echidna flame protruding from his breast. Silence filled the air, and all onlookers were dazed and confused. Zenith, seeing his chance, instinctively dove onto his sword, grasping it, forcing it deeper into the chest of the elder, all his body weight pushing behind it. Abruptly, it slipped, cascading through the armour, penetrating the flesh beneath. Screams evicted the silence as the elder recoiled, scraping himself backwards from Zenith, dislodging the Echidna flame from within his chest. Zenith twisted the blade, wrenching it clear, fracturing the bone Armour, splintering it into a multitude of fissures and flaws, watching as they appeared all across the chest plate, weakening it, exposing weak spots, placing the Elder at a disadvantage.

Still, the elder came again, this time his axe in both hands, carving the dirt as it pulled up, throwing dirt into the air and into Zenith's eyes. Had Zenith not deflected it, no doubt it would have severed deep into his lower thigh, even amputating it. Knocked back, Zenith caught a chance to breathe, subconsciously screaming, "Synergy, please aid me." A power flooded his body; the Echidna flame responded, and the blade's edge sparkled, gaining a renewed shape. The carved flames of the blade shaft began to twist and turn, dancing from pommel to tip.

His Grip intensified the sword, feeling more at one in his hand than it had ever felt before; his mind cleared, and within his new clarity stood Synergy, uttering instructions to him.

"Focus the blade, Zenith.
Summon my flame to it.
See where you strike.
Not only by sight but by foresight."

Focusing his mind, he envisioned the moment he struck the elder, seeing it clearly, predicting it. The Echidna Flames' head turned blue. The flames shot from it, blistering the very air around it, linking with a path that led straight into the elder's now-shattered armour.

The blink of an eye would not have been enough to describe the speed of movement before the elder had seen Zenith move, the Echidna flame projected itself into his very core. Smelting the bone armour liquid, severe heat permeated every section, melting it away yet somehow protecting the elder inside of a bubble of cold yet bright blue flame.

As the final piece of bone fell from the elder he stood stone like unable to move or speak, his own body had been delinquent in its act, his mind black, he had been there but not in control, trapped inside his own conscious screaming to stop, once the flames danced from the blade he knew this was the real general.

Somewhere inside, a lingering thought that he should have been the one to receive the visions and the quest. The one to see the general reunited with the Echidna Flame. Thinking it should have been him, not a lowly monk such as Thaddeus. Realising he had left even the slightest sliver of a gap in his faith, letting Rycore in through his jealousy, letting Rycore contort and control his body. How could he face the general now, attacking unprovoked, having attempted to slay him?

30
THE WAY HOME

Brent barely slept for the rest of the night, sat amongst the men that hung around one of the several camp-fires, making sure always to face Lemma's tent, "I... I can't even believe what my own eyes saw. What in all the benevolence was that beast? The star it... It responded to Princess Lemma's every move and command without her speaking. How can it do that? It looked like it moved on its own."

The foe could have easily maimed and killed nearly half of the forces in camp. Its size was that of three men; its strength seemed unbound. It was pitch-black, with a lizard-like appearance. The creature was pure evil incarnate.

"Then there were the bright lights that shone, pulling the figure of a man up to the sky, from whence the creature died; this must truly have been the workings of Rysand, his grace granted as the spirit relinquished its sin." Brent just couldn't process any of it, trying made his head pound like a storm raged inside it.

No sooner did the sun peek above the horizon than Brent

had the soldiers breaking camp, loading the horses and carriages, and reconstructing the awnings from the sheets and pikes. The only tent he ordered left standing was Lemma's. "The Princess still sleeps soundly, let her be." Lemma lay Undisturbed by the hustle and bustle of dressing down camp, showing no sign of waking any time soon. Brent granted the men time to cook and eat while they waited for her.

The vast heat of midday sprawled over the plains as Lemma awoke, eyes slowly opening and taking in the surroundings of the tent. Bemused, "How did I make it back to the camp and tent? I swear, moments ago, I was fighting for my life, did I dream it?"

Rising from her ornate bed, calling out. "Guards, come please," as politely as possible, although she hated the pomp of being royal; the soldiers respected it. Without delay, the guards entered, bowing their heads to her. "How did I get to my bed?" one of the guards had to reply, "My lady Brent carried you here asleep in his arms, in the early hours. Should we fetch him?" Nodding to them, the soldiers turned, leaving the tent; she was alone again. *Brent carried me in his arms? From where? Why?*

Moments later, Brent appeared through the cloth at the tent entrance, carrying a waterskin and a tray of fresh-roasted meat. "I guess that you will be famished, my lady." Peering at him, Lemma motioned him over to her table. There he set the meat and waited for Lemma to take a seat and to be asked to sit.

Lemma tucked into the meat famished, acting most un-royal-like, she spoke between chews. "Y-y-you ha-ave my dee-pest than-nks for aid-ding m-e let's just not bur-den Pri-nce Zen-ith Wi-th the Det-ails." Taken aback, Brent didn't know what the best way was to reply, so he only smiled and nodded, remaining silent. He released a huge sigh while hearing his voice talking to him, "I'm in no hurry to get on Prince Zenith's bad side, I'm quite happy to forget it all."

Meal eaten, Lemma rushed to have her tent dismantled and stored. They had already lost half a day because she overslept. Once all had been made ready Lemma mounted Rath and lead her men onwards towards home, several hours had passed. When finally the northern outpost moved into view, once they arrived, the men busied themselves restocking the foodstuffs and water carriers, no one wanting to remain here, eager to push on into the night and make up some of their lost ground before making camp again.

Lemma and Brent both felt the same as the men once they had all restocked. Brent ordered them to move out. Lemma had decided that tonight they would sleep under the stars, once the moon reached the pinnacle of its arc, meaning they would be marching for at least the next four or five hours. This would actually put them back on track, if not slightly ahead by her calculations. Brent agreed with her assumptions. "An extra five miles a day will see us back in Sciran a half day earlier, and me back with Zenith that slight bit sooner." Her voice betrayed her, speaking louder than she meant to. Brent overheard and didn't speak, but his face said he heard all the same, giving Lemma a pause for thought. "Oh gods, he heard me now, he thinks I'm going soft."

Halted at the moon's pinnacle, guards were posted, fires made, and Lemma curled up in Rath's wings, lulled to sleep by the soft cooing sounds Rath made as she slept. Morning soon broke, and all woke refreshed and ready, food consumed and fires doused, they made off, a renewed spirit in all their steps.

The following day pasted unimpeded they walked at a fast pace, the makeshift awnings aiding the men to keep a modicum of shade above them, come the cooling of the evening all pushed a little harder making extra ground, sleeping under the stars despite Brents attempts to have Lemmas tent set up she constantly refused, preferring the comfort and warmth of Raths feathers.

Soon enough, the final night of marching had ended, and every man was bedded down, staring up at the stars. Lemma looked up, wishing on them, "I wish to be held by Zenith's arms, feel his warmth against me. Please let me return to him post haste." These days of marching had brought on an unexpected loneliness inside, truly feeling his absence and growing fonder at each fleeting thought, still being whisked off to sleep by the warmth wrapped around her from Raths' tentative embrace, at least let her rest and dream in comfort.

All of them woke up, quickly made a meal, then prepared themselves, eager to move towards Sciran. Rath was a little hyper, not keeping pace with the soldiers, speeding off and returning to the group. Lemma smiled and laughed, enjoying the enthusiasm in Rath's steps. "Come on, girl, is that all you got? I swear you ran faster in the gorge. Is this tame life making you chubby?"

It was as if Rath heard her and took offence as her speed sent her into a blur of greys, Lemma screaming at the top of her lungs, holding tight. "Rath, you little..." her words cast aside by the wind forced into her lungs. The soldiers all smiled to see their Princess acting like a teenager, adding a slight, almost unseeable bounce in their step, although none could keep up with her pace; some chose to chase Rath and play like little children.

The plains seemed to smile at the jubilation of the soldiers and Rath, the sky shining a little brighter, the grass looking greener, flowers coming into bloom as they passed by, and the whole area seemed lighter and fairer.

Before long Sciran's walls came into view the gleaming white stone, shimmering in the evening rays of the sun, the large eastern gate swinging wide as the unit approached, ahead of them many people, looked on scouring the lines of men marching, looking for their loved ones, smiles filling their faces as they saw the ones they loved. Husbands, brothers, wives, mothers, fathers or sons alike were being flocked to by those who waited. Those who could not find their loved ones, slumping to the floor, tears flooding from their eyes, knowing they had lost them.

Lemma sat high on Rath, watching the crowd, and could not hold back the sadness; tears filled her eyes, and sobs left her breathless. Feeling worse for those who cried, she found herself wishing she could comfort them.

Lemma climbed down from Rath, moving among those who wept in the street, holding their hands, whispering condolences to them, and hugging those who placed their arms around her; it seemed second nature, almost as if she felt maternal to all of them.

Brent had dismissed the soldiers, letting them go with their families. Continuing to wait, Rath stood aside, silent, watching over Lemma. Brent could see Rath just watching the princess, mouthing silent words. He spoke to Rath, looking in her eyes, to know that she guarded Lemma just like he did. "This is why her people loved her. How much love does she feel for each of them? No other royal would act this way; they love their people and have their respect, but they live as royals first. So, you would never see them interact this way."

Without thinking, he spoke out loud before he could edit his words. "Wheat sacks, I will swear my sword to you, princess, my bow will be yours to command, even if you don't want it." Lemma startled, stumbled to her feet, face flushed red "Erm, Brent, where did that come from? Why on earth did you curse at me? You are flaming lucky it's me, not the Queen. You utter mud muncher. You know I'd never ask that." No reply came, just an awkward silence between them, Brent smiling, "Oh, Dung heaps, that wasn't supposed to come out, especially that way." Brent's eyes, serious and unmoving. His words were now his vow. Lemma just left Brent to his embarrassment. "I've got more important people to tend to anyway."

Once Lemma had seen to all those that she was able to, she made her way along the cobbled streets heading for the castle. She urgently needed to speak with her mother and gain command of all the freemen she could. Zenith needed a conquering force to command.

Two thousand monks and two thousand Errant men wouldn't be a sight enough to scare Quinten. No army had ever conquered the city in hundreds of years; a siege was more likely to fail, as Errant kept farms within the walls, and wells were abundant. It could last for years when under siege, and no standing army had a chance of outlasting it.

Lemma expected that Catherine would spare the forces without issue. Silently thinking. "*Mother hates Quinten almost as much as Zenith after all, and besides, anything we don't have already built, the forces mother provides will be able to produce it in a matter of hours upon our arrival at Errant's gate, it is something they trained daily for.*"

31
THE AYR ROSE

Zenith, having defeated the elder that had become one of Rycore's minions, hastened into the Ayr Rose compound, the wall sealing shut behind him. Those monks who floated around him, all still in awe of the arrival, whispered between themselves. "The general of the Echidna Flame has finally arrived, predestined to come and face the trials."

These trials were established at the cloisters' founding so that the newest general could fully connect with Synergy; they would test his physicality and mental prowess, pushing him to accept the powers he was preordained to possess. Zenith, of course, didn't know about any of this and just walked amongst them, ignorant, with a rather nonchalant look on his face.

Thaddeus spoke in a gravelly and coarse voice, "Zenith, finally, you are here. Maybe now my brothers will forgive my transgressions against the order in bringing you the sword. The time has come for you to know the true purpose of the Ayr rose, its boon to you in the form of warriors, and how we shall forward you to your true powers."

Zenith's face contorted in confusion; *Arriving seeking warriors, yes, but what did Thaddeus mean by 'true powers?* The fact remained that acquiring the two thousand-plus warrior monks to help him release Errant from his uncle Quinten's clutches was essential. Always expecting the need to persuade and convince them of this, even so, they had already pledged their loyalty without any of that.

The church within the rock stood proud, light pouring from each of the windows and carved doors beckoning him in. The monks filed in behind, filling the pews, so many that hundreds still filled the stone courtyard, all eager to see and hear their general. Pulled through the crowds Zenith was hoisted upon the stone stage and alter at the back of the building by now he must have been inside a great cavern within the bowls of mount Valen, uncarved stalactites hanging from the upper most portions of the craggy ceiling above, stalagmites standing proud from the floor pews placed about them, massive naturally formed columns supporting the cavern where the two had met.

A voracious voice boomed out into the chamber bouncing off the walls resounding to the farthest areas of the courtyard, Zenith jumped out of his skin this voice seemed to come from nowhere disembodied, flinging his body around searching the space for the voices owner, there above him in a carved Varinder stood an old gent dressed in splendour compared to the other monks. His voice boomed out again, filling the room once more. Zenith gazed on in amazement, trying his best to listen to the words being spoken.

"Today, my fellow brothers, is one for joyous praise; he has come, he hath joined us. Thaddeus had foreseen this and was justified in taking action. Too many of us doubted and swore to seek blood on

his life. Now we see that we were wrong. Forgiving and punishing him has been our undoing, forming cracks in our cores; we shall all need to seek his forgiveness. Unfortunately, some among us held too much doubt, falling into the evil's embrace; those who still harbour any ill will be tested; your resolves should be hardened after that, which many have witnessed this night. The twisted form that became of our dearly departed elder was all in difference to his doubt and the vile cunning of Rycore. Reaffirm your vows here and now to Rysand and his general, who now stands before you victorious and proof that the legends are true."

Below Zenith stood enthralled in each and every word. The Ayr rose truly were devout and lived the way of Rysand in fact, they could probably teach many from his home country or even Sciran a lot about how to live in the light of Rysand, already knowing all too well that daily life would present the ordinary folks with many more temptations than affirmations that could lead them to Rycore.

The monk continued his speech, throwing his arms out in front, waving his hand, exaggerating each sentence.

"Tonight, we will mourn our lost brother, but we will also celebrate the coming of the general and the battle in which he proved his worth. Tomorrow, we will send the general up the mountain to the trials, that he may prove himself further before Rysand and his oath-sworn brother."

The night became full of merriment and glee, each of the monks vying to get an audience with Zenith. Zenith, however, didn't feel the joy or glee, just wishing to rest from the arduous journey here and the intense fight that he had just survived.

His body ached, his mind yearning for the sweet rest of his dreams. Perhaps his dreams would once again instruct him on what lay ahead in these trials, even if he didn't know where they were coming from. Completely unready and utterly taken aback by the elder monk's proclamation, pretending interest and that he was present in the moment. Whenever a chance came, pausing to take a breather in the momentary breaks between monks introducing themselves, glancing at Thaddeus, who, even tho beaten and bruised, emitted an aura of triumph and vindication as each brother bowed before him, begging forgiveness.

Finally, Thaddeus, in return, looked to Zenith's direction. In that fleeting moment, realising Zenith's plight, moving purposefully toward him, offering his hand, pulling Zenith free of the crowd. Well, if you can call it that, falling on his rear because of his hobbled leg, he attempted to pull himself up. Laughing wholeheartedly, Zenith returned the favour, helping his friend regain proper posture and composure before asking him if he could arrange lodgings for him.

Pushing their way through the crowds of monks, most of whom now had a merry look about them, like being sober was a distant memory, the mead soaked the floors and their clothing. Zenith, led by Thaddeus, made it into the cold, crisp air of the night in the courtyard.

Making towards an entrance in the side of the walls, Thaddeus opened a door into a small yet roomy bedchamber, well-furnished on one side with an ornate desk, and on the other a basic bed covered with cotton blankets.

"Sleep here, Zenith. Use my room. I will spend tonight in the communal bed chambers. I can't have you amongst them all. You will not get any rest." With that, Thaddeus turned and left his cane clunking on the stone floor as he did.

32
THE FIRST STEPS TO
AN ARMY

Making for the doors into the castle, Lemma pushed past multiple guards and the castle attendants. Blind fixation on the throne room, people soon got the message, quickly shifting from the path; obviously, her sole focus was on Catherine.

Sitting upon the throne, Catherine diligently worked on the stack of papers on a small table beside the throne—tasks that had piled up, managing the kingdom, issuing edicts for the latest deployments, and granting permissions for township development. The celebration of Lemma's wedding brought Sciran a boon, a growing desire among people to build and set up their futures, all of which was boosting the country's economy, but was making her work much harder.

Standing, lifting her head, pushing out her chest, rolling her shoulders back, putting on her most formal stance, below the throne, letting out a rather large, forced cough to prompt Catherine into noticing her and drawing her attention. "Lemma!" Jumping up from the throne, forcefully running down its marble steps, and wrapping both arms around Lemma before speaking again. "When did you return? Where is Zenith?"

Silently Lemma thought. *Well, at least she noticed Zenith was missing,* holding back the uneasiness she felt to explain the plans they had forged, detailing how, when, and why Renton was built.

Astounded, Catherine couldn't hold her tongue any longer.

"Quinten has gone too far; that town will be eviscerated in flames, and I will make sure Zenith is installed on the Errant throne. Any men and materials you need are yours, daughter!"

Trying to remain calm, relaying. "Mother! Renton is of no threat to Sciran. Asger has sworn fealty to Zenith, the very second he saw the sigil of Barathor on the armour, even aiding in planning and actioning of plans to take the Errant throne."

Catherine regained some of her composure, still holding anger. "Then, if you wish for the town to be saved, its ownership will transfer to Sciran; it should rightfully be under Sciran governance"

Lemma could only agree, thinking sure in her knowledge. *Zenith will see the sense in this. Surely, he will see it as a gesture of goodwill between the two countries and the meaning of my mother's words. Perhaps even solidifying our joint rule over the continent in the future, uniting the people under our banner. Well, if he doesn't, I'll kick his rear till he does.* The last thought elicited a slight chuckle.

Catherine looked at her. "Are you ok, my dear?" Lemma swiftly replied. "Just thinking how to persuade that rambunctious husband of mine to see it your way." A smirk crossed Catherine's face. "That's my child, make sure he knows who the real boss is."

Several days flew by in the blink of an eye, dispatches sent, engagement of services letters, conscription notices all flew out from the war room. Where Catherine now raged, planning to raise an army capable of helping Zenith and Lemma topple a tyrannical king and free the denizens of Errant from the ever-increasing evil polluting their kingdom.

Seeing that the goal was to increase the numbers she had ready in the standing army from three and a half thousand troops to a minimum of six thousand, adding these numbers to the six thousand monks and Errant soldiers already under Zenith's banner would certainly squash any resistance that Quinten could offer. His only choice would be to seal off Errant in hopes of outlasting a siege, but Catherine had planned for that.

Among the many subjects of the country, specific individuals stood out, their intellect and knowledge unsurpassed within the kingdom. Given even the shortest time, they would devise a method to get past the Errant walls, either through, under, or over, knowing that it was the most certain of facts.

Sitting in the farthest corner of the war room, Lemma gazed on in wonder at her mother. *This fury and rage, I've never seen mum do this ever. I can't even remember a day similar. She must be focusing a lot to remain transfixed on it, singularly on Quinten and the city of Errant. It must be a significant battle of wills; she hasn't even attended to Sciran, my uncle got that job, poor man is in over his head.*

This way, that way, in and out of the room, servants, soldiers alike flew in a flurry of panic and purpose, each one presenting or carrying a notice or order for Catherine's attention. Lemma had even witnessed several collisions between blindly moving people, storms of paper being sent into the air as they fell over each other. The ensuing rush to gather up the crucial documents created more issues as people bashed heads reaching down without due care and attention. Lemma couldn't help but laugh in these situations. She did try to help, but the people insisted she didn't.

The table that filled the centre of the room, easily twenty dinner placements square, covered in a humongous map showing all of Apprite. At its centre, the Rycliff Bridge hung across the gorge. Many days' walk from it, between the cities of Sciran and Errant. Between these points, notes on parchment, figurines to represent armies, and more minor black marks with names indicating other locations.

Lifting from her seat, Lemma strode to the table, bewildered at the organised chaos of the map. Lemma whispered to Catherine, going unheard. "Mother, you've been at this for days; Your notes are so thorough that a commoner could run the campaign. You're working so hard for me and Zenith. Just slow down and take a break before you make yourself ill."

Lemma's attention was drawn to the Rycliff bridge, piles of notes stacked, each one in a different script, but all plans or designs on how to disable the bridge without it being a permanent one. The one that Lemma thought her mother had chosen was placed separately from the rest of the pile. She picked it up, her curiosity getting the better of her.

"Why this proposal?" Reading further, it stated the intent to sever the connection, *sever it, and break the bridge. Wait what? I'd better read on, I'm sure it's not just to break it.* Further, on a description of how the Scirainian side of the gorge would be disabled and reattached to Trebuchet-style constructs with ropes long enough that they would be able to lower the bridge down into the Gorge. Lowered sufficiently that it would look to anyone on the Errant side that the bridge had yet again collapsed and was impassable. "OK, that's quite impressive, I'd never have thought of it." The drawing seemed very detailed; Lemma could make out the Trebuchet frames, the ropes from the bridge hanging from them, connected to wheels with spike-like shapes that varied in size. The wheels were then attached to a singular point that could be turned to raise and lower the bridge. "What the heck are those spikey wheels about? Something new?"

It was something that had never been used before to her knowledge — an invention — that sparked an idea of her own to suggest to Asger in the future. An ingenious idea, and once all the fighting was over, it was easily rectifiable, allowing travel to resume in a matter of hours. She noted this was a very similar idea to the one Asger had constructed to form Renton, except his required several horses to pull the chains; this one needed a single Mullock.

Catherine had finally received word from all corners of Sciran; thousands of men and women had pledged themselves to the country's defence and the defeat of Quinten. In the preceding day, having received notices covering more than ten thousand people, they were intent on service to the crown. These people, Nobel and peasant alike, would start to arrive at Scirans' gate over the next day or two.

Catherine had never expected such a quantity of volunteers. Orders issued from the crown had all the cities' smiths, fletchers, and weapon forges working at maximum capacity, producing hundreds of new weapons daily. From the windows of the war room, looking out over the town, you could see plumes of smoke rising from every direction, filling the sky with a black haze that choked the usual gleaming white of the city. The masters and the apprentices worked day and night at her request. Ironically, the issue now was that she hadn't accounted for this sudden influx; they would meet her demand for around two and a half thousand men, but they would never be able to produce over double the amount in the time available. Lemma took the opportunity to ask, "How will you use these extra bodies, Mother?" Catherine was swift with her reply. "Lemma, never you worry, I told you those walls would fall. The extra men will take Merik home and then be reinforcements to help take the walls when the time comes."

33

TRIALS OF BODY AND MIND

Zenith awoke from his rest in Thaddeus's bed quite refreshed and boisterous. The day ahead was going to be tough and long; this energy would prove him in good standing.

Leaving the room, the sun blazed brightly. It's light, forcing Zenith to squint and squirm whilst his eyes adjusted. Ahead, a lone figure, the old monk who had bellowed his speech the night before. His approach was purposeful and righteous, coming to take Zenith to the starting point of the trials.

Trudging through the stone courtyard, the monk walked ahead of Zenith. Passing the massive stone church, remaining silent until they stood behind it, hidden from view, a staircase. They led up and over the building's exterior and into the mountain, disappearing from Zenith's view. The monk's gruff voice instructed, "Ascend the stone staircase, follow the tunnel to its end. Once the mount opens before you, the trial will begin." Without a chance to question him, the monk turned on his heels, leaving Zenith standing alone in silence.

Zenith's attention was now raised above him, looking to

the tunnel and where it would lead, wondering. *Is this a final meeting with Synergy?*

Upwards, his feet moved sluggishly, trepidation slowing his movements; no matter what awaited him, his choice was clear. The trials allowed him to finally gain control of the blade, in turn preventing injuries to those he loved, like the one Lemma had received in the gorge, fixated on it, thinking. "I needed to conquer the blade to ensure their safety."

Finally, the top step and the tunnel in view, he pushed on his pace, quickened, becoming steadier. With each step into the darkness, it seemed to take longer; each second seemed to last longer and longer, as though time here warped in on itself.

Minutes seem to pass into hours, those hours seeming to last a day as he continues to walk, his willpower stretching thin. *Will this passage ever cease, and see me in the light again?* In the darkness, his sense of sight was greatly diminished, while his hearing was heightened, allowing him to catch a whisper, a quietly spoken word, striking past his ears, never fully hearing it.

The whisper, a menagerie of words, faith, strength, willingness and success, the only words caught. The suggestive nature saying he needed to prove himself in all of these areas, taking pause considering faith and desire to succeed, and what these meant to him. "All of these mean just one thing to me, my friends, my family, my wife, and all those who strengthen me." This, then, brought images to his mind. "The lake, the farm and the gorge. Had I not been there, I couldn't be here now."

The whispered words changed love, honour, vengeance and blood this time. Zenith finally realised, feeling the force of a waterfall crashing inside his head, that the trial had begun; these words held strong meanings for him. His mind whirring, "Love and honour that is entirely encompassed by my feelings for Lemma and how I can honour the sacrifices my friends have made, and I guess they will continue to make."

Vengeance and blood, strong, violent words, only causing thoughts of battles prior and to come. Provoking thought of Vengeance for his family, blood spilt for blood spilt. Yet something nagged and gnawed at that little spot right at the back of his brain, where you would say you felt the soul or conscience.

These two words didn't fit with the rest. His thoughts were full of anger: "So vile and reprehensible their meanings, it just doesn't sit right." The off feeling grew, pushing him to find further answers, one that felt good made him feel good. "Maybe I don't need the vengeance and blood to be satisfied." A flashing thought of his family before his mind. "Mum and Dad?" A random memory surging forth. Then Barathor stood clasped hands in front of him, smiling with Ake and Rathena on either side.

Dad was speaking to me when I was a small child, hearing Ake's words. "Zenith vengeance is the weak of wills' way out, blood for blood will just bleed a country dry and tarnish your very centre black, turning you into a victim ripe for Rycore to twist".

It struck him. *Did Dad predict this moment? Has it all led me to this?* This memory held the keys to his mind's freedom and body's escape. *Vengeance and blood are the actual tests?* In that very second, speaking firmly.

"I, Zenith Ake Ocard, stand here vowing that Vengeance is not mine to take; it is for my mother, father and grandfather to seek in the afterlife if they seek it. Quinten will not die by my hand, nor will a single drop of his blood touch the Echidna flame if that is possible."

. . .

Mind suddenly cleared, the menagerie of words vanished, and there he stood, a clearing, a small peak ahead of him, rising onward to the sky. "Does this mean I passed?" Succeeding in ridding his body and mind of vengeance and the thirst for blood.

The cool sense of relief flooded over him as Synergy spoke directly in his mind.

"Well done, brother, you have rid yourself of the need for blood. Now, the Echidna Flame will respond to you, releasing its powers without the need for your blood to be spilt. Call on the power now and see it firsthand in your waking state. Once this power is released and you understand its use, proceed forward. Your body is yet to be tempered and forged into one that can hold fast against all temptations."

This made little sense to Zenith, making him think hard. "This is like refusing a field mouse the excess wheat that fell from the stalk; it has no value. How can a body be tempered and forged? These are words for metalworking."

Zenith unsheathed the Echidna Flame hanging from his waist, focusing on the tip, recalling the fiery whirlwind Tripas had described, walking to Rockwall after the battle in the cave. The blade's length lit a deep blue and red, the point igniting. A small, fiery whirlwind grew as he moved the blade; the whirlwind followed its movements, dancing and twirling gleefully.

Commanding the flames to stop, Zenith now wondered *what lies further on this trail, ever climbing up Mount Vallen. Do I now need to face Synergy and complete some unknown tasks, or will it lead to nothing?*

Synergy in his complete majestic form sat at the pinnacle of Mount Valen, observing Zenith sitting in silent judgment, waiting for Zenith to reach his subsequent encounter, darkness and malice manifested in physical form, its only job to temper Zenith's anger, not physically but with his memories and feelings, twisted dark versions of them.

Synergy made sure not to speak to Zenith's mind, silently communicating his wishes to the air.

"I'm placing unending faith in you, Zenith, faith that you will overcome this obstacle and move past it. The final test is after that; you will need to forge a bond of trust physically with me."

In this clearing of rock, able to take a breath, Zenith pondered the words, the meaning he placed behind them, clearer, more defined. "The future is warmer, brighter and coming to meet me head-on, but here and now within my immediate surroundings, that isn't of concern."

A definite need to move forward, push on harder, and be more focused surrounded him. All he wanted was to return to that dearest to him, to hold Lemma in his arms, sit at a table with them, talk, drink and make merry, and just be. Onward he stepped, sure in himself that whatever the challenge came next would be easily overcome.

The small clearing was no wider than a cottage, those old-fashioned thatched types with white walls you would see in more settled areas in the Occardian grasslands and probably as long as 3 set side by side. It was possible to cross in a matter of several steps, then another climb again, but there was no clear path; it was just a gut feeling. Zenith looked to the other end of the clearing. "Up is my next destination."

Moving no more than twenty steps, his motion stopped. Unable to move forward, no matter how hard he pushed, something fought against him, pushing back against him. Hands placed out front, feeling something there; it was as if the very air itself had solidified, its physicality evident against the palm of his hand, "How does it make no sense? Nothing ahead, only a clear view, so which sense deceives now?"

Moving to each edge of the clearing to his left, the blockade still in place to his right, the same. Thinking about what to do. "Should I use the sword? Synergy mentioned it."

Removing the Echidna flame from its sheath, slashing with a wide arc across the front of himself, the sword slicing cleanly through the blockade unhindered, the force pulling him off balance and stumbling. Shouting out, "What? It's as if nothing is there at all."

From the corner of his eye, he caught a glimpse of a person on the opposite end of the clearing, shrouded in shadow. "Did I just see someone?" A dark, overbearing presence fixed its gaze, staring directly at him. A feeling of dread welled up inside his body, from where and why? Knots formed in his stomach, returning the shadow's gaze, locking his stare in place.

"You are a child of muck and excrement, a useless excuse of existence; you should have left this plane, not your father; he should be atop the throne. You caused this, you and that wench you called mother"

Sickening words flowed on the wind out in the open, his voice, words he would never speak, yet somehow, they rang truer than anything he had vocalised.

"Your grandfather would be turning to ash in his grave if he could see the useless salt weasel you have become, less of a man than a field mouse scurrying around begging for scraps at the coat tails of others far greater than you."

Zenith screamed in retort. "Damn you! You are only a shadow's imitation of me. How dare you speak such twisted truth and slander? This is my shame to bear and mine alone, but I will not wear it; those are the idiocies of a child who knew no better!"

His foot edged a step further as he replied to the voice and shadow. The shadows shape refining, taking a more masculine stance as he did.

"You are beneath her, not worthy of her love; she will only be disgusted by your actions, ridiculed in her own country for choosing you, a farmer, the lowest of humankind, a stain on her foot."

His anger almost taking over, Zenith breathed and replied again, "Such drivel, garbage and lies, yet all the same, a twisted truth that I hold deep inside. I may be a farmer, but I am more than that title suggests. I am a provider, a carer, a friend to the land and sky. One with the earth, respecting it, using it to better myself, feeding those around me through hard work and toil, I am a creator, a nurturer of things".

Each word he spoke reinforced his self-worth, helping to reduce the doubt that he harboured, but forced deep and locked away.

Another step forward, inching ever closer, the shadow just out of reach, even with sword in hand, but with each rebuttal, his body felt lighter, less oppressed by the air. Again, the barrage came at him, vile and putrid.

"How can you be a leader of men, you know nothing of it. Those that dare to follow you do so to their death or worse to the pits of doubt, where they can be food for a far greater being hastening his return. You will do nothing but aid him, feed him, help to restore him. Any who do survive, knowing you and following you, will be but shells void of life, just existing. Folly for the masses to hate and chastise as snivelling worms, sewer rats, enslaved to a new master, their pride stripped and their bodies naked, exposed to the vile of those you seek to destroy".

The shadow figure became clearer. Zenith stood before a blackened, twisted clone of himself, not an exact duplicate; its whole aura was rotten, dishevelled, heaped in dubious doubts and lies or half-truths. Still, Zenith controlled his anger; these lies may have held truth, but not his truth.

"I am no leader of men, I am just a person thrust into power, a power I did not want or ask for. Those who share the burden with me will guide me in the direction I need to tread; their friendships and love will guide them; they will be honest and true, directing the people against me if necessary. Those who turn to Rycore will do so of their own free will. I will not stop until I have rid the throne of its entanglements and misguided desires. I know that I can return Quinten to the light. Should I fail, others will push me forward repeatedly until we together succeed. That will not be the end, I will claim my unwanted destiny with them beside me, and any trial set will be overcome."

A tremendous shove from nowhere hurled Zenith forward, his feet free of the floor, as he flew directly at his shadow self, its fake blade drawn, pointed at him, with flames dancing along its shaft, ready to burn him.

A split second was all he had to think. "Focus on the Echidna Flame, envision the blade enveloped in flames, place it at the tip." Out in front of the blade, the flame he imagined appeared with a powerful intensity, a solid blue burning the very air, with no smoke to be seen. Colliding with the shadow's blade, the Echidna Flame liquefied it, passing through, plunging deep into the shadow's chest, the ribcage cracking as the bone sheared and mollified.

The sword pierced through the shadows, back as the heart burst open wide, exploding into blackened mist, the shadow dissipating away as it did. Zenith's body felt free, unburdened, his thoughts and movements entirely his own, a sense of satisfaction and jubilation taking over. Somehow, he knew that he had conquered his demons; now Rycore should never be able to tempt or taint his soul.

The tunnel at the other end of the clearing had disappeared, leaving no options but to climb upward to the summit. The next of his trials. If another one was placed in front of him. He swore then and there. "I will, I must complete them."

Looking to the rock's face, his eyes searched for even the most minor nook or cranny; the smallest of hand or foot hold was all he needed to begin the ascent. There seemed to be none in the rock, flat and shiny, offering no aid; if anything, it just sat there staring back at him, laughing, goading him, saying he could not succeed.

Slumping to the floor, deep in thought at the nothingness of the sheer face of the mountain. *Gods, why can I not be with them? I need to feel Lemma's breath be with her with all of them, back in Renton, Sciran, even the gorge, no, no, I must move forward, I will succeed. The thing that matters most is getting through this and out the other side so that I can reunite with her with them all.*

Still entranced in his thought, Zenith hadn't picked up on the faintest red glow at his waist, but the Echidna flame sensed something faintly in the area surrounding them. Pulling at the strap holding it to his waist, the sword struggled trying to free itself, but still, Zenith was too lost in thought to notice or feel it.

Synergy watched from on high, wishing he could help in some way, but Zenith had to finish this; otherwise, his trust could not be guaranteed.

Synergy began to think about planning. "Although I can't physically help him, I could snap him round from the delirium of thought and alert him to the actions of the Echidna flame; it cannot be done in an obvious way, as that will influence the outcome of this final challenge. I will have to consider how best to intervene without interfering; I need to give Zenith time to resolve this issue without my input. Maybe a nap to pass the time and create a plan?"

Still slumped over, Zenith despaired. His only wish was to get home to Lemma, holding her in his arms, looking in her eyes, hearing her sweet voice, all raced around inside his head. Suddenly, from somewhere, an almighty yawn pierced the heavens, sounding like the first clap of thunder, alerting all to the coming storm.

The sound caused audible shaking in the rocks, causing Zenith to collapse backwards, his head bouncing as it connected with the stone, shaking him from his fugue-like state. "What! My side feels hot, almost hot enough to burn me". The Echidna Flame wanted his attention. "How did I not feel the heat or movements? Was I that deep in thought?"

Pushing up on his arms, he regained his seated position and then stood, removing the Echidna Flame from his waist. The sword pulled him forward to the mountain's face, the light it emanated gaining strength as it did. The air in front shimmered. As the shimmer dissipated, a hole appeared.

Seeing the hole spurred Zenith on, moving the ignited Echidna Flame all around. More shimmers came and went, revealing hand grips and holes big enough for his feet to gain purchase, the feeling he had inside becoming even more familiar. "It's the same feeling I had back on the bridge before me and Lemma where attacked, the influence of Rycore, it has to be, that is the only way such a devious and maniacal illusion could be explained. Set here to prevent me from gaining the powers that Synergy will give me, or to prevent my return home," had the sound not shocked the surroundings and forced him to see the sword's actions. He may never have left this place.

Grabbing above his head Zenith pulled up with his left arm, pushing his feet into holes that they could reach, the Echinda Flame still brandished in his right hand its glowing still intense as he reached up with it dispelling yet another shimmer providing him the tiniest of hand grips, reversing his grip on the Echidna Flame holding it with his two smallest finger whilst wedging his pointer and index fingers in the crack pulling himself further up the wall.

A search with the Echidna Flame followed each troubled gain in height to find and dispel another shimmer covering his next foot position or place to hold. Time passed so slowly, but inch by inch he climbed, never looking back, face to the sky, the mountain's peak still not in view. Whispering to himself. "Will this climb ever be over?"

It seemed like he had been climbing for hours. Each step up this wall was fought for in excruciating pain from the cramps that had formed in his hand and throughout the joints in his legs, down to his individual toes. Seeing what looked like a shelf or the top of the wall several meters ahead, a place to rest or the place he would finally stop climbing.

Reinvigorated Zenith pushed on his speed, renewed, clasping each hold and jumping for the next. He soon arrived at the point he aimed for, exhausted, he hauled his body over it, collapsing in a heap as his feet finally passed. The edge behind him, gasping for breath, he rested for a moment, raising his head and looking forward. A creature lay in the foreground, its form familiar from his dreams. "Is that Synergy? It must be, everything my dreams have shown me lies in front of me."

Prostrated, he lay there staring at the magnificence of

Synergy sleeping not ten yards away from him. A pleasant yet soothing purr perforated the silence around them both. Zenith pushed on his forearms, lifting himself to his hand and Knees. From here, he was able to see the actual size of Synergy; he far outclassed Rath, easily the height of four of her and the length of at least three. Looking on, examining further, Synergy's body was covered in beige fur. At the end of each leg, ivory claws, the length of Zenith's arms, a long, slender tail curled around Synergy's body, and a surprisingly large tuft of fluffy orange fur covered the end. Synergy's head looked much like an eagle, his beak a golden yellow curving down his face, his nostrils black holes sitting just under his closed eyes.

Zenith tentatively shuffled forward, moving slowly. he stretched his hand out and placed it softly on Synergy's beak. It was cold and rough to touch, pits and falls acting like sandpaper against his hand as he rubbed over it, becoming familiar with his newest potential ally.

Synergy, roused by the feeling of his beak being rubbed, was surprised that it felt rather nice, like an old blanket being wrapped around his body. Synergy didn't want to open his eyes in case this was just a dream, honestly hoping it wasn't and that the person below him was the one it was supposed to be. In the meantime, Zenith had become accustomed to feeling beneath his hand and dared to move on, taking his hand and placing it on Synergy, feeling the coarseness of ungroomed fur. Curious, he pushed his hand deeper into the fur, feeling the depth down to the skin as his forearm disappeared into it. A warm sensation wrapped around it, a sense of safety and well-being filling his heart. *This feels right somehow. I don't know why, but it does. I can wholly trust just from this fleeting touch that I will be protected in this moment and into the uncertain future.*

. . .

Synergy began to feel a warmth he hadn't felt in so long coursing through him; he felt like he was back at the time of creation, being caressed by the generals of old, whilst Rysand stood over them all watching. The nostalgia he felt made him long for those days again. A blaring excitement and realisation built; he would once again have the company of those that Rysand had pre-ordained to fight when Rycore began to revive.

Stretching as if pretending to wake, Synergy nipped Zenith playfully, alerting him to his awakening. Zenith jumped back, not scared but ecstatic that Synergy had acknowledged him as a friend, not a foe.

Staring up into the eyes of Synergy, he could see nothing but a friendship that had been there since he could remember. "Synergy, my brother, finally I see you for the first time, yet it feels like I have seen you countless times throughout my life." Within his mind, Synergy's voice replied.

"Zenith, you have done well, you have forged your path to me, your mind and body both tested and attacked physically and mentally. Tests of your resolve and senses pushed your limits, yet you did not let them break you."

A smile formed in Synergy's eyes as he looked down at Zenith, congratulating him. "Now, Zenith, take to my back so that I may spread my wings and return you to the Ayr rose, so they can rejoice in your success and join your cause."

Jumping to his feet, Zenith moved to Synergy's side, grasping hands full of his fur, pulling himself up onto his back, watching in wonderment as Synergy's massive, dragon-like wings spread, spanning 20 yards out on each side of him. Quickly, Synergy moved, letting out a squawk, as they launched from the cliff's edge, first plummeting towards the clearing Zenith had climbed from, an updraft grabbed onto

Synergy's wings. With an almighty flap, they sawed upwards, as if they would pierce the heavens themselves. Clouds flew past as they circled downwards, their cold moisture condensing on Zenith's face, refreshing him. *Oh Lord, I haven't drunk at all since I left my bed this morning. No wonder the clouds quenched my thirst.*

The dust flew high and far as Synergy landed on the stone cobbles of the Ayr rose complex, causing uproar among the monks, who flooded out in their droves to greet Synergy and Zenith, seeing that Synergy had passed the trials for them. What Zenith didn't know was that two whole days had passed, and they thought he had failed.

34
THE ARMIES CONVERGE

The city of Sciran had become a machine of industry over the last few days; its workshops churned out all the armaments and armour needed for the over two thousand extra men that Catherine had promised to Lemma and Zenith's cause.

This was, of course, alongside seventy ballistae, fifty catapults, and twenty trebuchets, all crewed and stocked to the rafters; each had its own Mullock and sapper team to pull it.

So many men had arrived to aid in this conquest that a small township of tents and makeshift buildings had formed outside the city's gates, multiple muster points and inspection grounds had been erected. In turn, each of these had its own quarter master and their teams handling that unit's equipment and supplies.

Carts lined the city streets and queued outside the township, waiting to offload their cargo to the teams that awaited them.

Brent stood in the centre of the township, his charge the readying of this army. Brent felt so overwhelmed that he stressed thinking. "I've commanded a couple of thousand men at one time: now I'm in charge of approximately six thousand men and a full contingent of siege equipment. Princess Lemma, why did you foist this position upon me? Yes, you did it with the Queen's approval. But why?"

Catherine had felt that this was his due, as a promotion and a signal to the people that faith should be placed in him, showing the gratitude she felt towards him for bringing her daughter home safe. That had a lot to do with it, but also the fact that Lemma had come to trust him fully. Truly, Brent took stock in his thoughts while standing, watching the town ship. "The fact that once I have got this gargantuan army to Renton, I will have Cathal and Asger there to aid me in command. While I stand here, I will do my darndest to prove Lemma and Catherine's faith in me true."

The Army would be supplied and readied for its march within two days. The return journey should take at a good pace, around two or three days, and for sure, they would be making use of the awning again to keep the men and animals cool. This had made the journey home easier and seemed to be a logical choice for morale and comfort returning to Renton.

Lemma sat in hers and Zenith's wing of the castle, awaiting news on their departure. Rath was kept in the stables, ready to leave at a moment's notice.

Feeling uncomfortable over the last couple of days, pangs of guilt and sudden rushes of sorrow plagued her. There had even been a degree of pleasure and excitement; she had no idea where these feelings had come from, taunting her mind. "These feelings don't seem my own. I have no control of them;

I'm nothing but a slave to them. It's almost as if I'm connected to someone, somewhere being tested. I would not wish this on anyone."

Like a bolt from the blue, her mood had shifted further and further from one extreme to the other—a constant feeling of foreboding, as if she had an unseen foe within her body.

The star hadn't reacted at all, so there was nothing close that held the influence of Rycore. It was only this morning that the feeling had shifted, giving way to adulation and love. Love of a sibling or parent. Her mind was frustrated in the throes of meaningful thought. "I feel like I'm going crazy, all these feelings coming from nowhere." No matter what, the constant pressure and sadness of missing Zenith were still buried deep in her mind. "Oh, how I wish to see his fine chiselled jaw, to run my fingers through his black locks and be pressed against his chest surrounded by his arms, staring into his deep claret eyes. That alone would cure all my illnesses and afflictions."

Merik had spent his days in Sciran learning about the culture from Amabel; they had become inseparable. She took him all around the city, helping to invest in new clothing, tools, but most of all in developing innovative technologies for farming. Amabel's help and guidance had seen him collaborate with a master machinist who had long been working on a method to automate planting using a plough-type device pulled by a Mullock. The machinist could never seem to get the plough and planter working together, always ruining the soil or failing to sow the seed.

That was where Merik had come in, with his knowledge of farming and the techniques used within the industry, giving him the knowledge to adjust the device so that it would seed at the proper depth, flip the earth and return it, covering its newest charge. Then water it in with a single, smooth motion. The machine could do this, five rows wide, reducing the workload from a team of fifteen men to that of two or three.

It was a Marvel and had earned Merik much admiration; of course, the only admiration he craved was Zenith's; he would know the most accurate value of this, but until such time, he would make it ready to use back in Grissam. He was returning there once the army had marched from Sciran. He also hoped to persuade Amabel to travel with him.

Amongst all this, Merik had spent time with Lemma getting to know his sister-in-law, watching her changing mood had been nothing but strange. It had been like she had no control over them; Amabel had suggested one other option that could cause all of this, but Lemma was sure this could never have happened.

In Renton, Cathal and Asger sat together around a solid table reviewing all the information they had available.

Sat talking, Asger spoke. "The bridge I constructed gives us a direct link to the Occardian grasslands; this will be the quickest route to Errant. The main issue we face. Quinten will have a few days' advanced warning of any approaching army; with that, he will most likely withdraw all forces inside the city walls." Cathal had relevant questions, which he quickly posed. "What are the armaments, defences and army of the Errant walls?"

Asger's face pulled taught, even though he pledged allegiance to Zenith, Cathal was still much of an unknown quantity to him. Deciding that Zenith placed trust in him, he would as well, so put forward the information in plain formal speech.

"The walls of Errant are insidious; they stand ferociously tall, and just as solid at six meters thick, and easily hold thousands of archers. They always have tar and oil pots placed every ten meters; if this isn't enough, you have the Mangels and tower-mounted javelins at each of its built-in barracks, which hold roughly three hundred men each." Cathal couldn't believe his ears and blurted out the following words without a thought. "By Rysand, that is not anything I can imagine. In Vastuk, we are lucky to have a thousand guards for the bastion." Asger looked at Cathal and spoke, "You think I'm finished." Cathal just looked on and remained silent, letting Asger continue.

"This is one reason Errant has been able to outlast every siege in its long-storied history. The men who guard the walls spend their entire careers in the Errant military, devoting themselves to one thing: training to secure Errant's walls, willing to give their lives in the attempt. They are beyond devout. Then add in the city's design built with, outlasting sieges in mind, food, water, everything could be produced within the walls." Cathal Sat there, jaw dropped, staring at Asger, unable to form a clear thought.

The conversation became very one-way with Asger explaining one issue after another, like the Army that Quinten could field without Asger's contingent, estimating it would still be around the ten-thousand-man mark. Saying the total military strength of Errant was probably around twenty-five thousand at any given time, most of it trained for siege-resistant warfare. Once Asger's voice had become hoarse, he and Cathal turned to the Ale, proposing that a drunken idea would possibly work to overcome the walls.

Asger proposed slurring about it, seriously unsure to start with. "The armed forces of Errant, which I commanded, can act as the Trojan horse. We need to drop Quinten's guard and get them inside the walls." The main issue they had was not easily overcome. For all the sober and drunken plans they could make, the battle ahead hung on Zenith's success and Lemma's convincing her mother that it was a worthy enough cause.

In the Ayr rose compound, Synergy and Zenith had spent the day together, becoming further bonded and closer. Synergy shared stories of Zenith's life through his eyes, staying out of view but checking in now and then to ensure that Zenith grew into the man he was destined to be.

This time was well spent. When not listening to Synergy, he trained. Zenith could now focus the Echidna Flames' power without much effort. Under the tutelage of Synergy, he had managed to master the flame vortex, the snake's flame, and the air-slicing blade.

They had also worked on another technique, one that would gouge the very ground, throwing enemies skyward. Aptly, Zenith named it Synergy's claw since it left four distinct marks in the ground from where it scraped as he performed the low-to-high upward slash.

After midday, Zenith and Synergy instructed the monks about the plan to take Errant. Well, it was Zenith that spoke. Synergy that stood by him as an imposing statue. "I require the Ayr Rose to find this tunnel entrance. If it isn't there, continue to Renton and inform me. If it is, await my arrival in a few days. Hopefully with a massive army at my back. Oh, and before I forget, can someone please fetch Drake, my horse, from the waterfall basin?" The monks got as ready as they could and left the compound, following a hastily drawn map traced from the one that Zenith carried.

Zenith and Synergy took flight heading for Renton, and it would be less than half a day in direct flight. Sitting abridging Synergy's shoulders nestled amongst his mane and fur hands, free knowing that Synergy would not endanger him in any way. Reaching the clouds, Zenith's face and clothes were moistened by the water held within them. Above the cloud layer, the sky opened wide to the sun in full force, its heat drying Zenith in mere seconds.

Zenith wished so profoundly that he could share this with Lemma; the beauty he was witnessing was unlike anything anyone, except Rysand, had ever seen before. It seemed as if Synergy had read his mind, and Zenith heard his voice as clear as the sky ahead. "One day, brother. I will bring you and your love to the heights you now experience." To Zenith's delight, Synergy seemed eager to sweep Lemma into the unknown of the sky and bring joy to her as well.

The experience was all too brief, as before Zenith had even a momentary chance to gaze and ponder. "I know Lemma will love this view; it will be one of those things only we can share. A memory to share with the children in our future." Renton entered their view from above. Synergy paid attention to his surroundings, swerving and diving amongst the mountains that surrounded the town, selecting an outlying field in which to land, sparsely populated by crops and free of people.

The people of Renton thought a storm had rolled in; extremely strong, unseasonable winds blew through the town, followed by a scream, the shrill of it terrifying to hear.

Asger and Cathal sprinted from the village hall, Cathal asking, "What in the Benevolence was that scream?" Looking in the direction of East Renton, parts of the mountain blocked from view, an enormous creature stood proud, a figure waving from its back. Both shared a look at each other as they digested the sight before their eyes. Cathal fearfully spoke. "It can only be one person; if it isn't Zenith, I'd say we are done for." Whilst speaking, he was thinking to himself. "It proves the real battle is on the horizon."

No sooner had Zenith dismounted from Synergy's back than Cathal and Asger were on him. Cathal embraced him as a brother. Asger stood firm, raising his arm and hand across his chest in salute. Both stood back in awe as Synergy Lay down his head, brushing alongside Zenith, purring like a kitten. It sounded out of place. His majestic and intense form, then that sound, brought a chuckle to Zenith and those gathered around.

At the edge of the field where Synergy was strewn, all of Renton stood with looks of perplexity and wonderment in equal measure. All of the children hung eagerly on the fences, hoping to pet Synergy like they had Rath on her first arrival. Zenith stood by thinking. "Well, this is my fault. I let them play and fuss, Rath. No wonder they lack fear in the face of Synergy."

Zenith looked over at all their smiling faces and spoke to Synergy, "How do you feel about letting the towns' rapscallions play about your fur and make a fuss of you?" Synergy looked at them and squealed in approval. Zenith then shouted to the gathered crowds. "Come on, then, you rap scallions, Synergy says you can play." Without a second to spare, a barrage of children ran headlong to him. Soon enough, Synergy was covered in the little squirts, squirming and floundering through his fur and feathers. Synergy just lay there, relaxed, smiling with his eyes.

The day had drawn to evening, when Lemma and the six and half thousand approximately, strong Scirainian army reached the mountain entrance to Renton, The guards recognized her immediately, forcing the doors wide and standing at attention as they watched with shock as the forces began to march through the entrance, thousands of swordsmen, pike bearers, Toxites and Archers walked ten abreast marching in unison.

It took several hours for the walking army to pass, then the siege equipment began to roll by like thunder in the night, the sound echoing along the tunnel's walls.

Standing on the Renton side of the passage, Zenith waited and wondered. The signal had already come that the Scirainian had arrived, but he knew. *Even Rath at full pelt will take a good hour to arrive; this passage does cut through a mountain after all. Oops, sarcastic thoughts have a way of popping up now and then.*

The monotonous silence was broken by the steady rumble of a marching army that vibrated the arch in front of Zenith. This sound ignited his emotions; his entire demeanour perked up as he prepped and primed himself, sweeping back his hair into a rough-tied ponytail, adjusting his pants, and finally unbuttoning the top of his shirt, pulling the collar straight.

A quick look at Cathal and a nod of approval, his back straight, he looked forward in anticipation, a cheek-splitting smile adorned his face.

Rath's head was the first to pierce the tunnel exit. She cooed, seeing Zenith almost bucking in excitement, pulling towards him. There on his back sat Lemma, unusually dressed in a finery that Zenith would never get used to, thinking to himself. "Lemma, you are my warrior princess, not this damsel in a dress, more likely I'll be the damsel in distress", then letting a chuckle loose from his lips. So colourful and vibrant were the decorations that adorned Rath. It made Rath look like a parade cart; it must have been Catherine's doing. At least the look of frustration on Lemma's face suggested that.

Seeing Lemma like this didn't dampen Zenith's mood. He just wanted to grab her and hold her close, feel the warmth of her touch before taking her to Synergy. Lemma looked down on Zenith, and within a second, she leapt from her seat.

Lemma's flowing regal dress twisted and swayed as she fell from Rath's back towards Zenith's yet unopened arms. Plummeting downward, Lemma giggled, seeing Zenith's reaction, the shock horror in his face as he realised his current predicament, flinging his arms open wide too late to catch Lemma, his head disappearing in the folds of Lemma's dress.

The dress hooked around his shoulders, leaving Lemma dangling several inches off the floor with a husband-shaped form at her waist, covered in her Scirainian blue gown. The onlookers' faces all flushed red as rubies, watching as Zenith's body squirmed, his head bobbing and weaving, trying to escape his frilly prison, imaginations running wild, not being helped by Lemma's increasing laughter and movement as she swung left and right from hips to head, her legs latching around Zenith's body, smiling all the while.

35
THE PLAN TO MARCH

The fuss of Lemma's entrance to Renton all put to one side, and Zenith free, embracing her, pulling her close to him. Smelling her hair, that familiar scent of Byzantium rose filling his nostrils, igniting his senses. Taking Lemma by the hand, whisking her up into his arms, cradling her like the princess she is, passionately kissing her, making up for lost time and absence. Lemma lay in Zenith's arm, relaxed, feeling safe and secure, thinking. *Oh, how I need this, those feelings that plagued me, lingered till this moment. I knew he was all I needed to rid myself of them.* As Lemma's thoughts vacated, she fell even deeper into the kiss he had surprised her with.

Once they had all said their hellos and cordial greetings, Zenith led Lemma hand in hand through town, not telling her why. She followed him along, jovial, skipping, in a completely out-of-character mood. Zenith couldn't help but watch Lemma thinking. "Lemma, this isn't the you I usually get to see. I'm grateful for these moments we get you and me, I get to see the you no one else does, the you who places such trust in me to act so freely." Looking back, gazing lovingly at a Lemma, seeing the smile on her face betray her feelings of exuberance and love, no matter what lay ahead, forced the voice from inside his head to speak unfiltered.

"Lemma, my dearest love, I cannot say enough how much I feel the luck I had in meeting you. The fortune I hold in my heart, seeing the love you have for me. The dreams and life I wish for us to share, and the happiness I hope we can bring to those around us, but in this moment, you are the perfect picture of beauty and grace. A treasured portrait of honour and strength. You are a warrior, strong and mighty, a woman beautiful and unblemished and a Queen majestic and pure." Lemma's footsteps halted, fixed in place by Zenith's words.

A single solitary tear shimmering as it rolled down her red, flushed cheeks, her moist, emerald eyes gleaming, smiling unfiltered. The slightest of an upward curl at the side of her soft lips, hinting at the most genuine of smiles. A quivering bounce vibrating slightly within her upper lip, as if the words she could not form. The tip of her nose, twitching as though it tried to hide her embarrassment. The sentence left Lemma's pursed lips, spoken in the softest of whispers. "I love you, Zenith."

Zenith, unaware he had spoken out loud, replied in complete surprise. "I love you, too."

The field was still surrounded by onlookers and children playing on and around Synergy as Lemma and Zenith arrived. Lemma stopped dead, seeing the giant beast that was Synergy. A sudden pang of inferiority, just standing there, her mind struggling with conflicting thoughts. "God, I feel smaller than an ant, yet no fear? Who really can fear a creature that lies there cooing and lighting up as children clamber all over it?"

Zenith walked with Lemma to Synergy's face, placing their hands on Synergy's beak and speaking.

"Brother, this is my truest love and wife, Lemma. Hold her in your heart as I hold you. Please protect her as you would me," although Lemma didn't hear the words inside Zenith's head, the look of stern admiration Synergy gave said all that needed to be said, knowing entirely she was safe with him. Zenith, however, heard him clearly,

"Brother, though she is your wife, she will be as a daughter to me, for you or her my last breath will easily be given."

After spending some time with Synergy so he and Lemma could become familiar with each other, they left, heading for the town hall. Within the confines of the small-town hall sat the rest of the group, all awaiting Zenith and Lemmas' arrival. Brent piped up, gaining the others' attention. "Their Highnesses have arrived."

Zenith took up a seat as head of the table at the farthest end of the room, whilst Lemma sat to his left. Zenith had already explained on the return walk to Lemma that he intended to consider all points before offering any options. Once comfortable, Zenith addressed the room. "I will not be speaking, I wish to listen, digest all that you planned."

Asger began the meeting speaking slowly with purpose. "Cathal and I have considered many options, most of which bore little to no fruit. They would ultimately fail at the city walls with the limited forces we had readily assembled; there were too many unknowns for us to factor in."

Cathal cut in, "Let's just get to the point! We got nowhere fast except for your one drunken option, which we now know is indeed possible." The feeling of being sniped made Asger snap back. "Alright already, I was being free with the information"

Once said he continued. "The plan Cathal refers to uses me

and the men of Renton as a Trojan horse, but will not work without the cooperation of the Scirainian siege units and workers"

Lemma interjected, "Uses the siege equipment as a Trojan horse, how? Won't Quinten see that as an attack!" Asger looked at her straight in the eyes, "Not if I've captured them, he won't. You see, it relies on the information I'd previously sent to him."

Inquisitive Lemma asked, "Oh, what information might that be?" Asger lay down on the table for Lemma to see copies of missives detailing the recent assault on Sciran, only detailing a victory showing many prisoners of war taken.

Infuriated, Lemma slammed the table "Prisoners of war, you want my men to demean themselves!?" shocked, Asger replied, "No, not demean, act the part. Please, princess, allow me to explain. Suppose I and the men of Renton escort them. We can get them in front of the walls just out of range of the defences, but within their range." Lemma saw sense in his words, slowly coming around to the idea, her next thought being said without realising.

"Ok, so that gets three to four hundred of my countrymen inside the Errant borders safe, did you forget I bought six thousand more with me?" Asger admitted to being unprepared for the numbers that had arrived. He deferred the room to Lemma, asking for any relevant information to improve upon his and Cathal's work.

Lemma was quite happy to lay out the ideas she had, speaking firmly,

"The Scirainian army will march with me and Zenith, we will follow behind your detachment by a day so that we can surprise Errant in one foul swoop as we arrive, the siege units will begin their barrage. That is as long as you defend them whilst they set up the defensive wall that they carry to protect them." A confused but intrigued look crossed over Cathal's face as he spoke. "Siege equipment with a defensive wall of its own making. I've never seen anything of the type inside the gorge. Can u describe it? It sounds fascinating."

Lemma had quite forgotten that Cathal was a citizen of the gorge and that his knowledge would differ from those gathered here; he was just a part of the furniture now.

She granted his request quite eagerly, almost boastfully.

"Each siege engine carries thick shielded interlocking squares, enough that when built together, they form a six-meter-high wall that provides cover for the men and engine. These can be connected along the line of siege engine, forming a full shield wall."

Just the very thought of the wall amazed Cathal; he had full intent to take this back to Vastuk, and soon, if Rysand should see it done.

Lemma then continued the planning that Catherine had given her instructions on.

"Due to the volume of volunteers that joined up to aid in this campaign, my mother had around four thousand extra forces, which she had yet to equip when I left Sciran fully. Her intent is once kitted out to send this extra force across the Ryecliff bridge and to station in Grissam for the village's protection as well as escorting Merik home." Hearing this, Asger's mind whirled. If possible, his ears would have smoked as a further plan formed; he interrupted the flow of the meeting, interjecting forcefully, forgetting etiquette.

"Quinten will respond to this with force, and that I'm sure of. He will send at least half the standing army to meet them. If timed right, we can put them between me and the Scirainian army. This also presents another opportunity, I'm almost sure it will be Fortna who will command them."

Brent piped up, "Who is that?" Asger continued, "Fortna is

a commander I trained and just like me, a man who would see the Throne in better hands, if we send a message to that front with my seal on. He may turn coat and fight with us."

Brent stood, leaving the room at a pace, soon returning with a single Scirainian man, sleek and athletic. Brent gestured to the man as he spoke.

"Give this man that letter; he is among our fastest runners, and he will catch up to those forces and make sure it is delivered." Asger grabbed a quill and paper from the desk at the side of the hall and wrote the missive for Fortna. Dripping blue wax from the candles, he pressed his signet ring into the fold and across the join. He placed the message in the runner's hand and wished him Godspeed.

All back at the table, looking to Zenith, who had yet to speak, his face full of thought. Zenith remained silent, mulling over all he had heard. Zenith pulled the map from the bag that he had hung upon the chair where he sat. Lemma and Cathal recognised it immediately and wondered how a map of ancient Apprite could help now.

Asger and Brent lost watching this situation, wondering what Zenith was about to show all of them, and where his mind might be heading.

That familiar glow emanating from the map, as Zenith placed it on the table, caught Cathal and Lemma's attention. They noted that it had changed its topography, now newer, with the old cities gone, replaced by the current ones. Brent and Asger looked at the map, bemused, wondering about the glow that the others ignored so easily, as well as the fact that it seemed no different from any map they'd seen before, except for one notable difference: to the west of Renton.

Zenith took some loose objects from the tables dotted around the hall, small enough to use as tokens on the ancient map to indicate differing armies. Taking the tiny model of scales, he placed it on Grissam, saying one thing. "Sciran." Next, using the minute statuette of Rysand's likeness, putting it on the Renton crossing bridge and speaking again, "Asger." Next, taking a child's miniature horse and placing it randomly on the hill surrounding Renton's western side. This time he spoke at length. His voice was somehow regal and commanding.

"You may observe here that I have only indicated two of the armies you have discussed while I listened to you all have your say and voice your plans or information." Asger looked at him, speaking plainly. "I can see that you incorporated Sciran and my forces, but what of the Ayr rose and Lemmas' forces?"

Nodding in acknowledgement of Asger's questions, Zenith again spoke. " Yes, Asger, indeed I have, we will be using both of your ideas. I aim to reduce casualties as much as possible. The plan you presented does this in two ways. First, by putting our siege equipment in place without the need to fight. Second, if your message to Fortna works even in any percentage, we will then not need to fight them." All the group hummed in agreement, seeing the way Zenith pushed the campaign.

Cathal was next to pose a question: "Why does the horse just sit on the mountain?" Asger and Brent echoed his sentiment, and Lemma just looked to Zenith, whispering. "I trust you". Sizing up the room, Zenith placed his hand on the horse and ancient map, pulling them to one side, revealing the battle map Cathal and Asger had used while planning underneath it.

Next, he took the quill from Asger's vicinity. On the battle map, he drew two large circles, labelling one and saying "Entrance" and the other "Exit." He then joined them with two lines to show their connection. Before speaking, he also drew a crude rose at the entrance.

All looked at Zenith, his face sure. They're faces, full of

doubt and confusion. "What are you doing?" They all thought in unison. Zenith firmly spoke, "What I guess you didn't see is, that on the prior map a tunnel runs from here to Errant, it hasn't led me wrong, it even guided me to the Ayr rose by a swifter route, none here knew, including me." Cathal, Asger and Brent, all still unsure, listened intently whilst Lemma just sat there smiling cheerfully, trust in Zenith unwavering.

Zenith took a second to breathe before beginning his explanation. "This is that tunnel, the Ayr rose now waits for me and any men I bring. Their instructions were simple: find it. If it is there, set up camp and wait; if not, join me here. They haven't turned up, so that is all I need to know; the tunnel is real. Lemma, Cathal and Brent, along with the six thousand Scirainians, will take this route. By my calculations, it will have us at Errant's western walls in eight and a half days."

Asger was the first to speak, confused, "You mean, you can get there just after I've arrived, and the Errant forces will still be focused on me?"

Brent spoke second, eager and excited, "We will travel beneath the land from here to Errant, no one will ever know we are coming," Brent's face lighting up with glee. His inner child was thrilled at the chance of an adventure.

Zenith just smiled, taking back the floor to continue. "If we all leave in three days as Scirans' extra detachment do, you will arrive if I am predicting Quinten correctly, one day after he sends Fortna to meet them in Grissam, stopping him from recalling them." Pausing to take a breath, then continuing.

"Fortna should receive the message the next day, giving us the day to see if he will switch and fight with us or stay an enemy." Asger followed along, nodding in agreement. "That will also give Asger the day to set his Trojan horse up, also, I thought for you to enter Errant and see if you can gain any traction with those inside its walls."

Zenith caught Asger off guard with this; he hadn't considered speaking to those he knew in Errant to garner favour, but he liked the idea so eagerly agreed. Once the others all caught up and saw the sense of the plan so far, Zenith took to the floor again, circling the table as he spoke.

"Finally, on the eighth day, my companions and I will emerge at the western cliffs and begin the assault on the unprepared western walls." Stopping behind Asger and placing his right hand on his shoulder, directing his speech to him. "Any help there, Asger, would be appreciated." With that, Zenith finally finished laying out his plans to take Errant with as little bloodshed as possible.

Lemma sat dumbstruck, still seated, lost in her thoughts. *Who was this man, carrying such command and bravado? I see the same man I love. That meek farmer still sits in his eye, but in these last weeks, he has grown in strength and resolve. How did I miss it?* Snapped from her delirium as a large wooden plate clattered on the table in front of her, three women had entered the room while she had been unfocused, bringing with them food and drink for all those in the room.

From the door, a scraping sound as a burly townsman dragged in a large ale barrel. Cathal joined him, helping to lift it to the tabletop at the opposite end to where Zenith sat. The burly man pulled from his leather apron a mallet and beer tap, smashing the tap into the barrel's waxy seal, checking the ale flowed well, then offering a quick bow and leaving. Asger took to his feet once the ladies left the room, speaking to all present in a formal yet excited tone.

"My King, My princess and friends, I offer this meagre banquet and ale in celebration of the forthcoming battle and our continued friendship." The group made merry. Asger

summoned a flute player from the town and had him play
traditional Ocardian songs. Zenith took Lemma, pulling her up
from her seat, placing one hand at her shoulder, the other
riskily low on her back. From outside the town hall, a shrill
scream. Breaking from their dance, Zenith sprinted back to his
seat, grabbed the Echidna flame, and darted from the room
following Lemma, almost tripping over the drunken bodies of
Brent and Cathal back-to-back in the centre of the room.

Asger was the first into the town square. Screaming townsfolk
lay all about, injured, and others ran about trying to aid them
to safety. Asger, taking in the situation, saw a large, visceral
creature and bellowed out to those present. "Take the
wounded and leave." Then ran to the nearest person, offering
them aid.

Lemma came sprinting into the Square—Asger, alerting
her to the creature standing on top of the dolomite podium.
Lemma looked at the beast, black scales covered its strangely
hourglass figure, swords sat where hands should be. It looked
no taller than an average woman, shrill screams of pain and
anger flying out from its hidden mouth, somewhere within the
flat disfigured mess sat on its shoulders, black blood oozed
from the top of its head, flowing down its body, pooling about
its webbed duck-like feet.

Lemma could sense it, somewhere deep inside her mind,
this was a citizen of Renton. Lemma, seeing Zenith's imminent
arrival, screamed to him, "It's a Creature of Rycore, but something is different; the taint isn't as strong, the person fights
from within." Hearing Lemma's words gave Zenith a pause.
"The person fights, can we free them without death?" He
wondered while drawing the Echidna flame. From the podium,
the beast jumped, aiming its sword-like hands for Lemma.

Zenith saw the movement lunging to the front, holding the Echidna flame horizontally, blocking the blow, staggering the beast. Lemma, released the star watching it curl close by Zenith, his hair shifting from the breeze it created.

The star plunged for the beast's right arm, lifted high in front of it to block the star's incoming attack. Lemma moved to Zenith's side, waving her arm downward. The star followed the unprovoked command, dropping by an inch or two, connecting with the beast's wrist, severing it clean off. The sword blade fell to the floor, twitching as it spurted out the last of its blood from the open wound as the lightning struck, melting it from existence. Zenith spoke, "Lemma, try not to kill. We need to try and save the person inside."

Lemma nodded as the star returned to her hand. The beast still came at them again. Zenith pointed the Echidna flame out, summoning the Snake's flame, binding the creature in place, and mollifying the scale armour slowly. Lemma gasped, "There, Zenith, by the flames, I see skin, what did you do?" Zenith looked to flames, sure enough, he saw it, Skin. Gripping the Echidna Flame, imagining the fire shearing the entire body of scales, they began to move, minute movements at first, like they tested that they could perform the order.

Next, they twisted and moved, elongating, not letting the creature move from its grasp. At the beast's left foot, the flame curled and flowed over the scales, liquifying them, revealing the skin beneath them, continuing to move upwards and extend around both legs. Zenith exclaimed, "It's working." Then, abruptly, screaming at Lemma. "Wheat sacks, Lemma fetch clothes or a towel." Lemma looked at Zenith, a complete discombobulation all over her face, until the thought hit her and she screamed out loud. "Mulock, dung, she's gonna be naked if this works! On it," Lemma turned sprinting to the nearest house, slamming her whole body into the door, bursting it open and surging inside to search.

Zenith had watched the flames liquify the scale from the woman's body, thinking. "Hurry Lemma. I'll hold the flames away from her seed patch and chest till you get here. I am not dealing with that conundrum." The flames read his thoughts clearly, leaving the groin and chest areas covered in scale. Moving to the face slowly, the fire revealed the woman's face. Zenith recognised her speaking. "You're the woman from the meeting who doubted me!" A meek voice barely above the silence replied. "Yes... yes... My prince, please help me. I don't want this."

Zenith heard her plea and called to her. "You are the one who must fight. Reject Rycore, announce your sins so that Rysand can cleanse you." Lemma rushed to the woman's side with a large hessian bag in hand. Zenith saw it and questioned. "Lemma, really a bag?" Lemma looked him straight in the face and shouted. "Would you prefer the see-through chain vest?" Zenith recoiled, embarrassed, thinking. "See through chain vest, yep, I just made a husband mistake again."

The woman, still wrapped in flames, screamed out loud, "Rysand, forgive my sins, I should not have doubted the prince, your general. Please save me." Lemma rushed to place the bag over the woman's head as she saw it, the flames chipping small sections from her groin and chest, turning it into a see-through scale vest. Once covered, Lemma ran to Zenith, slapping him hard across the left cheek and screaming in his face. "Get that mind of yours out of the mud and fix her." Then, whispering in his ear. "Anyway, I'll be the one wearing that chain vest later."

Zenith's cheek reddened, eyebrows raised in response—the pain of the slap, reasserting his concentration on removing the rest of the scales. From the sky, the purest of white light shone down, pulling the liquified mess at the woman's feet upward and away from her, watching in amazement as her severed hand returned unstained and without scar. A sense of serenity coursed through her, leaving a strong, pure feeling. She had been accepted into Rysand's grace, purifying her body and mind. Into the sky, her echoed words floated, "Thank you, Rysand, for your forgiveness and the miracle you grant me."

The blackness gone, Zenith released the flames, freeing the woman, who raced to Lemma, hugging her, begging forgiveness. Lemma's reply was short and snapped. "My forgiveness isn't what you need. Kneel at my husband's feet and beg his forgiveness as the man you besmirched."

Turning to Zenith, she knelt, speaking. "My Prince, you saved me from myself, even though I cast doubt on you, I am lower than a mud muncher. Punish me as you see fit, but please, I beg thee, forgive me." Zenith looked down on her and spoke. "Do not beg forgiveness of me, you have been forgiven by one far higher than I. You will not be punished; you did no wrong. Another being controlled you through weakness that you have now sealed." The woman threw herself to the floor at Zenith's feet, tears streaming from her face, and saddened screams of emotion tore the air as she attempted to speak again. "My...Pri....Prince....Th...Than....Thank you."

Lemma couldn't help it; she felt the woman's pain and sadness all too much and dropped to the floor, cuddling her, whispering kind words to her, trying to soothe her broken heart. Asger made his way back into the town Square, moving to Zenith and seeing Lemma sitting on the floor, cradling the woman, asking, "What happened? Zenith just waved him off and said, "Fetch this young lady's family so that we might end this day and rest."

. . .

Calling the town and army together before they returned to the inn building, Zenith took to the dolomite podium, speaking proudly.

"All of you who gather here to aid me. I cannot express the gratitude I feel deep inside my heart for each of you. In three days, we march to war. A war to free our lands for many, and a war to free a kingdom for others. Whichever reason you fight for these three days are Yours to do as you wish. I will be spending my time with those I call family and friends. I suggest that you all do the same, for I do not know how long we will be away. Now my Friends go from this square to your homes or tents and make merry, enjoy the calm before the storm we aim to create."

The people who stood listening cheered in reverence of Zenith before departing the square, all aiming to do as Zenith said and spend this time in the best way possible.

36
TUNNEL VISION

Three days had whisked by, and now the army had lined up ready to march. Asger stood at its head, roughly a thousand troops behind him, then the almost two hundred siege engines, with their four hundred sappers ready, fake iron chains trailing behind the machines, ready to make the Trojan horse seem real. The rest of Asger's men then filed in behind them.

Zenith, accompanied by Lemma, rode atop Rath, Brent and Cathal on their finely armoured steeds to the left and right, the six thousand-strong Scirainian army standing in row and column, ready to march. Synergy has insisted that he would join them in eight days; he could fly there in half a day. Zenith took the way he spoke to have other motives, and Synergy didn't deny them. Simply remaining silent at the suggestion, he only wanted to stay behind to interact with the children.

Zenith gave it some thought after the conversation "He's become more active with them over the last few days, giving them rides on his back, swinging them on his tail. I'll forgive him this, knowing Synergy has spent decades alone and now enjoys being accepted and loved. It's quite the sight to see, and why ruin it?"

Asger called the horns to sound, and the march began. One and a half days lay ahead, with each other passing through the hills and valleys until they split, where the chains would be needed, and Zenith would join the Ayr Rose monks and descend to the mystic tunnel's depths.

The first day's march went faster than expected. The road formed in the years that Renton had been hidden had proved more than helpful. The siege engines moved smoothly at a modest pace, even with its uneven surface, putting them slightly ahead of schedule, meaning either an early camp or a later start the next morning. Asger opted for the early camp, giving them extra time to set camp while the sun still shone overhead.

Zenith, Lemma, and Cathal sat around relaxing and talking, all feeling an ominous and haunting feeling over the sun's position in the north, not the west; Zenith braved it, bringing it to the conversation's forefront. "The sun's aura has started to change, its usual bright yellow colour looks dimmed to an off orange. I think it's got to mean that things are beginning to switch, Rycore's awakening is becoming more likely."

Lemma took a serious tone. "We can't focus on that Zenith for now, we need to be here in the moment. Anyway, I get the feeling it's all being made worse by the fact that it goes seemingly unseen by the ten thousand men around us." Cathal butted in with his opinion. "Honestly, I've seen this in the gorge, not quite in the same way, though. It's just been getting darker and darker, whereas normally it is the brightest time of the year." Lemma Tutted and snapped, "I said we need to leave it, Cathal, regale us with more of your misadventures."

Zenith took the moment that Lemma's snap created between them, wondering, *What was that?* looking at Lemma with Concern, and spoke. "Lemma, you know I love you with all my heart. I feel something is wrong. Please tell me what's wrong so that I can help." Lemma was already thinking, *I shouldn't have snapped.*" Lemma, turning her face to Cathal, said, "Cathal, I'm sorry I should not have snapped. We haven't faced the wait before battle together yet." Cathal looked at her and waved it off. Lemma then turned to Zenith and spoke again. "Zenith, my love, you still haven't seen this side of me. I know you have yet to learn it. Before any battle, I prefer not to speak of the future in any form. I spend the time focused on the day, the people, and making sure everyone is content. Talking of darker things offsets that rhythm." A new understanding dawned on Zenith. *My wife only thinks of her people and that this may be their final days, so today, she focuses on them.* Zenith looked at Lemma, renewed faith and compassion in his eyes. "Ok, Lemma, I think I understand. Let's make this a night they remember."

The day turned to night, and soon enough, the campfires were lit, the men made merry, campfire songs rang out in the dark, the hills surrounding them adding the perfect acoustics. Eventually, Asger had to be the bad one and call the evening tattoo to play, signalling to all that it was time to rest.

The morning's onset seemed to come too soon for most, who had been overly rambunctious while making merry, not deterred. Even those whose heads hung heavy soon had their camps disassembled and formed up with the units, as all made ready to march. The morning flew on by as they rounded the second valley's pinnacle. It was time to split.

Asger rode to the front of Zenith's detachment and bid him adieu, safe travels, stating, "Within the next ten days, sire, you will be king as you should have always been."

With that, he turned his horse and returned to the front of

the Errant detachment. Lemma shouted after Asger, "safe journeys and fortunes."

As the army began to split, the chains of the sappers were applied; their freedom was secure, but the vision of a mass prisoner-of-war train being escorted by the two-thousand-strong Errant army that now surrounded them was in full effect.

As soon as Asger's army had left their view, Zenith and Lemma turned Rath towards the Tunnel and the eventual arrival in Errant.

Thaddeus waited at the tunnel entrance, watching the valley for any sign of Zenith's arrival.

Soon enough, Rath, carrying Zenith and Lemma, came into view. Thaddues alerted the brothers of the Ayr rose, who broke camp immediately, cries of jubilation running rampant, as they celebrated the arrival. Zenith stood on Rath's back and called out.

"Greetings, Thaddeus and brothers of the Ayr rose. We have no time to waste. Fortunately, I see that you have no camp set per se. This makes it so much easier. I ask you to join my army's ranks so that we may move forward to victory."

Moving together, the Ayr Rose brothers manoeuvred themselves into the ranks between Zenith and the Scirainian forces. Zenith issued the order "Move out" as soon as the brothers had amalgamated with the army.

Into the tunnel the army descended, Zenith at its head. Forward they marched in perfect unison, the darkness enveloping them as the sun's light diminished. Springing to life row after row, the torches seemed to light up instantly with a synchronicity that made it seem almost magical; the tunnel became brighter with each new light source piercing further into the looming black of the tunnel.

Hours passed, and still the army filed in, ten abreast, side by side, a determined look on each of their faces, a soaring spirit emanating from everyone. The wonder and intrigue this tunnel promoted made it an adventure for each.

Once the rear horns sounded, signalling the final man entering, Zenith calculated that they would march for another four hours before sunset. The perfect opportunity and time to make came, the tunnel could support the camp, but if they could find one, a cavern would improve the conditions.

The first night in the tunnel passed without incident; everyone remained in an exuberant spirit, the fantasy of being several miles underground and protected from the night boosting each man. It was the monotony of marching endlessly in only torchlight on the fourth day of travel that began to drag morale down.

Every soldier doing their best to boost their cohorts back to a level footing, Lemma had noticed the drop and had begun to sing a Cadence. "We march, we march, to Errant we will go, we march, we march, through tunnel we must go, we march, we march, over Quinten's walls, we march, we march into Errant we will go." The tunnel echoed as the words travelled the length of the army, repeating so many times that the sound of the song boomed off the walls. Its echo and acoustic vibrations became deafening, stifling the jubilation. Silence fell as the mundane returned. Aboard Rath, Zenith spoke with Lemma. "At least we are far enough along to make camp again. We will let the men drink, boost their spirits. I'm sure you, my dearest wife, will think of suitable punishment should any take too many liberties."

Zenith issued orders to be passed down the line. Tonight,

the men could drink but within reason. Also, ensuring that Lemma's promise of punishment was issued. Stating that any man who went beyond this would be carrying three men's equipment the next day. This news spread down the rank and file at a blistering speed, the smiles returning to almost all faces. The faces that didn't turn to joy grimaced, not wanting the alcohol induced dreams this tunnel may produce.

Zenith promised those under his command they would be able to unwind on every second night, knowing the men needed to be relaxed and free of distraction if they were to make Errant in four days. This news boosted morale even further. The men all began to talk and mutter that Zenith was a commander worthy of their respect. Lemma, always being one to mingle with the men, heard this. Her thoughts becoming overjoyed. *Finally, my countrymen have accepted Zenith; they even acknowledged him as one of their own, a leader to them. He's become a Prince of Sciran in more than name now.*

The fifth and sixth days of marching had passed, and only a select few soldiers had dared to ignore the warnings, overindulging and instantly regretting it, having thought that their direct commanding officers would not notice them. Carrying three men's equipment was not fun in the slightest; it weighed them down and forced them to exhaust themselves to keep pace. No other man dared to try and test their command chain's patience from Zenith downward to the unit commanders. The punishments had been issued without the slightest delay or sign of weakness. Some even believed it to be too quick a response as if the commander knew before it happened.

The seventh night was different; the campsite was within a gargantuan cavern. Its wall glittered with crystals of all colours. Every person present was in awe at the way the torch-light bounced off them, forming rainbows in the air.

Paths of all colours formed on the floors, every nook and cranny lit up in the fantastic display of illumination.

This night would be the easiest for all resting here, except for Zenith; his night had only just begun.

Zenith held Lemma in his arms, their private tent setup for the first time since they had departed. The soldiers had expressed a wish for their prince and princess to spend the eve of battle in comfort. Lemma caved to the demands, as many of her people hounded their commanders to express their feelings to her.

Lemma had genuinely enjoyed it; the evening had been spent among the men and with those deemed to be among her closest friends, with the constant thought of flirting at the edges of her mind. *I'm getting to spend the night with my husband in an intimate way.*

Once they had given in to the night, lying in each other's arms, exhausted and ready to sleep. Lemma was first to drift off, lulled and fooled into a relaxed state by Zenith stroking just above her forehead, whispering lullabies to her. Once sure Lemma was asleep, Zenith finally relaxed and lay back in the bed, staring at Lemma before falling into a deep sleep.

Unfortunately for Zenith, this deep sleep was going to be the stuff of dreams and nightmares.

Zenith's eyes opened within the dream, finding himself standing at a black gate, all around him engulfed in impenetrable fog, behind the gate, a hint of Jade light, barely visible.

The gates remained barred. It would not budge, even pushing with all his might.

From the fog came growls, snarls, and other guttural sounds, the sounds of claws grinding on unseen stone, moving within the places he could not see, getting ever closer. Zenith reached for his waist but found nothing. The Echidna Flame, gone. Zenith, panicking, pushed at the gate, franticly kicking, thumping and screaming, still it did not budge. Continuing to struggle more, from the fog, a Slither leapt, claws swinging, aiming at his head.

Zenith rolled away with no weapon to defend himself with. Trying with all his emotions to summon Synergy to his aid, but his call went unanswered. He was truly alone. A second creature emerged from the fog, trampling the Slither, a giant beast with a figure similar to a man's, several times taller, and a single eye in the centre of its forehead. Four arms protruding from its torso reached out, Zenith could not avoid its grasp. Lifted into the air, the creature pulled him towards its gaping mouth, dozens of razor-sharp teeth, blood-stained and white, on display. His mind filled with the thought. "If I die in this nightmare, will I wake in my bed, Lemma still beside me? The beast's mandible began to close around him, the first of the teeth piercing his skin, and intense pain filled him, causing his mind to flee.

His eyes opened again, and he sat on a golden throne at the top of red sandstone steps. Below him, people bowed low, many on one knee, their heads hung low. "Where is this? It seems familiar but somehow different." His mind was not quite able to grasp the location. There to his left sat Lemma on a smaller, no less grand throne, her belly round and full, a glow to her skin and a star-like shine in her eyes.

Looking back at the people assembled, there amongst them Merik in regal and official clothes holding a parchment, checking a list of some sort. After the people had bowed to him, they circled to the edge of the room, and yet more people stepped up. A golden rattle was offered to them, a well-dressed man taking it, turning, and ascending the steps, where it was handed to Lemma, who spoke, "Thank you for such a gracious and wonderful gift."

Again, the person moved to the right. Now, a woman dressed in regal finery stepped forward, a foal on a lead trailing behind. Again, the man took the gift and showed it to Lemma, who spoke again, "Thank you, M'lady, I am sure the foal will prove to be a noble steed." The foal was led away from the throne room, and the next person presented a gift, followed by the person after that. So on and so forth, the gifts kept coming for what seemed an eternity.

Suddenly, an announcement was called across the room. "Queen Catherine of Sciran has arrived." Lemma stood, her face delighted to see her mother. Catherine looked like she was floating as she approached. Behind her, carried by four men, an ornate, dark wooden crib filled with quilts covered with Scirans' colours.

Zenith's mind flashed again, spiriting him away this time. When his eyes opened, he was standing at Errant's Western wall, his army writhing in flames, the western wall filled with archers, loosing fire arrows over the field of battle, the Mangels and javelins atop the towers, firing in quick succession. Plumes of dirt rising in the air obscuring his view.

As the dirt settled, he had to stand there watching as Rath raced by, her feathers smouldering where arrows had pierced the skin beneath them. Lemma nowhere in sight.

Zenith's eyes bursting open, the dreams still playing in his mind, frantically searching the bed, not finding Lemma, jumping from his bed, bursting from the tent. His face panic stricken as he scanned the camp, looking everywhere. Taking to a sprint heading to Rath, frenzied in the search around where she lay and slept. His eyes finally settled on a familiar shape protruding from under Rath's nearest wing.

Heartbeat slowing, beginning to settle while watching Lemma sleeping soundly beneath Rath's wing, there looking content and happy; she must have woken whilst he dreamt. Snuck out of the tent to join Rath, having already voiced concerns over Rath being lonely even before they had retired for the night. Rath had not settled any night within the tunnel until Zenith or Lemma, on some nights both, had snuggled up to her. This bird had become more of a child to them than she ever was a wild beast that once terrorised the gorge.

Zenith was more awake than ever; he just sat watching Lemma sleep, his mind concentrating on the dream. *What was that black gate? I keep seeing it. It seems connected to the city in the fog; my earlier dreams have shown as much.* Speaking to himself. "That city will undoubtedly mean revisiting Rockwall to talk with the old Scribe about how to capture one of Vermont's wolves after I have secured Errant, or as to how I can gather information." He returned to his thoughts after hearing a moan from Lemma. *Perhaps I was a bit loud. I can't figure it out. Is this a dream about the future? Do my dreams predict things to come?*

The more concerning thing his thought focused on for the moment flew around his head. *If this dream predicts the future, does it show the truth of the forthcoming battle? If so, how can the rest be true?"*

The dream showed him the slaughter of thousands and Lemma being lost to him, trying to shake off the negative thoughts. Placing his focus on the throne room, trying to figure out how he knew it, suddenly the pieces fit. *I know it from childhood; Once I was the one settled at the base of the stairs, looking up at my grandfather. It's the throne room within Errant Castle, but it only has one throne.*

Choosing to place his belief in his forces and compatriots' abilities, he shook the feeling of dread, choosing to focus on how beautiful Lemma looked, full-bellied and heavily pregnant.

No sooner had he spent his mental energies on working through his dreams than Lemma began to stir.

Zenith switched his facial expression from one of longing and love to one that portrayed comical annoyance, so he could mess with her as she woke. She nagged him enough behind closed doors back in Sciran; he was due some payback.

Lemma opened her eyes to see Zenith intently staring at her, wagging his finger less than an inch from her face. Lemma, bleary-eyed, acted on instinct, before she registered, it was Zenith. Sinking her teeth into Zenith's finger. Once she woke up properly, the guilt became plastered all over her now teary face. "Zenith, oh gods, I'm so sorry, I didn't know it was you." Zenith sat, shocked astonishment all over his face, cradling his bleeding finger in the folds of his shirt, thinking, "Ok, another husband lesson learned. She doesn't wake up nicely when startled." Lemma wrapped her arms around him, holding on tightly, speaking again in a panic, "Zenith, don't ignore me, please. I'm sorry." Zenith finally spoke to reassure her. "Lemma, tis but a scratch, don't worry, I should have known better. Let's get breakfast.

The soldiers all began to wake around the encampment, preparing for the final day of marching. Their battle would soon be upon them. This soon turned into a jubilant final march, every man eager for the light of day.

The sunlight began to burn Zenith and Lemma's eyes as it finally began to surge in the tunnel's exit on the western cliffs. It took a few minutes of stillness waiting for their eyes to adjust. Once they had, Lemma exclaimed in joy about it, "It's astounding. It's the ocean, the waters are as blue as the sky above." Zenith looked on, loving this sudden burst of freedom in Lemma's voice, and asked. "Have you never seen the ocean?" Lemma shook her head and shot him a stern glance to which he replied, "ok, we will save the talk for later."

To the left of this exit, the cliff jutted out over the drop. Unfortunately, it would slow the march substantially, as only lines of five men side by side could safely walk up it. The path gradually ascended the cliffs, more of an amble than a strenuous hike. The only other issue Zenith could see was the loose chalk on the dusty white cliff path they had to climb; this could cause injury in the best-case scenario or death in the worst-case scenario if men fell over the edge. A mental note was made to secure this route before anyone could return via it.

Fortunately, Zenith's knowledge of the local area would aid in hiding his men as they all filled over the cliffs' top. Above the cliff lay a substantial woodland, providing a hiding place for his troops, allowing them to rest before the assault began.

37
THE EVE OF WAR

Asger's detachment and the fake prisoners of war had entered the Occardian grassland without issue, pitched up where they had intended to, approximately one hundred and fifty meters from the Errant walls, placing them just outside of the tower defences' maximum range. The Errant men encircled them on all sides, making it look real to anyone watching that they indeed had captured nearly two hundred siege engines and all their sappers.

Asger had spent the last day in talks behind closed doors and dark alleys with those in influential positions, sizing up who could potentially be the insiders —the ones to open the floodgates or drop the ladders over the walls, so to speak. Achieving a degree of success in this endeavour, one of the landowners of West Errant was utterly opposed to Quinten, but in public, a stalwart supporter, providing the Western wall with supplies and several hundred men.

Helping to formulate a plan for abandoning positions and creating a weak point in the wall, they needed to take Quinten quickly. Admittedly, Asger had to promise grandeur and position to make sure the landowner would follow through.

Meanwhile, Merik had arrived in Grissam, succeeding in convincing Amabel to join him; the two of them had become overly close in recent days. It was more uncommon to see Merrik without Amabel. She now spent more time attached to him, swooning and displaying interest in all he did, making her feelings Clear.

Merrik had this intent, but he had sworn to see Zenith on the throne before making his declaration and asking for her hand. The spare Scirainian army had taken up defensive positions around the village. The marching army of Errant stood firm in the distance, having arrived within hours of Quinten hearing they had crossed into his territories, thinking they had come to rescue the prisoners of war. Unknowingly to Errant forces, they had become trapped between two pincers of the same army.

The messenger sent by Asger and Brent had already caught up to Merrik and the troops a day prior and handed over the missive from Asger, which laid out the plan plainly in its setup and execution.

The Scirainian commander had received the instructions Brent had issued, but did not know how to approach Fortna, the Errant commander. This was where Merrik had taken the initiative and offered his hand in help.

Merrik believed that as a local, he would likely remain unharmed, especially if he flew the white flag of surrender over his head.

Merrik took Asger's missive from the commander, strode out into the open field carrying a white shirt hastily attached to the largest tree branch he could find above his head. The

Errant army paid great attention to him as he approached. Fortna had been notified of this questionable action, which occurred on the future field of battle.

Fortna, being a man of honour, took to his horse and rode out to meet Merrik in the field. Fortna paid attention to Merrik, noting his clothing and facial expressions, realising that this was not a Scirainian but an Occardian. "What on Apprite is happening?" he thought to himself. Once his horse came face to face with Merrik, dismounting and stepping toward Merrik.

Merrik bowed his head in respect, silent, just holding the message out in front for Fortna to see. Fortna's eyes scanned the message, his eyes drawn to the blue wax marked with the signet of Asger. In astonishment, Fortna spoke, "Where did you get this from?"

Merrik lifted his head so he could respond, "The Scirainian army behind me received this Yesterday from a runner, with instructions to deliver it to you."

Fortna snatched the missive from Merik, rapidly breaking the seal to what was written within.

As he began to read, it was as if Asger stood beside him; he could hear his words.

Fortna, my friend, I know you will find the receiving of this odd, and the situation in which I now find myself even more bizarre. This message comes from my hand. I write it as I help to plan the installation of Errant's true ruler, the son of Ake.

He isn't dead and hails from the very village your unit now looks over. Even though we lost our prince in years past, his son, Zenith, lives. The same child I once watched over as I did you.

If all the plans we have set in motion have reached fruition, your unit will now be between my army and several hundred siege engines at Errant's walls, and a vast number of Scirainian troops.

All I ask of you is to make a choice. Fight for Errant for its people and its true ruler, or stand aside.

Ideally, I would like to have you fight at my side, student and master, but I will be glad even if you choose life over blood. Zenith wishes to minimise bloodshed as much as possible.

With hope and honour
Commander of Renton
Asger

It took Fortna several attempts to read the letter and fully grasp its contents, his mind running rampant.

"Asger has somehow found Zenith alive, how?!"

Asger was like an uncle to him, and Zenith had been a dear childhood friend before his father, Ake, died. He would need to consider this news deeply, but if even one ounce of truth was written within. He would not, could not fight his own country's forces. "I hate the idea of facing Asger on the battlefield." Released to the air in muttered words.

Realising that the choice would put his loyal soldiers in a position to fight their countrymen, he was deeply hurt. Making his own choice easy, he would ride to join Asger, no doubt lay in his heart, of that anyone could be sure. Each of his men would need to choose for themselves.

Fortna looked up from the page, a heartfelt look on his face as he spoke to Merik again. "Sir, if what this letter contains is true, you are not and the Scirainians are not our enemy this day, but liberators?"

Merik nodded, a smile emerging across his face. It seemed the letter had hit its mark, so he enquired. "What does the letter contain that convinces you so easily?"

Fortna, taken aback, looked at Merik with a bemused expression on his face at his statement. "Sir, you truly do not know the content of this message you deliver?" Merik again nodded, allowing Fortna the opportunity to continue. "It comes from a man for whom I hold the deepest respect, my master and friend. That is not what perplexes me so. He tells me that my childhood friend and the crown princess lives. He intends to take the throne by force."

Merik started to laugh heartily from the bottom of his stomach. He had heard Zenith called many things, but the crowned prince was not one he was accustomed to. Through calming laughter, he spoke very nonchalantly, "Oh? Do you mean my brother Zenith by chance?"

Fortna's mouth slammed wide open when he heard this, dropping to his knees. He looked up at Merik, unable to find the words he needed.

"Yo...you.... your... hi...high...ness" the stutter left his lips amongst gasps for breath, shocked to his very core.

Merik, on the other hand, just stood there, boundless laughter as he responded, "I'm not a prince, I am Zenith's step-brother. I hold no royal lineage, so stand up."

Understandably, Fortna didn't have an answer; he stood up and returned to his horse. He jerked the reins, turned the horse, and was off at a canter back to his men, message in hand.

Merik stood motionless for a few seconds, watching Fortna, turning on his heels and marching back to town, in the hope he had been able to do Zenith even one small kindness in what would be his brothers' darkest day.

Fortna returned to his ranks, still mounted, calling for those who served under him to direct their attention to him. First, holding up the message for all to see, with Asger's seal in the blue wax fully visible. The men who had the clearest view all recognised it immediately, starting a chain of whispers that travelled the length of their lines.

"A Missive from Asger has arrived. Do we march on Grissam?" They all wondered until Fortna broke the silence with his commanding voice. "My soldiers, you see here in my hands, the strangest of messages."

The whispers started up. What did he mean by strange. Fortna continued to speak amongst the whispers. "This missive is not to attack or return, just simply a choice for each to make. One that I have already made, so I offer you this choice. Asger has asked us to choose between him and the king." Shouts erupted from the men gathered, "Asger is no traitor, do not lie", coming from multiple voices within the crowd.

Fortna waved them to silence, asking them to listen further.

"Men, Asger has made a damaging discovery that Ake's son, the prince royal, is still alive. He did not die as the current king claimed"

The shock of his announcement reverberated through the entire assembly. It rocked their very cores. This same statement could undo the decline of the last decade and more. The older soldiers remember Barathor's rule fondly; those who had been but children at his death didn't truly understand the ramifications.

Once he had given them a chance to digest the information, Fortna called for silence again, offering the choice for the second time, and added that those who did not wish to fight could stay in Grissam; none who did would be considered deserters.

It took almost two hours before each man had made their own decision, some because of loyalty to the crown, others because they didn't want anything to come back on them or their families if the coup failed, and many other reasons, all valid. Fortna kept to his word; these men would stay behind.

Still, nearly two-thirds of his men said they would follow

Fortna. They all knew that if Asger was involved, it meant something. He wasn't the kingdom's highest-ranked commander for no reason. He had proven over many years his strategies and ability to lead, which were beyond those of most ordinary men.

Once these men had separated, they hoisted a white flag high and marched into Grissam, where the villagers welcomed them. The Scirainians moved to join with Fortna's troops, forming up at their rear, quite a sight to see—a joint force comprised of men who, until moments ago, had been enemies. Almost totalling eight thousand men moving in unison, like they had marched this way a thousand times before.

The joint force soon appeared on the horizon in Asger's view. This could only mean one thing: the battle would soon begin. Quinten would hear that the Scirainian's had arrived alongside Fortna. Any blood shed now would be unavoidable; only Quinten's demise would see it stop.

A Messenger was swiftly dispatched from within Asger's ranks to the spot where Zenith should be waiting, told to tell him the Western wall would be either abandoned or aiding them, but the landowner didn't indicate which.

This was of no consequence; both options would allow Zenith and those with him free entry into the western district and a direct run to the Castle. Asger had the messenger ask Zenith, hoping it would happen that the eight thousand men Zenith bought would swarm the wall and crush any resistance swiftly.

38
A BLOODLESS BATTLE

A sger's messenger had returned dutifully delivering a response from Zenith, informing Asger that he would wait for the ruckus of battle before attempting to assail the western wall.

Asger was more than happy to oblige this request, sending his first order out to those he commanded and the prisoners of war, who still waited with bated breath to relinquish their fake chains of oppression.

The order instructed them to defend the siege engines at all costs once the horn sounded; his soldiers knew this meant to tighten their encirclement. The sappers had their method of defence to set up.

Once time enough had passed, Asger raised his war horn high, one enormous almighty blow into it, signalling the start of battle. His men all stepped backwards in smooth motion, tightening the encirclement. Each man raised his shield overhead.

The sappers joyously threw off the chains, sprang to their feet, all four hundred or so of them pulling a giant metal-plated board from beneath their siege engine. The first rows of the board planted their spikes, burying deep into the ground. Then a second and third row clipping into place, running the length of the siege line, extending a good six meters upward, covering the ballistae completely behind the constructed shield wall.

Except for a window where a couple of boards had not been placed. The ballistae had a clear line of sight from which to fire. The bases of the catapults and trebuchets, completely enclosed behind the wall, provided a haven from any incoming fire.

The sapper soon had each of the engines loaded and ready; they just awaited the order to fire. Asger's men marvelled at the siege wall that appeared as if from nowhere, built with a well-practised precision. They moved to the siege engines' flank, all men instructed to take up a bow.

The need for steel on steel would be staved off as long as humanly possible, for none wished to come to blows with their countrymen even if they were fighting on the right side of history.

The order came, and as it did, the first volley from the trebuchets flew whistling into the air. Huge chunks of stone soared in an almost beautiful way over the field. Their targets, the tower-mounted Mangols and Javelins. The first volley held true, multiple targets reduced to nothing but logs and rope, and towers crumbled. Those that did miss their target careened into the city beyond, smashing into the field, where the rest of Errant's standing army had formed up. The confusion flushed the men in all directions, forcing a temporary retreat to safer ground and a chance to regroup.

As the first crack of stone on stone was heard, the catapults released their payload. Smaller piles of rocks pelted skyward, aimed for the walls' central mass, and the gate that barred entry.

The Catapult's assault peppered the red sandstone walls with gashes and scars the length and breadth of them. The gate held firm still, splinters of wood flying up and away, each piece a crack in the gate's ability to stand. The Errant towers that still stood loaded up and fired; Javelins flew with speed and grace, while arrows rained down from the Mangols.

Their projectiles proved, as Asger had predicted, futile and useless, a few lucky shots making it past, where he had expected, wedging into the shield wall. The wall bending under the pressure of the bolts striking it, a wave reverberating along its length as the shock dispersed. Asger stood at the centre of the siege line, thinking. "What a marvel of engineering it stands firm yet flexes like a tree in the wind under the assault."

The Ballistae and Bowmen stood silent, waiting for their order from Asger to enter the fray. Not a single shot had been freed from them yet. The second wave of Trebuchet rocks flew clean through the air again, striking multiple towers. The catapults had not let up, firing continuously, smashing chunks from the wall and gate. The gate stood battered and broken, its top half hanging out front, held on by sinuous wood alone, defiant.

The towers of the Errant fell silent; those that had survived the onslaught stopped firing, beaten into submission. The walls still stood firm, chipped and blasted, not a single access had been beaten through them. Asger ordered the Trebuchet to halt their fire, the men that manned them to aid the catapults, and when the time came, the Ballistae's.

The upper part of the gate finally fell with a thunderous clap as it smashed to the ground. The Catapults refocused their efforts on the remainder of the gate. Soon enough, it crumbled, obliterated in a hail of stone from all angles.

Seeing that the Errant army had now regrouped and surged forth from the decimated gate, Asger issued orders for the Catapults to switch ammo. Errant men came charging headlong at the siege engines, only for their number to be halved by a hail of Ballista bolts and the Catapult's secondary projectile, glass and metal shards.

Those who survived retreated behind the walls to safety; unfortunately, the first known blood of this battle had been drawn. Asger swore his oath, shouting it to the air. "These men will be given full honours as they fought for a cause as valid to them as mine is to me."

Fortunately, his and Fortna's men's bows had not been needed, but now the Scirainians' bows would be. Asger called out, "Scirainian Archer to the front, we need the range of your bows. Line up spread as far as you can, form up in three lines." This order echoed through the Sciranians from their unit commanders, who were stationed with them, eager to engage.

The first line loosing their arrows and immediately took a knee, the second line loosing their arrows and dropped to a knee, the third line loosing their arrows. Four thousand arrows skirted through the air, filling the sky with black, darker than a storm cloud.

One arrow after another disappeared behind the walls' parapets. Blood-curdling screams were all that could be heard for mere moments before the sky turned black as the Errant defensive army returned fire.

A call came from the Sciran commanders. "Shields." The Scirainians swung their shields above their heads, many too slow to act; the lines broke and splintered as Scirainian blood began to stain the Occardian grasslands.

The Archers that survived released arrows as quickly as

possible to provide even the smallest amount of cover for Asger's and Fortna's surging troops, who charged for the gate.

The sounds of intense battle filled the silent void around Zenith and his army, still hidden by the trees; the battle had begun, signalling his need for haste to reach the western wall.

Focusing his mind, he called for Synergy. "Synergy, I need your aid to dismantle the towers just in case the western lord fails me." No sooner did he call and look to the sky than it seemed as if from nothing. Synergy was there, his giant wings casting a shadow fifty feet across, blocking the sun from view.

Synergy flew towards the battlements, gaining height as he did, the Errant walls darkening as he approached. His first dive caught those below off guard. Sending many men scuttling over the rear edge, falling to their most likely demise. Turning, he ignited his breath, scorching the Javelin stand black as he passed by.

Synergy regained his height, swooping in again, clasping the Mangol on the next tower over in his rear claws, ripping it from the tower, and dropping it on the outside of the wall. Repeatedly, he climbed scorching towers as he did, diving back down, ripping defences clean from their mooring until none were left.

Men had abandoned the wall, none daring to attack him for fear of being burned to ash by his breath. The guards that the landowner had on payroll had hidden within the towers, waiting for their cohorts to flee and Synergy's onslaught to dissipate.

Once the last tower had been rendered unusable, Synergy stopped his attack, choosing to land inside the walls, swatting at those stupid enough to advance on him with his front paw, hurling them into the air to crash back to Apprite out of anyone's sight. Soon enough, he was being left alone, so he stood watching and waiting.

Zenith and his army had steadily advanced, while most tripped over each other watching Synergy in action. Time and time again, soldiers fell to the ground, busy watching the sky, each one dragging themselves back to their feet and returning to the march.

The walls encroached, filling their view, their grandeur not lost on anyone, the march halted as not a soul could see how to scale them.

Zenith thought maybe Rath could jump it, but didn't see the need to risk it if it wasn't necessary. The Archers stepped forward, instructed by Brent, "Archers, prepare the rope arrows, we may need them to climb yet!"

Zenith nodded in agreement, and the Archers set about deploying the ropes. Moments later, the first ladder clattered down the wall, a cacophony of wood on stone as one by one a hundred ladders fell. Asger's plan had worked. The Western lords' men stood above them, waving them on.

Zenith issued the advance, thrusting his arm forward, rushing to the wall on Raths' back, leaping up to the first ladder he met, Lemma following as soon as he had climbed far enough. Brent and Cathal latched onto ladders left and right of them, hauling themselves up the walls and over the parapet to meet them. Reaching the top, unable to quite reach the inner edge of the parapets, Cathal had managed to get wedged in place. Lying half on the wall's top, his leg flailing behind him. His foot connected with the next man on the ladder's head. Feeling his foot hit metal, Cathal called behind him. "Give me a boost, these dam walls are too wide for me to reach."

Zenith issued orders to Brent. "Direct the bulk of the force to take the wall, subdue them as bloodlessly as you can." With that, turning away and witnessing Cathal's plight. Pulling Lemma over to him and showing her, they both laughed as Zenith asked, "Cathal, are you ok over there?" and Lemma taunted, "Is the wee man stuck? You really look like a general of Rysand right now." Cathal called back, "Oi, you pair of mud munchers, get over here and help."

Zenith strode over to the gap where Cathal lay stuck, grasping both of his wrists and pulling. Cathal's iron armour scraped the stone as he moved forward, sparks flying from his sides. The man behind began to push him, his hand slipping. Cathal screamed, "Watch where those hands end up!" With one last pull, Zenith had him free. Both falling to the floor, the sound of Cathal's armour meeting his, deafening all those about. Zenith, now flat on his back, face to face with Cathal, spoke. "If you want a kiss so badly, Cathal, just ask; otherwise, get off me!"

Lemma and Brent couldn't help themselves, nor could the men standing around, all bursting out in fits of laughter.

Cathal rolled off Zenith, both standing, looking at each other very sheepishly, both red in the face as Zenith spoke to all. "Ok, fun's over, can't let Asger have all the glory. Brent, you have your orders. Brothers of the Ayr Rose, follow his direction. Lemma, Cathal, with me."

The Scirainians and Ayr Rose flooded along the wall, knocking as many soldiers out as possible, killing or harming only when necessary, advancing faster than most would have expected. Most Errant soldiers unable to fight, barely even loosing an arrow in return.

The men of the Wall seemed to lack any hand-to-hand combat training, as though their commanders had lost all fear that the wall would be breached. Brent pushed ever onward, trudging past each tower, moving to the southern wall. Errant soldiers surrendered one after another, laying down their arms. Brent began to think. "This is going to go well, it's just too easy."

Brent had jinxed himself with that thought; ahead of him stood a seasoned veteran Errant commander, prepared to lay down his life. His sword stance was firm and practised, showing that he had been at it for years. The Errant commander charged toward him, gaining ground fast. Brent, stunned, stepped back, pulling his shield from his back, raising it to block an incoming downward slash aimed at his shoulder. Shoving it away with the shield, forcing the sword to the side, and then thrusting forward with his blade to be parried by a small dagger he hadn't seen the commander carrying.

In came the next strike, sweeping from his right, cutting the air as it smashed into his shield, forcing another step back with its strength. A second blow in quick succession from the commander's left hand, the point of the dagger piercing the shield and wedging there its point sticking out inside of Brent's shield level with his eyes.

Twisting the shield, Brent dislodged the blade from his assailant's hand, pulling the commander off balance. Brent then swept his sword low to the ground, aiming for the commander's left thigh. Brent's sword connected, but only enough to cut into his leg, the blood seeping out, soaking into the cloth between the commander's armour pieces.

Undeterred, the commander struck again with his sword, getting behind Brent's shield, then ripping it back, pulling the shield from Brent's arm. Luck smiled on Brent; the commander used too much force, setting himself up for a fall.

Straight on him, Brent tackled him, slamming his shoulder into the commander's gut, taking the commander to the ground, righting himself. Brent brought the hilt of his sword down into the soldier's skull with a force strong enough to knock him unconscious. Brent remembered Zenith's words. "As bloodlessly as possible."

Zenith made his way down the stairs of the tower, exiting at the base into the interior of the city. This part of Errant was relatively sparse, consisting mainly of farms with some other small, essential industries scattered here and there.

Moving to Synergy, who had now calmed and lay in the field awaiting him. Anyone who had been near had either fled or hidden in the buildings, seeking shelter.

Standing next to Synergy, Zenith spoke with Lemma and Cathal. "Ok, we've made it inside, but the forces we had are gone. Taking the wall and holding our entrance point has used all of them. So, what do we do now?" Lemma and Cathal understood Zenith's reluctance and doubt; neither of them foresaw this happening with such ease.

Lemma looked at Zenith, his current stature looking regal and more poised with each moment that drew them closer to Quinten. It was like his body grew in confidence, but his mind hadn't caught up. Knowing what he needed to do, surprising flashes of command and brilliance had got them this far. She could not let him falter and fail himself now.

Lemma spoke softly to him, "Zenith, you have me and Cathal with you all of Rysander standing together, then you have those who have sworn loyalty fighting for you at this very moment." She looked up into Synergy's big black pupils, hoping he would help, but he just stared at her.

She continued, "What a fool you must be to forget Synergy is here; we could ride on his back to the castle without fear."

Cathal spoke up, his voice spooked and fearful, "I'll even get on its back if you wish it, but don't think you won't owe me several drinks after, I hate being off terra firmer, you know that."

Zenith began to barrel laugh, seeing the image of Cathal on Synergy's back in his mind. *Tears of fear flowing down from his eyes, wrapped up in Synergy's fur, white-knuckled and red-faced, made this almost worth it. The gruff, formidable warrior of the gorge, afraid of heights, what a picture that did produce.*

Lemma couldn't help but begin to laugh with Zenith, having imagined a very similar situation to the one that had almost brought Zenith to tears with his laughter. Cathal stood stunned and confused, wondering what he had done to provoke this reaction. Synergy even chuckled in his way at the merriment.

Once Zenith regained his composure, agreeing with Lemma's assessment. Synergy was their current best option; he could carry them through the city without incident, and if anyone were foolish enough to approach, a simple flick of Synergy's paw would soon see them turn tail and run.

All three climbed up Synergy's side to his shoulders, Zenith at the head, Lemma gripping his waist, taking the opportunity to nuzzle into his back, hugging him tightly. Cathal, on the other hand, practically used Synergy's fur as ropes, trying to tie his feet and waist in place with some success. Cathal made sure he grabbed hold of the fur in front of him and squeezed tightly.

Up stood Synergy, walking onwards to the castle at the centre of the city, mindful to avoid buildings and crops where he could, making use of trackways and eventually the cobbled roads.

The buildings became denser as they left the open farming areas, small shops and cottage-style houses lined the roads, most built from a combination of red sandstone and the white chalk stone from the Western cliffs. This, in turn, led to the development of larger homes and businesses. It was like walking through the stages of fortune and snobbery.

Those nearest the castle were the most well-to-do, next they crossed into a wide-open cobbled square lined with shops selling everything fancy you could imagine. Clothing stores with windows full of all the latest fashions, jewellery providers displaying emeralds and rubies the size of hands, all the finer things the city could offer.

The castle was bearing down on them, only a block away, and it overshadowed even Synergy. Its tallest tower, easily three or four times his height and twice his girth, the main building immeasurable, cast an aura of strength across the skyline.

Asger watched the walls eagerly awaiting any sign that Zenith's men had taken them so that his forces, alongside Fortna's, could rush the rest of the gate guards and subdue the remaining military inside. Once this had happened, he was sure the city would be theirs; all that was left was to meet and aid Zenith in defeating Quinten.

The sign he had waited for: a rush of alarm and surprise rose from the battlement, as the Errant men were caught off guard by a sudden pandemonium. The arrival of thousands of Scirainian troops flooded over them to secure the gate, knocking men out before they could bring arms to bear.

Asger sounded his horn and screamed, "Charge!" The units under him and Fortna surged forward through where the gate once stood, splitting left and right as they did. They pushed into the Errant ranks. Those who remained of the Errant forces, trying to make it up the tower's steps to the walls, hoping to join their brethren in fighting the Sciranians, only to be caught off guard by the attack biting at their rear.

Most of those Errant men who still stood dropped to their knees on the ground, placing any weapon they had in front of them, feeling the obviousness of their defeat nearing. There, however, were those who refused to acknowledge this and continued to fight, forcing their blood to be shed needlessly.

Brent came down to Asger via one of the towers. The walls had been secured; His men would remain on guard in case of any further action by Errant soldiers. Brent's men's orders hadn't changed. They would still only draw blood if necessary. Asger instructed Fortna to take control of all the men in the city, overseeing both the Errant and Scirainians alike.

Asger spoke his Orders loud and clear to Fortna, "Oversee the collection of personal effects, so that once this war is done, they can receive proper burial rites and their families taken care of, for no matter which side they have stood on, all of them had fought for Errant."

Gathering around one hundred of his troops, Asger, along with Brent, started the long walk to the castle loop wall that separated the southern district from the others. This part of Errant was by far the worst part of the city, the most run-down and crime-ridden area. It produced small amounts of food, had barely any industry, and consisted mainly of rows of homes and shanty-style buildings. All the people here fought for scraps, eking out a daily existence.

The main population of Errant dwelt within the castle loop wall. Asger spoke with Brent in depth as they walked through the muddied streets, the air filled with the smell of rot from the water and food discarded in the streets. Rats and other such critters ran rampant here. Disease ran rampant among the population, with barely anyone having access to even the most basic sanitation. Another consequence of Quinten's lack of care. Even with the healer visiting daily and the help of the church, thirty per cent of the folks living in this area would be riddled with dysentery and scabies. Asger held hope, thinking Zenith would consider improvements for the sake of the people that Quinten had forgotten.

As they moved closer to the castle loop, a small force of around twenty Errant soldiers came out of one of the houses. They had hidden there during the assault, abandoning their duties and leaving their comrades to suffer. Asger spotted them screaming in their faces. "Cowards, how dare you desert?"

Asger could not abide such apparent cowardice and abandonment of duties; the only thing preventing these men from being put to death was Zenith's longing to avoid blood wherever possible. Asger issued his orders. "Detain them, do not hurt them, if they fight, they do so at their peril, any blood spilt will be on their hands, not mine."

Only two of the twenty chose to fight and soon died on one of Asger's men's swords; the rest were just young recruits, barely out of the academy. A feeling of pity washed over Asger as he saw the fear writhing all over their faces.

After moving past this and leaving ten men to watch them, they arrived at the castle gate, wide open, and no guards were to be seen. This could only mean that Quinten had pulled any available men back to the castle for one last stand in hopes of turning the attackers away, or they had fled in the face of the overwhelming force behind the gate.

Ahead stood Synergy at the main castle doors with Zenith, Lemma and Cathal aboard, waiting for them to arrive.

39
THE THRONE ROOM

The group assembled at the base of the castle steps, Zenith lifting Lemma down from Synergy's back. Cathal just tumbled as his armour's boot caught on the descent, "Honestly." Lemma thought he was trying to lighten the mood.

Cathal had already had her and Zenith in a fit going on about riding Synergy. Cathal wasn't being humorous at all; he had honestly hated that ride and swore never again. Gathering himself and dusting himself down, he stood with the others.

Asger spoke, "Zenith, my liege, what are your intentions for Quinten?"

Zenith had to make this clear so that everyone here knew what he intended and where it would leave them.

He summoned his courage to speak, "I do not wish death upon Quinten. I gave up my vengeance; it was not mine to start with. It belongs to my father and grandfather. If Rysand wills it, they will see it done in the great benevolence."

They all understood; the intention was not to kill Quinten.

The choice would be Quinten's: submit and declare his crimes, or give them no other choice.

The group began to climb the tall red stone Castle steps, a large dark wooden door at the top closed tightly, bolted on the outside with a massive iron lock. Asger spoke, already expecting this. "It's part of the defence for the king's plan. I don't see much point in the external lock. On the inside, it will also be barred and secured with logs placed in a row along the length and reinforced by a diagonal one dug into the ground to apply pressure." This would be the first of the obstacles they would need to overcome, or so Asger thought.

Zenith had little patience for trickery at this point. Pulling the Echidna flame from his waist, he summoned up the air, cutting blade, and sliced the lock. The Echidna flame cut into the lock, slowly moving through it, the very metal melting around it, molten iron globules falling to the floor.

Pushing the door, trying to budge it, "yet more tricks and deception." Zenith Said while thinking out loud, Quinten was testing his patience now. Taking a breath, turning to Synergy and announcing to the others. "Move aside, I'm going to destroy the door, if I can't, Synergy will in my place" Synergy nodded in approval.

Watching Zenith in awe, his mastery of the Echidna flame swinging the sword in an arc from the ground upwards. Four lines of flame followed the sword's path, carving through the ground, shredding up into the door and through the wood like a knife through melted butter, leaving behind what could only be a claw mark, ringed in flames that continued to burn along the cut's edges.

Cathal, ready to charge, took his staff and smashed it into the centre of the remaining door with his full strength, watching it crumble and explode inward, splinters of wood flying in all directions.

Striding into the castle, the entrance hall was expansive and lined with statues of previous kings on marble stands. In the centre stood what could only be described as a twisted mess of body parts.

A disturbing, hideous form that of nightmares, multiple bodies meshed. The six arms were filled with iron weapons, fixed and attached to three torsos standing on three individual legs. The eyes and mouth of the beast were positioned oddly within its chest; it appeared to have once been human—the sounds it made, ear-splitting and vile, screams of anguish and pain.

The creature's visage caused Asger and Brent to throw up and bleed from the ears. Both had to leave the room, running back outside, unable to even help in this battle, the influence of Rycore just weighed too heavily on them.

Each of the Rysander weapons had begun to glow fiercely, sensing the influence and ready for battle. Lemma was first to strike, casting the star out, aiming for the creature's left torso as it began to charge them, each hand filled with a weapon.

Somehow, the creature managed to deflect the star's first strike, batting it away with a mace. The star reaction seemed angry, redirecting itself, dipping under the front of the two leftmost arms, slicing right across the left torso's rear, flashes of blue lightning searing the skin.

Cathal charged next, sliding under the legs, striking the creature from underneath as it slammed a massive war hammer down at where Cathal had just passed, stunning it. The star had returned to Lemma's hand. Letting it fly back at the same target, this time taking advantage of Cathal's attack, having stunned the creature.

The star scored its way up the front of the left torso, lightning again following. Passing where the head should have been, it dug in, spinning in place, surging angry blue lightning entering the torso, arms flailing, dropping the sword and mace, before the torso was scorched and then slumped over dead. Lemma Screamed, "It's still not enough, the other bodies still fight."

Cathal spinning around, swiping the rear of the three legs, knocking the creature's balance off-centre, wobbling, slamming down the Warhammer, cracking the brick under it to bring itself upright.

Zenith pounced on the opportunity, sending the snake's flame forward from the Echidna flame's tip, wrapping around the right-hand side torso, snagging the front right leg, restraining the creature's movement.

The flame seared the skin, hissing and steaming. The skin burst into flames where the snake's flame touched. Burning the creature down to the bone on that leg, it screams, unbearable to the ears. Lemma recoiled, feeling the pain of three men projected at her as the creature suffered; she screamed, "We need to finish this quickly, they are suffering. Find its power source!" Zenith Span searching the room, "There to its left, Lemma, the shadow leads to the walls."

In the blink of an eye, the star was sent flying low to the ground, its blades chipping the stone, forming a gauge as it sailed towards the beast's power source. Spinning faster as it came upon the shadow, cutting deeper into the floor, the star passed through the beast's connection to its power. Guttural screams erupted, filling the room as the shadows shrivelled back to normal. The gaping maw of the creature was wide open, showing human-like teeth and a forked tongue lashing about in agony. Lemma recalled the star to her hand and screamed to Cathal, "Now take it."

Cathal responded instantly by smashing his staff through the bone Zenith had already severely damaged. The bone snapped, cracking fully through, sending the shin and foot sailing in Zenith's direction. Zenith dodged the flying leg by a hair's breadth, blood spewing out of its amputated end, covering his face and staining his armour as the creature tumbled, unable to stand.

Cathal dived on it, slamming the end of his staff through the creature's open mouth, piercing straight through the back of the centre torso, pinning it to the ground. Lemma sent the star slicing through the same torso, whilst Cathal leapt to a safe distance, leaving the staff behind, avoiding the lightning strikes. The centre mass, exploding a gaping hole left where a human's lungs would have been.

Screams erupted as the creature writhed upwards in its final defiance of death, collapsing back to the floor.

The room filled with light as the creature released its final breath; the souls of the three soldiers were released, free, they began to ascend, smiling, all their regret gone. The smell of death filled the air as Cathal retrieved the staff from the corpse. The group moved forward, moving towards the throne room.

The throne room's door stood magnificent in its design, made from thick iron etched with depictions of the crown upon Hagan's head. Showing him young and battle hardened after creating his kingdom upon the Occardian grasslands.

Examining the door, Lemma saw something on the frame around it —a recess shaped oddly like the Echidna flame and the star together, well-weathered from the hands that had crossed that area over the years.

Calling over Zenith, indicating the depression, and spoke, "Do you think it's a key? The castle has been here since Hagan's time."

Looking curiously at the depression pulling the Echidna flame from its scabbard, "Worth a try, let's see if it fits." Lemma dropped down to her knees, averting her gaze from Zenith's bulbous groin, and pushed the star into the slot left behind.

Placing the star over the sword's point, forming a rudimentary key shape. "It fit, but now what?" Lemma asked. Zenith replied, "Give it a moment, like you said, the Castle is ancient."

A click and a whirring sound started up the wall, moving quickly from the floor up and around the door frame. Zenith stood smugly "See, I told you to wait." Lemma really took issue with Zenith attitude, kicking him in the shin. "I beg your pardon?" Zenith tried to reply, but was interrupted when, unexpectedly, the brickwork began to lift from the floor directly to the left of the massive door, revealing a passage that led parallel to the throne room, with a small amount of light permeating it at the far end. Cathal just stood there looking at them both, thinking to himself. "These two, I swear I've never met anyone luckier, if I'd tried that, well I doubt it would have gone so smoothly."

Entering the passage, the three of them had to shimmy with their backs against the passage wall, their noses almost grinding on the opposite side. Cathal also had an issue due to his short, rotund stature, meaning he had to suck in his stomach, making it hard to breathe, whispering to the others. "Why do they never make secret passageways for the plumper of people?"

Shimmying along, they approached the opposite end, where the light began to illuminate the passage, giving them a glimpse into the throne room. Quinten was sitting on the golden throne at the top of a red sandstone staircase. Zenith whispered. "I don't see anyone else, not even a single guard, it's odd." Lemma did her best to face him, asking. "Are you sure?" Zenith nodded, "Yep, only Quinten."

They continued shimmying as far as possible, stopping when they hit a wall. Zenith could feel a draft from the wall that faced into the throne room. Fingers slipping into a hole no bigger than three fingers wide, touching a cold metal lever.

"There is a Lever here, inside the stonework." Lemma scowled at him. "Open it then. It's starting to get claustrophobic in here." Cathal snapped quietly, "Starting! I'm wedged tighter than a Mullock's arse hole, and you think it's starting to get claustrophobic now."

He flipped his finger to the left, the switch moving slowly, then hearing an ancient lock stuttering and grinding as it moved for the first time in probably a thousand years. Once the lock finished releasing, the wall pushed forward and slid slightly to the right. Zenith gave the door a push, forcing it open the rest of the way.

Stepping out into the throne room behind where Quinten sat. Able to stretch and breathe, they took a moment to get the lay of the room. Zenith spoke quietly, "We can get around either side of the throne and be in front of Quinten, the only issue is not knowing if there are any men stationed that side for his protection." Cathal had made the same assumption and replied. "Well, who gets to go first, and they had better be quiet."

Zenith moved in close, whispering directly into Lemma's ear, "You're of the lightest frame and the stealthiest of us, can u sneak and take a look at the area up ahead?"

Lemma nodded and turned, crouching low as she stepped slowly and lightly towards the rear of the throne, ensuring each step was solid and silent, making it look effortless. Peering around the right-hand side, she could see no sign of any armed men.

Then, moving to the left and peering around the side, seeing two large men fully armoured holding two-handed swords held in front, pointing to the floor, watching the door to the Throne room. Turning back to Zenith and Cathal, indicating silently with her right hand what lay beyond the throne. Zenith moved to the left slowly, as quietly as he could, Cathal to the right, placing his back to the throne's podium and whispering. "I'll take the second guard, Lemma, take out the first at range and draw the second towards you."

Lemma spoke to Zenith before they moved. "Rycore is rife here, those guards may still look human, but they aren't. They are completely twisted. As for Quinten, I can't tell, most likely he is, as the influence is so oppressive, the worst I've ever felt." Springing from her hiding spot, the star flew straight and true, slicing through the first of the two guards' throat armour and the skin underneath. Blood spurted from the wound, covering the ground as the guard gurgled, falling to the floor. The lightning flashed, missing completely, striking the wall behind him.

The second guard sprang into action, running in Lemma's general direction after seeing the star return to her vicinity. Once the guard had passed the midway point, Cathal sprinted from his location on the opposite side of the Throne, scraping the staff along the floor to draw attention. Screaming out. "Oi, big boy, come and get me if you dare?"

The guard pivoted almost a complete half turn and charged at Cathal. Cathal meeting the challenge head-on. Charging directly at the guard, colliding near the centre of the room. Cathal was first to strike, levelling a stern swipe to the guard's midsection, sending the guard reeling back, swinging his broadsword overhead, aiming directly for Cathal's head. A roll to the side saw him cleanly away as the sword dug into the ground, sparks flying into the air. Taunting the guard, Cathal called out. "Come on, is that the best you've got?"

Cathal swiftly to his feet launched with all his strength into the air at the guard bringing the staff down on to the side of the guards Helmet, crushing it in around the eye socket, the guard screamed in pain as a transparent liquid with the slightest traces of blood began to eek its out of the crushed slit where the eye should have been.

Not giving the guard a chance to recover, Cathal struck again, this time lofting the guard from his feet with a forceful upward arcing strike from below into his groin region. Zenith watched from behind the throne, his only thought. "Right in the wheat sacks." As he grasped at his groin in sympathy without knowing it.

The guard clattered to the floor, his armour rattling him about inside as he did. Swiftly, Cathal despatched him with one last attack, a blow to the neck severing his spine, the guard's body lay limp on the floor at his feet as a tremendous black wave of energy hit him. Thrown clear across the room, Cathal collided with the wall, sliding down it, slumping over at the base of it, unconscious.

Zenith tuned instructing, "Lemma, stay behind the throne, it offers a small amount of safety. While I confronted Quinten, I hope to reach him with words rather than action." Lemma held little hope for words and voiced it out of concern. "I very much doubt words to be strong enough, Zenith, but ok, try it if you must, I'll get to Cathal if a chance presents itself. Good luck. I love you."

Zenith stood and straightened his back and stepped out into the open, speaking as he did, "Uncle, I am here for the throne that belongs to me and should have been my father's before me. That is all I came for. We need not fight; I have already taken the city. You are all that remains of the cruel regime that was your rule. Step down, do not fight."

Quinten remained silent and stoic, standing in front of the throne, staring down at him. A callous and morbid look on his face. His skin, grey and withdrawn. His eyes, white, with no pupil to speak of. The crown lacked lustre atop his head, hanging low over his dishevelled forehead. Scraggly locks of almost grey hair twisted and tangled. There he stood in his royal garbs, the purple faded, and the gold-coloured edging cracked and browned like rust.

Zenith's senses fired off in every direction as he faced his uncle, years of not knowing the truth about his parents' deaths. Emotions he had kept forced down resurfaced: anger, sadness, and overall disdain for his uncle's condition. It was now so evident that another had guided all of Quinten's actions; his body didn't even look like it belonged to him.

Still, he had to try to bring this to a peaceful end. If even one iota of Quinten remained, he must try to reach it. Stepping forward up onto the first step, he looked onward at Quinten.

"Uncle, if you are still in there, listen to me, you are not yourself, Rycore has twisted you."

Quinten's face twisted a look of pure, unadulterated malice, crossing his grotesque face, launching down the steps, straight jumping directly at Zenith. Quinten landed a single step in front of Zenith, wrapping his clawed fingers around Zenith's throat.

Zenith clasped at Quinten's arms, attempting to extricate himself, wrestling, he pulled back, pushing his arms between Quinten's. Shoving upward, he broke Quinten's grip, and a swift punch to the gut pushed Quinten back a single step.

Grabbing Quinten's wrists, screaming at him. "Uncle, wake up, fight him, do you not see the evil he has wrought with your name?" Quinten's white eyes flickered for but a moment, and a small black dot appeared in the centre; immense sadness was all they showed.

There was but the smallest showing of hope; something remained of his uncle—nothing but the tiniest spark. In a split second, Zenith thought. *Will it be enough to break through to?* Smash, Quinten's forehead connected with his, stunning him, giving Quinten the advantage. A decisive, powerful blow with both hands shoved Zenith backwards, his heel catching in a small crack, causing him to fall, throwing his arms behind him to keep from falling entirely to the flat of his back.

Quinten pounced on him in a blink, his hands back at his throat, squeezing tightly. Zenith rasped for breath, gasping for air, speaking between laboured breaths. "Uncle...... I saw you.... in their...... fight.... back I.... implore you...., for the.... Sake.... of your...... father... and... brother." Again, Quinten's pupils flickered into view this time for a second or two.

Zenith let himself fall backwards, taking Quinten with him, pushing his legs up into Quinten's Stomach. Gaining purchase with his feet. Zenith forced his legs outward, lifting Quinten from the floor and launching him flying. Watching as Quinten crashed down onto the steps below the throne, several snaps echoed across the room as bones shattered from the impact.

Yet Quinten still stood. The pain of his injuries had some tiny effect, allowing Quinten's consciousness to push through. A strained voice, just above a whisper, spoke, "Zenith," a small recognition of the man in front of him.

That was a way in, a minuscule crack in Rycore's control. Zenith snatched the Echidna flame from his waist, summoning the snake's flame before he had even brought it to his front. The flames ensnared Quinten, tying him to the spot. Total Concentration and effort on restraining filling Zenith's face, as he fought to avoid contact with Quinten's skin, trying not to burn him.

Quinten struggled against the flames' grip, thrashing wildly to no avail. Zenith spoke, "Uncle, I've seen you come forward, let me hear you give your regrets a voice." Though his body continued to thrash, Quinten's voice and consciousness fought through to the surface. His black pupils seemed to reflect the pain and anguish of the internal struggle taking its final toll.

Speaking directly to Zenith with only three words. "Forgive

me, nephew!" His consciousness slipped away. Zenith implored him for more. "Fight ill, hold Rycore, take back your mind." Nothing. Quinten's eyes had returned to white. It was only Rycore's will that resided there now.

The Snake's flame snapped, vanishing back into the Echidna flame. A solo flame held on, still burning on Quinten's left shoulder, fighting for air as it attempted to keep alight. A surge of black energy flung forward, emitted from Quinten's hands. Zenith quelled the attack, slicing it through with his blade, the blade consuming it, sucking it into itself.

The Energy converted, seemingly moving invisibly through the air, passed to the flame on Quinten's shoulder, which intensified, bursting into a small yet powerful burn.

The sudden blast from the flame knocked Quinten to the ground, searing the skin on his face before being snuffed out. Still, Quinten stood again. Lurching forward, it was as if the body were moving alone, its movement jarred and odd. Zenith had to defend against the thrusting arm aimed at his face. Zenith realised, "It's just a soulless shell I fight now. Quinten is lost; nothing but darkness fuels his body now." It left Zenith with minimal choice. The only way to release Quinten now was to free his body and soul from this world.

Hesitating, Zenith struck a blow to the mid-section of Quinten's body; it didn't even flinch, just carried on pushing towards him, impaling itself on the Echidna flame. Zenith could feel each movement of the blade as it cut through the internal organs of Quinten's body, a squelching sound filling his ears as the stomach gave way, orange bile leaking from the wound mixed into the blood, an eventual popping sensation and an unexpected forward movement from Quinten had Zenith near face to face with Quinten's snarling teeth and the reek of rot blasting straight up his nostrils from Quins rotten breath as the Echidna flame pierced out of Quinten's back.

Wrenching and bending over, just as Quinten's clawed hand grasped his shoulders, forcing him to the ground. Quinten fell with him, pinning Zenith to the floor.

A strange aura surrounded the body, with thick, black, almost solid blood pouring from every orifice, Black tears pouring forth, gaining intensity as if building to a final crescendo.

Lemma chose this moment to run, snatching the limp body of Cathal by the ankles, pulling with all she had. Cursing out loud. "By the gods, Cathal, how does such a wee man weigh so much?" dragging him backwards behind the throne area to safety and thinking. "I've got to help Zenith!" Sprinting from cover, she threw the star, spinning its way to Zenith's aid.

The star struck the back of Quinten's body, lightning crashing down, but it did nothing, the black energy deflecting it upward. The lightning smashed through the ceiling. Revealing a creature, Sat, watching from its lofty position, a black wolf, its eyes fixed on the battle, seemingly recording it.

As if sensing Lemma had seen it, the wolf disappeared. In that instant, the ceiling erupted outward, ripped from the very rafters.

Synergy clawing it apart, frantic to get into the throne room. Synergy's mind rife with panic. "I must get in there, I sense it, that power, the one that almost killed Angelus in the last war." Finally tearing away enough of the castle roof to fit his front half into the room, Synergy snarled at Quinten's body, grasping it in his beak, crushing it almost in half. Retreating from the castle into immediate flight, rising higher and higher.

Quinten's body still squirming, the black Aura continuing to intensify. Hitting the cloud layer, Synergy tossed Quinten's body out into the open sky.

Swooping away and back toward the mystified Zenith and Lemma as Quinten's body disintegrated in a cataclysmic explosion, Darkening all the seeable sky. Both Exclaimed. "By Rysand, what in all benevolence was that!" The darkness took several moments to dissipate, replaced by a brilliant white light that vanished in an instant. A profound sense of relief and contentment swept over the entire city.

Every soul within Errant stared upwards in that moment, seeing what could only be described as the acceptance and forgiveness of millions of sins.

40
A RULE BEGINS

Zenith pulled himself up from the floor, embracing Lemma in his arms. "Is it truly over? Have we expelled Rycore from Errant?" Lemma just snuggled close, not answering, realising how close to losing Zenith she almost was thinking *I will need to find a way to thank Synergy, but I don't know how yet.*

The metal doors of the throne room burst open, and Asger and Brent fell through them, followed by Asger's troops. Many of them toppled over each other like a chain of dominoes. The door just gave in without resistance, not what any of them had expected.

Lemma and Zenith couldn't help but smile at the scepticism of grown men falling one after another; it was just the right timing bringing a certain lightness to the sombre air.

Synergy had reperched himself above where the roof once was, watching on, sounds of delight and congratulations echoing down, but in Zenith's mind, his words formed. "Zenith, you may now be king, but we have much more left to do. Enjoy the peace for now, but soon we must-"

Synergy stopped, not wanting to ruin this for Zenith. Zenith already knew more would need to be done in the coming years; his dreams foretold it. Turning to Asger and the troops holding Lemma at the waist, he hoisted the Echidna flame above his head and roared.

Just roared, no words, a sound signalling the end of battle, the relief of seeing it through. Freeing his home, cleansing the evil god's maleficence from the throne, cherishing his people, all of it expressed in just one sound.

The scream echoed Zenith's sentiment: it passed forward, each man and woman raising their weapons high and screaming with all their lungs. From outside the castle, more screams of delight erupted, all the way out of the southern walls, the Scirainians joining in. Cathal was jarred from his still unconscious state by the roars of thousands.

Delirious, he rose to his feet, staggering from behind the throne, still grasping the staff in a fighting posture, determined he wasn't out of the fight yet. This sight left the entire room in stitches; even the men still lying on the floor couldn't help but laugh.

Lemma took a sharp breath to calm the laughter. "Oh, Cathal, what shall we ever do with you? The fight's over. Did you enjoy your nap?"

Cathal, overcome by the embarrassment, tried his best to hide it and retorted with some bravado. "Well, I had to leave some for you two, didn't I?" With that, he joined, clasping both Lemma and Zenith's hands and holding tight.

The jubilation of the day pushed events forward fast. Runners were sent from Errant to all corners announcing the victory and accession of the true king in Grissam; those who stayed behind were allowed to join with those in Errant. Ready to aid in rebuilding and rectifying any wrongs they had done.

Merrik and Amabel walked with them, eager to join Zenith

and Lemma. Catherine received the news and rushed from the castle, a carriage pulled by the fastest horses, ready and waiting to carry them to Errant.

The people of Renton flooded from town, journeying across the gorge via Renton's bridge, singing and dancing all the way.

Rath had been bought from outside the walls and stationed at the castle steps, decked in finery. Synergy retired to the tallest tower, sleeping whilst the rivalry continued.

A week passed, and the city's damages were assessed and distributed to those able to complete them. The joint armies rebuilt the gate, making it stronger and more resilient, using the combined knowledge of both. Scirainian sappers helped to reconstruct the tower defences, adding improvements and permanent shields to the tower frontage.

The wall defenders lashed Scirainian and Occardian flags to the battlements, a declaration of the union of the kingdoms under King Zenith and his Queen, Princess Lemma of Sciran.

Soon enough, the only repair left was the roof of the throne room. It was indeed a giant undertaking, but Zenith felt that something wasn't right; he didn't want it to be put back the way it was. He knew from his dreams it needed to be different, but he couldn't quite remember how. He just knew in his dream that the room was always bright and welcoming.

He had spoken with Asger at length about it, and Asger had utilised his engineering skills alongside those of the Scirainians to complete a design for installation. A fully glass ceiling supported on fine metal rods. Zenith loved it.

The issue was that the parts needed couldn't be produced in Errant easily, so they had to wait for Sciran to create them.

This didn't deter the people of Errant, though they wished to see their king on his throne.

The crown of Hagen had been lost when Quinten had

exploded. A new crown was being manufactured for the occasion, but it was taking time.

Typically, Zenith had forgotten his role and helped in the fields of Errant, accompanied by Merik. Excited to use Merik's invention. At the front of the self-planting plough, Zenith walked the Mulock along in his usual straight line, monotony, Merik, monitoring the seeds and water barrels. Lemma and Amabel lazing around the field's edge sat on a blanket, the boys' lunches prepared and wrapped, ready and waiting, acting like young ladies in their prime, gossiping in hushed tones, blushing when the conversation turned to discussing men enjoying the freedom and warmth of the sun.

Errant's people looked on in wonder, those who knew his father, Ake, seeing his father in him. Everyone else was confused and wondering if this truly was their king. Cathal, on the other hand, gazed on, thinking to himself about how a new day had dawned in Errant, indeed, perhaps a new chapter for Apprite was soon to begin and of course, how he would get home.

EPILOGUE

Tripas sat amongst the stone buildings of Vastuk, watching the rebuilding efforts that had nearly been completed. Captain Green and most of his men stood watch on the bastion wall, some also stationed at the village's entrance. Some, however, had seen the lives of those in Vastuk and decided to make it their home from now on. Working in the station mine, helping to improve the flow of elemental iron that they could sell in Rockwall.

Tripas had relayed Remi's message as promised to his brother and mother. They left Vastuk three days after Tripas's return with several of Green's men as guards, aiming to live in the comfort of Rockwall. The village's miners had asked them to seek a trade contract with Remi to secure future sales of iron. This was returned with glee by Remi, who sent the Contracts back with the Green's men.

Happening within the first three weeks of his return, it had all gone by in a haze and left Tripas contemplating Cathal's return out loud. "It has been well over a month since leaving them all in Rockwall. The entire village expected Cathal to have returned by now; surely, he would have completed whatever tasks the Toplanders had to do." Green walked over, hearing Tripas, and replied to his rhetorical words. "The Toplands really couldn't be that big a month away; that's like walking the length of the gorge from the bastion to the apex."

Tripas looked up at Green and returned his words. "Still, once Cathal does return, he will have many tales and stories to tell." Excited wasn't the word for how Tripas and the other younger members of the village felt; the waiting drove them crazy.

They all knew, however, that the new village walls and gate would please Cathal, and the improved defences would aid in preventing another Slither attack on the scale of the last one. Captain Green and his men had also decided, after seeing the bastion that defended against the dark, that they would all become Bastion members. Its numbers had dwindled with the last Slither incursion, anyway, Cathal had promised them a place among the guard as a reward for aiding Vastuk.

Vex walked the streets of Sciran, a half-free man as Catherine had promised, permanently escorted by a guard. His relief at not being needed to bring down Quinten left the most horrible taste in his mouth after he heard that Errant had fallen to Zenith. He felt that he would be unable to atone for his sins fully, even with the forgiveness of Zenith and Merik.

Catherine had also found a new way to torture him and have him give back, which utilised the skills he had developed in his old life. Catherine had expressed a need for people with his skills to help protect the joint kingdoms, from the southern areas of the continent, that may see them as weaker now that Zenith, such a young person, sat on the throne.

She had placed him within the Raven's nest, the home of

all those employed in spy craft and subterfuge. His instruction was simple: teach them the ways of a vagabond by any means necessary, make them even more unnoticeable, and help them blend in with those whom nobody saw. He taught there two days of the week, the use of chemical agents to disable crowds, tinctures and drugs to quell violent minds, lethal poisons and plagues to dispatch unwanted foes. The one part he hated most was the instruction of physical persuasion, although he didn't commit the act, the screams he could hear from prisoners used for practice haunted his dreams and waking moments. Everything he had done before arriving at Catherine's prison was now being used for the protection of the people, which gave some solace. He still felt the presence of Lemma and Zenith with him, always as their joiner; he felt some of their emotions on occasion. Sometimes he wished he didn't, as those intimate feelings should be theirs alone. Honestly, though, even with all his guilt, he felt free and useful; all he did, he now did for others.

Asger had retired from the military in the week after the battle, becoming an advisor to the throne and the royal engineer. He had seen the merits of Rycliff bridge first hand, taken all of them and combined them using the circular machinery to improve Renton's bridge construction and improve its speed and operation. Those spiky circles had brought an age of invention forward. Between him and the sappers, they named them gears. Using the gearing system and a whole lot of men, he had begun a vast project on Zenith's commission to aid Cathal in his return to Vastuk. Aiming to bring the Gorge access to the Toplands. The Scirainian trebuchet-style bridge moorings were ideally suited for the project. Asger had carefully reversed their engineering and improved them by using different gear sizes to speed up and slow down the ropes they carried.

He had already built two of them on the eastern side of Errant, where it met the gorge, tall enough that they stretched out over the gorge. Once the metal-infused ropes arrived from Sciran, the metal and wooden cages could be hung from trebuchets, dangling. Using the gearing system, one would lower to the gorge's floor while the second one would rise from the depths to Errant, making all things possible and tradeable that the Toplanders had available to the gorge, and the same was hoped in return.

Merik had returned to Grissam a prince, his hand now promised to Amabel. In Grissam he promoted his mechanical Plow system to all of the continent making a swift and enduring name for himself, at the same time bringing even more renowned to Grissam as its newly elected mayor, the village itself had begun to grow larger, already approaching the size of a small town, mainly because people of Errant and Sciran had complete freedom of movement and could choose where to live. Many people had also fled from Arathy, south of the mountains, having heard that war was headed their way and that the north was prospering.

The brothers of the Ayr Rose returned to their home, swearing to aid Zenith when he next called, safe in the knowledge that he was truly the Bearer of the Echidna Flame. Thaddeus had risen through the ranks and was now known as the son of Kastow and revered as the one who would receive the divine messages. He had fully healed from his beating by the time they left Errant; many a brother had begged forgiveness and spent time lashing themselves in solitude for their disbelief.

Cathal had spent these weeks eager to return. Contemplating a lone journey via the apex back to Vastuk. Zenith and Lemma had dissuaded him from it, especially considering they had elevated him to a never-before-heard-of rank. An ambassador, the Gorge's representative in Errant, given a home and lands that Ake once owned. Zenith had appointed the lands as Vastukian sovereign territory, Cathal's to do with as he wished. Cathal walked through his gardens, enjoying the flowers, still so fascinating to him. Zenith approached from the front yard gate, calling his name. Cathal turned to speak. "Ahh, Zenith, is it time already? We get to relax and talk alone." Zenith nodded, "Where shall we sit? I hope you can regale me with stories of the gorge and Bastion." Finding a bench around the edge of the Pond full of colourful fish, Cathal began to explain the foundations of faith in the Gorge. Zenith wanted to rush him, so he interrupted. "Tell me of the Bastion." Cathal shook his head. "That's a story for another time." Zenith looked at him. "Why?"

A NOTE FROM THE AUTHOR

Thank you so much for taking the time to read my first foray into the realms of authoring. It has taken me over ten years to get here. When I say over ten years, I mean I spent over nine of them stopping and starting, losing motivation, and the determination to complete it. In the last four months, I have gone from having only sixty per cent of a book completed, with no hopes of ever finishing it, but thanks to those mentioned in the acknowledgements and others who have pushed me, I completed and edited the book. Oh boy, can I honestly say when I started this, I never knew just how much it would drain me, test me and have me wanting to give up.

This book began as a way for me to be creative, a hobby if you will. Inspiration would come at me from any direction: old RPG games, movies, anime, and other books I would read. I still don't honestly know what created it, or where the idea originated. If you do, can you let me know? I do know, however, that it was also used to express how I would want to be if I ever ended up in another world. A background character content with his lot, no need to be anything more than that. Grateful to have family and friends around me.

What would you choose if you had the option?

Anyway, that's enough of me waffling on; I will end, though, on a positive note. I thank you from the very bottom of my soul for taking your precious time to read my book, and I hope that you enjoyed it. There is more to come. I'm already working my way through book two.

If you can, would you please leave me a review on Amazon, Goodreads or anywhere else that you use to review the books you have read. Leaving an indie author a review is one of the most powerful and informative things you can do as a reader. It not only lets the author know your thoughts but also helps other readers decide if the book is for them.

Anyway, enough from me. See you back in Apprite soon. I promise. Familiar faces will be back with just as many up and downs and random encounters. Once again, thank you so very much.

Andrew D Stevens
17/08/2025

P.S. If you have any questions or ideas, don't hesitate to contact me via email A.D.Stevens@outlook.com. I can't promise to reply to all, but I will always try my best.

Printed in Dunstable, United Kingdom